Dear Reader:

I'm delighted to present to you the first books in the HarperMonogram imprint. This is a new imprint dedicated to publishing quality women's fiction and we believe it has all the makings of a surefire hit. From contemporary fiction to historical tales, to page-turning suspense thrillers, our goal at HarperMonogram is to publish romantic stories that will have you coming back for more.

Each month HarperMonogram will feature some of your favorite bestselling authors and introduce you to the most talented new writers around. We hope you enjoy this Monogram and all the HarperMonograms to come.

We'd love to know what you think. If you have any comments or suggestions please write to me at the address below:

HarperMonogram
10 East 53rd Street
New York, NY 10022

Karen Solem
Editor-in-chief

HE WOULD MAKE HER BELIEVE

For several seconds, Jake struggled to say something, anything. When he finally managed, all he could get out was her name and three words, "I love you."

Jake tightened his arms around Indigo, glorying in the feel of her velvety skin beneath his hands. He traced the fragile ladder of her ribs and smiled. Courageous as she was, she was still a long way from fearless. But wasn't that what love was all about, taking risks?

Also by Catherine Anderson

Comanche Moon
Comanche Heart

Available from
HarperPaperbacks

CATHERINE ANDERSON

Indigo Blue

HarperPaperbacks
A Division of HarperCollins Publishers

This is a work of fiction. The characters, incidents, and
dialogues are products of the author's imagination and are not
to be construed as real. Any resemblance to actual events or
persons, living or dead, is entirely coincidental.

HarperPaperbacks *A Division of* HarperCollins*Publishers*
10 East 53rd Street, New York, N.Y. 10022

Cover illustration by R.A. Maguire

First printing: October 1992

Printed in the United States of America

HarperPaperbacks, HarperMonogram, and colophon are
trademarks of HarperCollins*Publishers*

❖ 10 9 8 7 6 5 4 3 2

To my husband, Sid,
who came to me from where the sun rises
and who will walk with me to where the sun sets,
always my guiding light, always the strength at my side,
always the impetus behind me. When I am but a whisper
on the wind, listen closely, for I will be calling,
"*Nei-na-su-tama-habi.*"

PROLOGUE

Oregon, 1866

Rain lashed Jacob Rand's face, the streaming rivulets on his cheeks blending with his tears to puddle in a salty pool in the cleft of his upper lip. A soppy hank of black hair dangled in his eyes. His vision blurred so that he could no longer clearly see his mother's grave. Not that it mattered. The downpour had made fast work of flattening the freshly mounded dirt. If not for the rock he had used to mark the spot, her burial place would have looked no different than the other churned-up mud. He wished his pa had taken time to whittle a cross, but as always, there was work to be done. Pa had helped with the digging, stayed to get Ma laid out right, and said some prayers. But cross whittling had to come later, after the daylight ran out. Times were hard, and it was up to Pa to feed them all.

Doubling one fist, Jacob scrubbed at his eyes, determined not to cry in front of his sisters. Now that Ma was gone, looking after the girls was up to him, the eldest. He had promised to do a good job, and he knew Ma was counting on him.

He glanced down at three-year-old Sarah, who stood beside him sniveling. He wished he could switch places with his younger brother, Jeremy, and be down at the creek working. Why did he have to be the one to finish up and say the final words? He didn't shine much to talking. He had already said the Lord's Prayer. Most of it anyways. He didn't know any others except for the supper blessing, and that didn't seem fitting. He reckoned he ought to finish up by saying something nice over Ma, but he couldn't think what. If only Jeremy was there. Right now, his gift for tonguing a subject to death would come in handy.

Sarah mewled again. He wished she'd hush. Fat chance. She looked like she was sucking alum. A string of snot dripped from her nose to her upper lip. He didn't have a handkerchief, so he made a quick swipe with his sleeve. Sarah snuffled, then sobbed, which made air erupt from her nostrils. He made another swipe.

Poor Sarah. Her black high-tops were clumped with red mud. Her tattered shirt, a castoff of Jacob's, clung like a sodden second skin to her bony shoulders. Beneath the hem, her knobby little knees were as red as apples from the cold. She gulped and shuddered, her tiny face twisting.

Jacob drew her close. Ma claimed a hug spoke a thousand words. The smell of urine floated up to him, and he realized she must have wet herself last night. Guilt washed over him. He had promised to take care of her and here she was, soaked, freezing, and as smelly as a cow pen in August. A fine job he was doing so far. She nuzzled her face against his side. He knew she was wiping her nose on him. Ma always scolded her for doing such, but he didn't have the heart.

Fresh tears burned behind his eyelids, and he

dragged in a breath. He remembered quarreling with Mary Beth yesterday, right before Ma started feeling poorly. Then he recalled how he had played with Jeremy up on the hill, putting off his chores until later. Now Ma was gone, and there was nothing he could do to bring her back. Nothing. He couldn't even say how sorry he was.

His stomach churned with hunger, and his knees knocked with weakness. It didn't seem right, feeling hungry, but he hadn't eaten since yesterday at noon, and grave digging was hard work.

Almost as hard as mining for gold . . .

"It's muddy down there." Sarah gazed at the grave, then looked up, imploring him with her big brown eyes to set her world aright. Dripping strands of black hair stuck to her cheeks. She shivered so hard her teeth clacked. "Why do we gots to put her in the mud?"

Jacob had no answers. If there was a God, he was a far piece from here. Somewhere in California, more than likely, where the sun never stopped shining. If Jacob was God, that's where he would be.

From the far side of the grave, eight-year-old Mary Beth said, "Ma ain't here anymore, kitten. She's gone away to heaven to live with angels."

Jacob watched Mary Beth, willing her to say more. Something about harps and gowns and streets paved in gold. If Sarah kept picturing Ma with mud all over her face, she'd be plagued by nightmares for a year. As always, Mary Beth did just the opposite of what Jacob wished. Her mouth settled into a grim line, and she said no more. Still hopeful, he slid his gaze to six-year-old Rebecca, but she stood as still as a statue, gaze fixed, face white, her black hair hanging in wet streams.

It looked as if it was up to him. He gave Sarah's shoulder a pat. "Heaven's a fine place. There's nothin' but white horses up there, and the angels are all gussied up in fancy dresses the likes of which you ain't never seen."

"What kinda dresses?"

Jacob hesitated. The entire scope of his existence was mining towns, but once a long time ago, he'd gone looking for Pa at the saloon. "I reckon they're red with black lace."

Mary Beth, face mud-smeared and swollen from bawling, puffed up like a toad eyeing a fly. "They ain't neither! Angels wear white, Jacob Nathaniel! Don't go tellin' lies as gospel."

"What difference does it make, Mary Beth?"

"It just does, that's all. Red's one of Satan's colors, and only bad women wear it."

"White then. And quit flarin' up over the top of Ma's grave. You might as well walk on it."

Sarah, apparently oblivious to their bickering, was still stuck on heaven. "Why didn't Ma take us with her?" she demanded in a shrill voice. "She taked the baby! Don't she love us no more? I wanna red dress with black grace."

"Lace," Jacob inserted. "Someday when I'm rich, I'll buy you one, kitten. An angel dress, any color you want."

Jacob's throat ached. The raindrops felt like pinpricks on his face. Angels? All he could see was mud, and more mud. And when he closed his eyes, all he saw was his mother's blood.

"Someday when you're rich," Mary Beth scoffed. "You're startin' to sound just like Pa. We ain't never gonna strike it rich, Jacob, and you know it."

"Then I'll get rich doin' something else. Hush yourself, Mary Beth. You'll make Sarah start takin' on again."

"Better that than makin' her promises you can't keep. She don't even got a coat."

"I'll buy her a coat, and dresses, too. Just you watch. I'll buy you all dresses."

Mary Beth's eyes filled with tears again. She stared at him a moment, then lowered her gaze. "Even if you tried, Pa'd take your money and spend it on mining gear. All he cares about is finding color. He didn't care if Ma hurt herself and the baby by workin' so hard. And he don't care about us. Sarah won't never have a coat, nor dresses, neither. The only thing Pa'll ever give her is a shovel with her name on it. Same for me and Rebecca."

Jacob had thought the same himself, but hearing it said out loud frightened him, especially now, after promising he'd watch after his sisters. He hadn't been big enough to do Ma's share of the work, but surely he would be by the time Mary Beth's turn rolled around. She was going to be a small fry, just like Ma. Working in the digs would kill her.

Jacob eyed the grave and remembered the desperate, pleading look in his mother's eyes last night just before she died. With her only remaining strength, she had clutched his hands and whispered, "Take care of them for me, Jacob. Promise me you will. Don't let your father . . ."

Her voice had trailed off, and her beautiful dark eyes had fluttered closed, the remainder of her request left unspoken. Jacob had held tight to her hands, hardly able to speak around the sobs that had torn up his throat.

I'll take care of them, Ma. I promise I will. I won't let it happen to the girls, Ma. I swear I won't. It's going to be all right. You'll see. Everything's going to be all right.

Even as the words passed his lips, Jacob had known he was lying. His mother was dead. His father had killed her and her unborn child chasing a fool's dream. Nothing would ever be all right again.

1

INDIGO BLUE

Portland, 1885

Though darkness had not yet fallen, the gas lamps in the study were lit to ward off the gloom of yet another rainy February day. Burning the lamps was the one luxury, aside from the two comfortable chairs and an occasional brandy, that Jake allowed himself in this room. Otherwise, he maintained an austere simplicity, evident in the knotty pine walls, his handmade but serviceable desk, and the rough plank bookshelves.

He had selected the decor, if one could call it that, to create balance in his life and strike a mood totally at odds with the opulence of the rest of his home. The fireplace mantle was fashioned from a myrtlewood burl he had found years ago in southern Oregon. Above that a large painting of snowcapped Mount Shasta held court over a collection of nature scenes that took up every inch of available wall space, his favorite a crystalline mountain stream winding its way through a stand of dappled cottonwood trees.

His fiancée, Emily, complained of the clutter and

insisted, quite rightly, that he should redecorate. But, so far, Jake had put it off. He couldn't explain why, wasn't sure he even knew why, but he needed this room, every ugly, ill-matched inch of it. He felt at peace here as he did nowhere else.

Jake usually kept the study door locked while he worked, and his family honored his wish to be left alone, but today had proved an exception. Earlier, two of his younger sisters had popped in with their broods in tow to bid him farewell before he left town on another business trip. Now Mary Beth had demanded an audience.

Disgruntled because he had a great deal of work to do before he departed for southern Oregon, Jake loosened his cravat, tugged on the waist of his gold silk vest, and leaned back in his chair to regard the eldest of his sisters over his steepled fingers. Just in from a shopping trip and still wearing a walking suit of wine-colored lightweight wool, she looked like a princess perched there on his extra desk chair. A very unhappy princess. Though they both had their mother's ebony hair and dark brown eyes and, according to some, shared the same insufferable stubborn streak, Jake had never yet come anywhere close to understanding Mary Beth. Her mood swings were as difficult to predict as Oregon's constantly changing weather.

After Joseph Rand's first gold strike, their circumstances had taken a drastic turn for the better, and Jake had endeavored tirelessly since to keep it that way. She had everything she could possibly want. But was she happy? Hell, no. At twenty-seven, she should be accepting one of her many suitors and marrying so she could have a child before it was too late, not getting addlebrained notions about attending college.

"Mary Beth, I'm expected to give Jeremy a briefing in ten minutes so he can handle everything here while I'm gone. I haven't even begun to pack. I really don't have time for this right now."

"And I have nothing but," she replied sweetly.

"I thought we discussed this to our mutual satisfaction last year."

She toyed with the silk-covered buttons of her suit. "We discussed it to your satisfaction, not mine."

A picture of his mother's haggard face flashed in Jake's mind. "You know how I feel about women working."

"Practicing law isn't work. It's a profession. A calling."

He picked up his pen and repositioned the papers he'd been working on. "I won't have my sister shouldering a man's load. I provide for you nicely. There's nothing you can possibly want."

Her fist slammed down on the surface of his desk with enough force to make his pen squiggle. Jake assessed the damage, then drew up an eyebrow. He had backed men down with his glare. Mary Beth didn't so much as flinch. Mary Beth, the bane of his existence, the one person who could goad him into losing his temper. Why she was his favorite sister, he hadn't a clue.

"Don't go back to your work as if I'm not sitting here!" she cried. "We're going to have this out here and now."

Jake laid down the pen and settled in his chair. He could only wonder what her strategy would be this time. After their last confrontation, she had shattered every glass object in the formal dining room. The time before that, she had taken to her bed for three days, refusing to eat. He had known all along, of course, that her maid, Charity, was sneaking her food. Mary Beth was nothing if not inventive.

"I don't run your life. You can do anything you like."

"Except work."

"Yes, except for that." He noted the high color on her cheeks, a sure sign she was about ready to let fly. "You're such a lovely woman. Isn't there a single solitary man in Portland who catches your eye? I don't care if he's a street sweeper."

"And you'll go buy him for me, I suppose? Just as you have all else. For once, I'd like to accomplish something on my own." She clasped her hands in her lap. "Besides, if the marital state is so blissful, why haven't you married Emily? You're thirty years old. Now that she's out of mourning, there's nothing holding you back. You've been engaged for over a year."

"Leave my relationship with Emily out of this." Jake sighed and rubbed the back of his neck. *Emily.* Like redecorating his study, she was another piece of unfinished business. For reasons totally beyond him, he couldn't muster the enthusiasm to set a wedding date. Regarding the mountain of paperwork on his desk, he said, "I've plenty on my plate. You have nothing but time on your hands, time which you utilize to concoct fantastic notions."

She shot from her chair. "Fantastic notions? Damn you, Jake. Sometimes I come so close to hating you, it's frightening."

He flashed her a conciliatory grin and gestured at the books lining the wall. "Have you considered becoming a novelist? A poet? Why don't you take up painting or sketching. The work Emily does is lovely. I don't want to restrict you, Mary Beth, just protect you. Can't you see that?"

"I'm not another Emily. She's so complacent, she makes me nauseated. Well, that's not for me. If I study law, I can make a real difference in the world, Jake, I just know it, if only you'll give me a chance."

"Honey, you've already made a difference. Think of all the people in this family who love you—who need you."

"That isn't enough." She threw up her hands.

The beginnings of a headache centered behind Jake's eyes. He rubbed absently at his forehead. "We've been over this ground a hundred times."

"And you know what's best for me. I have the response memorized." Her mouth twisted in a bitter smile. "And then you return to your work, forgetting my existence." She waved a hand at the study. "And why not? You have the life you want."

Did he? In his peripheral vision, he could see the waiting paperwork. Tomorrow he was bound for a mining town to negotiate yet another acquisition for his father. When he returned, his desk would be piled high with still more papers. What was the point? To acquire more wealth? To make Mary Beth happy? The first made a cold bedmate, and he was clearly failing miserably at the second.

"Mary Beth, what is it, exactly, that you want? Is it to be a lawyer? I doubt it. You'd detest it after six months."

She took a step toward him. In a quavery voice, she said, "Would I? Who are you to decide? What I detest is being made to suffer because you are trying to absolve yourself!"

This was a new wrinkle. Jake narrowed an eye. "Absolve myself? What in hell does that mean?"

"Exactly what it sounds like! Keeping me imprisoned in this tomb, protecting me from what you regard as the harsh realities, won't bring our mother back. And it will never undo what our father did to her. Or that you stood by and watched it happen."

That stung. Jake rose slowly from his chair. "You, young lady, are an ungrateful, spoiled little brat. How dare you bring up what happened to our mother?" He braced his fists on the desk. "You ask why I haven't married Emily yet? Think about it. When have I had time for a wife and family? If not for me, an empty belly would have driven you to those tent saloons in the mining camps. You'd have danced for your supper, and possibly more. Was that my sin? Working a second job to keep food on your plate?"

"The threat of starvation ended so long ago that nei-

ther of us can even remember what hunger felt like."
Tears filled her eyes. "I'm not a child anymore. Yet you
address me as young lady? How long has it been since
you really looked at me?"

"Don't be ridiculous. I'm looking at you now."

"Are you? You've become blind to everything but
your own obsessions. As for sacrifices? Oh, yes, you've
made them. So many that I could weep, not the least of
which was your ethics. Do you know what breaks my
heart the most? You've despised him all your life, and
now you've become just like him."

Jake knew she referred to their father. The comparison was like a slap in the face. "I think we'd better postpone this little talk until we're both a bit calmer."

"When? You're leaving in the morning to visit another hellhole mining town. God knows Ore-Cal Enterprises needs every acquisition it can get its grasping hands
on."

"That's part of our business, Mary Beth, acquiring
mines."

"Stealing them, more like."

The accusation knocked Jake clear off balance. "Stealing them? I've never stolen anything in my entire life!"

"Haven't you? If you want to pretend you're blind to
what's going on, that's fine by me, but please don't further destroy our relationship by lying to me about it."

With that, she went to the door.

"Where do you think you're going? You can't say
something like that and then walk out."

She froze with her hand on the doorknob. "Maybe
I'll go down to the waterfront and"—she tossed him a
glare over her shoulder—"dance for my supper. Prostitution *is* a feminine pursuit, is it not?"

Until that instant, Jake hadn't realized Mary Beth
even knew about the seedy activities that went on down
at the waterfront.

"Surely you can't argue with my doing that. That *is*

all we women are good for. Correct? Females, whom men either protect or use, depending upon their nature. You, Jake, are a protector. And I am your victim. If only you would marry poor Emily. Then perhaps you'd make her life miserable instead of mine."

With that, she walked out and slammed the door with such force that the walls reverberated. Jake stood there, frozen and feeling strangely numb. His victim?

He sank into his chair. The ache behind his eyes intensified. With a vicious sweep of his arm, he cleared the papers from his desk. They fluttered aimlessly to the floor. He watched them land, knowing damned well he'd be picking them up in a minute. Propping an elbow on the desk, he rested his head on his hand.

Scarcely a moment passed before he heard the door creak open. His brother, Jeremy, dark hair aglisten with raindrops, brown eyes dancing, poked his head into the room. "What the devil's wrong with Mary Beth?"

"Nothing compared to what will be wrong with her. One more word, and I swear I'll throttle her."

Jeremy chuckled. Draping his gray frock coat over one arm, he stepped in and closed the door. The smell of rain, fresh air, and lavender swept in with him. Jake knew without asking that his handsome brother must have had late luncheon with one of his many ladies fair. Judging from the heavy scent of perfume, perhaps a bit more than luncheon.

People claimed Jake and Jeremy bore a marked resemblance, both of them extraordinarily tall, broad at the shoulder, narrow of hip, with ebony hair and naturally burnished skin, made even darker by their mutual penchant for being outdoors. Jake couldn't see the likeness, though, aside from the slightest of similarities. One look from Jeremy sent women spinning onto their backs like unbalanced tops.

"Jesus, Jeremy, you smell like a French whore."

His brother tugged on his starched white collar and stretched his neck, the picture of satiated masculinity.

"Athena does go a bit heavy on the scent. A woman of excesses, that's Athena, bless her generous heart."

Jake searched his mind for a woman of their acquaintance who bore that name. "The dairyman's daughter? The one who looks—"

"Who noticed her face? The girl's glorious from the chin down. And don't preach. In case you haven't noticed, I'm old enough to tend my own stew."

Jake gave it up as a lost cause. "Your stew stirring is the least of my troubles."

In response to Jeremy's questioning look, Jake gave him a quick account of his argument with their sister.

Jeremy's teeth flashed in a grin.

Tugging up a gray pant leg, he perched his hip on the edge of Jake's desk. "At least she's gotten past the scalpel stage, and it's nothing bloody this time."

Jake sank into the soft leather cushion of his chair and leaned his head back. As he let his eyes drift closed, he asked, "Am I wrong, Jer? Is my way of thinking so terribly unfair?"

Jeremy took a moment to answer. "I don't think it's a question of right or wrong, fair or unfair. There are times, though, when I believe it's possible to love people so much that we make the mistake of trying to wrap them in cotton."

A heavy silence fell between them. Jake recalled Mary Beth's words and was plagued by uncertainty. He had felt guilty about his mother's death. To this day, he could remember shirking his chores the afternoon she died to play with Jeremy. His mother had gone to the creek and hauled the water herself. Though nineteen years had passed and he could look back on it now as an adult, realizing that any overworked eleven-year-old boy probably would have done the same, Jake couldn't quite forgive himself. It was frightening to think he'd spent all these years trying to atone for his father's sins. It was even scarier to think he'd forced Mary Beth to do penance with him.

"Tell me . . ." he said hoarsely. "If you were I, Jeremy, what would you do about Mary Beth?"

Jeremy sighed. "I don't know. The hard part is that I can understand both sides. Mary Beth feels that her life is meaningless. But I can see how you feel, too. I can't blame you for wanting to keep her home, where you have some control."

Control. Was that how everyone saw it? "You know what it'd be like for her if I let her attend school. She'd meet with more opposition than she can possibly imagine getting admitted to the bar."

Jeremy picked up the gold nugget from Jake's desk that served as a paperweight. "Mary Beth's a little bored, Jake, but boredom won't kill her. She'll get over this, just like she has a dozen other times. Why are you so upset? You've always laughed it off before."

"Because I want to do right by her." Jake sat more erect, not quite able to put his feelings about Mary Beth into words. "Why does it have to be my decision, anyway?"

Jeremy laughed and held up his hands. "Oh, no, you don't! Leave me out of it."

"She's making me feel like a jailer."

"Don't pull me into your battles, Jake. Either way I go, I can't win. You're the eldest, and it's your responsibility."

"Maybe I'm tired of the responsibility." Jake pushed up from his chair and paced a moment. Raking a hand through his hair, he paused before the window to gaze out into the street. A carriage passed by, its wheels sending up twin sprays of muddy water. "At least you can reason with her. God knows I can't. When she gets on these tangents, the first thing I know, I'm so furious all I can do is yell. She had the audacity to accuse me of underhanded business tactics. Can you believe that?"

Jeremy made no response. Curious, Jake glanced

over his shoulder. His brother kept his head bent, studying the gold nugget. Jake turned and waited. Jeremy remained silent.

"Well, aren't you going to laugh?" Jake asked. "I've never done a dishonest thing in my life."

Jake walked slowly back to the desk. "Jeremy . . . ?"

Sliding from his perch, Jeremy returned the nugget to its place, his broad shoulders stiff beneath the gray silk of his vest. The sleeves of his white shirt stretched taut over the bunched muscles in his upper arms. "Now isn't the time, Jake."

"Now's the perfect time. What in hell is all this about?"

"Damn Mary Beth and her mouth." Jeremy pinched the bridge of his nose and closed his eyes. "You're putting me in a hell of a spot."

"That's too damned bad. We've never kept secrets in this family."

"Maybe you and I haven't," Jeremy said in a strained voice.

"And what, exactly, does that mean?"

"That Father isn't so candid around you as he is me."

"Meaning?"

Jeremy's lips thinned. "Meaning I've overheard certain things, seen things, that have made me—" He swiped his sleeve across his mouth. "I have reason to believe our father *assists* small operations in going under so he can buy them out."

Jake stared at him. "Have you any idea what you're saying?"

"Yes." The starch went out of Jeremy's shoulders. "Take Wolf's Landing, where you're headed tomorrow? About two months ago, as I was approaching Father's office, I heard a conversation between him and Hank Sample. Wolf's Landing was mentioned. I remember the name because it's unusual. Father said 'take care of it, Hank.'

Now, you're headed there to make the owner an offer."

Jake waved a hand. "So? It's a fair offer. And he'll be damned glad to get it. The owner's laid up with an injury and can't work. He won't be able to for months. Our stepping in may save him from financial ruin."

"How was Hunter Wolf injured?"

"You know the man's name?"

"I've done some investigating, yes. How was he injured?"

A trickle of uneasiness inched up Jake's spine. "A cave-in, I think."

Jeremy nodded. "One of several. Just small ones. Little inconveniences, costly but fixable. There has been a rash of accidents in and around that mine this last month."

Jake knotted his hands into fists. "That's a despicable accusation, and you know it. Hunter Wolf was nearly killed. Father may be greedy. God knows I'd be the last person to defend him. But he's no murderer."

Jeremy's gaze didn't falter. "That's a risk with arranged accidents. Sooner or later, someone is bound to be in the wrong place at the right time."

Jake could see by the look in his brother's eyes that he truly believed what he was saying. He slumped against the desk.

"Check the records," Jeremy challenged. "There've been no injuries in the past, but practically every acquisition Father made was preceded by a string of bad luck that put the business in the red. I'm certain of nothing, but in every instance, the bad luck miraculously ended the moment Ore-Cal took over."

For a moment, Jake was swept back in time and standing by his mother's grave. Mary Beth's voice rang in his mind. *All Pa cares about is finding color.* "I couldn't be that blind."

"Maybe I'm seeing what you don't because Father isn't quite so careful around me. I've seen him tidying his desk before you enter the office, stashing papers, covering them with other correspondence." Jeremy threw up his hands. "Just think about it, Jake. How is it that Father always knows, Johnny-on-the-spot, when a business is in trouble? It's not only mines, you know. Three months ago, it was a hotel. In every case, he steps in with an offer at just the right moment. Do you think people facing bankruptcy send out notices to prospective buyers?"

Jake stared at the ceiling. There was a ring of truth in what Jeremy said. His father did seem to have an almost uncanny sense of timing, moving in for a takeover at the perfect moment. And Jake knew Jeremy well enough to feel certain he wouldn't say such things without reasonable cause. *Dear God.* The study seemed to close in around him.

"I'll check into it," he said.

"And do what?" His brother's voice sounded shaky. "I'm sorry, Jake. I never intended to drop it on you like this. I wanted more proof. But if I'm right, what are we going to do? We have to make amends and keep it quiet somehow. The scandal will ruin us. You can scotch your engagement to Emily."

Right now, Emily was the least of Jake's worries. As a boy, he had once run head-on into a tree, and he felt exactly the same now, dazed, disoriented, unable to remember what he had been thinking an instant ago. Scarcely able to feel his feet, he circled his desk and lowered himself into his chair.

"Jake, are you okay?"

Was he okay? Jake bit back a harsh laugh. His sister had just ripped him wide open, and now his brother was telling him that he'd been orchestrating unethical business acquisitions. Hell, no, he wasn't okay. He thought of all the times he had dealt the death blow to businessmen, buying their livelihoods for a fair market price, believing he was doing them a favor because he was saving them from inevitable financial ruin.

You've despised him all your life, and now you've become just like him. Everything within Jake rebelled against that thought. He loved his father in a detached way, but he had never liked him. And therein lay the problem. He was happiest when he didn't see the man. Until this moment, Jake had been content to keep a separate household and tend the management of their enterprises, sparing little if any thought for his father's end of the business, acquisition and investment.

"I should have spent more time at the main offices," he whispered hoarsely.

"That's famous. Blame yourself. Good old Jake with the broad shoulders. Overseeing a few mines would be a gargantuan undertaking. He's loaded you down with nearly forty, plus several other nonmining enterprises. When you're not worrying about safe working conditions, you're doing accounts. Has he ever once offered to hire someone to take over part of the load? Has he encouraged me to do so? Hell, no. And now we know why. He wanted to keep you so bogged under, you wouldn't have time to notice anything he did."

Jake's mouth felt dry. He tried to swallow and couldn't. "We can make excuses all day, but the bottom line is that I should have seen what was happening."

"What are you going to do?"

"I'm going to Wolf's Landing, just as I planned, and check into it."

Jake knew he was repeating himself, and that it wasn't a solution. But beyond that, he hadn't a clue. How did one rebuild destroyed lives?

2

Wolf's Landing, 1885

Lightning slashed the sky, then thunder clapped. Indigo Wolf settled herself on a patch of grass and looped her arms around her knees. With a cleansing sigh, she leaned back to catch the rain on her tongue. Water streamed from the brim of her leather hat down the nape of her neck. She shivered and straightened her spine. Somewhere above her on the hillside, lightning struck. A tree, split asunder by its force, gave a loud pop and crashed to the ground. The rumbling vibration and the smell of scorched pine reached to where she sat.

Her pet wolf, Lobo, whined and pressed closer to her thigh. Buffeted by the wind, she placed a hand on his rain-soaked ruff and closed her eyes to absorb the electrical rage that eddied in the air. For a moment, she didn't feel quite so impotent against the forces that threatened to tear her life apart.

Today had been one of the longest she remembered. Every minute she had spent up at the mine had seemed like an eternity, her thoughts centered on home and what might be happening there. Now that she had finished work for the day, here she sat, afraid to find out.

She wished the storm could last forever, but within a few minutes, the thunder grew more distant, and the rain began to abate. She opened her eyes to see that the blackest of the clouds were moving south. An anemic ray of sunshine shafted through the gloom, then blinked out. Her father would say the glimmer of light was a promise from the Great Ones that all would be well. Indigo lacked his faith. Things weren't going to get better unless she fixed them herself. The question was, how?

She sighed and pushed to her feet, gazing somberly at the settlement that clustered below her. Home. The word probably conjured different images for different people; for her, home meant Wolf's Landing. A few more dwellings had gone up over the years, but otherwise the town looked the same. The sprawling house that her father had built after coming to Oregon over twenty years ago had held up well, its log walls seasoned to burnished umber, its patched roof a confused checkerboard of weathered gray and blond shakes. From her vantage point, she could see her ma's chicken house and garden spot out back. Farther into the trees stood her father's lodge, the cone of leather honeybrown with age, its poles crisscrossed among the lofty pines. Out by the woodpile was the scarred stump she and her brother, Chase, used as a practice target for their knife and axe throwing.

Indigo couldn't imagine living anywhere else. Yet, right now, her father might be signing the papers that could change her life forever. If he hadn't already. Ore-Cal Enterprises. She had first heard the name only a month ago, and already she hated it.

Feeble strings of gray smoke drifted skyward from the town's many chimneys and canted southward with the wind. She turned her gaze in that direction, filled with dread because she knew a different world lay beyond those distant snowcapped peaks. Here, only a snobbish few looked at the color of her skin and found her lacking. In the digs, no one tried to restrict her because she was female. If her father followed through with his plan to sell his mine, the life she had always known might be snatched away. In all her nineteen years, she had ventured no farther away than Jacksonville, a distance of ten miles.

Selling the mine wasn't necessary, but thus far she had been unable to convince her parents of that. She could get things running again and manage alone until her father recovered. She knew she could. If a bunch of narrow-minded people were bent on closing them down, let them do their worst. She could battle them as well as any man. If her parents would only give her half a chance, she'd prove it.

Filled with frustration, she stroked Lobo's wet fur. He leaned against her, the ridge of his back as high as her hip, an unwelcome reminder that she had inherited her mother's slight build. She hated being small, especially now when so much rode on her ability to cope. Every afternoon since her father's accident, weariness had ached across her shoulders, but she had never once complained. Yet her father still intended to sell out? It wasn't fair, it just wasn't fair. She didn't want to leave here.

Lobo lifted golden eyes to hers, his expression uncannily human and far too intelligent to ignore. They were a pair, she and Lobo. A wolf would never be accepted in that world beyond the mountains.

"Well, my friend, shall we go home and see how bad the news is? We can't avoid facing it forever."

Indigo struck off down the hillside, taking care where she placed her moccasins so she wouldn't slip in the mud. Lobo paced beside her, a silent silver wraith that blended with the gloom.

As Indigo turned onto the main street of town, she

saw Shorty Dixon reclining on the bench in front of the general store. As was his habit every day after work, he was having a chew with his two cronies, Stretch and Stringbean. Acutely aware of the strange buckskin horse tethered to the hitching post out in front of her house and none too anxious to meet its owner, Indigo wished she could run down the street and linger on the boardwalk with the old men. She could almost smell the delicious aromas that would be coming from the hotel restaurant at this time of day. She lingered a moment in the rain. Stringbean's laughter floated on the wind to her, and she smiled, fairly certain Stretch was probably telling another of his outlandish stories.

The slamming of a door caught her attention. She glanced over her shoulder to see her mother on the front stoop. Indigo broke into a run. As she neared the sprawling log house, the strange buckskin, frightened by Lobo's approach, shied and whinnied. Casting a wary look at the sidestepping horse, the wolf slunk under the porch.

Indigo nudged her hat back, pleased to see that her mother was smiling. Not a halfhearted smile, but ear to ear, as if something grand had happened. "What is it?" Indigo asked, afraid to hope for good news, yet heartened by the twinkle in her mother's blue eyes. "Ma, don't just stand there grinning. What are you so happy about?"

"Oh, Indigo, you'll never guess in a million years."

"Ma!" Taking the steps two at a time, Indigo joined her mother on the porch. "Don't play guessing games. I could use some good news for a change."

Her mother pressed one hand to her slender waist, the other to the swirl of golden braid atop her head. "The Lord answered our prayers with a miracle. We don't have to sell the mine."

Indigo gave an involuntary gasp of pleasure. Then a dozen questions sprang into her mind. "What kind of miracle?"

"A man named Jake Rand. He happened to be in

Jacksonville yesterday and heard about your father's accident. He's between jobs and down on his luck. He's got lots of experience running mines. He's offered to be our foreman until he's saved enough wages to move on. It's a perfect solution for us and him."

Indigo knew she should be happy, but instead she felt as if a giant fist had hit her in the stomach. Rather than count on her, her father preferred to hire a complete stranger? After all that had happened, how could her parents be certain this Jake Rand could be trusted?

"Anyway," her mother went on, "Mr. Rand needs to familiarize himself with things. Your father volunteered your services. You won't mind taking Mr. Rand on a tour, will you? No one knows more about the mine than you."

That was true, and it rankled that she was expected to hand over the reins. "Ma, I can run the mine. We don't need an outsider coming in. This will only mean more wages."

Her mother's mouth twisted. "Oh, darling, I know you've dreamed of running the mine yourself, but dreams aren't always practical. No matter how capable you are, you're still just a girl. You can't expect a crew of men to take orders from you."

Indigo could, and would, but she could see saying so would change nothing. She swallowed down an angry retort. These last few weeks hadn't been easy on her parents. "When does Mr. Rand want to go up?"

A relieved look crossed her mother's face. "Immediately, I believe. He'll be taking over first thing in the morning." She placed a hand on Indigo's shoulder. "Don't look so crestfallen. Your time will come when you're older. For now, be proud that your father has chosen you to be Mr. Rand's right arm. That is what you'll be, you know. You'll provide the answers to all his questions. Why, if you think about it, you'll be running things through him."

That seemed like idiotic thinking to Indigo, but then

life was pretty insane sometimes, especially for a woman. She knew the mine as well as the lines upon her palm, yet she was supposed to instruct another in its operation? It wasn't enough, but she knew she must settle for it. Her father was seriously injured. Their mine was teetering on the edge of disaster. Her mother was holding things together with a prayer and a smile.

"You can count on me, Ma."

"Was there ever a question?" Her mother took a deep breath of the rain-touched air. "Things are looking up. I can feel it in my bones." Her brilliant blue eyes met Indigo's. "Would you like to come in and be introduced to Mr. Rand?"

Indigo brushed at her buckskin pants. "If I'm going back to the mine, there's no point in cleaning up. I think I'll just wait out here rather than muddy up the floors." A thought occurred to her. "Ma, what happened to the man from Ore-Cal? He was supposed to come today. Didn't he ever show up?"

"No, thank God. They wired saying he'll be delayed a couple of weeks. Imagine how we would have felt if we'd sold the mine to Ore-Cal and then Mr. Rand had knocked on the door."

Lantern light touched the bedroom with amber, a pleasant contrast to the stormy gloom that spilled in through the window. The rain started up again, tapping an uneven tattoo against the polished glass. Soothed by the lamp's steady hiss and the cozy warmth coming from the stove and fireplace in the other room, Jake settled himself more comfortably in the rocker beside Hunter Wolf's bed.

He couldn't recall ever having seen another home with this one's simple charm. Everywhere he looked he saw evidence that Loretta Wolf's hands had been at work. When Jake considered the extraordinary amounts spent on decorating his house in Portland and compared the resultant cold elegance with his present surroundings, he felt strangely lonesome and hollow.

"You have a nice place here," he said to his bedridden host. By Portland standards, the place was little more than a shack, but he liked the colorful rag rugs and rustic log walls. They gave him a feeling of timelessness. And something more, an unnameable something that made Jake want to linger.

Hunter Wolf's indigo eyes warmed with affection. "My woman has magic in her hands." He shifted his broad shoulders and winced as he tried to get his bandaged right arm into a painless position. He settled his gaze on the wedding ring quilt stretched across his lap. "She puts great love into everything."

Yes, Jake thought, that's what I feel in this room, a great deal of love, something all the money in the world can't buy or duplicate. Suddenly uneasy and uncertain why, he rocked forward and braced his arms on his knees.

Hunter Wolf wasn't what bothered him. Jake liked the man, so much so that he couldn't credit anyone wanting to kill him. Yet the proof lay before him. From the looks of Wolf, he had more broken bones than not.

Regret filled Jake. Even if his father wasn't responsible, he hated to see such a strong, rugged man confined to bed with little hope of leaving it for weeks to come. Jake knew how he would feel if he were forced to rely on a woman Loretta Wolf's size. He'd be reluctant to request the simplest things, even having his pillow fluffed, for fear she'd try to lift him.

"What makes you think the trouble around your mine may be due to racial prejudice?" Jake asked softly.

Wolf toyed with a tuft of blue yarn on the quilt. "Why else? I feel certain the accidents have been—"

When Jake saw that his host seemed to be searching for the correct word, he quickly supplied, "Engineered?"

A cool smile touched Wolf's mouth, then he nodded and grew pensive. "I've made no grief behind me. If someone wants to cause trouble for me, my blood is the only reason." He met Jake's gaze. "Many people have come to these hills. Some have brought bad feelings. If you stand beside me, you will be hated as well. I almost died in the last cave-in." A question entered his eyes. "Knowing that, most men would not take this job."

"I'm not one to shy from trouble." Jake knew no one could possibly connect him to Ore-Cal. The Rands did all their business using the company name. But that knowledge didn't reassure him much. Wolf's gaze peeled off a man's layers and made him feel transparent. Jake couldn't risk having his true reason for being here revealed—not yet. "I'm desperate for temporary work, and you need a foreman. It seems like a perfect solution for both of us."

Wolf seemed to consider that. "After all that has happened, I am looking always behind me. Your eyes speak to me of friendship, though. And you have an honest face."

"Is that why you considered selling out? Because there's no one you can trust and because of the danger?"

"Not because of danger to myself. If it was just me, I would hold on until I healed, then reopen the mine. But I have mouths to feed."

It had been a long while since Jake had worried about providing the basic necessities for loved ones, but he still remembered how that responsibility had preyed upon his mind.

"My daughter, Indigo, has been trying to supervise my men and get repairs underway," Wolf went on. "I believe she could do a very good job, but after so many accidents, I worry. Her mother worries even more, and with me unable to work, her burdens are already great." He lifted his uninjured hand in a helpless gesture of defeat. "The doctor says it will be a long time before I walk. Sometimes, a man must put his pride behind him. He must say *suvate*, it is finished, and look at the horizon."

Loretta Wolf was a little slip of a woman. Jake couldn't blame her husband for feeling protective of her. He hadn't as yet seen Indigo, but imagining a girl inside a mine that had already suffered several cave-ins made his guts knot. He'd be insane with worry if that girl happened to be his daughter.

"Well . . ." Jake's voice trailed off and he gazed sightlessly at the floor. He couldn't bear the thought that his father might be responsible for this family's misfortune and could only pray Wolf was right, that the cave-ins were the work of locals who had it in for Indians. "I'm just glad I happened through Jacksonville before you sold out."

"I am glad with you."

The simple honesty of that response touched Jake. It was indicative of a man who dealt in truth, even if it humbled him. What would happen to this family when Jake had to leave? While making his plans to come here, he hadn't thought of the people at Wolf's Landing as being real, nor had he considered that he might like them so much.

"If something should happen—if it ends up that I can't stay until you're completely recovered, isn't there anyone—a friend or a relative—who could help you out?"

Wolf closed his eyes for a moment. "Many friends, yes, but they must feed their own families. My son would come home, but if I ask that of him, he will lose all he has worked for in the woods. My brother-in-law, Swift, works in the timber as well, and he is needed there to help Chase fill the orders. I cannot ask others to lose everything in order to help me."

Clearly, Hunter hadn't quite managed to put his

pride behind him. "Sometimes, we have no choice but to call on family."

"Not to save a mine that could play out next week or next month. Timber is my son's future. It may end up being mine."

No one knew better than Jake how insecure a mining venture could be. He sighed and nodded. "Well, for as long as I'm here, maybe your son's help won't be needed."

Wolf's eyes warmed again. "My woman believes her God sent you to us. If that is so, then he will see that you stay until our need is finished, yes?"

He could have said anything but that. Feeling horribly guilty, Jake stared out the window for a moment at the slanting rain. He was tempted to tell Wolf the truth about who he was and why he had come, but if he did that, the half-breed would send him packing. And, under the circumstances, who would blame him?

"Well . . ." Since beginning this conversation, *well* had become his favorite word, Jake decided. A deep subject with a hollow ending, a word that said everything and nothing. Anxious to escape his new employer's penetrating gaze, Jake rose from Mrs. Wolf's rocker and retrieved his rain slicker from the floor. He felt angry, impotently angry. All this man wanted was to make a modest living for his family. It didn't seem fair that some people had so much while others far more deserving lost what little they had. "I hope you'll be happy with my performance." Jake meant that from the bottom of his heart. "For as long as I can stay, I'll give you my best."

Wolf's eyelashes fluttered. For an instant, Jake thought he might drift off to sleep before their conversation was completely finished. The laudanum sitting on his bedside table seemed to be doing its job.

With what was apparently a great effort, he focused. "The work has piled up—at the mine and here. Since my son and brother-in-law left, I've been shorthanded. I got the roof patched this fall, but there are other things—"

"Don't worry about the work," Jake interrupted. "I'm pretty handy. If I see something that needs fixing, I'll work it in."

"Indigo—she tries. But it is a heavy burden for a girl."

"I'm here now, Mr. Wolf. You just concentrate on mending yourself. I'll worry about everything else."

Because his right arm was in a sling, Wolf extended his left to shake hands. Though weak and a little shaky, the Indian's fingers closed around Jake's in a firm grip.

"To my friends, I am called Hunter."

The last thing Jake wanted was to forge a new friendship. His mission here would be difficult enough without his loyalties being divided. "I go by Jake."

Wolf smiled. "It is good." His grip on Jake's hand relaxed, and his arm dropped heavily to his side. "I will rest easy now, eh? Because you have been sent to us."

The half-breed's eyes closed, and his features fell into repose. Jake stood over him, feeling like a condemned man who had just heard the cell door clang shut behind him.

A movement drew Jake's attention. Loretta Wolf glided into the room. Though she wore simple clothing and no jewelry, she was radiant in her quiet way, the kind of woman who made a man feel like smiling. Jake could see why Wolf's eyes warmed when he spoke of her. So fragile of build a strong wind might blow her away, she was no match for the rugged man lying on the bed. Yet Jake had the feeling she probably ruled the roost. It'd take a hardhearted man to say no to those blue eyes of hers.

"Our daughter, Indigo, has agreed to show you around, Mr. Rand. She's far more familiar with goings-on at the mine than I. She'll be able to answer any questions you might have."

Jake cast a glance at the window. "It's pretty nasty weather for a young lady to be out and about."

A mischievous twinkle brightened her eyes. "Indigo doesn't let bad weather slow her down. She's waiting for you out front."

Jake immediately snapped to, imagining someone very like Mrs. Wolf shivering on the porch. "I'll be on my way then."

"You'll be joining us for meals, of course, since you'll be using our son Chase's bedroom for the duration of your stay. We have our supper promptly at six."

Jake disliked the thought of further depleting their stores of food. He knew without being told that the Wolf family was hard put right now. "I appreciate the offer, Mrs. Wolf, but I already made arrangements to stay at the hotel."

"Nonsense," she retorted. "The moment you get back from your tour of the mine, you go over and tell Mr. Bronson you've had a change in plans. Mike's rates are more than fair, but they're far too steep for a workingman who needs lodging."

Jake was no workingman, and he already liked the Wolf family far more than he felt he should. If he stayed in their home and took meals with them, it could only complicate matters. "That's very kind but—"

She held up a hand. "I'll not hear another word. You're staying with us, and that's final." With that, she swept past him to lean over her sleeping husband. After pressing the inside of her wrist against his forehead, she glanced up and flashed a beatific smile. "I haven't seen him so at peace since the accident."

Jake didn't like being cast into the role of savior. He backed out of the bedroom and softly closed the door.

3

When *Indigo heard* the front door open, she forced a smile, determined to be pleasant to Jake Rand if it killed her. Though his arrival had usurped what she considered to be her rightful place, she knew it wasn't truly his fault. The moment she settled her gaze on him, however, her good intentions scattered like dandelion fluff on the wind. He was nothing like she expected.

Miners came in all types, colors, and sizes, of course, but most weren't so handsome. None in her memory had been taller than her father, and those with enough experience to supervise a dig were usually older. She stared up at his sun-burnished face, taking in the squared line of his jaw, the tiny creases at the corners of his coffee-brown eyes, the jut of his straight nose. The clean, sharply chiseled planes of his features reminded her of a seasoned wood carving. Not a trace of gray showed in his ebony hair. She guessed him to be in his late twenties or early thirties.

Though his red-plaid wool shirt and faded jeans weren't new, they were spanking clean. A miner's clothes, even freshly washed, usually bore earth stains. After shutting the door behind him, he took two long strides and stopped, so tall that the porch overhang barely cleared his head. After giving her a brief nod in greeting, he darted his dark gaze left and right, then frowned and stared through the sheeting rain toward town.

She thought it rather rude the way he ignored her. She didn't think it was proper for a lady to address a gentleman first. Ordinarily, she wouldn't have fussed about something so trivial, but folks from outside Wolf's Landing put a lot of stock in manners. She began to wish she had gone inside and muddied up her mother's floors so she wouldn't be faced with this dilemma. The last thing she wanted was to make a bad first impression.

Still looking up the street, he pursed his firm lips and whistled a little "Yankee Doodle." She took advantage of the moment to study him. The wind whipped his wavy black hair across his forehead. The faded denim of his pants rode low on his lean hips and stretched taut over the powerful contours of his thighs. Tucked neatly at the waist, his shirt hugged his broad chest and shoulders. His stance one of energy and purpose, he stood with his long legs braced apart, arms akimbo, his slicker hooked over one wrist.

A sudden feeling of dread swept through Indigo. She couldn't say why, but somehow she knew nothing would ever be quite the same again now that he had come.

When he continued to remain silent, she decided to speak first, even if it wasn't proper. "Hello."

She would have said more, but he inclined his head in her direction—sort of in her direction, anyway—and started whistling again. Ending the tune with a sour note, he sighed with resignation. Then he raked a hand through his hair and draped his canvas slicker over the porch rail to fuss with the sleeves of his shirt, straightening the folded cuffs so each rode his corded forearms at just the right spot. When he started to whistle again without speaking, she began to grow angry.

Out of the blue, he said, "Nasty out there, isn't it?"

His deep voice, coming so suddenly when she wasn't expecting it, made her jump.

"That's February for you," he added. "You're soaking up sun one minute and diving for cover the next. Looks like the cloudburst caught you off guard."

Before she could think of a response, he shifted his attention to the broken pick handle leaning against the porch rail. After studying the cracked oak a moment, he heaved his weight onto one foot to test the weak plank under his boot. Next he grabbed a rafter of the porch overhang and gave it a shake. She surmised he was checking it for sturdiness. He clearly thought the place needed work. Indigo hadn't been raised proud, so his appraisal didn't bother her. A little dry rot was nothing to be ashamed of, after all. But she didn't think it was very nice of him to find fault with her home right in front of her.

He slid a hand into his pants pocket and quickly checked his timepiece. "How long have you been sitting out here?" he asked.

"Not that long."

She wondered if he meant to put her to work. Her ma said some men were born to be chiefs and others Indians. Jake Rand was definitely the authoritative type. An aura of power surrounded him, evident in the decisive way he paced, in the way his dark eyes skimmed over the inconsequential and settled with burning intensity on what drew his interest. She had the feeling he was accustomed to running things and that few people dared to buck him.

His gaze touched briefly on her muddy pants, then flicked to her moccasins. "I don't suppose you were already here when Miss Wolf left, were you, son?"

He thought she was a boy? Momentarily taken aback, Indigo stared up at him.

Clearly taking her silence as a negative response, he scanned the street again. "Damn, I wonder where she went." As he contemplated the rain, his mouth, bracketed by deep crevices, drew down at the corners. "It's pouring buckets out there."

She pushed up from the step and joined him on the porch, confident he'd realize his mistake once he saw her standing. "You're Jake Rand, I assume?"

Jake glanced down. The boy wore a wet leather hat pulled down low around his ears. All he could clearly see of his face was a small but stubborn chin. With surprising maturity, the slightly built youth extended a hand.

Still worried about the missing Indigo catching her death, Jake reached to shake and lowered his gaze. A soaked doeskin shirt clung to the boy like a second skin, delineating scrawny shoulders and what were unmistakably two of the most exquisitely formed breasts he had ever seen. Nipples, erect from the chill, thrust proudly against the pliant leather. For several endless seconds, he stared like a mindless idiot.

"Mr. Rand?"

Jake gave himself a hard mental shake and forced his gaze upward to peer at the shadowed little face beneath the hat brim. He knew he should speak, but nothing came to mind except that this particular he had turned out to be a she, a very charmingly shaped she who gave a whole new meaning to the word drenched.

"I'm sorry. When you called me son, I realized you didn't know who I was. I'm Indigo Wolf."

Jake swallowed and said, "I see that." He cringed as soon as the words left his mouth. "I mean—" Just what, exactly, did he mean? "Of course you're Miss Wolf. I realized the moment"—he felt heat rising up his neck—"the moment we shook hands."

With one slender finger, she nudged the sopping brim of her hat back, giving him his first good look at her face. Her eyes were large like her mother's, an incredibly light color that put him in mind of milk glass tinted with the barest touch of blue. Outlined by silken, dark lashes, they struck a delightful contrast to her dark complexion. She had fragile but striking features, a feminine version of her father's regal, high-bridged nose and sculptured cheekbones, a deliciously full mouth, and her mother's delicate jaw—not a combination one would term beautiful, but appealing, just the same. He found himself wanting to jerk off the God-awful hat so he could see her hair. Was it dark, blond, or a shade in between?

She tugged to get her hand free. With a start, Jake realized he still held her slender fingers in his grip. He immediately released his hold. "I'm sorry. It's just that—Well, you took me by surprise. I thought—"

"I suppose where you're from, women don't wear buckskins."

"No," he admitted. Nor were they streaked with mud and dripping wet. Jake stared down at her, fascinated without quite knowing why. Feature by feature, she wasn't the most beautiful girl he'd ever seen. But there was something, perhaps the odd contrast she struck, a china doll in buckskins. Mostly, he thought it was her eyes. They shone up at him, large and candid, revealing far more than she probably realized. She wouldn't last three hands in a game of poker. "Now that I think on it, I don't know why I expected a dress. That wouldn't be too practical for a mining dig. It's just that you're—" Jake caught himself and broke off before he pointed out how dirty her clothing was.

As if she sensed what he had nearly said, she brushed at her britches. "I worked the sluices today. Aside from the rocker boxes, they're all we still have up and running, and we need all the yield we can get."

Wind gusted under the porch eaves, bringing with it a spray of rain. She clamped a hand over her hat. The wind funneled when it hit the house and backlashed, drawing the front of her wet shirt taut.

Jake's mouth went dry as powder. He felt disgusted with himself for even noticing. She clearly had no idea how revealing the wet leather had become.

"Ma says you want to tour the mine. If you'd rather not get wet, it might let up out there if we wait a bit." She wrinkled her nose and regarded the sheeting rain. "That's one nice thing about Oregon. If you don't like the weather—"

"Just wait and it'll change," he finished for her. "I'm not worried about getting wet. I've got the slicker. But I am worried about you taking a chill." Before he thought, he glanced down again and had difficulty looking away. "You're soaked."

She shrugged one shoulder. Odd that. Only a few seconds ago, he'd looked at that shoulder and thought it scrawny. Now it seemed just right. Except for her ample bust, she was built like her mother, slight with fragile bone structure. He doubted she'd tip the scales at a hundred pounds even in the wet buckskins.

"I'm used to the rain."

As Indigo watched, his lips slanted into a boyish smile that deepened the lines bracketing his mouth and transformed his face. His intent brown eyes delved into hers. An unnameable something arced between them. It reminded her of how the air had felt during the storm, a charged sensation eddying around her.

Suddenly, the thought of spending hours alone with him, miles from town, didn't seem such a grand idea. She didn't like the way he looked at her, or the way she felt when he did. She couldn't name the feeling. She just knew it frightened her.

Apparently her father trusted him. There was an innocence about Hunter Wolf, though. Duplicity was beyond his comprehension. It wasn't beyond hers. A friendly smile could hide a black heart. No one knew that better than she.

Remembering the strong grip of Jake Rand's fingers,

she dropped her gaze to his hands where they rested on his hips. How could a man eke his existence from a hole in the ground and not have calluses?

She glanced at the mountain. A mist wreathed its forested slopes. In three hours it would be dark. She doubted Ma would understand if she said she couldn't go with Jake Rand because he made her legs feel weak. Her parents would think she was making excuses because she wanted to run the mine herself.

She squared her shoulders. "Well, if a little wet doesn't bother you, we may as well go."

"I don't mind waiting for you to change into something dry." Especially a shirt, he added silently. "No point in getting chilled. I'll lend you my slicker if you don't have one."

"Wet leather is surprisingly warm. It acts like a second skin."

Jake had noticed that, yes.

She plucked at the shirt. "Usually I keep everything waterproofed, but here lately, things have been so crazy I haven't had time."

He gestured at his horse. "If you could show me the barn, I'd like to get Buck settled. After the train ride to Roseburg and the long ride here, he deserves a dry place to rest. The traveling accommodations for stock aren't as comfortable as for people."

"Where did you travel from?"

Jake hesitated to mention Portland. "From up north."

She struck off down the steps. Not about to wear a slicker if she wasn't, Jake left the coat on the railing and fell in behind her, hunching his shoulders against the rain. After untethering Buck, she led him toward a looming gray building adjacent to the house.

Halfway there, Jake gave up trying to keep dry. Instead, he watched the jaunty swing of Indigo Wolf's hips. Her stride was long and graceful, her body a harmony of movement. He tried to picture her in one of Mary Beth's fancy dresses and grinned. If a bustle were perched on that fanny of hers, the resultant swing would be enough to make a man go cross-eyed.

Once inside the barn, she became a whirlwind of efficiency. Momentarily distracted by the excited oinking of three white pigs confined in a pen under the loft, Jake stood just inside the door and breathed in the long-forgotten smells. The stables at home were kept clean enough to serve high tea on the floors. Not so here. From the odor, Jake guessed the stalls were badly in need of mucking, yet another sign of Wolf's inability to keep up.

Suddenly, the enormity of the situation hit him. Two small women couldn't possibly handle all this work.

"Why don't I finish up with Buck while you wait on the porch?" Jake said.

"You don't know where everything is."

Indigo uncinched Buck's belly strap. Jake caught her arm before she lifted the saddle. "I'll get that."

She stepped aside. Jake draped the rain-soaked riding gear over a rail and grabbed a nearby rag to rub it down. Intending to do the same to Buck before putting him in a stall, he turned just in time to see Indigo wrestling with a bale of hay.

"Whoa." He dropped the rag and hurried over. "A half-pint like you'll get hurt hefting that." Getting handholds on the wire, he swung the bale off the stack. "Where do you want it?"

She stood back and studied him. In the shadows of the barn, Jake couldn't be sure, but he thought she looked perplexed. She pointed toward an empty enclosure with remnants of hay on the floor. "There'll do fine. Once you cut the wire, we'll fork him some hay into that end stall and give him some grain."

As he hauled the bale across the barn, Jake inquired, "Where's the pitchfork?"

Slowly coming to realize Jake Rand had no intention

of letting her help him, Indigo directed his gaze to the pitchfork that stood in one corner. His calling her a half-pint hit a sore spot. Her brother, Chase, called her that, and she absolutely hated it.

"I'm stronger than I look, Mr. Rand, and I'm used to doing the lifting out here."

"I'm sure you are. Your father tells me you're quite the little worker."

Quite the little worker? And a half-pint. Indigo ground her teeth. "I'm full-grown, nineteen years old this month."

"All of that?" He forked hay over the dividing walls, hitting his mark in the end stall with amazing accuracy. Through the gloom, he flashed her a grin. "You don't look that old."

Without being obvious, Indigo tried to stand a mite taller. "Well, I am."

He paused mid-swing, a forkful of hay poised over his broad shoulder. She couldn't read his expression. "I didn't mean to offend you." He finished the throw and forked another mound of hay. "A tiny frame like yours is attractive on a woman. Until I saw you and your mother, I thought my sister Mary Beth was small. Alongside you, she's an Amazon."

"I'm medium, not tiny."

This time he stopped, rammed the fork tines against the planks, and leaned on the handle to study her. After a long moment, he grinned and said, "Okay, medium. I have the feeling I have offended you. If so, I'm sorry."

The apology made her feel childish. He'd learn soon enough that she didn't let her size hinder her. "While you finish that, I'll get Buck some grain and water."

She felt his gaze follow her to the feed room. The fifty-pound sack of grain was nearly empty. Indigo jumped up onto the stack to get another. She had just gotten her arms under each end of a bag when she felt large hands settle lightly on her waist. The unexpected touch startled her.

She glanced over her shoulder, directly into Jake Rand's dark eyes. She could feel the steamy warmth of his breath stirring the hair at her temple. The expanse of his chest filled her vision, and she was suddenly conscious of how large a man he was. She could feel the untapped strength in his fingertips.

"I can get that," he said in a low, vibrant voice.

With a twist of her hips, Indigo escaped his grasp and lifted the bag, determined to show him how hardy she was. "I handle these sacks all the time, Mr. Rand."

He stole the burden before she could turn. "And you handle them very well."

At her elevated position, she stood as tall as he, her face a scant few inches from his. From up close, she could see the tiny lines at the corners of his eyes and the weathered texture of his skin. She felt oddly breathless and jumped off the sacks to put some distance between them. As he watched her back away, his firm lips twisted in a lazy grin that flashed gleaming white teeth, and his eyes filled with what looked like amusement.

He leaned the sack in a corner, pulled his knife from its scabbard, and slashed the burlap. She noticed that he handled the knife with the same practiced ease that she did hers. With each movement he made, muscle bunched across his back, drawing his wet shirt tight. Indigo stepped around him and darted out the door while he removed the measuring tin from the empty bag.

Unnerved and uncertain why, she waited for him at the front entrance, conscious of his movements behind her as he got Buck settled in. She wished she could postpone their trip to the mine. Tomorrow, the other miners would be there. If they went this afternoon, they'd be the only two people on the mountain.

Though she could detect nothing sinister in Jake Rand's compelling dark eyes, something about him frightened her.

4

The walk to the mine proved to be the longest in Indigo's memory. In some places, the way grew quite steep and the rain made it slick, which precluded conversation. While Jake Rand seemed comfortable with the long stretches of silence, she wasn't. It seemed to her that the air crackled with tension. By necessity, she led the way, and more times than not, she imagined she could feel his gaze on her person. Becoming increasingly self-conscious, she also grew awkward, which was silly. If she had walked this trail once, she had a thousand times.

Having already put in a grueling day's work, Indigo began to grow weary on the last stretch of incline. Her soaked buckskins had grown so heavy it took an effort just to move. She noticed that Jake Rand still breathed easily, so she trudged ahead, afraid to admit her legs were giving out.

He already had referred to her as a half-pint. If his manner in the barn was an indication, he didn't think women should turn their hands to much of anything. If she lost steam climbing a hill, it might reinforce that opinion. What would she do if he forbade her to work at the mine?

A stitch started in her side. She clamped a hand over the spot and focused on the crest of the mountain. She could make it if she placed one foot in front of the other and didn't think about how tired she was. She *could*.

"I need to rest," he said suddenly.

Short of breath and trying to conceal it, Indigo glanced back at him. The rise and fall of his broad chest was even, unlabored. To escape the rain, he ducked under the boughs of an evergreen and sat with his back braced against the tree, one arm draped over his bent knee. She eyed the semidry bed of pine needles and longed to join him there. He patted the ground beside him.

"Come on. I don't bite."

His white teeth flashed in a teasing grin. The hair on her nape prickled. He looked deliciously handsome sitting there with his black hair wet and wind-tossed and his rain-soaked shirt molded to his shoulders. He was nearly as dark as her father. It would be all too easy to forget he was a white man, something she could ill-afford to do. He might pretend not to notice her skin tone, but a cordial demeanor couldn't fool her. Not anymore.

Brushing her hand over her hip to be certain her knife still rested there, she moved toward him. She didn't have to duck as he had. The pine boughs cleared her head by a generous foot.

He didn't look winded or weary. Had he stopped because he knew how exhausted she was? Pride burned its way up the back of her throat. He'd think her a weakling and ban her from the digs. She just knew it.

"It's not that much farther," she said. "We have to get back before dark. Ma'll be fit to be tied if we don't."

He patted the ground again. "I'll have you home

before dark. A five-minute rest won't hurt. Take pity on an old man."

He didn't look old. He looked— Indigo clamped down on the thought and jerked her gaze from his darkly handsome face.

To keep her distance, she sat facing Jake Rand, forgoing the support of the tree against her back. The sharp scent of pine surrounded her. When she shifted on the evergreen needles, she smelled the moldy underlayer of the woodland floor. The network of boughs was thinner above her than where he sat, so more rain trickled through, plunking loudly on her hat.

After telling him how warm leather was, she'd never admit it, but she was becoming chilled. By this time of day, she had usually had a hot bath and was sitting before the hearth, warmed by the fire and Ma's hot cocoa. She hunched her shoulders, acutely aware that he watched her, his dark eyes warm, yet relentless.

"Your father tells me you know this mine like the back of your hand," he said.

"Yes."

"He seems to think someone caused the cave-ins. What's your feeling?"

Indigo wished her father would learn to be less candid. Judging from the look in Jake Rand's eyes, she supposed he had been told everything. If so, there was little point in her being evasive. She tried to hide the shudder that coursed through her. "I agree with my father. I'm not positive about the others, but the last collapse was no accident."

His attention shifted to her shoulders, and she wondered if he could see her shivering. "You sound mighty certain."

"I am. There were axe marks on the timbers, fresh ones. Someone deliberately weakened them."

Jake gazed past her at the rain. He didn't believe in burdening women with men's concerns, but in this instance, he didn't see a way around it. "Do you believe someone intended to kill your father?"

The ugly hat concealed her eyes. She pursed her lips. He noticed that a faint trace of blue now outlined them.

"Honey, are you cold?"

Indigo started. Outside of her family, only Shorty ever called her honey. She knew that Jake Rand's doing so was indicative of his attitude toward her. If she were all white, he would never dream of addressing her in so familiar a way. "Only a little," she replied. "As to your question, if someone had wanted my father dead, why not just kill him? They had no way of knowing he'd go into that shaft. No one should have but me."

Jake considered that. "Why no one but you?"

He saw her mouth quiver, from the cold or unpleasant memories, he wasn't certain. She looked so young and defenseless sitting there, shoulders stiff with pride. If he had worn his slicker, he could take it off and drape it around her.

"We planned to dynamite that morning. I'm the powder monkey and should've been the one who went in to place the charges."

Jake tried to conceal his surprise and knew he did a poor job of it. The powder monkey? One mistake, and she'd blow herself and everyone else to kingdom come. It didn't seem right that a girl should be allowed to take such risks.

"It was one of those freak things," she went on. "When I was about to go in, I couldn't find the fuse spool. The night before, I'd asked Shorty to round up everything I'd need from the powder shack and have it ready."

"And he didn't?"

"He thought he had." She waved a hand. "Shorty's memory's about an inch long. Anyway, I went up to the powder shack to see if I could find the fuse."

Her small chin came up a notch. Though Jake sensed

how difficult it was for her to continue, he couldn't help but smile. Somehow she reminded him a little of Mary Beth.

"While I was gone, Father decided Shorty might have taken the spool down the night before to the spot where we planned to blast. He went to check. I had just returned to the main entrance when—" She took a deep breath. "We all heard the cave-in. At first, I didn't realize my father was in there." She grew so quiet for a moment that Jake wondered if she meant to continue. "It should have been me down there, you see, so it couldn't have been an attempt on his life."

Did she feel guilty because her father had been injured instead of her? He hated to press her further. "How can you be sure it wasn't an attempt on yours?"

"Who'd want to kill me? For that matter, who'd want to kill my father?"

"Who is this Shorty fellow? Can you trust him?"

"Absolutely."

"You're certain he didn't deliberately forget the fuse spool so your father would go into the mine?"

Indigo bit back an angry retort. Jake Rand had never met Shorty, so he couldn't know how outlandish a suggestion that was.

As if Jake Rand read her thoughts, his expression softened. "I don't mean to elbow my way in and start making accusations. It's just—" He sighed and swiped a wet hank of hair from his forehead. "It's not too often I take an instant liking to people, but there's something special about your father." His mouth quirked at the corners, suggesting a smile. "He has a way of looking at you, a rare honesty. I want to help him if I can."

He could have said a dozen other things, all of which she might have discarded, but this had a ring of truth. There was something special about her father. She had seen that look herself. Rare honesty seemed as good a way as any to describe it, though Indigo had always thought of it more in terms of goodness. Some of her reserve fell away. Maybe her father was right in trusting this man. She had a bad habit of being too suspicious of strangers.

Still, there was something in Jake Rand's eyes—a hooded look, as if he was hiding something. That bothered her. Lots of people were a little reserved with strangers, though. She shouldn't form an impression too quickly.

"Shorty is an old friend. My father trusts him, and so do I. I think whoever was trying to sabotage the mine weakened the timbers, hoping the shaft would collapse when the dynamite discharged. If a powder monkey doesn't know what he's doing, he can collapse an entire tunnel. Because I'm a woman, everyone would've figured I made a stupid mistake."

Her assessment of the situation didn't set well with Jake. Just as Jeremy had guessed, someone had been in the wrong place at the right time. "So, instead of causing anyone physical harm, you think the intent was to cause damage to shut you down?"

"Some folks don't like having Indians nearby, and they're particularly leery of my father because he's Comanche." She gave a slight shrug. "I'm sure you've heard the tales about us, the most bloodthirsty of the lot. If you turn your back on one of us, you can kiss your scalp goodbye. If something comes up missing, they're certain we stole it." Her mouth turned down and deepened the dimple in her cheek. "They don't want him dead, mind you, just out of here."

"One thing bothers me. How could anyone have known you planned to blast that particular morning?"

"We don't make a secret of it. To the contrary, on blasting days, no one's allowed into the shafts until we're finished, so we let the miners know in advance that they can come in to work a little later than normal that day."

"So everybody in town probably knew."

"Yes. Just as everyone knew nobody would be in the mine."

Jake focused on her lips. The little hoyden was fibbing about not being that cold. "They knew you'd go in, though. Correct?"

She nodded.

"Then it *is* possible that you were the target."

"Like I said, who'd want me dead? No, whoever took the axe to the timbers just weakened them too much. They probably had no idea anything would happen until the charge went off. By then, I would've been safely outside. Shafts are funny things. If the timbers grow weak, the earth above them can shift. Then the smallest vibration can cause a collapse. It was my father's misfortune that he went down there and began moving things about, searching for the fuse spool."

It was Jake's turn to take a deep breath. He tried to imagine how terrifying it must have been for her when she realized her father was inside the mine.

"Is there anyone in particular you suspect?"

Indigo hesitated. She already had revealed far more than she felt comfortable with. Jake Rand had a way of dragging out answers. She looked into his eyes and could detect only concern.

"You can trust me," he inserted, once again giving her the unsettling feeling that he had read her thoughts. She was used to it being the other way around. "I need to know everything if I'm going to be of any help."

"The Henleys, maybe," she admitted. "It's just a wild guess, and I wouldn't want it repeated. It's not right to accuse people when you haven't any proof."

Jake considered that attitude pretty charitable since she had just admitted the same wasn't true in reverse. "It won't go beyond me. Why do you suspect them?"

"It's not a suspicion, exactly. They're just likely

because they have a mine not far from ours, and they don't cotton much to breeds."

Breeds. Jake winced. The word had such an ugly sound.

"Did any of the workers seem reluctant to help dig your father out?"

She gave a bitter little laugh. "All of them. Except for Shorty and Stringbean, of course. They're like family. The others ran in the opposite direction. When one part of a shaft collapses, the rest might. We all knew that. Many of the men have families who depend on them so I couldn't blame them."

Jake went over the story slowly, trying to pick up on anything that didn't fit. One thought blocked out all else. "You knew another collapse might occur, yet you went in to get your father out and returned to examine the timbers afterward?"

"Naturally, I went in after my father. And I had to know what caused the cave-in. It wasn't the first, you know. We had already begun to suspect tampering. We have a number of men working for us. If other shafts had been tampered with, their lives could have been at risk. What would you have done?"

Jake shifted his shoulders against the tree trunk. "The same, I suppose. It's just that—"

"I'm a woman?" she finished. "Understand something, Mr. Rand. I've been working with my father since childhood, at both sites. I don't stand aside while others do the dirty work."

"I'm sure you don't. That doesn't negate the fact that you took a terrible risk."

She made a fist on the wet leather of one pant leg. "Would it have been less tragic if a man had gone in and died? Besides, what choice did I have? I couldn't ask Shorty and Stringbean to do what I wouldn't. I had to either go in or close down."

Jake couldn't fault her for lack of courage. He studied

her a moment and decided the brief rest had restored her sufficiently to move on. There would be time later for more questions.

Pushing up from the ground, he offered her a hand. She hesitated and then placed her slender fingers across his palm. Jake pulled her to her feet, amazed at how little she weighed. Her hand, small and pliable within the circle of his fingers, felt icy cold. In an attempt to warm it, he held on longer than necessary as he drew her from beneath the tree. He noticed her skin was chapped. Like his mother's had once been.

"It's stopped raining," she said.

Jake hadn't noticed. He released his grip on her so she could move away, which she did with all speed. He nearly smiled again. She had braved a dangerous mining shaft, but the touch of a man's hand unnerved her.

Fully prepared to give Jake Rand a rundown on her father's operation, Indigo was perplexed when he bypassed all the things she had hoped to show him and instead insisted on seeing the pile of removed timbers. After examining them at length, he concurred with her that someone had taken an axe to them.

"The weather's darkened the blade marks, of course," she explained. "But they were fresh right after the collapse."

Crouching by the pile of rubble, he glanced up to meet her gaze. "Even though they've darkened, I can still tell that they're recent."

The touch of his gaze on hers was unsettling. He seemed more troubled by the collapse than a stranger should. She looked away. Dusk was beginning to fall. Deep within the woods, the colorful tangle of myrtle, laurel, and madrone blurred into a black void that seemed to stretch forever. The air smelled of night's crisp coolness. She should give him a rundown on what he needed to know so they could head home. Why was he examining timbers that had nothing to do with the work scheduled for tomorrow? There wasn't that much daylight left.

Unlike most parents, hers allowed her to do pretty much as she pleased, but they were strict about some things, especially social mores. One rule they adhered to was that young women didn't stay out after dark in the company of gentlemen. It simply wasn't done, no matter how trustworthy the man. Samuel Jones, who owned the general store, had ended up the groom in a shotgun wedding because he had taken Elmira Johnson on a picnic and been delayed in getting her home when his horse broke a foreleg. Indigo didn't think Jake Rand would like saying "I do" with a gun barrel poked up one nostril.

"Would you like to see the sluices?" she asked.

"A sluice is a sluice. I'd rather see the collapsed shafts."

Indigo hid her exasperation. Did he plan to run this mine or give it a eulogy?

When they reached the main entrance, she lit two lanterns, handed him one, and then led the way into the bowels of the mine. Forgoing the use of the skips, the small rail cars used to transport miners and equipment, she picked her way on foot alongside the rails so he could get a better look at everything. The cloying smell of cold, damp earth pressed in around them. Their voices echoed back at them. Indigo noticed that his shadow stretched longer than hers. Her uneasiness mounted. In the surrounding blackness, it was impossible to tell how quickly the daylight was running out, and he didn't seem in any hurry.

"You can only see two of the collapsed shafts down here," she explained.

"Is the air foul farther in?"

"We haven't tunneled that deeply yet," she called back. "And there are plenty of ventilation shafts."

"Where did the third collapse occur?"

"In the other mine."

"Where's it located?"

"Over the hill from here, five, maybe six miles. Father had Chase stake a claim there, just in case this location played out. We're obligated to do a certain amount of mining over there to hold the claim, but we haven't the men to work it full-time."

When they reached the accident site, he took his time examining the rubble that hadn't as yet been hauled to ground level. In an attempt to ward off the cold, Indigo shifted her weight from one foot to the other. His interest in the debris bewildered her. She might have understood it if he'd seemed interested in how extensive the repairs were going to be. Instead, he was far more concerned with the fallen timbers and the general layout of the mine before the two cave-ins.

"Where did you plan to do the blasting?"

"Farther in. That part of the mine is collapsed now."

He straightened. "I guess I've seen enough."

He hadn't seen anything thus far, anything that mattered, at any rate. How did he hope to be foreman for a crew when he didn't know squat about the work in progress? She bit down on the question.

"I'd like to see that other tunnel," he said.

"It's too far to go there tonight. I have to get home."

He held his lantern high and settled his gaze on her. With the light thrown across his chest and face, he seemed large and forbidding. And she felt exposed. The endless blackness behind her had icy fingers that curled around the nape of her neck.

"I'm sorry for taking so long." His gaze shifted to her lips. "You must be freezing in that wet leather."

A denial crawled up her throat, but she was too unsettled to voice it. Touching a hand to her shoulder, he walked by her and led the way out.

"Can we go over to the other site tomorrow afternoon?" His voice echoed back at her, each syllable overlapping, which made it sound as if he said each word three times.

"We aren't working over there right now."

"I'd still like to see it."

"I can take you. But since we're not digging there, it'll be a waste of time."

He swung around. The lantern light arced across her, then bounced onto the earthen walls. "I guess I'm not making much sense to you, am I? The reason I'm so curious about the cave-ins is that I want to know how they were caused. Forewarned is forearmed. I can't stop further vandalism if I don't know what to watch for. I think that takes precedence over all else."

Blinded by the light, she squinted and averted her face. "We can't afford a night watchman, if that's your idea."

He moved the lantern so it didn't play in her eyes. "Neither can you afford to spend days doing repairs only to have another collapse shut you down."

Indigo didn't need him to tell her that. "Since the last collapse, I check the timbers every morning before we begin work. What more can I do?"

She thought she glimpsed a smile tugging at his mouth. "I haven't gotten that far yet. Which is why I'm full of questions. I can see this isn't the place to be asking them, though. It's as cold as ice down here, and you're shaking like a leaf."

As he turned and continued walking, she fell in behind him and said, "Cold or not, I'd prefer you to go ahead now and ask any questions you have. My mother has enough to worry her."

"I doubt that avoiding the subject is going to ease her mind. She knows the last cave-in was no accident. You're working here. There's probably not a minute she forgets that."

"I'd still appreciate it if you wouldn't talk about it too much in front of her."

At the entrance, he doused their lanterns and stared out at the twilight. Indigo stepped past him, relieved to be in the open once again. Aware of his gaze on her, she glanced back.

"It's a heavy burden of worry for you to be carrying alone, isn't it?" he asked.

She straightened her shoulders. "I'm not complaining."

"No, I don't imagine you are." He stepped out into the gloaming. "If it'll put your mind at ease, I'll watch what I say while we're at the house. In turn, I'd appreciate it if you'd search your mind for anything you might've forgotten to tell me. I need all the ammunition I can get."

She didn't miss the fact that he said I, not we. He was already taking over. As if to drive home the point, he led the way back down the mountain.

They hadn't gone far when he closed his hand roughly on her wrist. With a violent jerk, he brought her reeling against his chest and clamped a steely arm around her. She tried to wriggle free, horrified when he drew his knife.

"Hold still," he whispered urgently. "We've got company."

Indigo froze and threw a glance over her shoulder to see what he meant. She could see perhaps fifty yards. Shadows turned to blackness beyond that point. Tree limbs swayed in the wind. Brush moved. He was startled by something, that was clear. She could feel his heart slamming.

For her part, she was relieved to know he'd grabbed her to protect her, and not for other reasons. Whatever it was that lurked in the woods, Indigo doubted it could frighten her as badly as Jake Rand just had. Earlier in the barn, she had sensed the untapped strength in him; now it was a reality. His body was padded with muscle and roped with tendon, all taut with tension. She felt surrounded by him and knew she hadn't a prayer of extricating herself from his hold until he chose to release her.

"It's a wolf," he whispered. "The biggest I've ever seen."

She tried to speak, but he was squeezing the breath out of her. The iron hardness of his thighs pressed against her. The heat of his body steamed through their wet garments.

"If I can draw him away from you, can you shinny up a tree?"

She worked a hand between them and shoved against his chest. "It's my—friend. Lobo—my friend. He won't hurt us."

His embrace relaxed, but only slightly. "Your friend?"

She managed to drag in a breath. Standing so close, she realized that her head barely cleared his shoulder. She could see the underside of his jaw and the whisker follicles along his throat. The scent of him surrounded her, a pleasant blend of wet wool, clean sweat, and male muskiness. His hand, broad and long-fingered, curled over her ribs, warm even through the leather.

"Yes, my friend." Even though his closeness unnerved her, she couldn't help but smile at the incredulous expression on his face. "His name is Lobo."

Jake sheathed his knife. She made the pronouncement as if everyone had wolves for friends, and she looked as if she was smothering a laugh. He felt like an idiot.

"Lobo," he repeated. "Your friend. Why didn't I guess?"

He glanced down and froze, still holding her fast. Her hat had been knocked off when he grabbed her. After trying to guess the color of her hair for most of the afternoon, he couldn't help but stare. It was neither mahogany like her father's nor a lighter brown, yet it wasn't what he'd call blond either. Tawny was the only word that came to mind, its overall shade that of dark, rich honey with wispy streaks of coppery gold throughout. During their brief tussle, it had come loose from its moorings and tumbled to one shoulder, a straight, silken mass still half wound in a coronet and caught with hairpins.

Oddly enough, its light hue struck such a contrast to her dark complexion that it earmarked her as part Indian, whereas a darker color might not have. With that tawny hair and those incredibly light blue eyes, anyone who looked at her would know she hadn't attained that skin tone from exposure to the sun.

Nature had played one of its jokes on Indigo Wolf. She was a rarity in that she had inherited the burnished skin of her Comanche ancestors and hair that belonged on a fair-skinned white woman. One of nature's jokes, yes, but Jake wasn't laughing.

Without the God-awful hat, she was the most striking woman he'd ever seen. She had a wild look, yet at the same time encompassed all that was feminine, so fragile and light in his arms that she seemed to have no substance. Except softness. He could feel warmth building wherever they touched.

He started to speak and then forgot what he meant to say when he looked into her eyes. So suddenly that it seemed to hit him between heartbeats, a rush of longing swept through him, and for several endless seconds, he couldn't think beyond that.

Because he was so tall, Jake usually found himself attracted to statuesque women, but Indigo Wolf felt perfectly right clasped in his arms. Her breasts, so warm and soft, hit him just below the ribs and burned through his shirt with white heat. With his arm vised around her waist, her pelvis was thrown forward to ride his thigh. For a fleeting instant, he imagined lifting her a bit higher, imagined her skin and how silken it would feel, imagined her legs looped around his waist as he buried himself inside her.

"M—Mr. Rand?"

Though he heard the uncertainty in her voice, Jake couldn't immediately surface and shifted his gaze to her mouth. Only the innocence that he had read in her eyes forestalled him from bending his head and kissing her. He could feel her heart pound and knew he was frightening her. She had gone rigid, her small hands fisted in his shirt, her back bent to put some distance between them.

"Mr. Rand?"

Jake blinked. He swallowed. He tried to breathe with lungs that didn't want to work. Then, with little grace and no warning, he released her. Caught off balance, she staggered. He grabbed her arm to steady her. She cast around for her hat, spied it and pulled away from him to fetch it.

What in hell was the matter with him? She was scarcely out of the schoolroom. When he looked at her, he couldn't believe she was nineteen and old enough to marry. Men who preyed on innocent girls disgusted Jake, always had and always would. He also disliked faithless men, and he had a fiancée waiting for him in Portland. Yet here he was, lusting after Hunter Wolf's daughter? He needed a swift kick in the ass.

Blood still racing, Jake watched as she wound her hair back up and pinned it. An instant later, she yanked the hat back down around her ears. He felt as if someone had just snuffed the only candle in a dim room.

Her hands were shaking, so he knew she had felt the change in him while he held her. He'd been with too many women not to realize when he ran across one who was man shy. God, how could he have behaved that way? She was just a kid. The problem was that she hadn't felt like one in his arms.

He glanced toward the trees and tried to think of

something to say to smooth things over. Nothing came to mind. She might be innocent, but not that innocent. Women had an instinct about things like this and, no matter how young, always seemed to know when a man had things on his mind that he shouldn't.

He spotted Lobo moving in the brush and decided the less said the better. Eloquent, he wasn't. If he started in on an apology, he'd probably fumble it and only make things worse.

"A pet wolf?" he asked in a deliberately light tone. "Don't tell me. I suppose you've got half the creatures in the forest trailing around after you."

She peered out at him from under the hat brim, her stance uncertain. Jake half expected her to bolt, and he wouldn't have blamed her.

"No, just Lobo. I feed a few wild creatures. The deer, of course. They're always beggars. Then there's an old cougar who's lost most of his teeth and a family of raccoons. They'll come up to eat from my hand, but they don't usually follow me."

"A cougar with no teeth. I take it his claws don't count?"

"He isn't a stupid cougar, Mr. Rand. If he hurt me, there wouldn't be anyone to feed him every day."

"And the raccoons? What's your pact with them? The ones I've seen have all been vicious."

"You probably frightened them. Anything can turn vicious if you scare it."

A girl, for instance? Jake laughed softly and shook his head. "I've never seen a wolf that large or with his coloration."

"He's from the Yukon."

Jake digested that. "How'd you come to own him?"

"I don't. We're just friends. You can't own a wolf— not really. They do the choosing. Wild things are like that, especially wolves." She moved a little farther away and glanced toward the brush where the wolf had disappeared. "An old miner from up north came through this way about three years back. When he moved on, Lobo chose to stay. We've been friends ever since."

So wild things were like that, were they? Jake shoved his hands into his pants pockets, hoping she'd feel a little less threatened. He'd lost it for a second. He admitted it. But did she have to act as if he had sprouted horns?

An apology was called for. There was no getting around it. He just hoped he got the words out right. "I'm sorry I grabbed you like that."

"That's all right. He took you by surprise."

So had she. "I'm afraid I gave you a scare." God, how he detested that damned hat. "If I did, I apologize."

"There's no need. You only meant to protect me."

She needed protection, all right. From him. He managed another laugh. "The truth? I thought we were going to be wolf dinner. I pictured a whole slew of the monsters—a pack of them, and every one hungry. It scared the hell out of me."

He thought he glimpsed a smile on her mouth. So far, so good. She didn't look poised to run now.

"He would never attack a man—unless of course he thought someone was hurting me."

A veiled threat? Jake knew he had no choice but to accept that. If she felt better by warning him off with her wolf, so be it. "I'll remember to mind my manners then." Would he ever. From here on out, he wouldn't so much as touch her. Glancing toward the sky, he added, "We'd better head on down. It'll be dark soon."

She didn't need any encouragement. Jake had to step smart to keep up with her.

The simplicity of the Wolfs' home life fascinated Jake. After a brief visit with Hunter, he did the evening chores. When those were done, he relaxed before the fire on a crudely fashioned stool and sipped a mug of steaming coffee while he waited for Loretta to finish preparing supper. Behind him, he could hear Indigo splashing in her bathwater, her only privacy a water closet Hunter had built in one corner of the kitchen. It amounted to little more than a privacy screen, enclosed to surround the tub and sink, without a ceiling, the walls about as high as his chin. She carried on a sporadic conversation with her mother. A woman from Portland wouldn't have dreamed of bathing in the same room with a man, privacy screen or no.

She emerged from the water closet in a flannel nightgown, a wrapper, and cumbersome, fur-lined moccasins that made her small feet look as large as snowshoes. When her mother handed her a mug of hot cocoa, she joined Jake by the fire on another stool, seemingly unaware that her attire was inappropriate. How incredibly sweet and uncomplicated she was. If only things were so simple and straightforward where he came from.

Not that she wasn't ladylike. She had positioned her stool as far away from his as possible—so far, in fact, that he feared she wouldn't get warm. And her nightclothes were certainly modest enough. It made no sense for her to dress again right before bedtime. As for the bath, if a person was smeared with mud and the only tub was in the kitchen, what choice was there?

Her tawny hair flowed in a straight, shimmering curtain to her fanny and looked so soft he longed to touch it. He kept his gaze on the flames and tried to pretend she wasn't sitting beside him. Every once in a while, though, he couldn't resist a peek. She made soft little sipping sounds as she nursed the hot cocoa, her dusky-rose lips bowing sweetly around the thick rim of the cup. Occasionally, the pink tip of her tongue appeared to flick her mouth clean.

Jake imagined those lips on his skin, imagined how warm and sweet her mouth would taste, and his guts tied into knots. What in God's name had come over him? He knew he had to put a stop to this. A man could imagine himself right into the boiling pot if he didn't watch his step.

After Loretta finished feeding Hunter his meal, she called Indigo and Jake to the table. Dinner proved torturous for Jake. He didn't know how, but Indigo Wolf managed to make eating look sensual. He ended up staring at his plate during most of the meal, scarcely aware as he shoved down mouthfuls of venison, potatoes and corn.

He couldn't keep his mind from wandering to the loft bedrooms above them. Separated by only a half-wall, he was to sleep in one room, Indigo in the other. All night long, he would be able to hear her soft breathing, listen to her stir in her sleep. And he would know she was only a few steps away.

Jake had never availed himself of a whore's services, but he was beginning to wonder if there shouldn't be a first time for everything. During his engagement to Emily, they had shared nothing but chaste kisses. Though Jake had considered pressing her for more, a vague feeling of uneasiness had held him in check. Emily was undeniably beautiful, gracious, well-bred, the perfect wife for him. Yet he felt no urgency to marry her.

His busy work and social schedule precluded a great deal of soul-searching, but occasionally Jake had paused to wonder, rather guiltily, if he truly loved Emily. Always before, he had shoved the question aside. What was true love, after all? A relationship like that of his parents, with his mother giving at every turn and his father taking? At least Jake cared about Emily's well-being. That had always seemed enough to him.

Until now.

Jake took a sip of coffee, his gaze still riveted on his

plate. There was a saloon across the street, the Lucky Nugget, if he recalled correctly. Maybe a sporting woman lived upstairs.

A light scratch on the front door brought Jake's gaze up from his plate. When Indigo excused herself from the table, Loretta smiled. "That'll be Lobo, back from visiting his wife and family."

The skin along Jake's spine prickled as he watched Indigo open the door. He'd never had the dubious pleasure of being in the same room with a wolf. To cover his uneasiness, he said, "Wife and family?"

"Oh, yes," Loretta replied. "Old Mr. Morgan's shepherd presented Lobo with seven pups about a month back. Wolves mate for life, you know. Lobo takes fatherhood very seriously and goes to stay with the babies several times a day while Gretel takes a run. He also provides her with fresh meat."

Lobo walked in. He was beautiful, with thick silver-and-black fur, a plumed tail and regal head. Jake stared into his golden eyes and wondered if the beast slept in the house. He hoped not.

Indigo dropped to her knees, encircled the wolf's neck with her slender arms and buried her face against his ruff. As if it was his due, the wolf accepted her adoration with kingly aloofness, never taking his eyes off Jake. Jake had the feeling that the wolf was taking his measure and knew he had been entertaining less than honorable thoughts about his mistress. The piece of venison in Jake's mouth grew to gigantic proportions and became too dry to swallow. He washed it down with coffee.

"He doesn't act like any dog I've ever seen," he commented.

"That's because he isn't a dog," Loretta informed him. "Wolves are a different story altogether. We had a time understanding him at first. He regards no one as his master, for one thing. He worships Indigo, of course, but even that goes only so far in dictating to him. He comes and goes as he pleases and does pretty much what he likes otherwise. Fortunately, his wishes usually mesh well with ours. He's a surprisingly well-mannered and solicitous animal."

After rinsing her hands, Indigo returned to the table and resumed her meal. Between bites, she explained the traits of wolves to Jake in more detail. Jake learned that wolves, unlike dogs, had vicious claws instead of toe-nails. They were fiercely independent animals, yet loyal to a fault. With the pack instinct so much a part of their makeup, they adjusted well to domesticity. Her voice flowed over him like mulled wine, soft and musical. He found himself wanting to hear her laugh.

"I'm not sure I'd want an animal I couldn't control," Jake admitted when she finally finished talking.

She arched a delicate eyebrow. "I don't imagine you would."

And what did that mean? Jake studied her thoughtfully. "Perhaps we differ on that. To my way of thinking, an animal should know its master and obey without question."

Two bright spots of color stained her sculpted cheeks. "Lobo doesn't need to be controlled. He's very intelligent."

The wolf lay by her feet, silent and unobtrusive. Jake peeked under the table at him. "He seems well-behaved."

"A perfect gentleman," she agreed. "And my very best friend in the whole world."

The love shining in her eyes was unmistakable. A pang of sadness sliced through Jake. Surely she had other companions, girls her age and young men coming to call. He promised himself he'd say nothing more derogatory about her pet. He just hoped the animal never turned on her.

"You say he's got pups? Do they look like wolves?"

"Only one out of the seven resembles Lobo." She wrinkled her nose. "The others look mixed."

Loretta excused herself and pushed up from the table. "That one little male is all wolf, though, a dead ringer for his papa. I worry that Mr. Morgan won't be able to find a home for him. He'll have to shoot him if no one'll take him."

"I'd never let that happen," Indigo cried. "Lobo's son?"

Loretta smiled. "I suppose we could feed another until someone adopted him."

"Or until he adopted someone," Jake inserted. "If he turns out like his father, he might not take up with just anybody."

Loretta groaned. "God spare us. If the pup gets his druthers, he'll tag right along with his papa after Indigo. She attracts wild things like honey does flies."

Jake shoved back his chair and helped clear the table, taking care not to disturb Lobo as he maneuvered his way around to gather serving dishes.

"He won't hurt you, Mr. Rand," Loretta assured him. "If he were the least bit dangerous, we couldn't let him run like he does. People around town were leery, too, at first, but Lobo has proven himself safe around children and pets. I don't think he'd bite unless provoked."

"Would you like to pet him?" Indigo asked.

With a good-natured chuckle, Jake said, "No thanks."

He strode to the dish board with the plates, scraped them into the slop bucket, and then nudged Loretta away from the sink. It had been years since he'd washed a dish, but he certainly didn't mind the chore. Tonight he had taken care of their livestock, which had lifted some of the load off of her, but even so, he imagined she'd put in a hard day. As had Indigo.

"I didn't think there was a man for miles around besides Hunter who'd condescend to wash dishes," Loretta said with a laugh. "You really don't have to. I can get them."

"It'll go quicker if we all pitch in," he replied. Plunging his hands into the sudsy water, Jake looked over at her. "I'd like to see your other mine tomorrow afternoon. I was wondering if you'd mind if Indigo took me over?"

Jake half expected her to say no. It was a long way for a young girl to wander with a man her mother scarcely knew. Loretta answered with one of her bright smiles, her large blue eyes nearly as innocent as her daughter's. Jake supposed it would never occur to her that he might be entertaining thoughts that he shouldn't.

"What a perfect opportunity for you to see some of the country!" she replied. "I'll pack you a nice lunch. Perhaps on the way back, you can take a different route and make an afternoon of it. What do you think, Indigo?"

Indigo, Jake noticed, looked none too thrilled by the thought. A smart girl, that one. She came slowly toward them, her hands laden with the cream pitcher and butter dish. "I guess we could come home by way of Shallows Creek."

"That'd be ideal," Loretta seconded. "That way, if it rains, you can take shelter in one of the shacks along the stream to have your picnic."

The moment the mess was cleared away, Indigo and Lobo disappeared up the loft ladder. Fascinated, Jake watched the wolf make the climb, amazed that he could manage the rungs. "How does he get down?" he asked.

"Out through her window." Loretta finished drying her hands and returned the towel to its rod. "She leaves it open for him so he can come and go as he pleases during the night. Here recently, he's torn between love of Indigo and his duties as a papa. He's gone some, visiting Gretel and his pups. The slope of the porch overhang isn't far off the ground, and Hunter put an old barrel out there so he can jump up and down."

"Doesn't she get chilled with the window wide open?"

Loretta laughed. "She's part Comanche, Mr. Rand. As long as she has plenty of cover, cold air agrees with her. I think that's why Lobo loves her so. They're kindred spirits, both of them wild in their way. Indigo isn't like most girls."

Jake had already concluded that, but until this moment, he hadn't realized just how very different she might be. Wild. He sensed that in her. Yet he also sensed an inherent sweetness and vulnerability.

He straightened his shirt sleeves. "I think I'll mosey over to the saloon for a couple of hours."

"A card player, are you?"

"I enjoy a hand now and again." Jake had no intention of playing cards. There was only one cure for what ailed him, and he intended to go get a dose. Though it went against his grain, hiring a woman to scratch his itch had to be better than ogling a girl Indigo's age. "If you'll leave the door unlatched, I'll close up when I come in."

"I'll leave a lamp burning, then."

Jake opened the door. "No need. I can find my way up to the loft without it. Good night."

5

Jake slipped back into the house three hours later, more than a little drunk and as randy as when he had left. The saloon had two sporting women plying their wares upstairs. Unfortunately, Franny, a little blond with dimples, looked as sweet and vulnerable as Indigo. The elder whore, May Belle, was fifty if she was a day. Uncomfortable with the thought of hiring Franny, Jake paid May Belle ten dollars for an hour of her time, figuring he could douse the lantern.

Maybe Jeremy could throw up a woman's skirt and forget all else, but Jake hadn't risen to the occasion. Fortunately, May Belle had a sense of humor, a kind heart, and plenty of experience in nursing the male ego. She cracked open a whiskey bottle, and by the time they'd worked their way to the bottom, Jake was well into his cups and dimly realized he had spilled far more than a little liquor on her nightstand. He had not only related his life story to her, but had told her about his engagement to Emily and his unexpected attraction to Hunter Wolf's daughter.

May Belle's advice had been short but sweet. She

patted Jake's shoulder and said, "Honey, you know what your problem is? You're too serious. If a gut feeling comes over you and it seems right, don't think it to death."

The advice had struck Jake as hysterically funny. But at that point, just about everything did. With a laugh, he replied, "I don't think a gut feeling is what I'm experiencing, May Belle. Not anything quite that profound, if you get my meaning."

"Yes, well . . ." She joined him in a chuckle. "You show me a man whose brains aren't between his legs, and I'll eat my black lace garters."

With that bit of wisdom to take with him, Jake had picked his way back to the Wolf home, picked being the operative word. Aside from an occasional brandy, Jake seldom indulged, and May Belle's private stock packed quite a wallop.

As he made his second attempt to scale the ladder to the loft, Jake grinned in the darkness, remembering May Belle's throaty laughter. He might go back sometime. She was a nice old gal and about as wise as any he had ever met. Until tonight, he hadn't thought whores could be sweet.

He reached for a rung and missed. His arm shot through the hole, he lost his balance, and all that kept him from falling was a rung in his armpit. Son of a bitch. Jake hung there for a moment, trying to find purchase with his boots. While he dangled, hooked by one arm and in danger of dislocating his shoulder, it occurred to him that only a drunken fool would try to climb to a loft when he couldn't walk on level ground.

Goddam ladder, anyway. He found toeholds and crawled the remainder of the way. When he reached the loft, he threw up one leg, pulled himself forward, and then lay on the floor, facedown.

It wasn't a bad floor, as floors went. He decided he

might rest there a while. Nice and cool. He just wished it would hold still. He didn't want to fall and land in the sitting room. It was the middle of the night. He'd wake everyone up. Not to mention the very real possibility that he might break his neck.

To be safe, Jake dug in with his toes and pushed farther from the ladder. Then he rested again, thinking of the follies of drink. The floor spun beneath him. He spread his hands upon it and assured himself it wasn't moving. He couldn't remember ever having been this drunk. Of course, he'd never failed to perform with a woman before, either. That called for a man to tie one on if anything did.

Maybe his manhood had atrophied. That was a sobering thought. His nose hurt. Jake peered down its length, wondering what in hell was wrong with it. Then he realized it was smashed against the floor. While he contemplated this new predicament, he heard a low snarly sound. For an instant, he thought it was air going up his smashed nostrils. Then the origin of the noise registered. *Shit.* That damned wolf.

Jake lay perfectly still on the revolving floor. The wolf continued to snarl. Finally, Jake dared to lift his head. Anemic moonlight shafted in through the window, spilling across Indigo's bed. The wolf stood at the bed's foot, swathed in shadow, approximately three feet from Jake's throat. Jake sobered up, fast.

"It's okay, boy," he whispered. "I'm just taking a breather here for a second."

Lobo was having none of that. Jake didn't suppose the wolf had ever seen a man slithering around on the floor of his mistress's bedroom. It had to be a strange sight. Jake blinked and tried to rise to his knees. The wolf's snarl remained constant, no louder, no less threatening. So far so good.

Standing up proved to be a problem, but with such encouragement to get his ass out of there, Jake decided not to be fussy and crawled toward his side of the partition. If he woke Indigo, how would he explain the state he was in?

The wolf stopped snarling and followed on Jake's heels to stand sentinel at the foot of the other bed, watching while Jake tried to mount the damned thing as he would a horse. Well, not exactly. He had never slid back off a horse. Determined, Jake threw a leg over the mattress and tried again. Of course, the ground never moved when he was climbing into a saddle, so it really wasn't a fair comparison.

When he failed on the third try, Jake dropped his head to the mattress and peered through the shadows at Lobo. "If you tell anyone about this, I'll shoot you. Understand? Bam, one dead wolf."

Lobo snarled once and sat back on his haunches. He obviously didn't intend to leave until Jake got into bed where he belonged. Jake had trouble focusing and sighted in along the bridge of his nose. "You did know what I was thinking earlier. Think you're pretty smart, don't you?" Working one hand loose from between his chest and the bed, Jake leveled a finger. "Understand something, you dumb mongrel. What I think and what I do are two different things."

Lobo licked his chops and snarled again. Jake made another attempt to climb on the bed and thumped back onto the floor. He groaned and laid his head on the mattress.

"I can't do it," he whispered.

Lobo growled.

Nausea rolled through Jake's stomach. He groaned again. "Go ahead. Kill me. Right now, it'd be a mercy."

Another low snarl was Lobo's response to that.

Jake closed his eyes. "Look at it this way, old chap. If I can't climb in my own bed, I can't climb in hers." A sick grin spread across his mouth. "And even if I could, I probably wouldn't rise to the occasion."

*   *   *

Typical of Oregon's unpredictable weather, the following afternoon turned warm and sunny. The air smelled steamy and sweet, a preview of spring that appealed to Indigo's senses and lifted her spirits after such a long, wet winter. After showing Jake Rand their second mine, which her father called Number Two, *Wahat* in Comanche, she led the way toward Shallows Creek, feeling more lighthearted and carefree than she had since her father's accident. Mounted bareback on Molly, her mare, she picked her way through the tall grasses and tree-studded slopes, guided toward the old Geunther Place by an inborn sense of direction. Jake Rand followed on Buck, speaking to her infrequently.

After spending yesterday and most of today in his company, Indigo was coming to realize that Jake Rand wasn't a talker. In fact, this morning he'd been almost surly. That suited her fine, for she wasn't given to chatter, either. She enjoyed conversation, of course, but she loved silence as well, especially while in the woods. The sounds of the wild animals and birds played upon her ears like music. The whisper of the wind carried her imagination to faraway places and distant times.

Sometimes, while in the woods alone, she pretended she was full-blooded Comanche, a respected woman of the tribe, riding a powerful horse across the Texas plains her father had described to her. She always felt a little foolish when her daydreams ended and she was forced to face reality. Molly was a far cry from a sleek stallion, and the gullies and hillsides hemmed a person in. But what did dreaming hurt? She didn't quite fit in this world, and it made her feel less lonely to pretend, if only for a while, that she lived with the People, that the color of her skin didn't matter, that no one would ever look down on her.

Today, with Jake Rand riding behind her, she was a little too nervous to indulge in daydreams. Instead, she took pleasure in the glimpses of spring and watched Lobo romp through the woods. The fair weather had him behaving like a pup.

Turning slightly on Molly's back, she called, "I thought we'd stop and eat at the old Geunther Place. Since it's so sunny, we can even sit outdoors."

Jake figured the ground would be wet, but he could survive that. After living through this morning, he figured he could survive damned near anything. "Sounds good to me. I've worked up an appetite. Is it far?"

"Just over that next hill. Tomorrow, you'd better try Ma's flapjacks. She's a wonderful cook, you know."

Since his head no longer felt like a bucket someone was thumping with a spoon, Jake could smile at that. "For some reason, I wasn't hungry this morning."

"You'll get over that. We put in long days here. You load up at breakfast to keep meat on your bones."

She had plenty on hers—in all the places that counted. Riding along behind her, Jake found it difficult to keep his eyes off her well-rounded bottom. She sat a horse as if she and the animal were one entity, lending a grace to horseback riding he'd never seen. Her slender, well-toned legs hugged the mare's belly, displaying a subtle strength.

Watching her, he found it easy to imagine her living in a primitive world, wild and free. It was also unnervingly easy to imagine himself making love to her, immersing himself in that wildness, tasting her sweetness. A grin settled on his mouth. There were some itches a man just couldn't scratch with a jug of whiskey.

When Jake saw the Geunther Place, he thanked the Lord it was sunny. The place was a shack, and he didn't relish the thought of eating in there. Indigo dismounted beneath a laurel tree, then looped Molly's long reins so the horse could graze. Jake swung down from Buck with far more grace than he had managed the mattress last night, unsaddled him, and followed Indigo's example by looping his reins.

The rushing sound of the creek sang in Jake's ears. Fern fronds and blackberry shoots lined the bank. Jake spread his feet on the velvety grass, took a deep breath of the air and closed his eyes for a moment to savor the taste. It had been years since he'd been out like this, riding for the sheer joy of it, surrounded by mile upon mile of wilderness. He had forgotten how wonderful it felt.

"Is something wrong?"

He focused on Indigo, who knelt on the grass, unpacking the saddlebag that held their lunch. She hadn't worn the hat today, and the sunlight ignited her loose hair to a blaze of copper-touched gold, nearly blinding him. He blinked and smiled. "The air smells so good, it makes me feel like yelling."

The words popped out before he considered how silly they sounded. She didn't appear to think him strange, though. Instead, she looked beyond him at the hillside they'd just descended, a distant expression in her beautiful eyes. After a moment she flashed him an impish grin. "Then perhaps you should yell, Mr. Rand."

He laughed at that, then jumped a foot when she let out a shrill, yodeling cry. He'd never heard any sound quite like it. "What in God's name was that?"

"A Comanche war cry. It's really not difficult, once you get the feel of it. Go ahead, give it a try. It's invigorating. There's only me and Lobo to hear."

With a chuckle, Jake narrowed an eye and sat beside her, pleased that she was beginning to relax. All morning, she had been reserved and wary. Not that he'd encouraged conversation.

"Maybe later. First, I want to eat."

Loretta had packed them each two sandwiches, chunks of cheese, a piece of chocolate cake, dried apple slices, and a small vinegar jug filled with juice. After Indigo laid out the food on a towel, he dug in and savored each bite. The juice, he discovered, was blackberry and tasted finer than any expensive wine.

He was beginning to realize that the Wolfs' lifestyle, simple though it seemed, was, in its way, far more pleasurable than his own. Jake figured he probably could buy a thousand mountain clearings but would never have time to enjoy them. Even if he made time, he doubted he'd find a picnic companion among Portland's elite. Emily wouldn't dream of sitting on damp ground to eat a sandwich. *Emily.* He couldn't envision her face.

The realization made him feel a twinge of melancholy. Until coming here, he thought he had everything. Now he felt a vague dissatisfaction. There was more to life than paperwork. The years had cheated him, and the realization made him feel frustrated. How could a man with his wealth be made to feel poor by a girl who drank blackberry juice from a chipped vinegar jug?

When Lobo joined them, Indigo peeled the newspaper wrapping from his lunch, a generous portion of raw meat, which Jake assumed was venison. The wolf devoured it.

"With your father bedridden, shouldn't you take care with the meat stores?" Jake asked. "How can you feed Lobo and a toothless cougar without running short?"

"There's always more where this came from." She wiped her fingertips on the towel and picked up her sandwich again. "I bring home most of the meat, so my folks don't mind my being generous with Lobo and the cougar."

His gaze dropped to her slender shoulders. "You shoot a rifle? I'd think the kick would set you on—" He broke off.

"Sometimes a rifle. I prefer to use a bow."

Jake considered that. She killed animals, which meant she probably gutted and skinned them as well. How in hell did she tote a deer? Because she no longer

seemed as tense as she had earlier and because he wanted to keep her talking, he asked.

"I quarter it, carry a section home and go back for the
rest on Molly. I don't go far. These hills are filled with
game."

What a puzzle she was, a girl who befriended a wolf,
who fed the wild creatures, and then had the heart to
slay them. Jake studied her small face, trying to understand her and failing. What bewildered him most of all
was that she seemed so nervous around him. Maybe
Jeremy was right and he glowered too much. Or maybe
she sensed how she affected him.

"Does it bother you? Killing animals, I mean."

Her mouth firmed and drew down at the corners.
"My family must eat. The animals, they are *tao-yo-cha*,
children, of Mother Earth. Sometimes, they must die so
we may live."

She truly did love the animals; he could see that in
her expression. "It hurts you to kill them, doesn't it?"

"It makes me feel sad, but only for a while. As my
father says, 'That's the way of it.' We can't question
nature's ladder. If I were a deer, I would probably be
eaten." Her gaze dropped to his hand. "Your sandwich
is made of venison."

Jake chuckled again. "Point taken. It's just that one
doesn't envision a young lady like yourself going hunting. That's usually a man's job."

"I'm a little different than most young ladies," she
admitted, "as I'm sure you've noticed. I gave up trying
to be something I'm not years ago. I walk my own way."

Jake thought it would be a shame if she changed. Indigo Wolf was an original. One day soon, a young man
would come along, take one look, and snatch her up. The
thought made him stop chewing. If only he were ten years
younger, he might have been in the running. There was
something about her that appealed to him in a way other
women didn't, in a way Emily didn't.

But he wasn't younger. And it was probably a blessing. A girl like her would be an outcast in his world, and the social restrictions would make her miserable. She belonged here beneath a laurel tree, with the breeze playing in her hair.

He took another bite of his sandwich and relished the taste. "*Tao-yo* . . . ?"

"*Tao-yo-cha*. Comanche flows nicely from your tongue." She regarded him a moment. "You aren't, by any chance, part Indian."

"I'm not sure. The Rands are so mixed, it's hard to keep track. My mother—she was Black Dutch. That's where I got my hair and eyes. My father is—God only knows. I believe the name Rand is an abbreviation of something foreign—Russian or Italian or something. My father told me once, but it was such a mouthful, I promptly forgot. And who really cares?"

"Black Dutch?"

"A darker strain." He searched her troubled gaze and smiled. "Heritage is extremely important to you, isn't it? You can't imagine my not knowing what I am or caring."

She averted her gaze. "Some must wear their heritage."

Beneath the stiff pride, he heard a world of hurt in her voice. He regarded her creamy skin. "You're beautiful, Indigo."

He wasn't sure where the words came from or why he had said them. But they were out. The moment he spoke, the fragile comaraderie that had begun to develop between them was shattered. She fastened those huge blue eyes on his—vulnerable eyes that belied her impish smile. He saw pain in those eyes, pain she tried desperately to hide. And fear. Of what, he didn't know.

The tension between them became almost palpable. Jake wanted to kick himself. He was afraid to move or say anything more. The breeze picked up and rustled in the tall pines. The sound seemed lonely.

Following her example, he applied himself to his meal, wondering what it was about him that unnerved her so. Even if she sensed that he found her attractive, she could surely see he wasn't the type to act on it. Or could she? Last night on the mountain, his behavior had been less than exemplary. Perhaps his size intimidated her. They were miles from town. Maybe she was afraid he'd make an improper advance and try to press the issue.

He had never used his strength against a woman. But she couldn't know that. Short of telling her, he couldn't think of a single thing he could do to ease her fears. He never had been good with words. If he so much as alluded to rape, she was sure to think he'd been entertaining the notion.

"Indigo, am I imagining it, or do I frighten you?"

She stiffened at the question. "Why would I be frightened?"

That was a good question. "You just seem nervous, that's all. If I've done something—"

"You haven't."

His mouth felt suddenly dry. "I hope not." Aiming for a lighter note, he said, "I'm harmless, really. Ask anyone."

He didn't look harmless to Indigo. Right at the moment, he seemed a yard wide at the shoulders. His denim-sheathed legs appeared endlessly long. The sleeves of his green wool shirt were folded back to reveal the tendons that roped his bronzed forearms. He sat a mere two feet away, close enough to snake out a hand and grab her when she wasn't expecting it. She hadn't missed the gleam in his eyes, and she knew what put it there. Once, a lifetime ago, another white man had looked at her that way.

"I'm not afraid of you or anyone else," she told him.

It was a lie, one of the few she had ever told. Everything about Jake Rand frightened her. She couldn't shake the feeling—a premonition, perhaps?—that he was somehow going to gain control over her life. The moment she first saw him, she had sensed it—an inexplicable something, a strange feeling of recognition—as if her destiny had finally come calling.

He wasn't a man to be taken lightly. Every pore of his skin radiated strength, every movement he made was ruggedly masculine. Oh, yes, he frightened her. She had seen women over at the general store looking at a new bolt of cloth in the same way that he looked at her. Tempted, but telling themselves no. Nine times out of ten, those women returned, again and again, and finally bought the cloth. A week later, they wore new dresses, patterned just the way they wanted them. Indigo didn't want her world torn apart, then reassembled to suit Jake Rand.

Recalling the steely power she had felt in his body last night, she nearly shivered. His collar hung open to reveal the burnished column of his sturdy neck. When he moved, the green wool of his shirt pulled tight, showing the delineation of bunched muscle in his shoulders and arms. She tried to imagine his strength being targeted at her and decided she'd have a better chance pitting herself against a stone wall.

"You're not afraid of anyone at all?" He studied her as if he found her response highly amusing. "I'm impressed. I thought just about everyone was afraid of someone."

The question jerked her back to the present. She gathered her composure and finally managed to reply. "Oh? And who do you fear, Mr. Rand?"

The question left Jake drawing a blank. "I'd appreciate it if you'd call me Jake."

"You're my elder. It wouldn't be respectful."

He winced. "I'm not exactly a Methuselah."

Having her refer to him as her elder rankled. He shoved an entire piece of cheese in his mouth. Thirty wasn't that old. He'd only been—he did a quick calculation—eleven when she was born. He knew men who were married to women twenty and thirty years their junior, for Christ's sake.

Following the cheese with a slice of dried apple, Jake regarded her once more and strove to recover his sense of humor. "Do I creak when I walk?" he asked with mock concern. "I rub my joints daily with axle grease. The doctor promised that'd cure the problem."

Her eyes were still wary, but he glimpsed a smile flirting at the corners of her mouth.

"I have it." He held out his hand and made it tremble. "You noticed the palsy, didn't you? Embarrassing that, but unavoidable for a fellow of my advanced years."

The smile finally broke loose and spread across her mouth.

Warming to the game, Jake lifted his gaze skyward and groaned. "Oh, no. It was all that rain yesterday, wasn't it? It washed the shoe blacking out of my hair. Admit it. You saw black streams running down my neck, didn't you?"

She rewarded him with a musical giggle, which she immediately stifled by biting her lower lip. The sound tantalized him. Lord, but she was sweet. He was happy to note that the wariness no longer lurked in her eyes.

"I didn't mean any offense, Jake."

She said his name as if it were an intimacy, and her cheeks turned a delightful pink.

"You're not *that* old," she added.

"Tell me I'm a handsome devil, and maybe I'll forgive you."

She giggled again. The sound warmed him clear through.

"You're a handsome devil," she replied. "A very *young* handsome devil, so young you're still wet behind the ears."

"You're definitely forgiven."

Lobo flicked his ears toward the hillside. Jake followed the wolf's gaze but saw nothing.

"Don't mind Lobo. He probably sees his dessert running around up there. Rabbits are his favorite food." She returned her second sandwich to the saddlebag, then started on her cake. After taking a bite, she skimmed her lips with her tongue to lick away flecks of chocolate. "Mr. Rand . . ."

"Are we off on that again?"

"Jake." The pink flush returned to her cheeks. "May I ask you something?"

"I'm thirty."

"No," she said with a laugh, "not about your age."

"Ask away."

She turned her cake as if studying it for flaws. "Can you explain why you don't have calluses like most miners?"

It wasn't what he expected. Jake looked down at a palm. A dozen lies swam through his mind, but for reasons beyond him, he couldn't voice them. He had come here knowing he'd have to lie his way into a position of trust, and he had thought himself prepared to do that. That had been before he had met Indigo and her parents.

"I, um . . ." He cleared his throat. "For the past several years, I've been doing desk work."

"Desk work?"

"For a very large mining corporation."

"What possessed you to quit?"

Jake felt as if he were drowning. "I didn't, exactly. It's more like a leave of absence. I, um—" He took a deep breath. "I came here hoping I could—" He looked into her eyes and, though he couldn't say why, knew he couldn't lie to her. "Have you ever had the feeling you've sleepwalked through your life?"

"No."

"Well, I did. I came here searching for the truth."

"The truth," she echoed. "The truth about what?"

"About myself, about everything I've believed myself to be. The truth about my work." He sighed. So far, he hadn't told her anything that wasn't true. "When you work within a large company, it's all too easy to assign a dollar value to everything. People become names on paper. A man can get so caught up in making profitable business moves that he notices nothing else. Something happened to make me realize that maybe I had lost touch with all the things that really counted. I had to find some answers. I ended up here at Wolf's Landing."

"By accident?"

Jake felt his pulse quicken. But after coming this far, he couldn't retreat into a falsehood, no matter how harmless. "No, not by accident. I had heard about the cave-ins at your father's mine and about his injury. I figured he might hire me on. From what I heard about Wolf's Landing, I thought it might be the place where I could find the answers I needed."

"So you didn't just happen to be in Jacksonville."

"No."

"You told my father—"

"I know what I told him." Jake braced his elbows on his knees and leaned forward. "Some things aren't easy to explain. What would he have thought if I'd said I was searching for answers? It was easier to say I was just passing through."

She gazed at him for what seemed an endless time. Then her expression softened. "I hope you find the truth you're seeking. And I won't embarrass you by telling my father."

Relief flooded through him. "You won't?"

"No. A journey within is a private thing, and I respect that. So would my father, if you told him." Her eyes warmed on his. "So many never question. They never look within themselves for any kind of truth. I'm not sure they even realize there's a truth to look for.

My father isn't one of them, though. He journeys to a place within himself nearly every day. And so do I and my brother. It's the Comanche way."

Jake eyed the remains of his sandwich. In his nervousness, he had pressed his thumbs into the bread. "A place within," he repeated. "You make it sound almost noble. Yet it feels so—" He broke off, uncertain how to finish. "When I take a good, hard look inside myself, I'm not too sure I like what I see."

She smiled. "If you don't like who you've become, set your feet along another path."

She made it sound so easy. But it wasn't. How could he turn his back on everything he had worked so hard for, on everyone he loved? Perhaps his world in Portland wasn't all it should be, but it was where he had come to belong. "It isn't always quite that simple."

"A journey within is never simple."

She searched his gaze. It took all Jake's resolve not to look away. He had the feeling she was reading him. After a moment, she broke the visual contact to finish off her cake. Silence fell over them. Jake concentrated on the remainder of his lunch, no longer enjoying the taste. He tossed a crust of bread at Lobo, who still sat beside Indigo, regarding the hillside. When the bread hit the wolf's chest, he let it drop to the ground and eyed it with disdain.

Stretching her arms above her head, Indigo took a deep breath, then rolled onto her side. As she did, the air around Jake seemed to explode with sound. A rifle shot.

For an instant that seemed years long, he couldn't react. His eyes registered the smallest details, imprinting the images on his brain like a camera did on a negative. Lobo, sitting beside Indigo one moment, thrown aside the next. Blood everywhere, splattered across the towel, on the grass, on Jake's face. Indigo screaming. The horses bolting.

Jake felt as if he were submerged in cold molasses. A rifle, dear God, a rifle. Blackberry juice flooded his lap as he released the jug with fingers that took forever to react. He dove forward to shield Indigo's body and had the crazy sensation that he was floating against a headwind and might never reach her. One thought tumbled inside his mind. If Indigo hadn't stretched out onto her side when she did, she might have taken the bullet in her chest. He covered her with his body and crossed his arms over her head.

Jesus, sweet Jesus.

No more shots rang out. Panting as though he had been running, he raised on an elbow, swiped the blood from his eyes and scanned the hillside. He saw a man darting through the trees. Leaping to his feet, Jake grabbed Indigo's arm and dragged her toward the shack, his one thought to get her under some kind of cover.

"Lobo!" She sobbed and tried to wrench free. "Lobo! I can't leave Lobo!"

Jake swore. "Forget the goddam wolf!"

He dove with her through the ramshackle cabin's yawning doorway. Once inside, he shoved her to the floor near a window and crouched over her to peer through the grimy glass. If the man was still up there on the hillside, he was well hidden. Something sticky clung to Jake's lips. He grimaced and spat, then brushed at his face. A cobweb.

"Lobo . . ."

The horror clouding Jake's mind fell away layer by layer. He glanced down to see Indigo holding up her hands. Lobo's blood flecked them. She shook violently. Jake groaned and drew her arms down. Then he gathered her close. Settling his hand on her hair, he registered two things—two totally insane, irrelevant things: one, that her hair was as silken as he imagined, two, that he felt nothing but fierce protectiveness now that he held her.

"I'll go back for Lobo, honey, just as soon as it's safe."

"Why?" she wailed. "Why did someone shoot him? He never hurt anyone. Never!"

Keeping an eye on the hillside, Jake ran a palm down her slender back, trying to comfort her in the only way he knew. Dear God. Had that bullet been meant for her?

She was so frantic about the wolf that Jake risked going back out into the open. As he bolted out the doorway, he veered to the left and dove into the brush. Blackberry vines snagged his shirt as he belly-crawled toward the laurel tree. Lobo lay where he had fallen. His left shoulder, once padded with muscle and thick fur, was now a gaping hole. Blood was everywhere. He could scarcely believe it when he saw the wolf still breathing.

After scanning the hillside, Jake rose, scooped Lobo into his arms, and ran back to the shack. Indigo met him at the door. He nudged her aside, barked at her to stay down, and took the animal to a corner. Indigo dropped to her knees beside him. Seeing how gently she hugged her pet nearly broke Jake's heart.

She didn't cry. Jake would have welcomed tears. Instead, she sat back on her heels and placed a reverent hand on the wolf's forehead. Jake stripped off his shirt.

Though he didn't particularly like the wolf and knew he would probably die, Jake couldn't let him go without a fight, not when Indigo loved him so. He made another trip to the window to check the hillside. Then he pulled his knife and cut a strip of wool from his shirt for binding. The remainder of the garment would do as a pad. With enough pressure applied to the wound, perhaps the bleeding could be stopped.

Returning to Indigo, he grasped her shoulder and

drew her out of his way. "Let me do what I can," he said softly.

The interior of the shack was cloaked in shadow, which gave him poor light to see by. Using his knife, Jake carefully probed for the lead. Indigo leaned forward beside him, her shaking hands hovering, her silence eloquent testimony to her grief. *My best friend in the whole world.*

Jake hadn't called on God for a long while, other than to take his name in vain. But he prayed now. Not for the wolf, but the girl. It was going to half kill her if Lobo died.

Jake's knife tip scraped the lead. Cautiously, he inched the mass upward. At last, the ball came free of the mangled flesh and *kerplunked* on the dusty wood floor.

Working quickly, Jake folded the remains of his shirt and clamped it over the wound. He held the pressure for a while in hopes he could stop the bleeding. The wolf was still alive, which in itself was unbelievable. Now that Jake had examined the wound more closely, he knew there was no hope. Most of one shoulder was gone. If Lobo lived, he'd be badly crippled. It would be kinder to let him go.

So why was he doing this? At best, he'd give Indigo hope where there was none. A glance at her face answered that question. Her blue eyes were huge and frightened, pleading with him to save her pet. Jake tried to remember being her age, and only one thing came clear. At nineteen, he had still believed in miracles. It wasn't up to him to disillusion her. Life would do that soon enough.

"I-Is he g-going to die?" she asked in a shrill voice.

"I don't know, sweetheart. It doesn't look good."

She laid a tremulous hand on Lobo's head again. "He can't die, he just can't. Lobo? Do you hear me, my friend? You can't die. You can't leave me . . ."

Using the strip of wool, Jake bound the wound, then moved back to the window and left her to her grief. What he heard made him feel sick. He wished she would wail and sob. Anything would be better than those heartfelt whispers and shaky pleas. He couldn't imagine loving anything that much, and the realization made him feel hollow.

He scanned the hillside and tried not to think. It was a time for craziness, he supposed. The feeling that he no longer knew himself or what he wanted, that his life was missing something vital, was a product of the madness. *You've despised him all your life, and now you've become just like him.*

As those endless minutes stretched into an hour, her whispers abated, and she slumped against the wall, holding a vigil that Jake knew would end in her pet's death. He regretted that, but right now, his main concern had to be getting her out of here. He kept seeing her, arms stretched skyward before she lay on her side. Had that bullet missed its mark?

The thought terrified Jake. All he had on him was a stinking knife. Why in hell hadn't he brought a rifle? And where were the horses? If that bastard walked up to a window and started blasting, Jake couldn't put up much of a defense with nothing but a three-inch knife blade as a weapon.

He peered at the hilltop. The sun had dropped. They didn't have much daylight left. Two hours, possibly three. What if he couldn't find the horses?

"Indigo, can we make it back on foot before dark?"

A shadow that blended with shadows, she stirred slightly. "We can't move Lobo."

Jake's gaze slid to the wolf. Didn't she understand that there was no hope? "Honey, we can't stay here with him." The time had finally come to tell her of his suspicions. "I think that bullet might have been meant for you."

She drew a sharp breath, clearly appalled. Then she looked at the wolf. "If Lobo dies, I'll wish it'd hit me."

Jake could only stare at her. "You don't mean that."

"Yes."

He combed his fingers through his hair, fighting down an unreasoning anger, not at her, but at that bastard on the hillside.

"Is there anyone you know of who might try to shoot you? Think hard, Indigo. Anyone at all?"

"No." She moved again, a shadow in the gloom, her hair a dim glow around her shoulders. "I think whoever did it meant to hit—" Her voice cracked. "A lot of people hate Lobo. They're afraid of him. He's been shot at before. Whoever did it probably thought killing him would be funny."

Funny. Jake felt as though he might vomit. As recently as yesterday, he might have shot the wolf himself. But he never would have done it knowing the animal was a pet. It was inconceivable to Jake that another man had. But it was easier to believe that than to think someone had meant to kill Indigo.

"Whoever did it took a big chance. If he had been a hair off, he would have hit you."

"A good marksman is seldom off," she replied. "If the bullet had been meant for me, it would have found me."

Jake prayed she was right.

"I still think we ought to get out of here."

"No," she said simply. "I can't leave Lobo."

Jake swallowed. "Honey, he's not going to make it. You know that."

"He might. The bleeding's stopped, I think. If we move him, it'll start up again. He'll die for sure."

Jake propped an elbow on the filthy windowsill, planted a hand over his face, and sighed. "You can't risk your life for a wolf, Indigo."

"You say wolf as if it's something dirty."

"I didn't mean it to sound like that."

"No, but it's how you feel. He's different, not a dog, so you don't like him."

Jake sighed again. "I'm sure I would've come to like him, given time. But even if he were a dog, my vote would be the same. Your life is far more precious than an animal's."

"I'm different, too." Her voice came to him in a thin whisper. "Lobo and I, we're alike. I know you don't understand, but we're friends. Not ordinary friends, but special. You don't leave your friend to die alone."

"If he loves you as much as you love him, he'd want you to go. It might not be safe here."

"And it might not be safe out there in those woods," she came back. "The horses have run off. If someone meant the bullet for me, we could get shot going out there to look for them. We're as safe here as anywhere, maybe safer. And—Lobo—he wouldn't desert me, no matter what the danger. I won't do less for him."

Aside from her irrational loyalty to the wolf, she had a point. Jake kept his gaze riveted to the hillside. He considered searching for the horses, but what if the rifleman came down to the shack while he was gone? More than likely, it was as she said, and she was in no danger. But that was a gamble Jake couldn't take. He considered striking off for Wolf's Landing to get help. He scotched that idea for the same reason.

"Who knows," he whispered. "Maybe you're right and staying put is the best idea. Your mother knew we planned to come back this way. Maybe she'll send someone out to look for us."

"She won't know where we stopped. The horses aren't here."

That was true. Jake slumped against the wall. Maybe, just maybe, luck would be with them. Maybe the bullet had been meant for Lobo. Maybe Loretta Wolf would send someone to find them, and the saddle would draw attention. Maybe the man who shot Lobo was miles away by now. Maybe everything would come out perfect.

It was one hell of a lot of maybes.

6

By midnight, Jake realized he had never understood the true meaning of the word endless. He measured the seconds by the muted and sluggish ticking of his pocket watch. The moon had surely frozen in one position. Even the wind had stopped blowing. Silence closed in around him, an awful, horrible silence that seemed to be waiting.

Jake had never been afraid of the dark, but tonight the moon-touched blackness of the woods seemed threatening. Though not a draft of air stirred, the shadows seemed to shift and move toward the shack. When he stared long enough at a shape, it took on the outline of a man. Sweat beaded at the nape of his neck and trickled down his spine. At times, his heart pounded so hard he felt sure it would beat its way through his ribs.

He kept seeing Loretta Wolf's guileless blue eyes. She had trusted him to bring her daughter safely home. Now, here he sat, armed with nothing but a knife when a madman with a rifle might lurk nearby. One well-aimed shot would take him down. After that, Indigo would be on her own.

Behind him, she sat in rigid silence. She seemed aware of nothing but the wolf. Her stillness unnerved him. Maybe it was the Indian in her, but the way she grieved didn't seem natural.

A cramp knifed up his thigh. He changed positions to ease it and accidentally thumped his boot on the floor. The sound seemed deafening. His arm brushed the grimy windowsill, and the dust filled his nostrils. Hunching his bare shoulders to ward off the cold, he kneaded his leg and stared at the hillside.

Sudden movement made him turn. Lobo, a silver-and-black wraith in the moonlight, shoved himself up with his uninjured foreleg. Golden eyes fixed on the window, he stretched his neck and let out a low howl that rose eerily to a mournful crescendo.

Jake had never heard a wolf howl from up close, and the sound sent a chill washing over him. It seemed to go on forever. Indigo moved closer to the wolf and hugged his massive chest. A ragged sob erupted from her.

"Oh, Lobo, my friend."

The anguish in her voice made Jake's throat ache. With a sinking sensation, he realized that the wolf was baying at the moon to herald his own death. Indigo, so attuned to him, had already concluded that and was helping him sit erect. Lobo tipped his head back and howled again. The effort clearly drained him. He slumped against his mistress, no longer able to hold himself up. His third howl was pitifully weak.

Indigo took up the lament, her voice shaky and shrill. Jake listened, unable to identify one of the languages she used. Some of what she sang sounded like Latin, which he recognized from his days at university. The rest, he guessed, was in Comanche. *Ein mea-dro. Ein habbe we-ich-ket.* A death chant, sung with tearful clarity for Lobo because the wolf no longer had the strength to do it himself.

As if Lobo understood, he leaned his head against her breast. In the moonlight, his golden eyes seemed to glow. Jake had the unnerving feeling the animal was beseeching him to do something, but he had no inkling what.

After a few minutes, Lobo's strength ebbed, and he sank across his mistress's knees. Measuring the seconds by the painful thudding of his heart, Jake watched the glow fade from the wolf's eyes. He knew the exact instant when the last bit of life slipped from Lobo's body. He said nothing; he couldn't.

Though she must have felt her pet's sudden limpness, Indigo never paused in her chanting. She stroked the wolf's head with gentle fingers and sang ceaselessly, as if the animal could still hear her. In the dim light, she looked like a full-blooded Comanche. Until tonight, Jake hadn't realized how deeply her father's ways were ingrained in her. He could almost hear the alien drumbeats of the Comanches thrumming in the night.

Jake had the crazy sensation she was made of moonbeams, and that if he stood and let his shadow fall across her she would disappear. Her chant went on and on. The minutes slid into an hour, the hour into two. She was still singing when the first pink streaks of dawn touched the horizon.

When it turned daylight, Jake deemed it safe to leave Indigo and search for the horses. Just as she had done all night, she was still kneeling and holding Lobo clasped in her arms when he returned. Jake slowly approached her, uncertain what to say.

"Indigo?"

Her lovely eyes didn't seem to focus on him.

"Indigo, I found the horses and got Buck saddled up. I think we should head back to Wolf's Landing now."

Her arms tightened around the wolf, and she whispered, "*Nei-na-su-tama-habi, nei-na-su-tama-habi. Kiss, hites.*"

Jake hunkered beside her. Dark shadows etched her high cheekbones. He heaved a sigh and skimmed a hand over her hair, wishing to God he knew how to make this easier on her.

"He's gone, honey. It hurts, but you have to face it."

She shook her head. "No. He isn't gone. Never gone."

She tipped her head as if to listen. The morning wind funneled under the eaves of the shack and made a whining sound. She closed her eyes as if she heard something Jake couldn't.

"Our sacred brother, the *esa*, doesn't die," she whispered. "He becomes one with the wind, the mountains, the moonlight. His spirit lingers always. If you listen, you can hear his voice."

<u>Esa</u>. Jake guessed that meant wolf. As irrational as her behavior was, the expression on her small face cut him to the quick. If only she would cry. He wished with all his heart that he could bring the wolf back.

"If he lingers, then you haven't really lost him."

When she opened her eyes, the pain he saw reflected there made him ache. "Yes, I've lost him. Though he may walk beside me, we will be a world apart."

Jake touched reverent fingertips to the wolf's thick fur. "Will you trust me to carry him?"

Her mouth twisted, and she swallowed convulsively. "Let me say my last goodbye to him first."

Jake rose and left the cabin. The chill morning air licked at his bare back and raised gooseflesh. He gazed at the steadily rising sun and drew comfort from the predictability of it. Creatures were born, they died, but the world went on. In time, Indigo would have only a dim memory of this morning.

Without a sound, she appeared at Jake's elbow. He

gazed down at the telltale moisture that glistened on her thick, dark eyelashes, the only sign that she had shed so much as a tear.

"I'm ready now," she said simply.

Feeling hollow, Jake returned to the shack for the wolf. She looked away while he strapped the animal across Molly's rump. When they mounted up, Jake noticed a marked difference in the way she rode, back hunched, shoulders drooped, head bent. The fierce pride that usually held her erect had been snuffed out.

Jake was surprised when she stirred from her listlessness and turned to speak. "I don't want you to tell my parents that the bullet barely missed me."

Jake nudged Buck into a trot to ride abreast of her. He glanced over at Lobo's lifeless body and tightened his grip on the reins. "I can't promise that, Indigo. I believe they have a right to know, just in case."

"In case of what?"

Jake ducked his head to miss a tree limb. "You know very well what. Say that bullet was meant for you?"

"I told you yesterday, a good marksman seldom misses. People have shot at Lobo before. And I haven't any enemies. It's ridiculous to think someone meant to kill me."

Jake avoided meeting her gaze. "I'm sorry, but I feel I have to tell them."

"And give them something more to worry about?" Her voice rose an octave. "They've enough on their minds as it is."

"And how would they feel if it had been you instead of Lobo? The mine and all the other worries would pale in comparison."

She made a frustrated noise and nudged her horse into a trot. Jake held Buck back. There was little point in continuing the conversation. He had to tell her parents, and that was that.

*   *   *

When they rode back into Wolf's Landing, Jake didn't expect to see so many people out and about. Nor did he anticipate the excitement his and Indigo's appearance would stir. As they rode down the hillside, he heard voices heralding their arrival. A moment later, he spied Loretta Wolf as she ran from the jailhouse into the street, her blue skirts lifting in the breeze.

"Indigo!" she cried.

There was no mistaking the tearful relief in her voice. Acutely conscious of his bare chest, Jake pulled Buck up in front of the house and swung from the saddle. The people along both boardwalks had stopped and turned to stare. After the day and night he and Indigo had just spent, the accusing expressions on their faces ignited his temper. Surely they could see the dead wolf across the back of the girl's horse. If they thought that he and Indigo had been off somewhere fornicating all night, they were narrow-minded idiots.

"Praise the Lord you're all right," Loretta cried.

Indigo turned her horse toward the barn. As Loretta drew up in front of Jake, she spied Lobo. Her steps faltered, and the color washed from her face. As quickly as he could, he explained what had happened. Loretta clamped a hand over her mouth and closed her eyes.

"Oh, dear God. Poor Indigo."

Two older women stood near the jailhouse. As they whispered behind their cupped palms, they shot knowing glances at Jake's bare chest. He ground his teeth.

Loretta followed his gaze. When she looked back at him, her mouth had drawn into a tight line. "Don't mind them, Mr. Rand."

They were a little hard to ignore. "You know what they're thinking."

Loretta nodded. "Yes, but it can't be helped. You mustn't concern yourself with it. I assure you that

Hunter and I aren't the kind of people who'd—" She pushed at her untidy braid. She'd obviously been up all night pacing the floors. "You took care of our daughter. We'll be eternally grateful to you for that."

Indigo came from the barn carrying a shovel. Without so much as a glance in their direction, she balanced the handle across Molly's withers, swung onto her back and rode off into the trees. Loretta stared after her.

"Bless her heart. She loved that wolf so."

"More, I think, than any of us can understand," Jake replied in a husky voice. "Will she be all right tending to him alone?"

Still gazing after her daughter, Loretta gnawed her lip. "I pray so. Regardless, it is their way. No one must intrude, at least not for a while." When she finally returned her attention to Jake, she raised both eyebrows. "Mercy, Mr. Rand, what happened to your shirt?"

"I used it to bandage Lobo."

"If you don't take a chill, it'll be a miracle. Come into the house and get warm. I've got fresh coffee made."

As Jake followed her up the porch steps, he shot one last glance into the trees where Indigo had disappeared. Was it their way to let a girl mourn alone? Maybe Loretta could accept that, but to him it seemed heartless.

Upon entering the house, Loretta went directly to Hunter's bedside. Jake could hear her relating what had happened. He stepped to the bedroom doorway and peeked in just as she concluded the story and began telling her husband how the people on the street were behaving.

"The old biddies!" she cried. "They make me so angry I could spit. Both of them axe-handle broad with three chins. They're just jealous, that's all."

Jake braced himself for Hunter's reaction. He knew how he would feel if Indigo were his daughter. Malicious gossip could ruin a girl's life, and if it got out of hand, there would be only one way to mend the situation. Jake wasn't certain how he felt about that. Obligated, yes. But resentful, too. He hadn't asked for this.

Hunter turned a concerned gaze toward the doorway and beckoned for Jake to enter. "It sounds like you had a very bad night, my friend."

"I've had better." Jake rubbed his shoulder as he strode toward the bed. "Indigo had a tougher time than I, by far." He saw Hunter's gaze drop to his chest. Since he hadn't heard Loretta explain his state of undress, he decided he should himself to avoid any misunderstanding. "I used my shirt for bandages. I did all I could."

The half-breed closed his eyes for a moment, then took a deep breath. When he looked back at Jake, there was no mistaking the sadness in his expression. "And Indigo?"

"She's taking it pretty hard, I'm afraid."

Loretta touched her husband's shoulder. "Mr. Rand says the bullet nearly hit her, Hunter. She moved in the nick of time."

Hunter caught her small hand and gave it a quick squeeze. Then he turned a questioning gaze to Jake. "You believe someone meant to shoot our daughter?"

Jake didn't want to alarm them needlessly. "I'm not sure what I believe. All I can say is that she would have been hit if she hadn't moved. Maybe the man was waiting for a clear shot at the wolf." He glanced at Loretta and noted how pale she had become. "That's probably how it was. But since it was such a close call, I felt I had to tell you."

Hunter seemed to consider that. "What is your feeling?"

Jake sighed. "That's a tough question. It scared the hell out of me, and right after it happened, I would have sworn—" He licked his lips and swallowed. "Now, looking back on it, I think maybe I overreacted. Indigo assures me she has no enemies. If that's the case, it's highly unlikely someone would try to harm her. I understand that Lobo's been shot at before."

"Several times," Loretta inserted. "Wolves don't inspire much good will."

Jake wondered if she hadn't responded a little too quickly. Yet he couldn't blame her for leaping at any explanation. No one wanted to think a loved one was in danger. "That being the case, we're probably safe in assuming Lobo was the target."

Hunter released his wife's hand and motioned for Jake to sit in the rocker. "We are grateful to you for all you've done."

Jake lowered himself into the chair, weary beyond all reason. "I didn't do much. And from the looks of things, what I did do has—" He broke off. "I'm sorry we didn't get back before dark. The horses bolted, and I was afraid to leave Indigo alone to go looking for them. Even if I had, she wouldn't have left. The wolf lingered for several hours."

"You did what you felt was best," Loretta murmured. "We don't hold you responsible."

Hunter nodded. "You took care of our daughter. If wagging tongues make something dirty of that, we will weather the storm."

It seemed to Jake that Indigo would be the one to weather the gossip, not the three of them. Did Hunter, being Comanche, fully understand the possible consequences? A glance at Loretta's face answered that question. The Wolfs understood, but they were too decent to hold him accountable for something he hadn't been able to prevent.

A wave of guilt washed over Jake. Before it ebbed, he wondered what in hell he had to feel guilty about. It wasn't his fault some trigger-happy bastard had taken a shot at them and hit the wolf. Nor had he had any choice in staying at the Geunther Place all night.

Still, he couldn't let it drop. The issue had to be

faced, and running had never been his way. He gestured toward the front door. "From the way those women were looking at us, I'd say they're bent on making things miserable."

"That is our trouble, not yours." Hunter looked up at his wife. "Where has she gone, little one?"

"To bury Lobo," Loretta replied in a tremulous voice.

Hunter shifted restlessly. Jake could see that he yearned to be on his feet so he could go after his daughter.

"If you don't think she should be alone, I can follow her," Jake offered.

Hunter closed his eyes and nodded. "In a few minutes, yes? Give her some time to grieve without eyes looking on. It is a private thing, and the way of my people."

Jake slid his gaze to the sunlit window. The well-scrubbed glass glinted in his eyes. His throat felt scratchy, and the smell of coffee made his mouth water. The sleepless night had left him drained. How much worse must Indigo feel? The warmth from the fires settled around his shoulders like a blanket. He glanced down at his hands. Blood and dirt stained his fingers.

"I'd best wash up and put on a shirt," he said.

Loretta circled the foot of the bed. "Are you hungry, Mr. Rand? I can fix something in no time."

Jake pushed up from the rocker. "Aside from a cup of that coffee, a kettle of hot water and a bar of soap will do for now."

A little over an hour later, Jake left the house and struck off into the trees. Molly's hoofmarks had left a clear trail to follow, and about a half-mile from the house, he came to a clearing. He drew up when he spotted Indigo huddled by a mound of freshly turned earth. She hugged her knees, head bowed, back bent. Exhaustion was apparent in every line of her body. Molly stood near her, tethered to a large fallen log.

Jake lingered in the trees, reluctant to intrude. Then he noticed the blood glistening on Indigo's right forearm. Fresh blood. His pulse quickened, and he hurried toward her. At the sound of his approach, she raised her head.

"Indigo, what—" Jake froze mid-stride and stared at the knife she clutched in her left hand. "What in God's name have you done?"

He dropped to his knees beside her, scarcely able to believe his eyes. The slash in her flesh appeared to be deep, and the sharp edge of her knife was stained with blood. He looked at the grave and saw dark stains where she had bled onto the dirt.

"Indigo, what the hell—"

He seized her wrist to examine the wound more closely. The bleeding had slowed, but the cut was deep and would require stitches to mend right. Even at that, she would carry a scar. Why? What had possessed her to cut herself?

"It is the way of the People," she said. "When a loved one leaves us, we make a mark in our flesh to remember them by."

Jake's stomach clenched as he stared at her flawless skin, defiled by a knife blade. A surge of anger swept through him. "Jesus. That's insane." Incredulous, he lifted his gaze to hers. "That's insane, Indigo. You don't take a knife to yourself, no matter what the reason."

"It is the way of my father's people."

"You aren't one of your father's people."

The moment the words passed his lips, he regretted saying them. Though her blue eyes and sun-touched hair belied it, Comanche blood flowed in her veins. Last night, he had seen evidence of that. He reached into his back pocket for his handkerchief, glad that he'd gotten a clean one from his bags before leaving the house. Giving it a shake to unfold it, he held the edges of her wound together and quickly wrapped her arm.

Sitting back on his heels, he studied her pale face. The calm in her eyes told him she had found some measure of peace in the grieving ritual, barbaric as it seemed to him.

"Are you all right?" It was a stupid question. Of course she wasn't all right. "Let's get you back to the house so your mother can stitch up your arm."

"No stitches."

Jake tightened his grip on her wrist. "What do you mean, no stitches? That's a damned deep cut, young lady. It'll never mend right without them."

"That is good."

Understanding dawned. She didn't want a thin, barely visible scar. For the rest of her life, she meant to carry Lobo's mark, and she wanted the whole world to see it. His guts knotted, and he felt as if he might lose the coffee he had drunk.

As if he wasn't there, she gazed off across the clearing. The wind picked up and played with her hair. Strands of coppery gold draped across her eyes and caught in her long lashes. Jake released her wrist and shoved the strands aside with a fingertip. Then he settled his hand on her shoulder.

When she didn't look at him, he gave up on convincing her to leave and sat beside her, using one knee as an armrest, his attention centered on the dusty toe of his boot. She wasn't in any danger of bleeding to death, after all. Maybe her mother could convince her to get the wound stitched when he got her back to the house. He could feel her nearness in every pore of his skin and wondered what she was thinking.

"He nearly died for me once," she whispered. "I stumbled across a big black bear and her cubs, and she came after me. Lobo got his belly ripped open trying to keep her away from me." Her breath caught. "Ma sewed him up. His fur was so thick, the scar didn't show. But I never forgot."

Jake swallowed. The sound made a hollow plunk in his chest. The wool of his shirt cut in at one armpit, and he shrugged his shoulder. "You'll miss him, I know."

"Even after he and Gretel had pups, he spent most of his time with me. When I fell asleep at night, I knew he'd be there to watch over me. When I woke up in the morning, he was always beside me. He loved my pillow. I had to fight for my half."

Jake remembered the night he had crawled into the loft and how fiercely protective Lobo had been. He could easily picture the wolf taking punishment from a bear to save his mistress. His gaze shifted to the grave. He wished he knew what to say.

The minutes ticked by. He sensed that she resented his intrusion, but since she still held the knife, he wasn't about to leave her. He remembered the slash on Hunter's cheek. A mourning scar? The thought appalled him. How could the man have raised this beautiful girl to believe in self-mutilation? And over a wolf, for God's sake. Jake understood that she had loved her pet in a way most people couldn't comprehend, probably in a way that even he didn't comprehend, but cutting herself was carrying things too far. He wanted to wrest the knife from her and throw it in the brush.

As if she read his thoughts, she sheathed the blade and pushed to her feet. He guessed that she was leaving sooner than she wished because he had come.

"Indigo."

Whatever he intended to say fled his mind. Dry-eyed and expressionless, she met his gaze, then circled him and went for her horse. He expected her to mount and ride off. Instead, she led Molly from the clearing. He rose, grabbed the shovel, and fell in with her, shortening his stride to match hers.

From the corner of her eye, Indigo watched Jake's boots as they touched the ground. He walked with a sure step, heel to toe, like all white men. The muscles in his thighs bunched and stretched the denim of his pants taut every time he moved. She glanced at his dark face and saw the brooding frown that pleated his forehead. He clearly disapproved of her father's beliefs.

Indigo set her jaw and quickened her pace. She could sense his shock and revulsion. He had no right to follow her and then pass judgment. All she wanted was to be left alone.

He seemed to loom over her, an unshakable and unwelcome presence. She hadn't missed the way he looked at her knife. He had considered taking it from her. From the scowl he wore, perhaps he still toyed with the idea. If he tried, she doubted she could stop him. He stood a head and shoulder taller than she. A glance at his broad chest reminded her of how it had felt to be trapped within the circle of his arms, surrounded by ironlike muscle. She had no doubt he could take anything he wanted from her.

A claustrophobic breathlessness came over her. Anger followed in its wake. He had no right to interfere in anything she did. No right at all.

So why did he frighten her?

As she pondered that question, the airless sensation in her lungs returned. She knew the answer. Even numb with grief, she couldn't shake the feeling that her destiny had come calling. A warning whispered in her mind like a chant. *Be careful. Don't trust him.* Her father would say the spirits whispered to her. Indigo wasn't certain if it was spirits or her imagination, but the words still bedeviled her. Jake Rand was dangerous, and the sooner he left Wolf's Landing, the happier she would be.

Jake expected Loretta to have a fit when she saw the cut on Indigo's arm. Instead, she doused the wound with whiskey and didn't scold. Indigo bore the pain without a sound.

"You should wrap it before you go to the mine in the morning," Loretta said softly.

"My sleeve will protect it." Indigo looked up at Jake. "Mr. Rand thinks I'm crazy."

Loretta patted her daughter's head and went to put the whiskey away. "I don't imagine he's far wrong. But it's a good kind of crazy." She closed the cupboard and flashed Jake a smile. "I'll bet you're starved. I've got some johnnycakes warming in the oven and some blackberries cooked up."

Jake's stomach lurched. "Maybe later."

"Some coffee then?"

"No thanks."

Indigo rose from the table and disappeared up the loft ladder. Jake gazed after her, his mouth as dry as dust. After a moment, he realized Loretta was watching him with a puzzled expression. Suddenly, he felt the need for fresh air. Someone ought to check on the mine, and the thought of a brisk walk appealed to him. He had to get out of here—away from the insanity. There was no other word for it. A young woman shouldn't slash herself, no matter what the reason, and no mother in her right mind should accept that she had.

7

Hours later, Indigo lay awake in her loft bedroom and listened to the rich timber of Jake Rand's voice as he visited with her mother in front of the fire downstairs. He had a nice laugh, warm and deep. But when she heard it, she felt trapped, the sensation very like the one she had experienced while ensnared in his embrace, helpless, with no avenue of escape. She rolled onto her side, filled with dread she couldn't explain. It was silly—ridiculous. Aside from his temporary position as foreman at the mine, he had no control over her, and there was absolutely no reason for her to fear him.

Lobo's scent clung to her pillow, and tears burned behind her eyelids. She buried her face to stifle a sob and made fists in the ticking. Cool air from the open window touched her back. Lobo would never leap over the sill and into her bed again.

Memories crowded into her mind, poignantly sweet, of Lobo bounding across the grass to her, looking up at her with his solemn golden eyes. She would never hug his neck or feel the rasp of his tongue on her cheek again. He was gone. Forever.

It was all Jake Rand's fault. Since his arrival, nothing had gone right. And things weren't likely to get better until he left. If he hadn't come, she wouldn't have stopped yesterday at the Geunther Place, and Lobo would still be alive. If not for him, her reputation wouldn't be in shreds. Ma had already told her the next few days were liable to be difficult, with people staring and whispering, some downright obnoxious.

She wished she didn't have to go with him to the mine tomorrow. She wished she never had to set eyes on him again.

The first person Indigo set eyes on the next morning was Jake Rand. So much for wishes coming true. She had just doffed her nightgown and tugged her chemise over her head when he came creeping around the partition, boots in hand. In the nick of time, Indigo jerked the muslin over her breasts. He spied her sitting on the edge of the bed and turned toward her.

Black hair tousled from sleep, shirt open to reveal a broad expanse of bronzed, furry chest, he stood there a moment and stared at her as if his senses had fled. Caught by surprise, she couldn't move. His bleary brown gaze dropped to the pink drawstring ribbon that edged the neckline of her undergarment. Stung into motion, she grabbed the quilt and drew it over her chest.

A slow smile tipped up one corner of his mouth, and his white teeth flashed. "Good morning."

Judging by the gleam of warm appreciation she saw in his heavy-lidded eyes, she suspected he had glimpsed more than just her ribbons. "Couldn't you thump or something so a body knows you're up?"

He raked a hand through his hair. "Sorry. I didn't know you were awake, and I didn't want to disturb you."

She curled her toes into a crack between the floor planks and wished with all her heart he'd leave. A lot of good wishes did her. His gaze dropped again.

"How's the arm?"

He wouldn't stand there and ask after a white woman's health when she wasn't dressed. Indigo averted her face. She could hear her mother downstairs, starting breakfast. The smell of freshly brewed coffee wafted up to the loft. She wanted him to go away . . . far, far away. Maybe then the breathless feeling in her chest would leave. With a voice gone strangely shaky, she responded to his question. "It's fine."

"You should probably put some salve on it."

It was her arm. She didn't need him to tell her how to care for it. She made an inarticulate noise and watched as he headed down the ladder, his back to the rungs. In stocking feet, that was risky. Her brother Chase's heel had slipped once, and he'd bounced all the way down on his rump. Jake Rand didn't slip, of course, but imagining him doing so brightened her mood considerably. She heard him bid her mother good morning. Then the back door slammed. She guessed he had gone to the privy.

Shivering in the chill air, she dragged on her buckskins and doeskin blouse. When she went downstairs, her first thought was of Lobo. Of a morning, he had always gone out the window and circled to the front door, scratching to be let in before she got down the ladder. Now, only silence awaited her. An ache sliced through her chest. She stood there a moment and listened, longing for his death to be a bad dream.

"It'll get easier as time passes," her mother said in a gentle voice. Turning from the dish board with a large bowl of batter cradled in one arm, she smiled understandingly. "Try to push it from your mind. It's harder if you dwell on it."

Indigo took a deep breath. The problem, as she saw

it, was that Lobo had been so much a part of her life that awareness of him hadn't taken thought. He had been like an arm or a leg, always there when she needed him. Her protector, a friend to talk to. And, like an amputated limb, his presence was going to be missed, no matter how hard she tried not to think of him.

Her parents' bedroom door stood open, and she could see her father sitting up against the pillows. She went in to say good morning. In the past, he had always been able to soothe her, and she hoped he could now.

He smiled and took her hand as she approached the bed. The warmth of his strong fingers curled around hers. She perched on the mattress and sighed wearily. To her surprise, her father didn't speak. Instead, he closed his eyes, as though he absorbed her presence and tasted the feelings roiling within her. Tears sprang to her eyes. She longed to burrow against him and weep, but that was not the way of the People.

They sat in silence. The urge to cry grew stronger, and she blinked. In the back of her mind, she heard the normal sounds of morning and resented the fact that things went on, as though nothing had happened.

As if he read her thoughts, he said, "That is the way of it, little one. The sun rises, and it sets. Mother Moon smiles upon us. Grief can make it seem that the ground becomes the sky, the sky the ground. But when Father Sun rises and warms you, you see it isn't so. It is a good thing, the sameness."

Indigo supposed it was. She turned her gaze toward the window.

In the same gentle voice, he added, "Tears are also a good thing."

She jerked her gaze back to his, unable to believe she had heard correctly. Always, he had spoken against weakness. "Only the faint of heart wallow in tears, my father."

His eyes remained closed. "When the flesh is

wounded, we cleanse it so it can heal. The wounded places in our hearts cannot be reached, so the Great Ones gave us tears."

She stared at his strong face, chiseled and dark, the mourning scar on his cheek lost in the weathered lines of life. She couldn't picture her father weeping. "But when I was small, you scolded me for crying."

"Ah, yes. A leaf fell from a tree, and you wept. The wind changed directions, and you wept. I scolded you because to weep over nothing is not good. Tears must be saved for big hurts."

"When have you shed tears?"

His lashes lifted. The dark blue of his eyes settled on hers. "Long ago, before your mother held you and your brother to her breast, she held me. I wept for those I had loved and lost."

"You weren't ashamed to weep?"

He freed his hand from hers to smooth her tousled hair. "Not when the pain was great. There is no shame in loving, Indigo. The only shame is when our hearts are so hard we no longer feel. I have taught you a great lie if you believe it is wrong to spill tears. Perhaps it is because the Great Ones have blessed us, eh? We have had no grief within these wooden walls. When grief comes, I will show you how to weep." He patted her arm, then settled back against the pillows. "I do it very good."

Indigo felt a smile tugging at her mouth. "I think I could do it very good, too."

"Go now and face the day. The hurting is like a storm. It will lay you low, but in time it will pass."

Indigo pushed up from the bed. The ache of loss still centered in her chest, but in a strange way, she felt comforted. Others had walked this path before her, and they had survived. Just as she would. "Thank you, Father."

Hunter waved her away. "Truth is not a gift, Indigo. No thanks are needed."

As she left the bedroom, Indigo's thoughts contradicted him. Truth was the most blessed of gifts, and no one could share it in quite the same way that her father did.

When she entered the kitchen, Jake was just coming in the back door. Moisture beaded his hair, and his face had a ruddy, just scrubbed look. She guessed he had found the pump at the spring and doused himself awake. His blue wool shirt, which enhanced the breadth of his shoulders, was buttoned and tucked, and he wore his boots.

"There's a four-point buck out there," Jake said with a laugh. "I thought he was going to run over me."

"That's normal around here," Loretta told him. "We get mighty popular at breakfast time."

Indigo circled him and headed for the back door. Her mother called after her. "You'd best step fancy, Indigo. Breakfast will be done here in a few minutes. On the way back in, can you grab me three more eggs out of the henhouse?"

Indigo pulled the back door open, uncomfortably aware of Jake Rand's eyes on her. She bounded down the steps. The cool morning air slapped her cheeks as she hurried across the yard.

When she returned to the house, a stack of flapjacks sat in the center of the table. She hurried to the sink and worked the pump to wash the eggs she had gathered. Motioning for Jake to sit down, her mother placed a plate of eggs before him. Indigo sat across from him, her eyes still sticky from sleep, her mouth dry. She noticed that Jake had grabbed a quick shave.

When her mother returned and slid a plate under her nose, she crossed herself and bent her head to whisper the blessing. As she finished praying, she made another sign of the cross and picked up her fork.

"You're Catholic?" He regarded her with amused curiosity. "I thought you embraced your father's beliefs."

Though she had no appetite, Indigo swallowed a bite

of egg and tried to ignore the tingling sensation on her skin wherever his gaze touched. "My father's Great Ones and my mother's God walk well together."

He reached for the warmed honey and poured a generous amount over his buttered flapjacks. "Seems like the church would feel mighty crowded."

Bristling with resentment, she commandeered the honey as soon as he finished with it. It seemed to her that he questioned her convictions at every turn. "Don't you believe in the Blessed Trinity?"

"Most Christians do, in one fashion or another."

"My mother believes in one God with three faces who reins supreme over heaven and earth. My father worships many Gods who band together into one mystic force of nature. One God with many faces, or many Gods with one face, is there truly a difference?"

He seemed to consider that. "No, I guess there isn't."

Indigo forced a smile, not quite sure why she bothered to explain. Jake Rand's opinion didn't matter a whit to her. "I have been raised to recognize God everywhere, inside my mother's church and outdoors in my father's cathedral. I don't feel confused, Mr. Rand, but blessed."

Jake looked into her eyes. There was no mistaking the pain reflected there. Yet she spoke in a steady voice as if her heart wasn't breaking. What a contradiction she was, this girl who crossed herself with the same arm that had been slashed only yesterday in a primitive grieving ritual. One God with many faces. She embodied two different cultures, somehow in harmony with both. One minute, she seemed as white as he. The next, she seemed pure Indian. The mixture fascinated him. In her simple way, she had just sliced through complexities that had baffled theologians for centuries. He recalled the long night they had spent at the Geunther cabin, the feeling of mysticism that had surrounded him. No other woman had ever managed to touch him as this wisp of a girl did.

Though she went through the motions, Jake noticed that she ate very little of her breakfast. When she rose from the table to scrape her plate, her mother handed her a dish of pork rinds.

"I thought it might cure Toothless of the hairballs."

Jake searched his mind and couldn't recall which animal was called Toothless. He watched as Indigo scraped her uneaten eggs onto the saucer. A sad expression crossed her face. "I reckon I won't have to hunt as much now."

"No, I reckon not," Loretta replied gently.

Jake waited until Indigo left by the back door, then he asked, "Who's Toothless?"

Loretta cast him a surprised look. "You didn't see him out back?" Laughter warmed her blue eyes. "You'd better take care, Mr. Rand. You won't see a snake until it bites you."

"Toothless is a snake?"

She chuckled. "Lands, no. Although there is a bull-snake that comes up now and again to sun on the stoop. If you're still around this spring and come across him out there, just step around him. Because of Indigo, he thinks he has squatting rights. Toothless is a cougar."

"A cougar." Jake slid an incredulous glance to the rear windows. "The mountain lion she feeds?"

She chuckled again. "He's an old fellow. Age has robbed him of his teeth, and arthritis has set in. He can't hunt well, so Indigo supplements his diet. Every morning, he comes up to the edge of the yard and waits for his breakfast."

Jake's nape prickled. "It doesn't worry you, her feeding a wildcat?"

"Indigo isn't like most girls."

Breakfast forgotten, Jake pushed up from his chair

and walked to the window. A few feet into the trees, he saw Indigo kneeling near a huge golden cat. In addition to the saucer of rinds and eggs, she had taken along a slab of meat from the smokehouse. Muscle rippling under his sleek coat, the cougar circled her, back and forth, impatiently watching while she cut the venison into manageable chunks.

"My God," Jake whispered. "One swipe from a paw, and she'd be ripped wide open."

Loretta joined him at the window. "I used to worry myself into fits. Over the years, I've grown accustomed to it. She was only knee-high—about four, I think—when the first wild creature followed her home. A coyote with a front foot that had been mangled in a trap. She ran in and asked her father to come doctor it."

The cougar moved closer to Indigo, and Jake caught his breath. He couldn't believe what he was seeing when the girl lifted her hands and let the cat lick her fingers clean. "She's crazy." He glanced at Loretta. "What did Hunter do?"

"What could he do? He went out and doctored its foot."

"Just like that?"

"Well, no. Indigo had to calm the coyote first. It took some talking to convince him Hunter was safe."

"Talking?"

"I can't explain it, Mr. Rand. Just take my word. She speaks with the animals." Her eyes took on a mischievous twinkle. "You haven't felt it when she looks at you?"

A chill shot up Jake's back. "Felt what?"

"She has a gift. If you have secrets, guard them well."

Jake recalled the feeling that had come over him yesterday, that she was reading him. Unnerved and trying to pretend he wasn't, he said, "She told me a sow bear tried to kill her once. Her gift didn't work that time."

"As with all talking, it takes cooperation on both sides."

Jake was relieved to hear that. He'd be careful from now on not to let Indigo look into his eyes for very long. The thought stymied him. He didn't really believe such nonsense. Did he?

Loretta went on to explain. "The sow had cubs. Indigo and Lobo stumbled across them accidentally. The sow panicked." She wiped her hands on her apron and turned back to the kitchen. "Believe me, it's the rare animal who turns on her. Sometimes, of a morning or late evening, I need a club to reach the privy. Skunks and coons, badgers and coyotes, and deer galore. They come hoping for handouts. The deer are the bravest. They'll walk right up and butt you, begging for flapjacks. A body would think we lived miles from town, but I guess they don't feel threatened here. She has a way about her."

Jake watched Indigo as she walked back toward the house. The cougar disappeared into the woods. "Why does she bother hunting? She could pick off a deer from the back stoop."

"Mercy, no. Not one of those who come to the house. That wouldn't be fair when they trust her so."

Jake rubbed his jaw. This family bewildered him more by the moment. Indigo entered. A rush of fresh air washed in with her. He turned from the window. He recalled his first impression, that there was something wild about her. He had been more perceptive than he realized.

When she and Jake reached the mine, Indigo realized that the next few days might prove even more difficult than her mother feared. At the entrance to the tunnel, several of the younger men stood in a group. The moment they saw her, they broke apart and returned to work, but she didn't miss the appraising looks they gave her or the knowing smirks on their faces. She wanted to close her mind to them. Losing Lobo was difficult enough.

In hopes of drawing strength from her surroundings, Indigo lifted her gaze to the thick timber that encroached upon the rocky hillside above the mine. Without turning to look, she absorbed the feeling of serenity that emanated from the tangled woodlands to her left and right. Peace filled her, and she straightened her shoulders, ready now to face the pocket of humanity ahead of her.

"Stupid asses," Jake muttered.

Indigo dragged her mind back to the present. "I beg your pardon?"

"Nothing."

She knew by the flush on Jake's neck that the smirks on the men's faces infuriated him. She prayed he wouldn't say or do anything to make matters worse. The best course of action in a situation like this was to pretend indifference. Jake would leave here in a few weeks. But this was her world.

Picking her way across the loose braid of rails, Indigo approached the toplander, who handled all the ore cars when they surfaced from the mine. The skip was full, which clued her that the track had been cleared so they could drill and dig in the west drifts. "Good morning, Topper. How's it going?"

Topper spat and slid his gaze toward Jake. "Things'll be better when we get the other drifts dug back out. Only being able to work one section is like trying to empty the ocean with a thimble. This is the first load the trammer has brought up."

"It's better than nothing. Did Shorty check the timbers before you started work?"

Topper nodded. "He always does if you come in late. We heard about Lobo, missy. We're all real sorry."

Contrary to what Topper obviously wanted her to believe, Indigo doubted that all the employees shared that sentiment. "Thank you, Topper." She turned to Jake. "You've met Mr. Rand?"

Jake extended his right hand. "I think we spoke in passing yesterday. Pleased to meet you."

"You the new boss?"

"Only temporarily. I'm filling in for Mr. Wolf until he gets back on his feet."

Topper spat again. One of the men who had just walked away hooted with laughter. Indigo turned just in time to see him glancing in her direction and nudging the fellow beside him. She could well imagine what they were saying, and humiliation scorched her cheeks. She returned her attention to Topper, determined to hold her head high.

Besides, what did it matter what they thought? Her interest in mining had never centered around the men she worked with. If they followed her orders, they could smirk all they liked.

She stood off to one side while Topper and Jake conversed. When she deemed it polite to move on, she tapped Jake's arm and turned toward the creek, where several of the younger men worked the sluice, some shoveling and picking, others hauling up loads in wheelbarrows. Better to face the gossipmongers now.

When Jake bid Topper goodbye and fell in beside her, she could feel the tension emanating from him. He obviously wasn't looking forward to this any more than she. As they approached the men, Indigo assessed their expressions. Unless she missed her guess, Denver Tompkins, a slender blond who had shown interest in courting her, was bent on being the most obnoxious. He drove the blade of his shovel into the dirt and leaned on the handle, flashing her a grin. She made straight for him.

"Good morning, Denver."

His light blue gaze slid boldly over her body. "Mornin'." His grin widened as he turned his attention to Jake. "I hear you two had an excitin' adventure."

"If you call getting shot at an adventure," Jake replied.

"Bound to happen sooner or later. A lot of folks didn't like that wolf."

"That gave no one a license to shoot it," Jake retorted.

Indigo resisted the urge to throw him a warning glance. If he lost his temper, there was little she could do about it. Corey Manning came up beside them and dumped a load of gravel. Dust billowed. She stepped to one side. Jake moved closer to the sluice to check the riffles. By the set of his shoulders, she could tell that he was angry. Not that she blamed him. She just prayed he would hold his peace.

Denver must have read Jake's mood as well. His cocky grin faded, and he pulled his shovel free. After drawing a comparison between the two men, she decided the blond was wise to err on the side of caution. Jake was by far the taller and more powerfully built. A small man like Denver would be foolish to rile him.

The other men at the sluice took their cues from Denver. The smirks and knowing expressions disappeared from their faces like chalk marks wiped from a board. Indigo relaxed slightly. Jake appeared not to notice. But when he finished examining the riffles, she saw him slowly and deliberately meet the gaze of each man. A warning flashed in his dark eyes.

As they walked away, Indigo didn't hear any more whispers or snickers. Jake caught her looking up at him and winked.

"The art of subtle intimidation," he whispered. "It works every time."

Subtle? Indigo hoped she was never one of his targets. She led him downstream to show him the mule-powered arrastra, which ground their ore. From there, she took him to see the two shafts that were located farther up the hill from the mine. After checking the pulley mechanisms on the two cages, he settled his hands on his hips and gazed down at the flume, which routed a controlled flow of water into the sluices.

The breeze caught his black hair and draped it across his bronze forehead. A speculative look entered his dark eyes as he settled his attention on her. Her belly twisted and felt as though it dropped to the region of her knees. She had no idea why she reacted so strangely to him.

"I'm really sorry about all that," he told her softly.

She glanced toward the sluices. She saw Denver watching them. He was smirking again. "It isn't your fault."

"No," he admitted. "But you didn't do anything to deserve it, either. I wish—"

When he broke off, Indigo focused on him, a little surprised at the emotion she heard in his voice. His eyes caught and held hers. What was it he wished? Looking up at him, the resentment that had been welling within her the last twenty-four hours fell away. It wasn't his fault. None of it was. He couldn't help that his arrival had coincided with events over which he had no control, and she had been wrong to blame him.

"Don't feel bad, Mr. Rand. It doesn't matter."

"I'm afraid it does."

Indigo took a deep breath. "If I were someone else, you'd be right. But I'm not, and regardless of what you think, their opinion of me isn't important. As long as they do their jobs, they can think whatever they like."

Clearly unconvinced, he searched her gaze. His quiet scrutiny made her feel exposed, and she turned to walk away.

"Jake," he called after her.

She stopped and glanced back. "Pardon me?"

"Jake—I'd like you to call me Jake."

She recalled their conversation day before yesterday, his teasing, her laughter, the feeling of comaraderie that had begun to build between them. Minutes later, Lobo had been shot. The memories flashed in her head, harsh and clear, accented with streaks of scarlet.

"Jake, then," she heard herself reply. "If you'd like, I can give you a tour of the powder shack. And I'd like you to meet Stringbean and Shorty. When we go back to the house, I'll show you the books. We order all our supplies in Jacksonville."

By noon, Indigo felt as if she had moved through the day in a blur. She had a vague recollection of touring the mine with Jake, of sitting at her mother's table with him after lunch to familiarize him with the paperwork, but none of it seemed real. Only one thing registered, and that was the awful feeling of emptiness. She was so accustomed to Lobo's presence that she had dropped her hand several times to stroke his head, only to realize he wasn't there. More than once, she took care where she stepped, expecting him to be underfoot. As the hours wore on, the pain within her grew until it seemed unbearable.

When her mother asked her to go over to the general store for a list of staples, she leaped at the chance to escape the house. Jake had stepped out for a few minutes. Since he hadn't mentioned their returning to the mine, she knew the remainder of the afternoon loomed before her. Unaccustomed to spending much time indoors, she yearned for some fresh air and exercise.

The walk up the boardwalk seemed altogether too short. Though aware of the stares she drew from customers inside the shops along the way, she enjoyed the breeze playing upon her face. Outside the general store, she lingered for a moment over a barrel of potatoes that had just arrived, then decided she had better not spend the money. Ma still had spuds in the gunnysack, if she remembered right, and with their funds stretched so tight, every penny had to be watched.

When she stepped inside the dim interior, it took a minute for her eyes to adjust. From out of the shadows,

Elmira Jones, the proprietor's wife, called, "Well, hello, Indigo. It's good to see you."

Indigo approached the counter. As always, Elmira was gussied up, her waist cinched so small by her corset that Indigo wondered how she breathed. Her dress, far too fancy for working, was a blue taffeta creation of layered pleats with a blue and white striped cotton overskirt trimmed with white silk fringe.

"It's good to see you, too," Indigo replied and handed over her list. "Is that a new dress?"

"Do you like it? Aunt Mary sent it to me. Made in New York, mind you, the latest in fashion. It's a resort dress."

A resort dress? A last resort, maybe. Indigo forced a smile. "It's lovely."

A movement to Indigo's left drew her attention. She turned to see Jake Rand standing at the glove rack. He glanced over his shoulder at the same instant, and their eyes met, his twinkling with amusement. He obviously agreed that Elmira's dress was a bit too fancy for the surroundings.

Seeing Jake inside the store drove home to Indigo how large a man he was. Outlined against the backdrop of shelving, which gave her a reference of measure, she noted that he stood a shelf and a half taller than Elmira, and the breadth of his upper back hid half a rack from view. His stance, though relaxed, was purely masculine, muscular arms loose at his sides and slightly bent, booted feet braced apart. The denim of his pants conformed to his long legs. The wide band of his leather belt sat low on his hips. Without trying, he cut an imposing figure.

Elmira fluttered her hand as she stepped daintily along the wall shelves to gather the items on Indigo's list. Indigo wondered where her husband, Sam, was. Since their shotgun wedding last autumn, he hadn't left Elmira alone to run the store but once.

"Do you happen to have these in a larger size?" Jake asked.

He held up a pair of heavy leather gloves. Indigo silently applauded his foresight. After doing desk work for several years, he would blister his hands up at the mine unless he wore protection. Elmira frowned and gnawed her lip.

"I'm certain Sam has others he hasn't put out yet, but for the life of me, I can't think where."

Jake chose another pair. "No problem. These'll do."

As he spoke, Doreen Shipley and Adelle Love, both wives of local businessmen, entered the store. Walking abreast, they formed a rather formidable rank, each corsetted into silk dresses embellished with far too many ruffles and flounces for women of considerable girth.

The instant they spied Jake and Indigo, they stuck their noses in the air. They made such a point of it, in fact, that Indigo wondered if they hadn't come in just so they could snub them. Several years back, Indigo's Aunt Amy had scandalized the town by publicly admitting to illicit behavior in order to save her lover, Swift Lopez, from a hangman's noose. Adelle and Doreen, with nothing better to do, still gossiped about it. Now, they had fresh meat to chaw.

Mrs. Shipley cupped a plump hand around her mouth and said, "Have they no shame at all? Why, if I were her, I'd be embarrassed to show my face."

Elmira, who had been victimized by this pair's snobbery last fall after her ill-fated picnic with Sam, narrowed her eyes. "May I be of assistance to you, ladies?"

Adelle Love sniffed. "I'm not at all certain. We were given to believe an establishment such as this catered only to decent folk."

Heat crept up Indigo's neck. Elmira smiled. "Your sources were absolutely correct. So perhaps you'd better leave."

With a look of shocked disbelief, Mrs. Shipley gasped and held her breath, putting such a strain on her bodice that her buttons nearly popped. "Oh-hh!" she cried.

"Well . . . we'll just see what Samuel has to say about this. I spend a great deal of money in this store, I'll have you know."

Elmira smiled again. "Do you? I hadn't noticed." She plunked a can of pepper onto the counter. "But don't fret. It's only ten miles to Jacksonville."

Mrs. Love's face flushed crimson. "Are you implying that we're not welcome in your establishment?"

Elmira glanced at Indigo. "Did I slur my speech?"

"We don't have to take this!" Mrs. Shipley cried.

"We certainly don't!"

In a huff, the two ladies left as quickly as they had come. A resounding silence fell over the store. Indigo couldn't bring herself to look at Jake.

Elmira slapped a bag of beans on the counter. "Don't pay them any heed, Indigo." She grabbed a tin of baking powder and set it by the beans. "Those old witches live to pick on people. Don't get the idea that everyone in town feels that way, because we don't."

"I hope Samuel isn't angry when he hears," Indigo ventured.

Elmira pulled the account book from under the counter and quickly made a list of the things Indigo was taking. "If Samuel had been here, he'd have given them a boot to help them on their way. They're both vipers, and everyone in town knows it. If it hadn't been for the likes of them, Sam and I—" She broke off and waved her hand. "Oh, well, it's water over the dam. Suffice it to say that they had it coming."

Still avoiding Jake's gaze, Indigo gathered her purchases. "Well, I appreciate your standing up to them. Thank you, Elmira." Forcing a laugh, she added, "I reckon I'll be on my way before you lose any more customers."

"We'll keep the ones who count," she replied.

After Indigo left, Jake stood and looked after her for a moment. First the men at the mine, and now the local women. Who would shun her next?

"I suppose tongues are buzzing in Jacksonville by now as well," he muttered.

Elmira held out her hand for the gloves so she could check the price tag. "No doubt. We got a wagonload of supplies in from there yesterday morning. Harry, the driver, always catches up on the latest over at the saloon. I'm sure he didn't waste any time spreading the news."

Jake clenched his teeth. When something like this happened in Portland, an honorable man set things right as quickly as possible. Despite the Wolfs' forbearance, Jake doubted things were done differently here.

Knowing what he ought to do and doing it were two different things, however. Marriage? The thought brought him up short. He felt certain Emily would recover quickly enough if he broke his engagement to her. Hell, she'd probably be married to someone else within the year. It wasn't as if theirs was a love match. But he couldn't for the life of him imagine how he could make a life with Indigo work. She belonged here in Wolf's Landing, with the wind playing in her lovely hair and the sun kissing her skin. Eventually, he would return to Portland. His family was there, his obligations were there, his home was there. Indigo would shrivel up and die if he carted her off to the city.

As he fished in his pocket for his money clip, Jake smiled to himself, remembering that first night up on the mountain when he had held Indigo in his arms. If he were brutally honest, he had to admit that the thought of marrying her wasn't totally repugnant. She appealed to him in a way he couldn't define. He could almost taste how sweet her dusky-rose lips would be, how silken her skin. A man could suffer far worse fates.

Jerking his thoughts into line, Jake paid for his gloves and left the store. He'd be wise to keep his mind on the practical. Only a fool allowed his reason to take second seat to his urges.

8

Her cheeks still afire with humiliation, Indigo jostled her packages to ease a cramp in her shoulder. She kept her head bent. If people were staring at her from inside the shops, she didn't want to know it. It was one thing to be set apart because she dressed and behaved differently. That was her choice. But to be scorned? She felt so alone. Wolf's Landing had been founded by her father. It was where she belonged. Yet suddenly the town felt hostile and alien to her.

It wasn't her fault that Lobo had been shot. Tears burned beneath her eyelids. The slats in the boardwalk blurred.

"Indigo?"

The sweet voice calling her name brought her head up. She turned to look at the second story of the Lucky Nugget. Franny's window stood open. The young prostitute leaned out and waved, her neatly coiffed blond hair flashing in the sunlight.

"I heard about Lobo. I just wanted to say how sorry I am."

Indigo glanced uneasily over her shoulder. Not many people knew about her and Franny's friendship. Indigo wasn't concerned so much for herself as for Franny. The fine, upstanding citizens in Wolf's Landing would run the girl out of town if they learned she had dared to speak to a decent young woman. Not that Indigo was considered decent anymore.

"Thank you, Franny. I appreciate that."

"I said prayers for you last night. I don't know if they'll count, but I said them anyway."

"Franny, how many times do I have to tell you to stop thinking badly of yourself? Haven't you read the story of Mary Magdalene yet? Of course your prayers count."

"Did they help?"

Indigo smiled her first sincere smile of the day. She knew Franny would have been far too busy after dark to have said any prayers. She guessed "last night" meant early evening. On occasion, even her father might tell a fib to lighten someone's heart. Since she had already told two lies in as many days, one to Jake yesterday and another to Elmira about her silly-looking dress a few minutes ago, Indigo decided she might as well go for three. "You didn't say them along about dusk, did you?"

Even from a distance, Indigo saw Franny's eyes widen. "Well, I'll be! How'd you know that?"

"I just ventured a guess."

Franny leaned farther out the window. "Indigo, tell me true. Did you feel something?"

"I did. But don't you go telling anyone."

"You did? Truly?" Franny flushed with pleasure. "Well, if that isn't something. I didn't think He heard the likes of me."

Indigo spotted Jake walking up the boardwalk. Her

heart took a nervous leap. "Franny, I've gotta go."

"Come see me soon?"

"I will. Maybe tomorrow after work."

Franny drew back into her room and started to shut the window. Then she poked her head back out. "I'll say more prayers for you."

Indigo couldn't help but smile again. Franny was as gullible as she was sweet. With a quick wave, Indigo hurried on her way. She hadn't mentioned her friendship with Franny to her folks yet, and she didn't want Jake Rand telling them before she had a chance. The Comanche people had never allowed the lone women in their villages to become destitute, so prostitution had been nonexistent. She felt certain that if she approached her father when the moment was right, he'd defy convention and offer poor Franny sanctuary in their home.

With her thoughts focused on Franny, she was scarcely aware of her surroundings when she stepped off the end of the boardwalk. As she drew abreast of the livery and the blacksmith's shop, a man darted out at her from the darkness between the two buildings. Before she could react, cruel hands jerked her half off her feet and into the shadows. Her packages scattered on the ground in her wake.

Indigo didn't have time to feel frightened. The man shoved her against the livery wall. Her head snapped back and hit the boards. The impact of his body with hers pushed all the air from her lungs. For a few seconds, she hung there, sandwiched in and too stunned to move. He pressed his forearm against her throat to keep her from screaming. Not that it would have done her much good. Right next door, the smithy was making such a racket that no one walking along the boardwalk would be able to hear her.

"Hello, Indigo."

That voice. She blinked and tried to place it. No. Oh, God, no. As her eyes grew accustomed to the shadows, the man's face came clear. Brandon Marshall. Indigo gaped. When he smiled, his scarred bottom lip puckered grotesquely. Her horrified gaze dropped to the slash mark on his chin. Years ago, she had thought him the most handsome young man she had ever seen, slender and blond, with laughing blue eyes and a wonderful smile. He had said such nice things, making her feel pretty and special. And she had believed every lying word.

"I promised you I'd come back. You still haven't crawled for me, Indigo. Surely, you didn't think I'd forget that."

She had heard he'd been living in Boston for six years. She had never dreamed he would hold a grudge all this time.

As if he read her mind, he removed his forearm from her throat and touched his scarred bottom lip. "Oh, yes, I remembered you, love. Every time I looked in a mirror."

Indigo's heart began to pound. She fought back the fear and slowly inched her right hand toward her knife. As her fingers touched the handle through the leather of her blouse, Brandon seized her wrist.

"Oh, no, not this time."

Indigo finally found her voice. "Let go of me, Brandon."

"When I'm ready. Meanwhile, forget the highborn act. I saw you talking to Franny. A whore talking to a whore."

She strained to twist away from him. He laughed and pressed harder against her. Another wave of fear rolled through her. She was no longer a thirteen-year-old. She had long since realized that her strength was no match against a man's. With a knife, she could hold her own. Without it, she was no more equipped to battle Brandon than any other woman her size.

Her father lay confined in bed. Her brother, Chase,

and her Uncle Swift were miles away, working in the timber. There was no one for her to turn to, no one. Unless—

"Jake!" she cried. "Ja—"

Brandon slammed against her. "Shut up."

Indigo gasped for breath. She had seen Jake on the boardwalk. Unless he had entered another shop, he should pass by here at any moment on the way to her parents' house. "Jake!" she cried again.

When Jake saw Indigo's packages lying in the dirt, he knew something had happened and broke into a run. As he drew close to the spot, he heard Indigo's frightened voice and whirled to peer into the shadows between the two buildings.

A man's voice said, "I told you to shut up, you stupid little bitch. Besides, why call for Jake Rand? Everyone in town knows he's already sampled the goods. They're even talking about it in J'ville. That's how I heard. You think maybe he'd feel jealous, seeing me with you? Wise up, Indigo. White boys don't mind sharing an Injun slut."

"No." She was sobbing.

"Oh, yes. Like I told you years ago, squaws are only good for one thing, spreading their legs for white men. And crawling, of course. Quarter-breed or not, that's what you are, nothing but a squaw. Being prettier than most doesn't buy you respect. I don't see Rand rushing you to the altar."

Sickened by what he had heard, Jake moved into the shadows. "Take your hands off her."

"Jake!" Indigo tried to twist free. "Let go of me, Brandon!"

The terror in Indigo's voice made Jake's guts clench, and he threw down his gloves. With two long strides, he reached her. The man released his hold on her and fell back, warding Jake off with outstretched hands. "Hey, mister, we've got no quarrel."

"I'd say we do," Jake replied in a dangerously even voice. He grabbed Indigo and drew her past him so she could go back out into the street. Then he went for the man. "I think you need some lessons in how to treat a lady."

"Lady?"

Jake planted his fist in the man's offensive mouth.

When Indigo heard Jake's knuckles impact against Brandon's teeth, she bit back a scream and hugged her waist. Her mind felt frozen. Brandon Marshall. After all these years, he was back. She wanted to run, but fear for Jake held her rooted. Brandon was the type to have friends hanging around as backup.

The fight, if such a one-sided confrontation could be called that, ended in only seconds. Brandon collapsed against the wall and folded his arms over his head, moaning and saying he was finished. Jake grabbed him by the jacket and lifted him erect.

"Understand something, you miserable little worm. If you ever come near that girl again, I'll make you regret the day you were born. Do you understand?"

"Yes! Yes, I understand!"

For a moment, Indigo thought Jake might slug Brandon one more time for good measure, but instead he tossed him into the dirt. Without so much as a backward glance, he turned and walked toward her, his expression one of concern.

"Did he hurt you?"

Indigo shook her head. Words were beyond her. She remembered all the things Brandon had said and wondered how much Jake had heard. Shame washed over her in a scalding wave. *A whore talking to a whore.* The years rolled away, and the memories rushed at her, as vivid as if it had all happened just yesterday. *Squaws are only good for one thing.*

"Honey, are you sure you're all right?"

"I—I'm fine. He didn't—You came before—I'm fine."

Only, of course, she wasn't. Tears filled her eyes. Suddenly, she couldn't bear standing there another minute. With a sob, she turned and ran. Away, she had to get away. Someplace where eyes couldn't follow. Someplace private where she could cry. Someplace dark so she could hide her shame.

Still shaking with rage, Jake watched Indigo bypass her parents' house and run into the barn. His first impulse was to go after her, but then he saw her packages. By the time he had picked them up, reason returned. If she'd wanted comfort, she would have gone to her parents. She probably needed a few minutes alone to regain her composure.

At a slower pace, Jake followed her. Composure. He needed a dose of it himself. His hands were still trembling. This was his fault, dammit. *Squaws are only good for one thing, spreading their legs for white men. And crawling, of course. Everyone in town knows he's already sampled the goods.* The words plowed into him. He climbed the front steps to the Wolf house, then stood on the porch a moment to take several deep breaths.

He knew what he had to do.

Loretta Wolf paced back and forth at the foot of her husband's bed. Her pallor alarmed Jake. "Brandon Marshall, here in Wolf's Landing? I don't believe it. I just don't believe it! After all these years? You're sure she called him Brandon?"

Jake had just finished telling them what had happened. He stood at the window, his arm braced against the sash, his gaze shifting from Hunter to Loretta as he tried to make sense of what they were saying. Who in hell was Brandon Marshall?

"It can't be the same man," Hunter said. "He's in Boston."

"How many Brandons have we known? One!" Loretta stopped mid-stride and whirled on her husband. "It's Brandon Marshall, all right." As if seeking confirmation, she turned toward Jake. "What did he look like?"

Jake ran his hand over his jaw. "Tall, thin." He dragged up a clearer image. "Blond hair, longish. He had a nasty scar on his lip."

Loretta threw up her hands. "That's him! I knew it. The moment you said Brandon, I knew. Are you sure she's all right?"

"She's fine, just a little shaken." Jake pushed away from the window. "Just who is Brandon Marshall?"

Loretta splayed her fingers over her eyes. "He's a lowlife bastard."

If the situation hadn't been so serious, Jake might have smiled. His impression of Loretta Wolf up to now was that she wouldn't say crap if she had a mouthful. "I'd already figured out that much."

She took a shaky breath. "Six years ago, he lived in Jacksonville for a few months. He began riding over this way every few days, and he took a fancy to our daughter."

Jake raised an eyebrow. "Six years ago? She couldn't have been more than—"

"Thirteen," Loretta finished. She sighed and lowered her hand from her eyes. "She was very young and extremely gullible. And Brandon was rich, charming, and handsome. She walked around with stars in her eyes for weeks." Loretta's mouth thinned. "We're not positive of all the details. Indigo never talked about it much. But from what we could gather at the time, he made an improper advance, she slapped him, and they quarreled. A few days later, he came back, all apologetic, and lured her into the woods. He . . . um . . ." She gestured with her hands. "He had four friends with him."

Jake winced. He remembered that first night on the mountain when he had sensed Indigo was afraid of him. Now he knew why.

"They didn't finish what they set out to do," Loretta went on. "Indigo fought them off. That's how Brandon got scarred. She bit him and slit his chin with her knife."

"Good for her."

Hunter broke in. "Under that longish hair, he also has a notched ear." Pride rang in his voice. "One small girl against five grown men. I taught her to practice every day. She's better than I am with a blade. She held them at bay until she could run."

"Only she fell," Loretta added. "She lost the knife in the brush. And they caught up with her. Luckily, Swift and Amy heard her screaming and got there just in time."

"Swift and Amy?"

"My sister and her husband. Actually, she's my cousin, but Hunter's people regard cousins as siblings." Loretta waved the issue away as unimportant. "Anyway, Brandon swore he'd get even. Then he moved back to Boston. Until you said his name a few minutes ago, I didn't think we'd ever see him again."

"It looks like you were wrong." It was Jake's turn to pace. He ran a hand over his hair, then paused to look at Hunter. "How long has he been back? Could he be the man who shot Lobo?"

Loretta gasped. "Oh, dear God, I never thought of that."

Jake's pulse quickened. A picture flashed through his mind of Indigo dropping just as the shot rang out. "Hunter, do you think he'd go so far that he'd try to kill her?"

Hunter's dark eyes grew troubled. "He'd have to be *boisa*." His gaze met Jake's. "*Boisa*, crazy. It makes no sense."

"A killer usually doesn't," Jake replied. "I think maybe we should report this matter to the marshal. It can't hurt. And I'd rather be safe than sorry."

Loretta pressed a trembling hand to her waist. "I think you're right." She looked to her husband. "Hunter?"

Hunter nodded slowly. "Yes, the marshal should be told."

Loretta pushed at her hair to tidy it, then began untying her apron. "I think he's over at the jail right now."

Jake drew a deep, bracing breath. "Before you go, there's something else I think we should discuss."

"What's that?" she asked.

As quickly as he could, Jake told them how the men up at the mine had acted. Then he related the incident in the general store. He finished by saying, "A decent man doesn't stand by and watch this sort of thing happen."

Loretta stared at him. "What, exactly, are you suggesting?"

"That I marry her. Unless you have a better idea." The room grew quiet. "I hoped it might blow over. But I can see it isn't going to. If I don't do right by her, the people in this town are going to crucify her."

Hunter shifted in the bed. Jake looked over at him. Silence blanketed the room again.

"It's very nice of you to offer," Loretta said shakily, "but I don't think—"

Hunter held up his uninjured hand to silence her. "You have spoken only of Indigo. What of you? When you take a woman in marriage, it is for always."

Jake took another deep breath and exhaled through pursed lips. "I'd stand behind my vows, if that's what you're asking."

"It isn't. I want to know what is in your heart."

Jake swallowed. "She's a beautiful young woman."

"Yes."

Jake planted his hands on his hips and stared at the toes of his boots. At last, he looked up. "I don't love her, if that's what you're asking."

"Well, of course you don't. You scarcely know her," Loretta inserted.

Once again, Hunter motioned her to silence. "Go on."

Jake was beginning to feel like a bug in a hot skillet. These people didn't even know who he really was. If he married their daughter, he would eventually have to do some mighty fast talking to explain. "You want the truth?"

Hunter inclined his head. "The truth—from your gut."

Jake slid a glance at Loretta, licked his lips, and plunged ahead. "She's a lovely girl. Any man with eyes would be attracted to her. The physical aspect of marriage with her wouldn't be a hardship for me." He cleared his throat. "That's it, in a nutshell. I'm not even sure how we'd make a marriage work. She's not your average young woman."

"No," Hunter agreed.

Jake sighed again. "On the other hand, though, I have to look at the right and wrong of it. The other night wasn't her fault, it wasn't my fault, but it happened. And unless I marry her, she's going to pay for it for the rest of her life. I can't turn my back on that. If I could, I wouldn't be worth the powder it'd take to blow me to hell."

Hunter nodded in agreement. "It is a fine thing for you to do, and your words tell me you have only good in your heart. But what of a bride price?"

Loretta threw her husband a horrified look. "What are you—Hunter, have you taken leave of your senses?"

"A what?" Jake asked.

"A bride price," Hunter repeated. "Among my people, it is the way. A man offers a bride price of great worth to the bride's father. The greater the bride price, the greater the honor to the bride."

Jake circled that. "You want me to buy her?"

"No, I want you to honor her."

Loretta made a strange little squeaking noise. Jake had a horrible urge to laugh. Here he was, offering to marry a girl to save her reputation, and he was being asked to pay for the privilege. "How much do you have in mind?"

Hunter smiled. "My daughter is very beautiful." He grew thoughtful for a moment. "But you are a poor man, yes? And you have only one horse."

"You want my horse?"

"No, a man must have at least one horse." His mouth quirked at the corners. "Perhaps you can pay the bride price from your wages, a little at a time."

"From my wages? How much are we talking about?"

"A man does not cherish that which costs little." The half-breed arched an eyebrow. "It is not my place to say the price. You must make an offer. If it isn't enough, I will say so."

Jake sighed. Money wasn't an issue. The point was, did he really want to do this? Jake knew the answer to that. He couldn't do otherwise and live with himself.

"How does five hundred strike you?" he ventured.

"Seven, and she is yours."

"Hunter—rr-r!" Loretta clamped a hand to her forehead.

"Seven it is," Jake agreed. He glanced at Loretta. "I'll be good to her, if that's what's worrying you."

Loretta fastened gigantic blue eyes on him, then turned toward her husband. "You both seem to be forgetting Indigo's say in all of this. She's not going to marry Mr. Rand. She wouldn't consent to marry anyone."

Hunter looked unruffled. "She will do as I ask."

"Oh, Hunter, you can't do this," she whispered.

"It is already done," he replied.

Jake shifted his weight and shoved his hands into his pockets. "Is there a judge here in town? I think we ought to take care of this immediately."

Hunter nodded. "Not a judge, though. My daughter must stand before a priest. If you ride over to Jacksonville and get Father O'Grady, he will come and say the words. It is early yet. If you hurry, we can finish this tonight."

"Tonight?" Loretta threw up her hands. "Tonight, Hunter?"

"Yes," he replied, "before the gossips in this town draw any more blood."

Jake's thoughts turned to Indigo. He tried to imagine how he could best break the news to her. Matter-of-factly, he decided. Indigo was an intelligent girl. If he approached it correctly, she'd see the inevitability of it. "I think I should go out and talk to her before I leave."

Hunter nodded. "When you have finished the talk, tell her I wish to see her."

Sunshine leaked through the cracks in the loft walls, striping the hay with brilliant gold. Indigo studied the dust motes that danced in the shafts of light. Now that she had cried herself out, the familiar smells of the barn worked on her nerves like an opiate. She was utterly drained. Her arms and legs were boneless and heavy. When she conjured images of Brandon, she felt nothing but contempt. Not even thoughts of Lobo penetrated. Cleansed. Her father was right; tears worked their magic.

Suddenly, the serenity in the barn was shattered. From beneath the loft, she heard the pig Useless begin to grunt in eager anticipation, as he did when slop was about to be poured in his trough. Buck whinnied. She heard Molly kick her stall and shove her rump against the gate. Someone had entered the barn.

No sound, other than those of the animals, warned her. It was more an electrical awareness in the air, much like she felt before a lightning storm. Indigo trusted her instincts. *Brandon?* She slowed her breathing and pressed her back against the wall. She heard one of the ladder rungs creak and knew someone was slowly climbing to the loft. With equal stealth, she reached for her knife.

When a dark head appeared above the billowing hay, Indigo returned her knife to its sheath. Jake. She released a pent-up breath. His broad shoulders, swathed in blue wool, came into view. Even in the dimness, she felt the impact of his dark eyes when he looked at her. She brushed at her cheeks.

"I thought I might find you here," he said with an indulgent smile. "There's no place quite like a hayloft to do one's thinking, is there?"

He stepped into the loose hay and made his way toward her, lurching when he stepped into bottomless softness where bales were missing. When he finally reached her, he sat and braced his back against the wall. The loft, which had always seemed spacious to her, was diminished by his presence. Stirred dust burned in her nostrils.

Indigo tucked her heels against her bottom and looped her arms around her knees. The huddled position made her feel safer. More than dust hovered in the air, an unnameable something. She sensed that his attitude toward her had undergone a change. She ventured a glance at him. He was studying her. She noted a peculiar light in his eyes that had never been there before.

His mouth curved as if he felt like smiling and wasn't sure he should. Crossing his ankles, he drew his heels under his thighs and rested his elbows on his knees. A nostalgic expression played upon his face as he took in their surroundings.

"Years ago, here in Oregon somewhere, my father staked a claim near a farm. I used to sneak into the farmer's barn of an evening after he finished his chores." He hunched his shoulders. "My father did placer mining, and we always lived in a tent along a creek. There were five of us kids, and it always seemed to rain, so we had to huddle indoors. At night, I felt like one of six yeast rolls, all shoved into one muffin cup."

He waited a moment, as if giving her an opportunity to speak. "Sometimes, if I didn't get away, I felt as if I'd suffocate. When I discovered the hayloft in that old barn, I thought I'd struck the mother lode. I'd spend hours up there, spinning dreams about someday when I'd be old enough to earn the money to take care of my brother and sisters without my father's help. I imagined having my own house. A huge one, with so many rooms we'd all be lost in it."

His voice rang with sadness. A distant look came into his eyes. Then he seemed to refocus on the hay before him.

"The trouble with dreams is that when they come true, they never live up to your expectations. I finally got the house, and I finally made the money to be independent of my father. But I still—" He laughed softly and shook his head. "I don't know why I'm telling you this. But until I came here, I still felt like one of six yeast rolls in a muffin cup."

Indigo's throat felt oddly tight. "Why don't you now?"

His dark eyes warmed to the color of mulled wine. "I don't know. Being in the mountains, I suppose."

Plucking a piece of hay, he ran his fingertips along the shaft. She couldn't picture him as a child and wondered what had prompted him to share something so intimate with her. That he had was indicative of the change she sensed in him.

Since her experience with Brandon years ago, she had erected an invisible barrier between herself and men. Until now, no one had challenged the perimeters. Jake Rand was not only challenging them, but had stepped over into the space she considered sacrosanct. She couldn't say why she felt that. She only knew it was so. He was pressing too close. He had just shared a private part of himself with her, and she had the awful feeling he expected her to give something of herself in return.

While he was preoccupied with the piece of hay, she skimmed his body with a wary gaze, noting the depth of his rib cage, the leanness of his waist, the roped tendons in his thighs that stretched the denim of his pants taut. Her attention shifted to his hands, tanned to burnished umber and dusted with black hair that swept outward into a silken, dark line to his wrist. Broad, sturdy hands with long, powerful-looking fingers—hands that had been fashioned to take hold and never let go.

"What do you dream of, Indigo?" He searched her gaze. "You must dream of something. About the right man walking into your life someday, about marrying him and having children? Or have you already met someone special?"

"Someone special?" she echoed.

"A fellow—someone you've given your heart to."

She shook her head. "There's no one."

"And what of your daydreams? All young women dream of Mr. Right, don't they?"

Indigo's stomach knotted. She felt like a hooked fish being led toward a net. If she made a wrong move, he might entrap her. "I don't dream of anyone."

He seemed to ponder that a moment. "Maybe that's just as well. Like I said, reality seldom lives up to our expectations."

"This isn't idle conversation, is it?"

He gave a sheepish chuckle. "That obvious, huh?"

He rubbed his jaw, averting his gaze. "I've never been good with words. This is one time I wish to hell I was. There's something you have to know, and I'm not sure how to tell you."

"How to tell me what?"

Why she asked, she hadn't a clue, because suddenly she knew. From the instant she saw him, she had sensed this moment would come. He turned to look at her. The gleam she had glimpsed in his eyes was still there, but more pronounced, smoldering like a fanned ember. She recognized it now as possessiveness. "Your father and I just had a long talk."

A cold feeling surrounded her heart, making it skip a beat and lurch. "About what?"

"About you." He discarded the piece of hay and reached to brush a tendril of loose hair from her cheek. His knuckles felt warm and slightly rough against her skin. "About all the gossip. Unless something's done, you'll be ostracized."

Indigo wanted to stop him from saying anything more, but her vocal cords felt frozen.

As if he now had the right to touch her, he traced a path to her ear with his fingertips, then followed the line of her jaw to her chin. Feathering his thumb across her lips, he studied her expression, then allowed another smile to slant across his mouth. "The thought of marrying me can't be as objectionable as all that, surely. You're looking at me as if I've grown a third eye in the center of my forehead."

She couldn't breathe. She parted her mouth to drag in air, and he touched the moist lining of her bottom lip with his thumb.

"Believe me, Indigo, we didn't reach this decision without your best interests at heart. I know I'm a little older than the husband you've probably fantasized about, but the age difference won't seem so great once you grow accustomed to the idea."

"I t-told you, I haven't fantasized about a husband."

"Haven't you? Well, I don't have to worry about measuring up to your romantic expectations, do I?"

Her romantic expectations? Her thoughts of marriage had never been that. "I d-don't want to be married."

He abandoned his exploration of her mouth and took her hand, enfolding her fingers in his. "I know," he replied gently. "And I wish things had happened differently. This isn't exactly what I had in mind, either. But life doesn't always dish up what we expect, does it? All we can do is make the best of it."

It hit her then, with the impact of a fist in her guts, that he and her father had decided her future without even consulting her. Married to Jake Rand? The prospect exploded in her mind like a short-fused stick of dynamite.

"No!" she cried on the crest of a sob. "No, I won't do it."

He tightened his grip on her fingers and lowered their hands onto her lap. The heat of his wrist burned through the leather of her pants leg. "Indigo, be reasonable. We don't have any choice. Your reputation is destroyed."

"No-oo-o!"

He took a deep breath and exhaled with a weary sigh. She tried to tug her hand free, but his grip was relentless. The fact that he held her when she didn't wish it drove home what he was telling her. No wonder his eyes glowed with possessiveness. He was anticipating that he'd soon be her husband.

"It may not be much comfort, but I'll do everything in my power to make you happy," he said huskily. "I promise you that."

The finality in his tone panicked her, and the panic lent her strength. She jerked away from him and, in one fluid motion, rolled to her feet. "My father didn't agree to this. You're lying!" Her foot hit soft hay and she lost her balance. Scrambling to right herself, she made her way toward the ladder. "I'll never marry you! Not you or any other man!"

"Indigo, listen to—"

"No!" She whirled to face him. "I won't listen! You're a liar. My father knows me better than I know myself. He'd *never* agree to a marriage without asking me. Never!"

"I'm afraid he's done exactly that. And if you'd just stop and think about it a moment, I'm sure you'll understand why."

She threw a leg over the top ladder rung, found a toe-hold, and grasped the side rails. "He didn't. He wouldn't!"

Loretta perched on the rocker and leaned slightly forward to study her husband's dark face. His mouth had settled into a resolute line that was all too familiar to her. She couldn't help but wonder if the regular doses of laudanum she'd been forcing upon him had addled his senses. He adored his daughter.

"Hunter . . ." She clasped her hands and rested them on her knees. "Surely you can't mean to carry through with this insane notion. Mr. Rand is so much older than Indigo, and there's no love between them to lessen the gap. They're little more than strangers. I realize you're concerned about the gossip and that marriage may put an end to it, but what of the other problems it's bound to create?"

He smiled in that knowing way he had. With a sinking heart, Loretta knew she might as well go argue with a wall. Once her husband reached a decision, nothing could dissuade him.

"Little one, you must trust me, eh? I know what I'm doing."

Loretta doubted that. "She'll hate you for this until her dying day."

"Only until she comes to love him. Then she will forgive." With his uninjured hand, he touched his left breast, which was still as hard and muscular as it had been years ago when she first saw him. "Sometimes, a voice speaks within me, and the path I should walk stretches before me. I know if I follow it that all will be well. I have looked deeply into Jake Rand's eyes. He is a good man with a kind heart. He does not know it, Indigo does not know it, but the Great Ones have led him here. I feel the rightness inside me."

"It isn't your place to decide that!" she cried.

"Yes," he replied. "I feel that inside me, also. I look at all that has happened, his coming, Lobo's death, their night in the woods together, his sense of responsibility toward her. It is the circle of fate, closing in around them. As the circle tightens, they walk toward one another. Now, though neither wishes it, they stand face to face. It is up to me to grasp the ends of the circle and tie an unbreakable knot, so neither can walk away. It will be as the Great Ones wish it."

"What if the voice inside you is wrong?"

"It has never been wrong."

"I can't stand aside and allow this to happen."

"Yes, you will stand aside." The firm tenor of his voice told Loretta he would brook no defiance. "Always, I have bent to your will, little one. Always, I have tried to grant your wishes." He gestured at their home. "I've honored your ways with every breath I've taken for over twenty years. Now, you will bend to me. Our daughter will marry Jake Rand. I have spoken it."

"And if I—"

He cut her off. "You won't. You will honor me, as a woman should honor her husband. You will not stand against me, not in your heart or in your actions."

"You know I'd never do that, Hunter, but I think you're making a terrible mistake."

"You will wash the thought from your mind. I love

our daughter, yes? You will trust me in this because you know her happiness is my happiness. I would die before I would lay her heart upon the ground."

Indigo stood at the foot of her father's bed, shock gripping her with icy fingers. Looking into his dark blue eyes, she saw none of the familiar things, his love, his warmth, his understanding. Instead, all she could read was determination.

"Y-You can't mean it," she whispered raggedly.

"You will marry Jake Rand," he repeated. "It is my wish. We have agreed upon a fine bride price. The time for talking is finished. You will go to the kitchen and wait for your mother to return from the jail so you can help prepare the wedding supper."

Suddenly weak in the legs, Indigo gripped the bed frame. "What have you done? The bride price is a Comanche custom."

"I am Comanche."

"Jake Rand isn't! You know how white men view that practice. If they pay a bride price, they feel they've purchased the woman. I'm not a thing to be bought."

"I have explained the bride price to him. He has honored you in the way of our people and will pay seven hundred dollars. It is a fine offer."

Indigo heard the front door open and close. The tread of heavy boots came toward the bedroom. Lowering her voice, she cried, "It's a fortune! He'll feel he owns every hair on my head. Just draw up a bill of sale and be done with it."

"The marriage paper will do." Her father flashed a smile.

Indigo felt as if she had been slapped. She heard hinges creak behind her and sensed Jake's presence as he stepped into the room. Still gripping the bed frame, she twisted to look at him. Survival instinct told her to fight for her freedom now or forever hold her peace. She wasn't about to pull any punches.

"So . . ." Her voice trembled with rage. "Behold my new owner! You must feel proud of yourself. Slavery was outlawed over twenty years ago."

"It isn't like that, Indigo," Jake said.

"Isn't it?" She released the bed frame and turned on him, not at all certain her legs would support her. "Explain then."

A question slid into his eyes. He glanced toward Hunter. "I agreed to pay a bride price. That is your custom, correct?"

"You *bought* me!" she cried. "That's how your people look at it. I'm more than half white, and I know how you think."

"I can withdraw the offer, if you feel so strongly about it."

"No," Hunter inserted. "This will be a true marriage in the eyes of both white and Comanche."

Indigo hugged her waist. A shudder ran the length of her. Glaring up at Jake, she whispered, "If you go through with this, you'll never know a moment's peace for the rest of your life."

Eyes aglitter with irritation, Jake turned toward Hunter. "I understood you to say she would agree to this once you spoke with her. If this is the way it's going to be . . ."

"Indigo?" Her father's voice rang like steel. She turned to look at him. "Do you defy me?" he asked evenly.

In the face of her father's anger, her own fled. Though her every instinct urged her to rebel, that was not the way she had been taught. She would do what he asked because to do otherwise was inconceivable. "No, Father. I will never defy you."

She heard Jake heave an exasperated sigh. "Indigo, forget your father for a minute and look at me."

There was no such thing as forgetting her father, not even for an instant. Feeling numb, she lifted her gaze to his.

"I didn't offer to marry you to make you miserable," he said softly. "My aim was to spare you. If you're going to detest me for it, I'll not only have failed in that, but we'll both pay dearly. I don't want to fight you every step of the way, before and after the wedding. I can't imagine you wanting that, either. To make life bearable, one of us must eventually win the war."

Indigo focused on what he had left unsaid, that he would, without a doubt, be the victor. She couldn't feel her feet.

"My father has spoken." Her voice didn't sound like her own. She swallowed, imagining herself and Jake, married and alone. Suddenly, Jake Rand seemed to loom like a mountain. She couldn't believe this was happening. "I will honor his wishes."

Jake's eyes offered her no quarter. "And mine?"

Something inside her balled into a painful knot. Just above her waist, it rested in her belly like a hot ember. Her pride, she realized. This was how it felt to swallow it. "Yes, and yours."

9

Indigo felt trapped in unreality. Events seemed to escalate to a frantic pace. Jake left for Jacksonville. Soon after, her mother returned from the jail, briefed them on her conversation with Marshal Hilton, and then began making a list of things that had to be done to get ready for the hurried wedding.

First on Loretta's agenda was preparing a wedding feast. Indigo worked beside her in a haze. Not even thoughts of Brandon jerked her out of it. She didn't care if Marshal Hilton had gone to Jacksonville to question Brandon. Nor did she care what the marshal might learn. So what if Brandon had been the man who shot Lobo? What difference did it make, at this point, if he had been behind the accidents? Only one thing mattered. In the space of a few hours, she would be married to a white man.

And not just any white man. If her father was bent on choosing a husband for her, why hadn't he picked a native of the area, slight of build and short on brains? Jake not only towered over her but was twice as broad, every inch muscle. *One of us must eventually win the war*. What war? Once he became her husband, she couldn't resist. That wasn't the way she'd been taught.

With trembling hands, Indigo sliced potatoes into the pot, amazed that she didn't hack off her fingers as well. Then she mixed a cake. Had she put in the baking powder? She couldn't recall and measured it in again. How did a cake taste with a double amount of baking powder? Like her mouth tasted right now, she guessed, dry and bitter as gall.

When all in the kitchen was ready, her mother insisted they prepare Indigo's Aunt Amy's house for occupancy. Completely furnished, it stood vacant now that Amy and Swift had gone away to the timber camp. It would make a perfect temporary residence for the newlyweds. Indigo's brain stuck on the word temporary. Jake Rand didn't plan to remain in Wolf's Landing. One day soon, he'd decide to leave, and she would have to accompany him.

Indigo made her second trip of the day to the general store and gathered the items she needed to stock Aunt Amy's kitchen. Salt, pepper, sugar, flour, rising powders, yeast, beans, honey. When Elmira learned of Indigo's forthcoming marriage, she opened a new account under Jake's name and assigned all the charges to him. Signing her name to the charges drove home the point to Indigo that within a few hours she'd be Mrs. Jake Rand.

When she returned home with her purchases, she piled the lot in a pillowcase for easy carrying. In another, she stowed perishables. When she went to the smokehouse for a slab of bacon, the reality of the situation hit her anew. Tomorrow morning, she'd be cooking breakfast for a husband.

Her mother didn't give her time to worry for long. Like twin whirlwinds, they attacked the Lopez house with cloths and brooms in hand. When the basic cleaning had been accomplished, Indigo arranged her clothing in the bureau drawers and changed the linen on the bed while her mother restocked the kitchen.

As she tucked the bedspread under the pillows and smoothed out the wrinkles, Indigo tried to picture herself sleeping there with Jake tonight. As ignorant as she was about the sexual act, she did know it took place in bed. She had accidentally gone to visit Franny once when a client was in her room. The loud creak of the bed had warned Indigo not to tap on the window.

Smoothing the last wrinkle in the bedspread with trembling fingertips, Indigo recalled the saying, "You've made your bed. Sleep in it." Now she knew where that old adage originated; a bride had undoubtedly come up with it.

A feeling of panic filled her. Submitting to her husband was going to be awful. She just knew it. It didn't take a genius to figure that out. Women talked freely about pleasant things. When the sun shone, everyone commented on it. When a fair was scheduled in Jacksonville, tongues buzzed for weeks in advance. When someone particularly enjoyed an activity, such as a social, she talked about it for weeks after. Such was not the case when it came to what transpired on wedding nights.

To the contrary, if and when women said anything about that aspect of marriage, they flushed scarlet, glanced around to be certain they wouldn't be overheard, and then whispered behind cupped palms. From that, Indigo deduced that performing one's wifely duty was horrible, so horrible that mothers didn't want their daughters to get wind of it, for fear they'd never get married and make grandbabies.

Babies. That was another curiosity Indigo had noticed, the long faces women wore when they heard one of their number was having difficulty conceiving a child. A few years back, when Alice Crenton couldn't get in the family way after her marriage to Marshal

Hilton, all the ladies in town had rushed to give her advice about how to cure the problem. Mrs. Love had given her a rock to put under her husband's side of the mattress. Old Mrs. Hamstead, the herbalist, had given Alice fertility powders. Indigo's Ma had even joined in, suggesting Alice eat more fresh meat. Everyone had acted as if it would be the end of the world if Alice didn't get pregnant, and soon.

Since Alice already had five children, which seemed plenty enough, that set Indigo to thinking. Why was it so all-fired important that Alice get in the family way? Every expectant mother Indigo had ever seen looked downright miserable, her legs spread when she walked to keep her balance, one hand clamped to the small of her back to ease the ache, her belly preceding her everywhere she went. During that endless last month, she counted the days until her nightmare would be over. If pregnancy was so awful, why were all the women so eager to see Alice suffer?

Indigo found the answer in the Bible where God commanded mankind to go forth and multiply. Right there in black and white, it said, clear as rain, that every God-fearing woman had a Christian duty to bear off-spring, and that it was her husband's duty to see she did. No wonder all the women in town had been so worried about Alice. As big a trial as pregnancy obviously was, trying to get that way must be even worse.

All in all, Indigo didn't think wedding nights came highly recommended.

She considered running away. But to where? The farthest she had ever gone was to Jacksonville. She couldn't fade into obscurity there. And the thought of journeying elsewhere panicked her nearly as much as the prospect of being bedded. Besides, her father would never forgive her if she did such a thing, and she had been raised to obey him without question. She loved him too dearly to disappoint him.

She had no choice but to suffer through, praying all the while that Jake didn't turn out to be one of those men who wanted a huge family. She couldn't imagine anything worse. What if she was like Alice Crenton and didn't take easily? When it came to female things, she had always been slower than a fly on tack paper, the last in her age group to get her bosoms, the last to get her curse. It'd be her luck that she'd be slow to take as well, and she'd have to suffer through a dozen times before Jake got the job done. How would she bear it?

There had to be a trick to it, Indigo decided. For every other misery in life, there was some kind of remedy, laudanum for pain, peppermint for a bellyache, whiskey and lemon for a cough. She considered asking her mother, but she knew how that would end. When approached with questions about sex, her mother always stammered, blushed, and said, "Just never you mind." Indigo couldn't be satisfied with that answer now.

She stepped to the window and gazed up the street at the Lucky Nugget. If anyone on Earth was an authority on male-female relationships, it had to be Franny.

"I think we're about finished."

The unexpected sound made Indigo start. She whirled from the window and pressed her palms to her waist. Her mother had an uncanny knack for reading her thoughts sometimes. "I, um . . . Yes, I'm done in here, at any rate."

Loretta smiled and smoothed her apron. "We'd best step fancy. I don't want my ham to overcook." She wrinkled her nose. "We should sprinkle some vanilla around in here. This house has been shut up for so long, it smells musty."

"Vanilla! It wasn't on my list. I'll need it for baking."

Loretta raised an eyebrow. "You, baking?"

Indigo licked her lips. "I might change now that I'm getting married."

"Maybe. One thing's for certain, you need a dash of vanilla in here to freshen the air. I reckon there's time for you to go over to the general store and get some."

Indigo could scarcely conceal her eagerness.

"Just don't get sidetracked," her mother warned, wagging a finger. "You've still got to bathe and dress. If I have things figured right, Jake should be back with Father O'Grady in a couple of hours. You can't get married in buckskins."

As her ma finished speaking, a wistful expression entered her eyes and she flashed a tremulous smile. From that look, Indigo knew her mother was seeing her for the first time as a woman. Love and pride shone on her face. The moment lasted only an instant, but Indigo knew it marked her passage from childhood. The realization made her feel alone, incredibly alone.

Indigo made fast work of going to the general store. Afterward, she tucked the vanilla into the waistband of her britches and ran to the north end of town to circle the buildings. A gnarled oak stood at the left rear corner of the Lucky Nugget. She shinnied up it, gained the roof, and crept to Franny's window. After rapping on the glass, she shrank against the clapboard siding so she wouldn't be spotted from the street.

Please, Franny, don't be downstairs.

She heard the window open. Franny's blond head poked out. "Indigo! I didn't expect you until tomorrow."

Indigo ducked under the sash and into Franny's room. "I'm desperate, Franny. I need to talk to you."

Franny's green eyes filled with concern. "Lands, Indigo, what's wrong?"

Winded from running, Indigo tried to pace her breaths. "Just don't tell me never mind like my ma always does. Promise?"

"I don't usually like to promise when I don't know what I'm promising." After considering Indigo for a moment, Franny finally nodded. "But you're special. Now tell me what's wrong."

"I'm getting married." Running the words together in her haste, Indigo told everything that had happened since she had seen Franny a few hours earlier. When she finally finished, she said, "Tonight's my wedding night, Franny. I wouldn't admit this to anyone but you. I'm so scared my knees are knocking."

"Oh, my . . ."

The compassion Indigo read in Franny's eyes confirmed her worst fears; wedding nights were an ordeal. Deep down, she had been hoping Franny might say the sexual act wasn't so bad.

"I scarcely know him," Indigo blurted. "How will I bear—well, you know. You're the only person I can turn to."

Franny's mouth twisted. "Because I'm not a lady?"

Indigo had never meant to hurt Franny. "Oh, Franny, no! You're my friend. I figured if anybody was an expert on how to bear up, it had to be you. There has to be a trick to it."

Franny frowned and pursed her lips. Then she finally smiled. "You're right on all counts. I am your friend, I'm also an expert on bearing up, and there is a trick to it. At least there is for me. I don't know a whole lot about other women." She drew Indigo toward the bed and patted a spot. "Sit down and get that horrified look off your face. It's not a pleasant situation, but living through it won't kill you."

"I'd wish myself dead if I thought it'd work."

"I've wished it a few times myself."

Franny straightened the lapels of her pink wrapper, tightened the sash, and perched on the edge of the mattress. Looking at her, Indigo found it hard to believe she did what she did for a living. She had an incredibly sweet face that made a body think of an angel. Her blond hair added to the illusion, a coronet glowing like a halo. At seventeen, she was two years younger than Indigo, and her huge green eyes shone with an artless innocence. She didn't belong in a place like this.

For several seconds, Franny studied the ceiling. A deep sadness crept across her pretty little face. At last, she said, "How to bear up? My, Indigo, when you ask a question, it's a powerful hard one to answer." She lowered her chin. "Do you ever make pictures in your mind and go into them?"

"Sometimes, when I'm idle, which isn't often."

Franny smiled. "Just as long as you know how, that's what counts. I learned a long time ago that a woman can live through almost anything if she goes outside of herself and into a pretty picture. It takes a little practice, but you can get so good at it that you don't even know what's happening."

"Truly?"

Franny narrowed one eye. "How else could I stand to do what I do? You don't think I like it, do you?"

"No, but pictures? It doesn't sound like a sure solution."

"It is." She gestured toward the door. "With the first knock on that door of an evening, the thinking part of me leaves." She shrugged her slender shoulders. "I go and sit by a sparkling stream somewhere and listen to the birds sing. Or I conjure me up a big field of daisies that dance in the breeze, and I lie on my back and watch the clouds drift by."

A dreamy smile spread across her mouth. "It's heavenly. And the men who visit are a blur. The same fellow could come five times in one night, and I'd never even realize. I don't see their faces, I don't hear their names, and I feel nothing."

"Nothing?"

Franny's smile suddenly vanished. "Except for twice,

which isn't a bad average. And that won't happen to you."

"What won't?"

Her mouth thinned. "In my line of work, every once in a great while, a mean-natured man comes along."

Indigo's heart caught. "What if Jake's mean-natured?"

Franny laughed. "He'll come calling at the Lucky Nugget, my luck! Relax, Indigo! If you cooperate with Jake and do as he asks, why would he deal harshly with you? Just lie back in a field of daisies, and it'll be over before you realize it."

Indigo gulped. "Tell me true. Does it hurt?"

"The first time. After that, it doesn't."

"How bad?"

Franny sighed. "It depends. If your husband has a care, it won't be bad at all."

"And if he doesn't?"

Shadows filled Franny's eyes. Indigo knew then that Franny's first man hadn't had a care and that he had hurt her, badly. The realization made her forget all about her own troubles for a moment, and when she came back to them, they didn't seem quite so monumental. But for the grace of God, she could be in Franny's shoes.

Franny licked her lips and didn't seem able to meet Indigo's gaze. "Even with an uncaring man, it doesn't hurt bad, Indigo. No worse than a thorn prick on the finger."

Indigo knew Franny was fibbing to spare her. In a tight voice, she said, "I love you, Franny."

Franny flushed with pleasure. "Do you, truly?"

"I've never had a sister. I think you're as close as I'll ever come. Thank you for talking to me."

Still rosy-cheeked, Franny flashed a dimple and said, "What is a sister for, if not to talk to?"

Wishing she could stay longer, Indigo threw a nervous glance at the clock on the bedside table. "I guess I'd better go before Ma wrings me out and hangs me on a post to dry."

Franny nodded. "Cheer up, hm? The next time I see you, this will all be behind you, and we'll laugh about it together."

"I hope you're right."

Franny pushed up from the bed. "Think of all the women who have gone before you. We've all survived. You will, too."

As Indigo started out the window, she paused and turned back to give her friend a quick hug before she stepped out onto the sharply sloped roof. Franny grasped the bottom rail of the double-hung window to draw it down. "Have a care. Don't slip."

"Right now, I'd welcome a broken neck."

Franny giggled. "Just remember, think daisies."

As Indigo shinnied back down the oak tree, she sent up a quick prayer of thanks for having been blessed with such a good friend. Franny, the soiled dove. For at least the hundredth time, Indigo wondered what had led such a sweet girl into a life of prostitution. Franny had never said, and Indigo respected her right to privacy, but that didn't stop her from being curious.

One thing was for sure. If Franny could survive what she did, night after night, by thinking about daisies, the same method was bound to get Indigo through the first night with Jake.

By the time Jake got back to Wolf's Landing, he was saddle weary and hoarse, the first because of the twenty-mile ride, the second because Father O'Grady was deaf and loved to converse. When Jake opened the front door of the Wolf home and called out to let everyone know he was back, he forgot to adjust his volume and startled Indigo. No explanations proved necessary. When Father followed Jake in and began booming "hello" and "what's that ye say?," it became apparent why Jake was roaring. Within seconds, so was everyone else.

Once Jake had quizzed Loretta about her visit with the marshal and had learned Brandon Marshall was being questioned, he was able to relax a little. The moment he did, he found he couldn't take his eyes off Indigo. She wore a white doeskin skirt and blouse with matching moccasins, all embellished with beadwork. With her hair brushed to a tawny, silken cloud that rippled past her waist, she was the loveliest woman he had ever clapped eyes on. She was also the palest. Her skin had blanched so white he couldn't be certain where the doeskin began and she left off.

Jake couldn't help but anticipate the coming night. Neither could he ignore the fear he read in her gigantic eyes. She seemed almost timid, which didn't correlate with the spirited, brave young woman he had come to know. He wished she hadn't ended their talk in the barn so abruptly. It couldn't be easy for her, being thrust into marriage with a stranger. The least he should have done was set her mind at ease. As if he could. He had enough of his own misgivings. *Marry in haste, repent at leisure.*

After embracing and bestowing his blessing upon both Loretta and Indigo, Father O'Grady went into the bedroom. In his lilting Irish brogue, he boomed, "Hunter, me good man, why is it that every time I see ye, ye're lying about like a lazybones?"

Not quite certain how he wanted to deal with Indigo as yet, Jake went to the bedroom doorway and leaned a shoulder against the jamb. It amazed him at how relaxed the priest seemed to feel in the Wolf home, as if he were a relative here for a visit.

"Good evening, Father." Hunter closed his eyes when the priest bestowed a blessing upon him. "It's good to see you."

"What's that?"

Hunter raised his voice and repeated himself.

"Especially on such a happy occasion, eh?" Father lowered himself into the rocker. "Oh, but the old bones do ache!" He glanced toward Jake. "'Tis a fine son-in-law ye're getting." Father rocked forward and gave Hunter a conspiratorial wink. Measuring off an inch between thumb and forefinger, he said, "Except for one wee flaw, that being that he's a Methodist."

The priest said Methodist like he might have said leper, but Jake took it as it was meant and chuckled. O'Grady settled back and set the chair into motion with a push from his stubby legs.

Casting a glance beyond Jake to make certain the women hadn't approached the doorway, the priest whispered, "Ye've heard the one about the nun who asked all the wee children what they planned to be when they grew up?"

Hunter smiled and glanced at Jake. Father's whisper was nearly as loud as a normal speaking voice. "No, Father, I have not," he replied, just as loudly.

"When asked, one wee girl said she wanted to be a prostitute. The nun gasped and cried, 'What did ye say?' The wee girl repeated herself." The priest began to chuckle so hard that Jake doubted he'd ever get the joke told. "When the nun finally understood her, she sighed in relief and said, 'Oh, praise God, I thought ye said a Protestant!'"

Jake laughed. Hunter, however, didn't. He eyed the priest with absolute solemnity and asked, "What is a Protestant?" The disgruntled expression that crossed O'Grady's face struck Jake as more funny than the joke, and he laughed all the harder.

"Hunter, me man, sometimes ye do try me patience. A Protestant is a non-Catholic, ye see."

"Why did you not say non-Catholic?" Hunter asked.

The priest waved a hand. "'Twould ruin the whole thing." He threw Jake a glance. "'Tis me hope that the point did not go over yer head like the joke went over his."

Jake grinned. "I told you I'd study the faith and give conversion a lot of thought."

Father nodded. "A great deal, I pray. A mixed marriage isn't at all the thing, ye know, and with the wee lass's Indian beliefs tossed in—well, a couple needs a bit of common ground."

Jake agreed. He rubbed the stubble on his chin. "If you'll excuse me, Father, I think I'll wash up."

The priest waved him on his way and turned to boom a question at Hunter about the mines.

Jake washed, shaved, and changed clothes in record time, thankful that no one downstairs wore formal clothing. In keeping with his assumed identity as a miner, Jake had packed only denims and work shirts in his saddlebags.

When he climbed down the loft ladder, he approached Indigo at the table, where she was intent upon frosting the cake. She lifted wary eyes to his. Once again, Jake was baffled. Was this the same girl who had braved a dangerous mining shaft?

"Can you leave the rest of that to your mother?" he asked. "I'd like to talk to you for a few minutes before the ceremony."

Loretta overheard and came to finish the cake. "Don't be long, Indigo. Father O'Grady will want to hear your confession."

Jake assured Loretta they would return shortly, then guided Indigo out the front door. Once on the porch, he led her to the railing and, before she guessed his intent, lifted her to sit on it. Bracing a hand on either side of her, he leaned forward until their faces were scant inches apart.

"I think we need to talk."

She leaned away from him and nearly lost her balance. Jake snaked an arm around her waist and caught her from falling. She gasped and planted her hands on his shoulders.

"Indigo," he began. "About tonight."

That was as far as he got. Father O'Grady opened the

door and said, "Now, now, there'll be plenty of time for that later, Jake, me man. 'Tis time for confessions and the nuptials."

"Just one minute, Father," Jake came back.

"I haven't a minute." The priest waved impatiently. "'Tis not a wonder to me ye've ruined the colleen's reputation. Look at ye now, making eyes on the porch, for all eyes to see. Young men were more clever in me day."

Jake swallowed his irritation. "I'd like to have a word with her. Then she's all yours."

"Ye'll have yer word after, lad." The priest gave them an exaggerated wink.

Defeated, Jake stepped aside. Indigo jumped down and hurried into the house.

From that moment on, Indigo felt as if everything happened with dizzying speed. Father O'Grady heard her confession. Afterward, he stood with her and Jake at the foot of her father's bed and performed the ceremony. Before she quite knew how it happened, the priest pronounced them man and wife.

"Now she's all yers," Father O'Grady said with a broad grin. "Ye may kiss yer bride and make eyes on the porch all ye like."

Indigo looked up at her husband. When he bent his dark head, she held her breath, recalling Brandon's kisses that fateful day when she bit him. Jake surprised her by taking her face very gently between his hands and scarcely brushing her mouth with his. As he straightened, she blinked. Surely, that wasn't all there was to it.

As if he guessed her thoughts, he smiled, took her hand and chafed it between his. "You're like ice."

She was clammy as well. She tried to pull her hand free, but he held fast and drew her to the bedside table to sign the documents in the presence of her parents. The pen dripped ink and made a splotch as she pressed the tip to the paper. She began to shake as the magnitude of what she was doing sank home. For a moment, she couldn't remember how to spell her name.

Jake settled a hand on her back. For some reason, his touch bolstered her. She slashed her signature along the line, then handed him the pen. Their eyes met, his warm and strangely reassuring, hers frightened. He bent to sign his name.

Father O'Grady rubbed his palms together. "'Tis official. Ye're wedded, in the eyes of God and state. Now we can partake of that delicious meal ye ladies have prepared." When he turned toward Loretta and saw the tears welling in her eyes, he cried, "Be joyous, child. Ye haven't lost a daughter, but gained a son. A fine one, too, aside from one wee little flaw, that being he's a— but enough of that. I'll not be accused of driving the point into the ground."

Jake laid down the pen and rested a hand on Indigo's shoulder, his long fingers curling warmly and applying the slightest pressure. It was done. She belonged to him.

A searing sensation rose up the back of her throat. She had become that which she most abhorred, a white man's squaw. If he chose, he could govern her every breath.

As if he sensed her terror, Jake, still gripping her shoulder, bent his head to hers. "It'll be all right," he said huskily. "Leave the worrying to me. Just enjoy the evening."

Enjoy the evening? It was easier said than done. With Jake's muscular frame looming beside her, she had one thing on her mind, the end of the evening.

10

The air felt damp and cold when they stepped out into the night. Slinging his saddlebags over his right shoulder, Jake took Indigo's arm, positioning himself between her and the street as they walked toward the north end of town to her Aunt Amy's house. The warmth of his hand penetrated the soft leather of her sleeve, the grip of his fingers gentle but hinting at latent strength.

When she glanced up at him, she felt breathless. To her frightened mind, he seemed to loom taller than he had before, a solid wall of power that could at any moment unleash itself on her. The decisive and crisp tap of his boots on the boardwalk seemed indicative of his mood, as though he had set himself to a task and intended to get it accomplished with little delay.

Indigo looked up at the Lucky Nugget. It might be wise to practice Franny's art of conjuring before the moment of reckoning was upon her. Using all her strength of will, she tried to block out Jake Rand's presence and concentrate. Daisies refused to come clear in her mind. Instead, she immersed herself in memories of

Lobo when they ran free together in the mountains.

Lobo. She had been so wrapped up in her own concerns this evening that she had scarcely thought of him. A lump welled in her throat, and she lost her train of thought. If not for Jake striding beside her, she would have wept for all she had lost, especially her freedom. Her days of roaming the mountains might well be finished now. That would be up to her husband.

Jake sighed and repositioned the saddlebags on his shoulder. For an instant, his thoughts drifted to Emily. He should write to her at the first opportunity. The trouble would be in finding a private moment to do it. He couldn't risk Indigo spying the letter and discovering who he was. And wasn't that a fine kettle of fish? He didn't like the idea of keeping secrets from her.

For the moment, though, he had more immediate concerns. The distant look in her eyes worried him. Beneath his hand, she felt brittle with tension. As they drew near the house they would temporarily call home, he tried to think of something he might say to ease her mind. Nothing came to him.

If only they knew each other a little better, he might have had a clearer understanding of what she was thinking. What did a young woman feel on her wedding night? Would she like to talk for a while? Should he take her hand, kiss her? Or would that make matters worse? Judging by her expression, she looked forward to the consummation of their marriage with about as much enthusiasm as she might have the extraction of a tooth.

For an instant, he considered giving her a little more time to adjust before he exercised his conjugal rights. Just as quickly, he shoved the thought away. At best, he would be willing to wait no more than a few days, and her attitude wasn't likely to undergo a significant change in so short a time. Since he had no intention of living like a monk, there was little if any point in postponing the inevitable.

He had already bitten off a large enough chunk of

trouble by marrying her. He didn't need sexual frustration added to the list. As Father O'Grady so wisely said, a couple needed common ground. What better place than the marital bed to find some?

Glancing down at Indigo, he recalled that first night when he had held her in his arms, how incredibly right she had felt, as if her body had been shaped especially for his. He sensed there were fires to tap within her. His only problem would be in getting her to relax long enough for him to arouse her. At the thought, a burning knot of longing centered low in his guts.

As they stepped onto the porch, he fancied he could hear her heart pounding. What in God's name did she think he intended to do to her? Before he opened the door, he turned to look down at her. The sharp scent of pine touched the damp night air.

"Try to relax, Indigo. Everything's going to be fine."

Her small face glowed like a white oval in the dim moonlight. She lifted wide, frightened eyes to his. Jake paused to study her a moment, not quite able to shake the feeling that something about her had gone way off plumb. Was this the same young woman who had tried to foreman a crew of grown men? The same girl who had stepped into her father's shoes and done a credible job of carrying out his many duties?

He pushed the door open and moved aside for her to enter. She stepped to the threshold and froze, peering ahead into the blackness. He nudged her inside and closed the door behind them. Acutely aware of her rigid body inches away from his, Jake waited for his eyes to adjust, then made his way toward a round table where a lantern perched. He set his bags on the floor and groped for the box of matches. In moments, the lamp hissed and light flared, throwing their shadows upon the walls.

Chafing his hands, he glanced around to familiarize himself with his surroundings and said, "It's chilly in here."

"I laid a fire," she replied in a shaky voice.

Jake turned toward the hearth. "So you did." He carried the matches with him and crouched to light the kindling. Flames leaped and rose toward the chimney. He grabbed the poker and repositioned the logs.

"Well, that's done." He knew he was stating the obvious. Conversation never had been his strong point. Pushing to his feet, he turned toward her. "It'll warm up in here in a minute."

Lifting the lantern, he left her to stand alone in the flame-touched shadows while he took a quick tour of the tiny house. It was a far cry from his home in Portland. When he returned to the sitting room, he placed the lantern back on the table and gravitated toward the fire.

Indigo didn't know if it was the firelight, the shadows cast by the lantern, or a combination of both, but he seemed more ominous by the moment. Flickering amber played upon his face and gave his sharply carved features a sinister look. His wind-tossed hair glistened like polished ebony.

When he caught her staring at him, a slow smile touched his mouth. "Come over here, Indigo."

She straightened her shoulders and raised her chin.

His smile deepened. "Come on. It's warmer over here."

Her feet felt as though they weighed a hundred pounds. She moved toward him, afraid to do otherwise. As she drew up by the hearth, he leaned a shoulder against the mantle and gazed thoughtfully at her. He was making her feel like a troublesome arithmetic problem that he was determined to figure out. The air suddenly seemed too close, and she found it difficult to breathe.

"Closer. You still can't get warm there."

She took two more steps. There was no mistaking what that gleam in his eye meant. Whether she wished it or not, he planned to have her. From the first instant she saw him, she had read him as a man filled with purpose, who accomplished what he set out to do. Now bedding her was his goal. It went without saying what the outcome of that would be. She couldn't help but remember how easily he had dealt with Brandon.

Brandon.

A film of cold perspiration broke out on her body. Images sprang at her from the past, of that never-forgotten afternoon when Brandon and his friends had jumped her. Because she had so little Indian blood and was tawny-haired with blue eyes, they had considered her a prize.

Looking up at Jake Rand's dark countenance, she couldn't help but wonder if he might not have an equally dark side to his nature. Under all his layers of polish, did he harbor wicked yearnings that he had never dared to reveal? She found that difficult to believe, but she knew some men could disguise the blackest of intentions with gentle words and charming demeanors.

"Are you getting any of the warmth?" he asked. "You can come a little closer if you like. I don't bite all that hard."

Dignity. Her father had made it sound so easy, but it wasn't. "I—I'm really not cold."

His voice laced with amused tolerance, he said, "Really. Then why are you shivering?"

"Am I?" She clasped her hands behind her and dug her fingernails into her flesh. The pain gave her something to focus on. "Perhaps I am a little chilly."

His eyes, warm and twinkling in the firelight, delved deeply into hers. Indigo tried to see into him, but it was as if he had drawn curtains so she couldn't look too deeply. Why would he do that if he had nothing to hide? Her trepidation mounted.

After a long, torturous moment, he lifted a hand to her hair. His touch felt weightless and unbelievably gentle. He plunged his long fingers into the strands and gripped the back of her neck to draw her toward him.

"Indigo, are you frightened?"

"Of w-what?"

Jake nearly chuckled at that. She was obviously frightened. It was also obvious that her pride would never allow her to admit it. Though her fears were groundless, he could see they didn't seem so to her, and he had to admire her pluck. No maidenly tears to gain a reprieve. No pleading. She stood before him, clearly determined to accept her fate. Rather like a Joan of Arc, he mused, which made him feel a little exasperated. He wasn't her executioner, after all.

Her show of bravado had the perverse effect of emphasizing her lack of stature. He had never known anyone so determined to lead with her chin when she had so little bulk as backup. Why did she stand there, head lifted in proud defiance, refusing to let her gaze waver from his?

The compassion he felt for her in no way dampened his desire. From the first instant he set eyes on her, he had wanted her. Now she was his. It was a heady feeling. All he had to do was lift her in his arms and carry her to bed. As unenthusiastic as she clearly was, he didn't think she would struggle, which was all to the good. With a little gentleness and patience, he could coax her to relax, and once she did . . .

His pulse quickened as he pictured himself peeling away her clothing like the skin from a delectable piece of fruit. Indigo—a curious combination of innocence and sensuality, trepidation and dauntless courage.

Not wishing to prolong her agony, he tightened his hold on the back of her neck and leaned toward her. Her scent, a blend of rose hips and fresh-scrubbed skin, intoxicated him. He bent his head and feathered his lips against her hair. Such perfection, and all of it his. Had he truly been reluctant when he offered to marry her?

He heard her breath snag in her throat. A shudder

ran through her body, and she made fists in his shirt as
if to hold herself erect. Nuzzling his way, Jake found the
velvety slope of her throat with his mouth. Closing his
eyes, he tasted her skin. His imagination hadn't done
her justice; she was far sweeter than he dreamed. An
electrical shock of white-hot need shot through him.
Focused on that, he slipped his other arm around her.

She arched against him like a drawn bowstring, so
taut he feared she might break if he tightened his
embrace. He couldn't hear her breathing. But he could
hear her heart—a wild thrumming that spoke eloquent-
ly of terror. Jake froze. This was far more than a maidenly case of jitters, surely. Not that he was an expert in
handling virgins. Maybe all women reacted this way
when they faced their first experience with a man.

He splayed his hand on her back, assailed by a wave
of guilt when he felt the frantic flutter of her pulse
throbbing into his fingertips.

"Indigo . . ." Uncertain what he meant to say, what
he could say, he simply held her.

"Wh-What?"

The sound of her quavery voice made him ache for
her. That damnable Comanche pride of hers. If she was
this frightened, why didn't she simply say so? He certainly wouldn't think less of her for it. Was this an after-
effect of her experience with Brandon Marshall and his
friends? What had the bastards done?

Abruptly, he straightened. Pulled off balance, she
leaned full-length against him, still clutching his shirt.
Jake cupped her small face between his hands.

"Indigo . . ." Feathering his thumbs along her cheekbones, he said, "Honey, I'm not going to hurt you." The
words no sooner passed his lips than he realized they
weren't true; he would hurt her this first time. "No
more than I can help, at any rate."

He winced at the way that sounded. Why, when he
most wanted to say exactly the right thing, did he

always bungle it? She made no response, but words weren't necessary. The dread he saw in her wide blue eyes made him want to kick himself.

Taking a deep draft of air, he said, "Would you like to talk for a while?"

She blinked. "Talk?"

Jake nearly smiled at the disbelief that crossed her face. "Yes, talk. We haven't had a lot of time for that."

"All right. About what?"

"Uh . . ." He set her away from him, then held her erect until he felt certain she had her balance. "The weather?"

She rewarded him with a high-pitched little laugh that sounded more hysterical than amused.

Jake's mind raced. There had to be a hundred subjects they could discuss. That was the problem, wasn't it? They scarcely knew each other. He came up with nothing. With the bedroom looming only a few feet away, he doubted she would be able to concentrate on a conversation anyway.

"I don't suppose your Aunt Amy kept any games here, did she?"

"G-Games?"

"A deck of cards, some dice." He repositioned a log in the fire with the toe of his boot, then glanced up. "I'm not really ready for bed yet. Are you?"

Her poorly concealed relief nearly made him smile again. That would be a fatal mistake. She might think he was laughing at her, and that was the last thing he wanted.

"N-No! I'm not the least bit tired." He could almost see her gathering the threads of her composure. "A game?" Her eyes brightened. "How about checkers?"

Jake hadn't played in years, and he never had particularly enjoyed the game. "Bring it on."

She nearly tripped over her own feet in her eagerness to find it. Jake hauled in two straight-backed chairs from the kitchen and positioned them at the table. When she emerged from the hall with the board, he moved the lantern aside to make room. Straddling his chair, he watched as she set up the game.

"Which do you choose, red or black?" she asked.

"Red." For unrequited passion.

She perched on the edge of her chair and carefully laid out the pieces. Her hands shook. As Jake watched her, a feeling of tenderness welled within him.

"You move first," she offered.

He moved out with a red disc, determined, for her sake, to concentrate on the game. Thirty minutes later, she had soundly trounced him. When she seized his last piece, she lifted wide blue eyes to his and said with obvious hopefulness, "The best two out of three?"

With a suppressed chuckle, he said, "I don't suppose you'd care to sweeten the pot with a little wager."

"I haven't any money."

"There are other stakes." He was thinking in terms of the loser forfeiting a kiss, but when he noted her wary expression, he said, "The winner gets to be served coffee in bed every morning for a week."

"I don't drink coffee."

"Hot cocoa for you, coffee for me."

"You're on."

Jake resigned himself to a long night. She was as nervous as a mouse in a roomful of cats, which didn't make for stimulating conversation. To sharpen his interest in the game, he pretended that the person who lost their wager had to forfeit an article of clothing, winner's choice. After several minutes of consideration, he determined that he would select her blouse. Remembering their first meeting and how she had looked in the soaked doeskin, he had little difficulty in imagining her nude from the waist up. His skill at checkers took a dramatic upturn, and he prevailed in the next two games.

When he executed the last killing blow and looked across the board at his opponent, he saw why he had won so easily. She was drooping with exhaustion, blue eyes bleary, her silken lashes aflutter in a hopeless struggle to stay awake.

"I guess we'd better call it a night," he said.

Her eyes opened wide, and she jerked herself erect. He couldn't have elicited a swifter response if he had jabbed her with a pin. "One more game, please? I deserve a chance to even the score."

Against his better judgment, Jake agreed. At the back of his mind hovered a purely selfish motivation. Maybe, if he wore her out, she'd be so exhausted by the time he took her to bed she wouldn't have the energy to be frightened.

No such luck. At the end of their fourth game, which he won, he had only to look at the rapid pulsebeat in the hollow of her throat to know that all her senses had revived to fine working order. Regardless, he was checkered out. This couldn't go on all night.

He pushed up from the chair. "Would you like a few minutes before I follow you in?" he asked, gesturing toward the bedroom.

"A few minutes for what?"

He stared down at her. The puzzlement in her eyes was genuine, he felt certain. In a voice tight with suppressed laughter, he said, "To get ready for bed."

She threw a horrified glance toward the dark hallway. "Oh." She dragged her gaze back to his. "I—Yes, that would be nice."

"Would you like to take the lamp?"

"No, that's all right."

As she walked toward the bedroom, Jake leaned a hip against the table and folded his arms across his chest. Cocking his head, he listened. The sound of a drawer being opened rasped through the stillness. He sighed and applied himself to counting the planks in the floor that ran from the wall to the braided sitting room rug.

When he felt he had given her plenty of time, he turned out the lantern and, guided by its diminishing glow, picked his way toward the bedroom. The smell of vanilla wafted to his nostrils as he stepped through the doorway. Indigo stood before the open window, her only armor a floor-length flannel nightgown. She hugged herself, as if to ward off the chill. She looked so young and defenseless. He moved slowly toward her.

As he settled his hands on her rigid shoulders, he abandoned all hope of lovemaking. A coldhearted bastard, he wasn't. He drew her against his chest and leaned forward to see her face. Her forlorn expression suggested that she was searching for something or someone in the darkness outside. He followed her gaze and studied the shifting shadows. A storm was blowing in. Looming black clouds hovered in the sky. The wind buffeted the house and whistled softly beneath the eaves.

Resigned, Jake guided her gently to the bed. She was trembling, from cold or nerves, he didn't know. He glanced back at the open window, thought about closing it, and then remembered her habit of leaving the window in her room open for Lobo. Despite the chill, he didn't have the heart to close it.

Tugging back the bedding, he gave her a nudge. With a notable lack of eagerness, she slipped between the crisp sheets. He glimpsed a flash of muslin and realized she was wearing her bloomers under her nightgown. Her chemise, too, no doubt. His bride, the temptress.

He unbuttoned his shirt, conscious with every flick of his fingers that she stared up at him, her eyes luminescent spheres of silver-blue in the moonlit shadows. He dropped his hands to his belt. She rolled to face the wall. Sitting on the edge of the bed, he unlaced his boots and jerked them off. The pants followed. He hesitated and then decided to leave on his knit underdrawers. There was little point in shocking her with total nudity when he couldn't put it to good use.

He stretched out on his side, pulled the bedding over himself, and studied her narrow back. She was still shivering. He pressed closer and settled a hand on the curve of her hip. At his touch, she jerked.

"You're cold," he said.

"N-No, n-not really."

There was a lump on Jake's side of the mattress. He shifted toward her to get off of it. "I've slept in better beds."

He slid his palm to her belly. She lay absolutely motionless. He bent his knees and drew her against him, so her bottom rested in the cradle of his thighs. Warmth cocooned around them, yet she still shivered.

"There's nothing to be afraid of, Indigo."

"I-I'm not afraid."

Her hair was draped across his pillow. He turned his cheek against its silkiness. God, she felt so good. He closed his eyes and willed his body not to react. Her soft butt pressing against him was sheer torture. With grim determination, he kept his hand where it was, even though he ached to cup her breast. What a hell of a way to start a marriage.

For some reason, thoughts of Mary Beth filled his mind. In ways, Indigo was a lot like her. Jake tried to imagine his headstrong sister thrust into this situation, married against her wishes to a man she scarcely knew. If that happened, it would be Jake's hope that the man would be understanding and take his time gentling her. That being the case, how could Jake do less?

Indigo felt Jake's arm relax and grow heavy. She held her breath and listened as the rhythm of his breathing altered. Was he asleep? She couldn't be so lucky.

His hand rested on her midriff, his fingertips touching the underside of her breast. Even through a double layer of muslin and flannel, the warmth of him seared her. She lay there in the clutches of panic, afraid he'd move.

Memories flashed, and she squeezed her eyes closed, trying to black them out. Brandon, his friends, the dizzying feeling of horror she had felt when the five of them had converged on her. She didn't want to be touched like that again.

Jake stirred, and her heart leaped. He murmured something against her hair. Feeling as if she might suffocate, she lay there and waited for him to do something— what, she wasn't certain. Remembering Franny's advice, she tried feverishly to conjure images of Lobo and daisies. The pictures flitted in and out at the edges of her mind.

Minutes dragged by. Then he began to snore. His robust breaths stirred her hair and misted the back of her scalp with warmth. He was asleep, really and truly asleep. She couldn't believe it. Why? The question circled endlessly in her head. He had intended to take her; she had read that in his eyes.

She stared at the wall, quite certain she would never be able to rest. When he didn't move or touch her in any other way, she started to relax a little. Her eyelids immediately grew heavy. She drifted for a while, vaguely aware, still not trusting him enough to totally let down her guard.

In the black of night, Jake awoke to a nagging ache in his side. Slowly surfacing to consciousness, he became aware by degrees. For a moment, he had no idea where he was. Then he identified the warm softness against his back, a woman's body. Startled, he opened his eyes. A slender arm was flung over his waist. He stared into the darkness. Then he smiled.

Indigo. . . . In his sleep, he had turned his back to

her. In hers, she had lost her inhibitions. He could feel her cheek crushed against his shoulder blade, her silken hair on his skin.

The discomfort that had interrupted his rest persisted. He recalled the lump he had felt in the mattress and realized he was lying on it. He tried to move, but Indigo murmured in her sleep and tightened her arm around him. He smiled again and imagined the expression that would cross her face if she woke up and realized how friendly she had become.

As much as he hated to conclude their cuddling, he wasn't going to get much sleep lying on the lump. Prying her arm from around him, he eased forward and succeeded only in transferring the discomfort to another spot. Damned if it didn't feel like something was poking him.

Slipping quietly from the bed, Jake slid a hand under the mattress to see if a section of the bed ropes had broken. His fingers encountered a length of board supported by the ropes. His hand curled around something large, cold and rough-surfaced. What the— He pulled it out. A rock?

Disgruntled, he set it on the bedside table, pulled the board out, and crawled back into bed. As if she had missed his warmth, Indigo snuggled up against him. Jake, never one to refuse a lady, welcomed her with open arms. She settled her head in the hollow of his shoulder and angled a bent leg across his thighs. Unable to resist, Jake slid a hand along her hip and slender thigh, tugged up her nightgown, and settled a hand on her knee. Bloomers. He grinned and fell back to sleep.

11

The following morning, Jake woke up to the smell of coffee. He pried open his eyes to see Indigo bent over him, holding a mug. With an uncertain smile, she said, "Our wager, remember?"

Jake flashed a sleepy grin and came up on one elbow to take the cup. Eyeing her over the rim, he indulged in a slow sip, aware, even through the haze of drowsiness, that she moved quickly away from him, as if she feared he might grab her. He was going to like waking up to her sweet face every morning, he decided. Even in her grubby old leathers, she was beautiful. He much preferred her hair loose, but with her delicate bone structure, she was every bit as lovely with the thick braid coiled at the crown of her head.

"I must have died," he said in a hoarse voice. Throwing a look at the rock he had removed from beneath him, he added, "It's not easy to sleep with a boulder poking you in the ribs. I wonder why your aunt and uncle had it under the mattress?"

A startled expression swept across her face, and she glanced at the bedside table. Taking care not to tip the mug, Jake grabbed her pillow, gave it and his own a punch, and settled his shoulders against them. "You're up and about with the chickens."

"We have to get up to the mine." She perched primly on the foot of the bed, well out of his reach, he noted, and watched as he took another sip of coffee. "Did I make it to suit you?"

Jake swallowed. "It's perfect." He studied her for a moment, his senses registering the myriad scents in the room, coffee, vanilla, and rose hips, a blend that conjured images of home and hearth. "Indigo, about your going to the mine."

"Yes?"

Jake couldn't miss the apprehension that filled her eyes. He smoothed a hand over the bedspread, then gazed out the window a moment. Yesterday, she had been Hunter Wolf's daughter, and her working at the mine had been a totally different circumstance than it was now. As of last night, she had become his wife.

Indigo wasn't like other women, though. Jake knew how much she loved going to the mine. He also knew it was a privilege she had come to expect. In the last few days, her whole world had been turned topsy-turvy. In addition to losing Lobo, she had been forced by circumstance to marry an older man she scarcely knew. How could he make her endure another radical change?

Shoving back his own feelings, Jake settled his gaze on her and forced a smile. "Nothing."

Her relief was evident in her expression. Jake wished he could solve all the problems between them so easily. All it had taken was his abandoning the convictions of a lifetime.

Pushing to her feet, she made haste toward the doorway, as if she wanted to escape before he said something else. "Breakfast is already warming on the stove. I'll dish your plate and get our lunch packed while you dress."

Minutes later when Jake strode into the kitchen, Indigo hurried to the stove, grabbed the coffeepot, and turned to refill the mug he held in his hand. Unaccustomed to such solicitous service, he arched an eyebrow in puzzlement and studied her as she moved away. Not that he was complaining. It was delicious coffee, and he had wanted another cup, but there was something almost desperate about her eagerness to please him.

He started toward the table, and at the sound of his boots touching the floor, she threw an apprehensive glance over her shoulder. Taking great care to make no sudden moves, Jake set his steaming mug next to his plate. Leaning a hip against the table, he folded his arms and regarded her, once again assailed by the odd feeling that the nervous girl before him was an imposter.

She was obviously imagining all kinds of horrors he had no intention of inflicting upon her. He pulled his timepiece and checked the hour. Nearly six-thirty. He had some time. He slowly straightened and moved in on her, determined to give her a taste of what he did intend.

Indigo felt his nearness before his hands settled on her shoulders. With her fingers still vised around the coffeepot handle, she twisted to look at him, then wished she hadn't. The blue denim of his shirt filled her entire scope. When she lifted her gaze, she found that he had bent his dark head so his face hovered only inches above hers.

"Did we say good morning?" he asked in a husky voice.

She couldn't misinterpret the slumberous, determined glint in his dark eyes. A breathless, mindless panic filled her. The silence of the house moved in on her, reminding her she was alone with him, horribly and completely alone. And even if she hadn't been, there was no one to help her, no one who would even try. She was his wife; anything he chose to do to her was his right, by law and in the eyes of God.

"I—yes, I think you—" His face drew imperceptibly closer, and she knew he meant to kiss her. Possibly more. "Good morning?" she tried hopefully.

With a knowing smile, he grasped her chin. "That isn't the proper way to tell your husband good morning."

"It isn't?" she squeaked.

"No, Mrs. Rand, it isn't," he whispered. "Let me show you."

His silken lips touched hers, lightly but with devastating impact. Keeping her mouth clamped closed, Indigo froze, afraid to draw away. He had every right to kiss her and might grow angry if she resisted. She would never forget how vicious Brandon had become when she had dared to tell him no.

Jake drew back and surveyed her with twinkling brown eyes. "Straining out bugs?"

"What?"

With a fingertip, he traced the line of her jaw, his eyes still dancing. Flashing her an exaggerated grin, he displayed gleaming white teeth, clenched tight. "Bugs. That's how I drink coffee on the trail. It works great at keeping foreign objects out of the mouth, but it isn't quite the thing for kissing. Not what I have in mind at all, in fact."

"No?"

"No," he affirmed, his voice dipping to a seductive timbre. He settled a hand on her waist and turned her to face him. When he noticed she still had one arm twisted behind her to hold onto the coffeepot handle, he arched a black eyebrow. "Are you planning to use that to club me?"

Indigo released the handle. "No. I just—your breakfast is ready. Fried potatoes and bacon and—" She tried to keep distance between their faces. "And eggs! With hot biscuits and fresh butter Ma made. And honey. Aren't you hungry?"

"Famished," he murmured and tightened his hand on her waist to draw her against him. "But the honey I'm hankering for isn't the kind you have in mind." Before she could react, he moved his other hand to the back of her head. "There's nothing to be afraid of, Indigo," he whispered. "I won't hurt you."

"I—I'm not afraid."

A low chuckle vibrated in his chest. "Then unclench your teeth and kiss me good morning. We have to begin somewhere."

"Why?"

The urge to laugh came over Jake and nearly made him forget what he had set out to do. "It's a law of nature. You can't finish what you never start." The tension in her body made her too rigid to mold against him. "Haven't you ever done this? A pretty girl like you should be an old hand at kissing."

"I never had much call to—"

"There's call now."

She leaned back, looking more alarmed by the moment.

Jake smiled. "There's nothing to it. I put one hand on your waist"—he tightened his grip there to demonstrate—"and the other at the back of your head. Then I pull you close." He drew her firmly against him. "All you do is close your eyes."

"B—But then I couldn't see."

"True. But in close quarters like this, anticipating my next move wouldn't do you a hell of a lot of good anyway."

She lowered her gaze to his mouth. "I—your breakfast will get cold."

He bent his head again. She strained against his hand, but he foiled her attempt to escape by knotting his fist in her braid. He wasn't another Brandon. His hold on her was like steel, and she couldn't twist away. His lips settled on hers, and she felt his tongue flick hers. She gasped and reared back, surprised that he allowed her to move. For an endless moment, she felt frantic and claustrophobic. Then the heat of the banked cooking fire seared through the leather seat of her pants. She jerked away, going in the only direction she could, which was forward. Her body pressed hard against his.

With a moan, he retreated a step, carrying her along. Then he slid his hand from her waist to her fanny and drew her closer so her pelvis rode his muscular thigh. At the grinding contact, her attention shifted from the alarming assault of his mouth to the strange, tingling warmth that pooled in her belly.

Shocked by the feeling and taken completely by surprise, she forgot he was kissing her just long enough for him to thoroughly invade her mouth with his searching tongue. A barrage of sensations hit Indigo with such sudden force that she couldn't muster her scattered wits to combat any of them.

She had to get away from him, she thought wildly. She had to get away before he—. The thought was lost to her. Unlike Brandon, Jake didn't conquer with strength alone. He used his mouth, his body, and his hands to disarm. A delicious, trembling weakness flowed over her.

As if he sensed her surrender, he dragged his mouth from hers and flashed a slow, sultry grin. "*That* is how you say good morning properly."

Indigo swayed against him, senses still reeling. She felt his arms quiver around her and knew he was as disoriented as she.

"Saying good night," he added huskily, "is even better. When we come home, I'll give you your first lesson."

That promise jerked her back to reality. She stared up at him, her mind racing ahead. A rush of dread filled her. With tremulous hands, she shoved against his chest to put some distance between their bodies.

"Don't look so appalled," he said with a teasing

wink. "It's a perfectly acceptable thing for married people to do, and it's far nicer than saying good morning. I guarantee it."

Releasing her, he turned back to the table where his breakfast waited. After sitting down, he took a large bite of egg and grimaced. "You were right. They got cold." He pinioned her with a warm gaze. "That kiss, however, was worth it."

Before going to the mine, Jake and Indigo had two stops to make, one at the jail to get an update from Marshal Hilton and another at the Wolfs', where Jake planned to do the barn chores for Loretta while Indigo fed her wild creatures.

The news from Hilton left Jake feeling frustrated. Brandon Marshall claimed to know nothing about the accidents at the mine or Lobo's shooting. He also had several friends who were willing to testify to his whereabouts the afternoon Lobo had been shot.

"That don't mean a whole lot," Hilton said. "The man's friends would lie for him. I'll be keeping my eyes peeled, you can count on that." He patted Indigo's shoulder and threw a meaningful glance at Jake. "Meanwhile, it wouldn't be a bad idea for you to take care. I don't trust that rascal, and I'm not real sure he doesn't have a brick or two loose."

Jake nodded. "I'll take every precaution."

"You do that. Me and the missus are right fond of this little lady. We wouldn't want to see anything happen to her."

Grasping his wife's elbow, Jake replied, "No fonder of her than I am, I'm sure."

As they left the jail and headed toward the Wolfs', Jake realized how sincerely he meant that. He had become fond of Indigo, so much so that he was glad to have chores to do while she fed her little friends. He wasn't at all certain he could watch her feed Toothless again without interfering. No matter what Loretta said, Jake didn't believe the cougar could be trusted, and the thought of his wife being laid open by those vicious claws made his knees weak. The farther he stayed away from the situation, the better.

Before they parted in front of the house, Jake said, "After you feed the deer, you eat a couple of those flapjacks yourself, Indigo. You never did light long enough to have any breakfast."

"I'm really not hungry."

Jake saw the sadness flash in her eyes and realized she was probably thinking of Lobo. "Will you eat at least one?"

"If I must."

"You must," he came back with a grin. "You've got a long day ahead of you. I'll meet you inside when I'm finished in the barn." Jake started to walk off, then turned back and cupped her chin in his hand. "Do me a favor and be especially careful while you're feeding the animals?"

She lifted puzzled blue eyes to his. "Careful?"

Jake narrowed an eye. "Yes, careful. I really don't approve of you feeding that cougar, you know."

"You don't?"

"No, I don't." He ran his thumb along the fragile line of her cheekbone. "Just thinking about it makes me break out in a sweat."

An alarmed expression crossed her face. "But, Jake, he's really quite harmless. He'd never hurt me."

"Harmless?" He gave a sharp laugh and released her. "He's wild, Indigo. You can't predict what he might do, and don't try to tell me you can."

"No," she admitted.

Taking a step back, he chucked her under the chin. "Then humor me, hm?"

With that, Jake strode off toward the barn. A few minutes later when he went back to the house, he found Indigo sitting at the table, the last few bites of a flapjack still on her plate. Jake put the pail of fresh milk on the dish board, stepped to the bedroom doorway to bid Hunter a good morning, then joined Father O'Grady to stand by the fire.

The priest gave him a nudge with his elbow. "'Tis a sad thing for me to confess, seeing that ye're a Methodist, but I understand we're of like mind about that cougar."

"She told you about that, did she?" Jake met Indigo's gaze and wondered why she looked so glum. "Does that flapjack taste that bad?" he asked her with a teasing grin.

With a notable lack of enthusiasm, Indigo lowered her gaze and put the last bite into her mouth. A moment later, Loretta emerged from the bedroom, carrying Hunter's plate. "Good morning, Mr. Rand."

Jake lifted an eyebrow. "Mr. Rand? I'd think we could move on to first names now that I'm your son-in-law."

Without her usual smile, Loretta swept past him and went to the kitchen. When she saw the pail of milk, she said, "I see you did my chores again. Thank you, Jake."

Because her tone was unmistakably cool, Jake frowned and replied, "You're more than welcome."

Father O'Grady reached up to touch Jake's shoulder. "'Tis never easy for a mother the first few days after a child marries," he whispered. "After all these years, she woke up this mornin' to discover ye've stepped into her shoes and that from now on ye'll be makin' all the decisions. Be patient, hm?"

"Decisions?" Jake turned a questioning gaze on the priest. "I have no intention of usurping her place in Indigo's life."

"No. Of course ye don't." Father O'Grady gave him a comforting pat. "She's just sensitive. All mothers are, right in the beginning. In a wee bit of time, she'll settle down and accept ye. Trust me to know. I've witnessed a few marriages."

Still troubled by Loretta's cool attitude, Jake turned his attention to Indigo. "Are you ready?"

She pushed up from the table. "Yes. It didn't take me as long as usual to get the animals fed."

Father O'Grady patted Jake's arm again and gave him a broad grin. "Did ye do any considerin' last night about convertin' to the faith? Since I'm already over this way, I'll be stayin' a few days to tend me flock. It'd make me a very happy man to begin yer instruction while I'm here."

Distracted by the question and amused by the priest's perseverance, Jake chuckled. "To be honest, Father, the last thing on my mind last night was religion."

The priest glanced toward the ceiling. "I suppose I asked for that."

Indigo returned from the kitchen just then. Jake took her by the arm and steered her toward the door. "I'll get back to you when I've made a decision, Father. That's a promise."

Once outside on the porch, Jake noticed Indigo's high color and realized she must have overheard his off-color comment to Father. Her wide blue eyes met his, then darted away. He nearly groaned. From her expression, he didn't think he had accomplished what he'd set out to by kissing her this morning.

"Well, are you ready for a long day?" he asked with deliberate lightness.

"Yes."

He couldn't help but notice that her voice rang with hopeless resignation.

When Jake and Indigo reached the mine and went their separate ways, Jake's first encounter was with Den-

ver Tompkins, who smirked, cast a lewd look in Indigo's direction, and said, "When we play, we have to
pay. I guess you learned that lesson the hard way."

Jake stiffened. "I take it you refer to my marriage?"

"Hell, everybody in town knew what was up when
you came riding in with Father O'Grady. The only surprise was that Wolf let you wait so long to do right by
her." He lifted an eyebrow. "It's double trouble when
you get caught messing with a squaw. How much did
her pappy get you for? A horse and a couple of blan-
kets?" He pursed his lips and whistled. "What a bargain, huh? She's a pretty piece of baggage, that one."

Jake froze with the shovel blade buried in the gravel.
His first impulse was to beat the man to a bloody pulp
and then fire him. Three things forestalled him from
doing that, the most important that he didn't want to
humiliate Indigo. Secondly, if rumors were already cir-
culating, pulverizing Tompkins would only add kindling
to the fire. His third reason, though less immediate, was
just as compelling. Of all the miners, he trusted Tompkins the least. Until he knew who had engineered the
cave-ins, he wanted the man underfoot to keep an eye
on him.

When Jake took so long to reply, Tompkins chuckled. "Not *two* horses? You really did get fleeced, didn't
you?" He gave a conspiratorial wink. "If you're smart,
you can triple your investment in a week. A squaw'll do
anything her man tells her, including bein' nice to his
friends."

Jake slowly straightened. For just an instant, blind
rage seized him, and he imagined how satisfying it
would feel to have his hands around Tompkins's throat.
His body had already tensed to leap when his reason
returned. He didn't want Indigo to get wind of this. If
he started a brawl, she most certainly would.

Counting on the surrounding noise created by the mining operation to muffle his reply, Jake said, "You've got

two seconds to retract that suggestion and apologize."

Tompkins took a step back. "Look, Mr. Rand. Maybe being a stranger to these parts, you haven't been around Injuns much and don't understand their ways. We do, and on occasion we joke about it." Tompkins lifted his hands in a shrug. "No one means any harm. Can't you take a little ribbing? Everybody knows you had to marry her and that her pappy, bein' Injun, probably made you buy her. That's how they do things."

Tightening his grip on the shovel, Jake said, "The bride price a man pays for an Indian wife isn't a purchase any more than the dowry a white girl takes into marriage is a bribe. If you weren't so damned ignorant, you'd know that."

A smug expression swept across Tompkins's face. "So you *did* pay."

Jake realized his defensiveness had cemented the man's suspicions. "I didn't say that," he replied.

"You don't have to," Tompkins said with a laugh. "The truth's written all over your face. God, that's rich. A shotgun wedding, and you had to pay to be the groom. With you being new to these parts, I would have loved to see your face."

Mind racing, Jake tried to think of a way to repair the damage he had just done. With a sinking feeling in the pit of his stomach, he looked into Tompkins's eyes and knew he couldn't. The more he tried to mend this situation, the worse it would probably get.

If anyone so much as hinted to Indigo that her husband had paid a bride price, she'd be bound to think he had mentioned it. After seeing the look in her eyes last night when she discovered money was changing hands, Jake didn't figure he would have a snowball's chance in hell of convincing her he hadn't. He could only hope she never heard about this. If luck went against him, however, he wanted to make damn sure she could at least take pride in the gossip.

Curiosity gleamed in the blond's eyes. "How much did he get out of you?"

Jake had the horrible feeling he was sinking in quicksand and cast around for Indigo to make sure she was out of earshot. "A small fortune, and I happily paid every cent. Another thing, just to get the story straight. There was no shotgun wedding. Any man with eyes knows that. The instant I met her, I knew I wanted to marry her, and when I finally worked up the courage to propose, she honored me by accepting. That's the God's truth, and I'll kill you or any other man who says different."

The blond held up his hands. "Hey, I'd be the first to admit she's a fine swatch of calico, or should I say buckskin."

"The finest." Jake strove to keep his voice even. "Don't ever make the mistake of referring to her as a squaw again. Not in my presence or in hers. There's not a female in this town, white or Indian, more chaste or God-fearing than that girl, and any man who doesn't have the decency to take off his hat to her will answer to me. Have I made myself clear?"

"Yeah."

"I'm glad to know we understand each other," Jake said silkily. "That goes for every rock-buster up here, so spread the word. And fair warning, Tompkins. If I hear one derogatory word about my marriage, I'll know it started with you." He jabbed a thumb in Indigo's direction. "If that girl sheds so much as a tear because of filthy talk, I'll take it out of your hide."

Tompkins looked uneasy. "It's not too smart to make threats about killing people. Someone might think you mean it."

"What makes you think I don't?"

"I have no control over what other people say. I'll tell it the way you want, but I doubt it'll change anyone's thinking."

With that, Tompkins struck off down the slope. Feeling helpless, Jake stood there and gazed after him.

"I reckon you'll do," a deep, gravelly voice commented from behind him.

Jake jerked around to see Shorty stepping out from behind a nearby wagon. "I'll do for what?"

As Shorty ambled closer, he scratched his earlobe, and then leaned sideways to spit tobacco juice. "As a husband for our little missy. At least you stood up for her." He drew up next to Jake and glanced at Tompkins's retreating back. "It's more than that no-good little pecker brain would have done. Half of what he said was envy talkin'. He wanted her for hisself. Offered her pappy three hundert dollars once."

Jake squinted against the sun. "What did Hunter say?"

Shorty hooked his thumbs under his overall straps. "Nothin'. He ain't much for jawin' when he's thinkin' murder. He just give him one of them looks of his—the kind that makes yer scalp crawl." He spat again. "For her sake, I'm right glad it was you she got stranded in the woods with and not Tompkins."

At best, that was a sparing compliment, and since the old man's manner didn't seem all that friendly, Jake wasn't certain how to reply. He ventured a hesitant, "Thank you. Do you always make it a habit to hide behind wagons and eavesdrop, Shorty?"

"When it comes to our little missy and her happiness, I ain't righteous. I been watchin' Denver flap his lip all mornin'. I figgered it'd tell me a lot about you if I could hear what ya said when he flapped to you. I knew he'd make tracks to needle ya the minute ya got here. All I had to do was stick close and wait." Shorty graced him with a narrow-eyed glare. "When I first saw you, I was afeard you had your eye on her. I guess I wasn't far wrong."

Jake wondered where this was heading. "No, I guess not."

"After overhearin' what I just did, I reckon I don't need to say this, but I'm gonna anyways. You'd best treat her good. If'n ya don't, we'll take ya to task, and don't think we won't. Just because her pa's flat on his back and all her other menfolk is gone, don't think there ain't nobody to take up for her."

Though Jake didn't feel particularly intimidated, he made a gallant attempt to appear so and bit back a smile. "Who's we?"

Shorty straightened his arthritic shoulders. "Me, Stringbean, and Stretch. Harm one hair on her head, and you'll answer to all three of us. And don't ya forgit it."

Striving to keep his expression carefully blank, Jake replied, "I won't."

"See that ya don't." The bulbous end of Shorty's nose turned red. "I s'pose you'll give me the boot now, first chance ya git. But somebody had to say it. It ain't right, a little mite like her, with nobody to take up fer her."

Jake could no longer hide his grin. "I agree. Rest assured, though. I'll take good care of her. From here on in, you don't need to worry."

Shorty nodded. "From what I heard you sayin' to Tompkins, I reckon I don't." He met Jake's gaze. "Just watch yer back. He's a sneaky little bastard, and his neck's been swole for better than a year over that girl. He'll be lippin' off to ever'body he sees now, mark my words. He won't be happy 'til he's got her in tears."

That was Jake's worst fear. He studied Shorty for a moment, decided he could trust the man, then cleared his throat. "If he flaps about that bride price, it's going to break her heart. Me being white, she didn't like the idea a damned bit, and I can't blame her. I'm worried that she'll think I was bragging. Or worse yet, complaining. I didn't think of it as a purchase, but that's what she'll believe if word gets back to her."

"Send her to me." A twinkle crept into Shorty's eyes. "Sometimes, atwixt right and wrong, there's a blessin'. In this case, it's my ears. I'll tell her what was said, just the way it was spoke." He offered Jake his hand. "Ya handled it right fine, to my way of thinkin'."

Relief washed over Jake. He clasped Shorty's out-stretched palm. "I appreciate the offer, and I might take you up on it. I'm afraid she won't believe a damned word I say."

Shorty's gaze held Jake's. "She was present the day Tompkins offered her pappy that three hundert. He walked right up, bold as brass, and tried to buy her. Try that on for size and see how it makes you feel." With that, Shorty hiked up his overall strap and strode off down the hill.

With a thoughtful frown and a shake of his head, Jake resumed his work, loading the pile of gravel near the arrastra into a wheelbarrow and taking it, one load at a time, to the sluice.

At noon break, he went in search of Indigo and found her helping to man a rockerbox, which was as exhausting a chore as it was backbreaking. Using all his self-control, he managed to swallow any objection. If he meant to restrict her from every job at the mine, he might as well send her home.

When she saw Jake coming, she spoke to her part-ner and abandoned her work. There was a question in her eyes as she walked down the slope. Forcing his gaze from the feminine swing of her hips to the narrow set of her shoulders, Jake remembered how fragile her ribs had felt beneath his palm last night. Then he recalled how soft and warm her little fanny had felt in his cupped palm this morning. She was his wife, dammit. He could buy her anything she needed, yet here she was, slaving in a two-bit mine. A fierce wave of protectiveness washed through him.

Lifting his gaze to hers, Jake set his jaw, determined not to say anything. He doubted Indigo would care a whit about all the things his money could buy her. His fancy home in Portland would no doubt impress her, but not favorably. To her, all the riches in the world were right here, and he couldn't in good conscience rob her of them. His one consolation was that she seemed more like herself now than she had since the wedding last night. She moved with confidence, and her gaze met his without faltering.

Indigo had little difficulty interpreting the look in Jake's eyes, and for at least the hundredth time that morning, she was filled with apprehension. There was no question what he had been thinking when he said, "About your going to the mine." He had come just that close to saying she had to stay home.

They sat together beneath an oak tree to eat the lunch she had packed. While she forced herself to nibble a piece of dried apple, she gazed at nothing and tried to imagine what her life would be like if Jake forbade her to come here. She knew he wasn't alone in feeling a wife's place was at home.

She tried to think of something she might say to sway him over to her side, but there was nothing. A wife's wants didn't carry a great deal of weight with most white husbands, a squaw's even less. Her only hope lay in prayer and his benevolence.

12

After the noon break, Jake returned to his job of hauling gravel. By making repeated trips from the arrastra to the sluice, he had opportunity to observe the other miners. What he watched for, he wasn't certain. Anything that looked peculiar, he supposed. Someone had weakened those timbers in the mine, and, as far as he was concerned, no one was above suspicion.

He couldn't help but hope his father had nothing to do with it. The possibility had been bad enough before, but now? Indigo already resented their marriage. She would detest him if she learned his father had nearly killed hers. Jeremy had promised to continue searching Ore-Cal's files while Jake investigated at Wolf's Landing. Jake hoped that instead of finding evidence against their father, Jeremy would find he wasn't guilty.

Each time Jake pushed a load of gravel to the sluice, he cast about for Indigo. Trust him to marry a slip of a girl who tackled everything. It took all his control not to interfere when he saw her helping Topper reseat a loaded skip onto the rails. To his surprise, she managed to lift her side. The weight was enough to break the backs of two men and a small boy.

Jake cringed and looked away. Then, though he knew he shouldn't, he slid his gaze back to her. As he watched, Denver sauntered down to the unseated skip. Indigo turned at something the blond said. Jake couldn't read her expression. He curled his fists around the handles of the wheelbarrow.

A cool breeze wafted against Indigo's hot cheeks. She gazed up at Denver, aware of the steel gray rain clouds gathering in the sky behind him. Tall pines whipped in the rising wind, heralding a storm. Denver's blue eyes glinted with cruel amusement, heralding unpleasantness of a different type.

"So you're married?" he asked. Tipping his head to one side, he flashed a smile. "How does it feel?"

Indigo glanced at Topper, who waited for her to resume their chore. She turned back to get handholds on the skip. "That's a strange question, Denver. It's like asking someone how it feels to have a birthday. One day is much the same as another."

"Really? I'm surprised you aren't wearing a leash."

Indigo's hands cramped on the side of the skip. She stared across the pile of ore at Topper's stony expression.

Denver chuckled. "You know, it's funny. Your father really had me fooled. He acted so indignant that time I tried to buy you. Remember that? I was convinced he'd never do such a thing. And all the while, he was just holding out for a better offer."

Indigo slowly straightened. As she turned around, her pulse quickened. "What are you saying? I haven't all day for games."

"I'll admit it made me angry at first. But now that I've talked to Rand about it, I don't feel so bad. In fact, now that I've thought it over, I'm kind of glad it happened this way. I'm not the marrying kind. I'd rather spend a few dollars to be with you and go home fancy free."

"Shut your mouth, Tompkins!" Topper interrupted.

Indigo held up a hand. "No, let him say what he came to say." She riveted her gaze to Denver's. "Finish. I'm waiting."

"What more is there to say? If I'm willing to pay the price, I'll get to spend time with you." He ran a knuckle along her cheek. "Not right at first. He said he wants to keep you for himself for a spell. But, hell, how long can it take for him to get bored? Besides, he'll be anxious to earn his money back. He paid a mighty steep price for you, the way he tells it. You'll have to do a lot of entertaining to earn his money back for him and start turning a profit."

Indigo jerked her head back. Denver caught her chin.

"Don't act too high and mighty, Indigo. When he starts renting you out, I'm going to be first in line. I'll take you down a notch or two the minute we're alone."

"That's enough, Tompkins." Topper stepped around the skip. "One more word, and I'm going to lay you out."

With a sarcastic laugh, Denver released Indigo and stepped back. "I've said all I had to say." He slid his gaze to Indigo. "You can bet I won't be playing cards and losing my paychecks from here on. Now I've got better things to spend my money on."

With a jaunty bounce to his step, Denver walked away. Indigo stood there and stared after him, unable to move, unable to think. As if from a great distance, she heard Topper's voice, but she couldn't grasp the words. She lifted her gaze to the hillside where Jake had stopped with a loaded wheelbarrow. When he realized she was looking at him, he raised his hand and waved.

"Denver's lying through his teeth, Miss Indigo," Topper said from behind her. "He's been building up to it all morning. Mr. Rand didn't tell him none of those things."

A horrible chill washed over Indigo's skin. How could Denver possibly know Jake had paid a bride price, let alone how much he paid, unless Jake had told him? The cold knot of fear that had rested deep within her since her wedding turned icy, and her insides clenched spasmodically around it. She knew many a white man had made extra coin by renting out their squaws. The practice was so common, in fact, that people joked about it. If Jake chose to do it, he wouldn't be the first, or the last.

Jake watched Denver Tompkins walk away. Relief filled him when Indigo turned back to the skip. With a little luck, maybe Denver hadn't said anything. Jake had no doubt that if and when Denver did, he'd make it sound as bad as he could. The only consolation Jake had was Shorty. The instant Tompkins said anything, Jake would take Indigo to her old friend and ask him to give her an accurate account of his conversation with Tompkins.

Heaving up on the wheelbarrow handles, Jake started to take a step. As he did, he thought he glimpsed movement on the rocky slope at the top of the cliff. He turned to look, and what he saw turned his blood to ice. A rock slide. The main entrance to the tunnel lay directly in its path. For an instant, Jake stared, scarcely able to believe his eyes. Then he dropped the wheelbarrow and broke into a run.

"Indigo!"

She couldn't hear him. The cacophony of sound in and around the mine drowned out his voice and the rumble of the rock slide.

"Indigo, run! Run!"

Jake felt as if he was having one of those horrible dreams where the danger advanced with lightning speed and he reacted with agonizing slowness. He could hear his blood pounding in his ears, his lungs whining. The impact of his boots on the slope jarred clear through his body.

"Indigo!"

At last, she and Topper heard him. Shading her eyes with her forearm, she turned to look. Jake made a wild gesture with his arm, never breaking stride.

"Run! A rock slide! Get out of there! Run!"

She cast a glance around and, seeing nothing, lifted her hands in bewilderment. "What?" she called.

Jake could see the rocks gaining momentum, dislodging others in their path. He imagined Indigo crushed beneath them. Fright lent him speed he didn't know he possessed. "Run, dammit! Run!"

She and Topper backed away from the skip, but, not knowing where the danger came from, they didn't move far enough.

"A rock slide! Above you! Get out of there!"

She looked up. When she saw what Jake was screaming about, she grabbed Topper's arm and whirled to run. The first of the rocks reached the edge of the cliff and peppered the ground around the skip. One hit Topper on the shoulder and dropped him to his knees. Indigo stopped to help him. Jake's heart froze. She was going to get herself killed.

With Indigo's help, Topper staggered to his feet. She draped his arm over her shoulder and half carried him along with her. A split second after they cleared the area, the bulk of the rock slide hit the edge of the cliff and spilled over like a giant and deadly waterfall. The skip and the surrounding ground for twenty feet in all directions were showered with stones.

Jake's legs went wobbly with relief, and he reeled to a stop about ten feet from Indigo and Topper. Dust billowed around them, searing their throats and lungs. The three of them retreated a few more feet, coughing and struggling to breathe.

Jake knew he never would have reached Indigo in

time to get her out of there. One more second, just one, and she'd be dead right now. The realization made him start to shake. He wanted to grab her into his arms, but fear had jellied his muscles.

When the air began to clear a little, Topper exclaimed, "That's what I call too close for comfort."

"Are you all right?" Indigo tried to check the toplander's shoulder. "Is anything broken, Topper?"

Several other men gathered around.

"I'm fine," Topper assured everyone. "Thanks to you," he told Indigo. "Most people would have said every man for himself. You saved my life, missy."

"Nonsense. We have Jake to thank for that." Indigo glanced around at Jake. "Praise God that you saw it coming!"

Jake tried to reply but couldn't.

She turned to look at the buried skip and went a little pale. "If we hadn't moved when we did—"

Shorty came limping over. "I been workin' this here mountain for fifteen year, and I ain't never seen a pebble so much as move on that slope."

Miners came crawling from the tunnel, coughing and waving away dust. Indigo cupped her hands around her mouth. "Are you all okay down there?"

One of the emerging men gave her a thumb up.

With a grimy finger, Shorty scooped a wad of chew from inside his lip and spat. He shot Jake a meaningful glance. "I say them rocks had a little help movin'. You wanna go with me and take a look-see?"

Jake, still not completely recovered from his fright, grasped Indigo's arm with a shaky hand and drew her into a walk. After such a close call, he was reluctant to leave her alone. "Yes, let's go check."

Thirty minutes later, Jake had seen all he needed to see. The slide had been caused by the displacement of a gigantic boulder. From all indications, it had been firmly seated, and it seemed unlikely to Jake that it had suddenly moved on its own.

"This was no accident." Rage made him clip the words.

Shorty scratched his head. "Don't appear like it. Could've been, though. We had a long spell of heavy rain a few days back. The dirt might've softened up around it."

Jake shot him a glare. "Do you really believe that?"

Shorty drew his bushy eyebrows together. "Nope, I reckon I don't. I jist hate to think somebody did it deliberate."

Indigo sank onto a nearby rock and gazed at the path of the rock slide. "You think someone did it on purpose?"

"Maybe so. Tryin' to block off the mine entrance would be my guess," Shorty ventured.

Jake didn't want to put his fear into words, but he had to. "Or to kill someone." He looked at Indigo. He'd never forget seeing that slope of rock rolling toward her like a giant wave. "Namely you."

Her eyes widened. "Me?" She threw a glance down the hill. "You can't even see the mine entrance or who's down there from here. It couldn't have been meant for me."

Jake gestured toward a group of trees to their left. "Someone could have been watching from over there."

She regarded him with ill-concealed exasperation. "I could have left, just that quick. Isn't that supposing a bit much? Topper was down there, too. Other people were coming and going. A rock slide can't be aimed at one person."

"Do you think a murderer would care who else he hurt, as long as he got the person he wanted?"

"Surely, you're not serious."

"I'm very serious."

Agitated, Jake swiped at his mouth. He didn't want to overreact, and her arguments made sense. But, dammit, how could he take that chance? At the best of times, working in or around a mine was dangerous. It was a perfect place to commit murder and make it look like an accident.

Jake recalled two other incidents that had nearly killed Indigo, the cave-in that had injured Hunter and the rifle shot that had taken Lobo's life. And now a rock slide. He kept imagining her, crushed under hundreds of pounds of stone.

With a feeling of unreality, he said, "You were reseating a skip, Indigo. If someone was over there in the trees, watching and waiting for the right moment, he would have known you'd be there for a while." He kicked a rock and watched it bounce and go airborne. "He would have had plenty of time to come over here and dislodge the boulder. It's only a few seconds' walk."

She braced her hands on her knees and pushed to her feet. "The rock could have come loose on its own."

Jake clenched his teeth. After a long moment, he said, "Maybe. But then again, maybe not. I'm not a gambling man."

"What do you mean?"

Jake didn't want to answer. He knew damned well how it was going to look, and that she was going to detest him for it. "I think you'd better go home."

She hugged her waist.

"You know it makes good sense. You can't watch your back here, and I can't watch it for you. There are too many people coming and going, too much noise, and too many dangerous situations. Until we get to the bottom of all this, I think you should stick close to the house."

"If someone wants to kill me, he can do it there."

"Not as easily. You'd have a better chance to see trouble coming, for one. With so many people within yelling distance of the house, only a fool'd try something in broad daylight."

Her voice rose to a shrill pitch, and she gestured toward the disturbed ground where the boulder had sat. "This is a steep slope. Boulders *do* come loose on their own, you know. You can't be certain the slide was started by someone."

"No. But my gut feeling—"

"You're just using this as an excuse!" she cried.

Shorty coughed. "I think this is where I say it's time for me to go back to work."

Jake watched him walk away. As soon as Shorty was beyond earshot, he turned back to Indigo. "Honey, listen to me."

She tightened her arms at her waist and averted her face. Jake sighed.

"Indigo, please don't act like this. Do you think I'd send you home without damned good reason?"

"Yes," she replied in a hollow voice. "I do. You didn't want me to come. You couldn't think of a good reason to send me home, so you didn't. But now a reason has dropped in your lap."

"That isn't true."

She fastened an accusing gaze on him, her mouth set.

Jake curled his fingers around the back of his neck. "I admit it, okay? I don't like you doing a man's job. I'd rather you didn't, but that has nothing to do with this."

In a toneless voice, she said, "I think it has everything to do with it."

Jake knew she probably had every reason to believe that. When it came to his feelings, he was fairly transparent, and the truth was, he didn't like the idea of her working in a mine. Regardless, though, there were other issues involved here, and he'd be a fool to ignore them. "Marshal Hilton advised me to take every precaution. That's exactly what I intend to do. As much as you

GET YOUR FOUR FREE BOOKS TODAY ($20.49 VALUE)

FILL IN THE ORDER FORM BELOW NOW!

YES! *I want to join the Timeless Romance Reader Service. Please send me my 4 FREE HarperMonogram historical romances. Then each month send me 4 new historical romances to preview without obligation for 10 days. I'll pay the low subscription price of $4.00 for every book I choose to keep – a total savings of at least $2.00 each month – and home delivery is free! I understand that I may return any title within 10 days without obligation and I may cancel this subscription at any time without obligation. There is no minimum number of books to purchase.*

NAME_____

ADDRESS _____

CITY_____STATE____ZIP_____

TELEPHONE_____

SIGNATURE _____

(If under 18 parent or guardian must sign. Program, price, terms, and conditions subject to cancellation and change. Orders subject to acceptance by HarperMonogram.)

GET
4
FREE
BOOKS
(A $20.49
VALUE)

TIMELESS ROMANCE
READER SERVICE

120 Brighton Road
P.O. Box 5069
Clifton, NJ 07015-5069

might hate me for it, my decision's made. Until this is settled and we're certain Brandon Marshall isn't behind it all, you're sticking close to house."

Her eyes widened. "H—How close?"

"No wandering off alone until I give the go-ahead."

"You mean I can't—" Her gaze shifted to the woods around them. "You mean I can't go walking? Or hunting?"

"No."

Jake watched the light dim in her eyes. For several seconds, she stood there with her lips parted, her throat working soundlessly. He fully expected her to light into him. He was surprised when all she said was, "Is that your final word?"

Agitated, Jake shoved his hands into his pockets to stop himself from touching her. Dammit, he didn't want this right now, not on top of everything else. "I always reserve the right to change my mind, Indigo. But in this instance, I have to say yes, it's my final word."

She bowed her head. He squeezed his eyes closed and swallowed.

"Indigo, it isn't the way you're thinking," he told her in a ragged voice. "I swear to God it isn't. I just want to protect you. The moment I think it's safe, I'll lift the restrictions."

She nodded and turned away. Jake stood there and watched her. Suddenly, Mary Beth's voice rang in his head. *I wish you'd marry Emily. Maybe then you'd make her life miserable instead of mine.* Only he hadn't married Emily. Instead, he had married a half-wild girl who had never been ruled by anyone.

Falling in behind her, Jake said, "I'll knock off early today and walk you home, all right? We'll talk things over."

She looked up as he came abreast of her. With an oddly blank expression in her eyes, she asked, "Is there a chance you'll change your mind?"

Jake wanted to say yes. But the truth was, he seriously doubted it. As upset as she obviously was and as much as she might detest him for it, his first concern had to be her safety. "It's not likely," he replied. "But maybe if we talk about it, you'll start to feel better about my decision."

Later that evening after Jake left to go visit her father, Indigo went out to the well to haul in water. As she drew up the bucket, she looked longingly toward the woods. The birds sang here in Aunt Amy's yard, but not as serenely as they did deep in the forest. The wind whispered here, too, but it didn't speak to her in quite the same way. She had to face the possibility that she might never again wander for hours in her beloved mountains.

A prisoner. That was what she had become. And it might be a life sentence.

Feeling oddly numb, she leaned her back against the well and stared at nothing. In the back of her mind, she wondered if perhaps she wasn't suffering from delayed shock because of all that had happened. But the question took too much thought for her to muddle through and decide on an answer. It didn't really matter. The numbness felt rather nice after all the turmoil.

Three days. How could one's life change so drastically in so short a time? She studied a clump of grass near the toe of her moccasin. Seventy-two hours ago, the grass had been just as it was now, several green blades, all sprouting from a matted root system. The sun was setting, right on schedule, as it had for centuries. The moon would rise when darkness fell. Nothing in the world had changed, and yet nothing was the same.

She tried to assemble all the changes into a meaningful whole, so she could grasp exactly where she stood and where she was headed. But she felt dizzy, the way Chase used to make her feel years ago when he grabbed her wrists and spun with her in a circle until she couldn't stand up. She had that feeling now, as if the ground and sky were whirling, and she couldn't find any place solid to plant her feet.

All the things she had always counted on had been snatched away, Lobo, the support of her parents, the home where she'd grown up, the mine, and her mountains. Even her name was different. Not Indigo Wolf anymore, but Indigo Rand. She felt like a cup that had been drained and left empty.

Denver Tompkins's taunts whispered in her mind, and she closed her eyes on a rush of shame. She tried to imagine the coming night, but her head refused to form the pictures. She only knew that making love with a man who regarded her as a possession to be used and lent out was bound to be horrible. She could only wonder why Jake had given her a reprieve last night. Was Topper right? Had Denver been lying? Or was Jake merely toying with her?

A cougar's cry lifted in the air. Indigo raised her head and listened. Toothless. Tears threatened to fill her eyes. Straightening her shoulders, she blinked them away, grabbed the bucket, and ran toward the house, sloshing water.

13

Jake went directly to the Wolfs' to speak to Hunter. Father O'Grady was out hearing confessions. Loretta greeted Jake with the same coolness she had that morning. Feeling uncomfortable, Jake didn't waste time on pleasantries before he went to the bedroom. After saying hello to Hunter and asking if he felt up to talking, Jake closed the door so Loretta couldn't overhear.

Taking care not to give a biased account of what had occurred, he told Hunter about the rock slide, how close a call it had been, and why he had restricted Indigo's activities.

As he finished laying the groundwork for the questions he meant to ask, Jake spread his hands and resorted to stark honesty. "I just left Indigo at the house. She's awfully upset." As briefly as he could and without bringing his past into it, Jake explained how he felt about women doing heavy work. "She thinks I'm using the rock slide as an excuse to keep her at home."

Hunter seemed to consider that. "If it were not for this danger, would you object to her mining or hunting in the woods?"

Jake shoved his hands into the hip pockets of his jeans. "I'd rather she had more conventional interests, but that isn't why I restricted her to the house. Marshal Hilton thinks Brandon Marshall is a card short of dealing with a full deck. He doesn't trust the man and told me to take every precaution. Since the shot that killed Lobo and the rock slide, how can I be sure she'll be safe at the mine or in the woods?"

"So this decision . . . it only stands until you are certain Brandon won't harm her?"

Jake nodded. "A temporary measure."

Hunter studied Jake for a long moment. "Why do you bring this to me?"

Jake laughed. "I want your opinion. Am I being unfair?"

Hunter smiled. "That is not for me to say. You are Indigo's husband."

"I want to be a good husband."

"With that wish to guide you, how can you fail?"

Jake wanted a direct answer, not talk that went in circles. "Do you think she might be in danger?"

Hunter nodded. "I believe it's possible. I also believe you have a good heart. Listen to the song it sings, eh? It is there that you will find the answers you seek."

Jake heaved a discouraged sigh. "I was really hoping you'd give me some advice, Hunter. She's your daughter."

"And I have given her to you."

Jake tipped his head back and stared at the ceiling. "You tell me to listen to songs? I'm not even sure there's one inside me. And if there is, it's bound to be different than the one in you and Indigo. I don't understand her half the time. How in hell can I make sound decisions about her happiness?"

"You must find the way."

Jake met his gaze. "That's why I came here."

Hunter smiled again. "So I can show you? And after

you have gone a great distance, what then? When you are deep into the trees and the way I pointed out is no longer clear, how will you direct your footsteps?" He shook his head. "You must find your own way from the start—a way good for you and for Indigo. Once you know how you should walk, you will never become lost."

Jake bit back a curse and jerked his hands from his pockets. "In other words, I'm on my own."

"No. My daughter walks with you. Choose your way carefully, yes? The trail ahead of you will be steep at times. At others, it may be rocky and narrow. You must be certain you go along a path that leaves room for her to journey beside you."

Jake sighed and sank onto the rocker. Dropping his head into his hands, he leaned forward and planted his elbows on his knees. "Right now, the path is pretty damned rocky. I'm ready to strangle her." He laughed softly and looked up. "She won't speak to me. That gets to me quicker than anything."

Hunter smiled slightly. "Ah, yes, the quietness. They are good at it. It is the way of things. We have strength of arm, they have strength of will."

"How do you handle it when Loretta won't speak to you?"

Hunter shifted his shoulders and winced. "I make the great fight for a while, and then I surrender."

A chuckle erupted from Jake before he could stifle it. When he saw Hunter's answering grin, he relaxed. "Sorry, but it struck me funny. If you sneezed at her, you'd lay her flat."

"Ah, but when she cries, it lays *me* flat." He closed his eyes for a moment. "I find ways to dry her tears, yes? And soon I find that I have surrendered."

"Would you surrender if you were afraid for her safety?"

"No. To keep her safe, I can be a very mean man."

"That's my position. I can't surrender on this."

Hunter inclined his head in silent agreement. "Perhaps you can surrender on small things. To be a husband is not easy, especially the first day." His knowing blue eyes grew solemn. "There are many ways a woman can come to harm, yes? You cannot keep her safe from them all."

"For instance?" Jake asked in puzzlement.

Hunter waved his unbandaged hand. "Indigo will not starve if she does not eat for a few days. Perhaps you could let her belly tell her when to put food in her mouth. When her throat wants to push the food up, and her husband says she must swallow it down, a strange thing occurs. My woman calls it gagging."

Jake stopped the rocker. His mind slid backward to that morning when he had asked Indigo to eat a flapjack. He arched an eyebrow. "Anything else?"

"You might let her feed her cougar. It would make me a happy man. He's been screaming off and on all day and waking me up. And my woman is pouting."

A muscle along Jake's jaw began to tick. "I see. That wouldn't be why Loretta treated me so coolly this morning?"

Hunter's lips twitched. "Indigo is her little girl. It didn't make her happy to watch her gag down a flapjack. And we have always allowed her to feed her animals. Suddenly, her new husband says no about the cougar."

"I see."

Hunter looked none too certain of that. "Do you? If Toothless isn't fed, he will try to rob the trap lines soon. If he does that, he may get a foot caught, and the trapper will kill him. Since he trusts only Indigo, we cannot feed him. We can only watch and worry."

"And be angry," Jake added.

Hunter smiled. "My Loretta is a good woman, and she will say nothing. But her eyes will give you frostbite.

Surrender on the little things, yes? Too many changes too soon can cause big trouble."

Jake shoved stiffly from the chair. "Thank you, Hunter. This visit has been enlightening."

Hunter nodded. "You will make talk with my daughter, yes, so maybe she will make talk with you?"

"Oh, yes. We're going to make talk, all right."

It was growing dark when Jake left the Wolfs'. He strode down the boardwalk, his boots hitting the planks with sharp retorts, his jaw set. Anger. It surged through him in hot, pulsing waves. She had lied to her parents this morning, out-and-out lied. The question was, why? Jake tried to imagine her sitting meekly at the table, gagging on bite after bite of flapjack, pretending that her brute of a husband had commanded her to do it. The picture made him all the more furious.

As he approached the Lopez house, he noticed that the lantern hadn't been lit inside. He swore and hurried up the steps, envisioning her running away or pulling some other fool female stunt. In his haste, he threw open the door with such force that it hit the interior wall.

He found her in the nearly dark kitchen. She stood at the dish board, calmly slicing a piece of venison, a picture of domesticity, except for her Indian attire, the lack of light, and the stricken expression on her face. Jake felt foolish. He shoved his hands into his pants pockets and watched her for a moment. She looked as if someone had just slapped her—bruised, shaky, and perilously close to tears.

His anger ebbed a little. Though it infuriated him to think of the embarrassing lies she had told her parents about him this morning, he had to admit the last few days had been miserable for her. She was probably fighting back the only way she knew how. The least he could do was bear that in mind and keep his temper.

He fetched the lantern from the sitting room, lit it, and carried it to the kitchen.

"Will you be needing more wood for tomorrow?"

Her expression didn't alter by so much as a twitch. "I'll bring it in."

Her reply came out in a monotone, clipped and unfriendly, punctuated by an eloquent *thunk* of the knife blade as it sliced cleanly through the venison and bit into the cutting board. Jake had the nasty feeling she was pretending that slab of meat was his neck.

"I don't mind getting it." Determined to be patient and reasonable, he went out and grabbed an armload of wood. When he reentered the house, she had finished slicing the meat and had begun peeling potatoes. With feigned cheer, he said, "The storm passed us over. So many days of sunshine has to set a record."

Her response was stiff silence. Jake clenched his teeth and went back out for more wood, cursing females and their war strategies. Maybe Hunter could laugh about it, but Jake couldn't. He'd be damned if he would put up with this from Indigo every time he crossed her.

Determined, Jake returned to the kitchen and carefully unloaded the wood into a neat stack in the woodbox. "There you are, Mrs. Rand. That'll get you through until tomorrow night."

She didn't say thank you. Nor did she acknowledge that he had spoken. Jake observed her thoughtfully as she clamped a lid on the skillet of potatoes and began laying floury pieces of butterflied venison across the piping hot griddle. Anger was evident in every line of her small body. Patience, he reminded himself. It occurred to him that maybe she was afraid to vent her feelings for fear he might retaliate.

He rubbed his neck. "Honey, I know you're upset."

Grease popped off the griddle, and she jerked.

Jake waited for her to reply, realized she didn't intend to, and pursed his lips. "Can't you look on the bright side? If you don't have to work for the next few days, maybe you can spend some time with your mother." He paused a moment, then added in an even voice, "Or time with your animals. Toothless maybe."

She threw him a startled look. Jake watched the expressions that flitted across her face. Guilt? He couldn't be certain. After a moment, she seemed to regain her composure. Shoulders set, she returned her attention to the venison as if he wasn't there.

"You don't have to be afraid I'll get angry at you for speaking your mind."

She didn't look up. "I'm not afraid."

That was hogwash, and they both knew it. Jake was growing more irritated by the second. "Well, if you're not, then at least look at me."

Though her eyes were bewildered when she turned her gaze on him, Jake couldn't miss the resentment in their depths.

"That's better." If a look could scorch, he decided he would be reduced to cinders. He knew damned well she had a temper and the communication skills to vent it. "How long is this infernal silence going to continue, Indigo?"

She licked her lips. "Only until I've something to say. Right now, there's nothing within me but"—her face drew taut and she threw him an apprehensive glance—"anger."

That was a step in the right direction. "Then express your anger to me," he insisted in a stern tone.

She threw him another startled glance. "Is that your wish?"

Accustomed to Mary Beth's feminine maneuvers when she wanted her own way, Jake eyed Indigo with sudden wariness. This subservient act of hers was really beginning to get to him. If it was her aim to make him feel like an ogre, she was succeeding admirably. If she hoped to rile him, she was coming perilously close to doing that as well. She had no idea how close. "Yes, it's my wish," he ground out.

Straightening her shoulders, she positioned the griddle away from the heat, wiped her hands on a towel, then turned to face him. "You won't get mad?"

"No. What's going to make me mad is if you don't talk."

She lifted her chin. "I think you are an arrogant, selfish bastard."

Her delivery was so well modulated and precise that for a moment the words didn't register on Jake's brain.

"I also detest you," she finished.

His throat felt oddly tight, from outrage or the urge to laugh, he wasn't sure. "Is that all?"

Obviously agitated, she stepped to the cupboard, took down a bowl, and then stared blankly at it. "No, that isn't all."

"Well?"

She flicked a glance at the stove, returned the bowl to the shelf, and pulled out a plate. "I'd like to burn your dinner, dump it on the floor, and bludgeon you with the hot griddle."

"That bad, huh? My, you really are upset."

"Yes."

He folded his arms. "But instead you just moved the griddle off the heat so the venison won't cook too fast?"

Her lips thinned with unmistakable distaste. "You are my husband. It's my duty to see that you eat."

"Even when you're so upset?"

"My feelings are only important if you make them so."

He narrowed an eye. Understanding was beginning to dawn. Guilt, the ultimate weapon. Mary Beth could take lessons from this little minx. "Don't tell me. This is the way of the People, right? A wife must be obedient, and if her husband is an arrogant, selfish bastard, her only recourse is to accept it."

Her eyes sparked more brightly. "Yes."

Warming to the game, he responded to the mutinous expression on her face with a slow grin. "Am I interpreting this correctly? You're so furious you'd like to—what was the word?—ah, yes, bludgeon me, yet you came in here, started my dinner, and didn't say a word. Is that the way a proper Comanche wife behaves when she'd like to murder her husband?"

Two bright spots of color flagged her cheeks. "Yes."

"She doesn't scream when she's angry?" His grin broadened. "She doesn't sass? She just does as she's told, no argument?"

"Yes," she replied.

"Repeat that. I didn't quite catch it."

"Yes!"

Jake studied her for a minute, still grinning. At last, he straightened. "That's every man's dream come true." Inclining his head toward the stove, he said, "I'd like toast instead of biscuits. Lightly browned." With that, he left the kitchen.

After he had changed from his work clothes and washed up outside, Jake returned to find that his beautiful, stonily silent, and sullen bride had prepared him a superb meal, everything cooked to a turn. He sat and spread his napkin across his lap.

With a smug grin, he said, "Aren't you going to eat?"

"I'm not hungry."

He chewed a piece of meat and swallowed, recalling Mary Beth's many hunger sieges. When it came to battles of will, he was a master. "And if I insist?"

She eyed the food with resignation. "Then I'll eat."

"Even if it makes you gag?"

Her startled gaze flicked to his. Jake nearly confronted her then. They both knew damned well that he hadn't commanded her to gag down a flapjack. He had been concerned because she hadn't eaten, and he had tried to cajole her into taking some sort of nourishment. For reasons beyond him, she had chosen to capitalize on that, following his words to the letter, no doubt to make him look bad.

Why? That was the question. Had she hoped her parents might decide to have her marriage to him annulled? Jake had no idea. The only thing he knew for sure was that he didn't like being made to look like a heartless ogre, and by the time he was finished with her, she'd never try it again.

"I don't suppose it'll hurt you to miss a meal or two. You're not what I'd term plump yet, but that fanny of yours could stand a little shaving."

She brushed a hand against her thigh, her dismay evident.

"I was afraid you might say you had to wait until your husband finished eating. That's another Indian custom, isn't it? The men eat first while the women hover nearby?"

"My father dispensed with that tradition. In his household, there is a comfortable blend of both white and Comanche ways, and he enjoys my mother's presence at his table."

Her father also surrendered when her mother grew angry and wouldn't speak to him. An authoritarian, Hunter wasn't.

"I see." He smiled up at her. "So, if I find a Comanche custom unbearable, we can alter it, correct?"

"Yes."

He shoved a piece of Loretta's homemade bread in his mouth. Chasing it down with a sip of coffee, he said, "Not that I'm complaining. I've never known a man yet who'd complain about having a completely subservient wife whose sole purpose was to please him and do his bidding."

The spots of color reappeared on her cheeks.

Jake hid a grin behind his coffee cup. "Tell me, what's expected of a husband in this kind of arrangement? Are there any rules he has to follow? I wouldn't want to disappoint such a dutiful, malleable wife by falling short of her expectations."

"There are no rules for a husband," she replied shakily.

"None? Surely a wife must have some expectation or ideal."

"It's her hope that her husband will love her and"—her gaze flew to his—"try in all ways to please her."

Bonanza. A subtle reminder of the promise he had made to her in the loft yesterday? How had he put it? *I'll do everything in my power to make you happy.* "I knew there had to be a catch."

"There's no law that says he must," she added in a tremulous voice. "A woman can only hope."

He set his coffee mug down with a decisive click, mentally applauding her. Her methods, intended to prick his conscience, he felt sure, had Mary Beth's tantrums beat hands down. Unfortunately for her, he had never been and didn't intend to be manipulated. She could keep this up for a month, and he wouldn't rescind his decision about her staying at home. Nor was she going to succeed in getting her parents to annul her marriage to him, if that was her plan. He'd make sure of that tonight.

Not that he had any intention of allowing her to continue on this course long enough for either goal to become an issue. She might not realize it, but there were methods available to him, underhanded though they were, to nip this little act in the bud.

"So, in a nutshell, my wishes prevail." He mused on that for a moment. "It's a damned fine arrangement for the man. Does it extend to everything? No matter how outrageous my request, you'll always obey me, without question or argument?"

A picture of stung pride, she appeared to be struggling to answer. Finally, she managed a weak, "Yes."

Jake rocked back in his chair and ran his gaze slowly and deliberately over her person. Lifting an eyebrow, he said, "That could prove interesting."

The startled look that crossed her small face told him she

got the gist. He was rather surprised when she showed no sign of backing down. When Mary Beth's ploys boomeranged, she usually changed tactics immediately.

He pulled his watch from his pocket and checked the time. "Do you realize we've been married for nearly twenty-four hours?" He looked her directly in the eye, pleased to note that she had begun to fidget. Innocent, she might be, but stupid, she wasn't. "Twenty-four hours . . . and I still haven't seen my bride without flannel or leather covering her from head to toe. What if I were to ask for an unveiling? You can be—my dessert."

She touched a hand to her throat, and her eyes grew as round as dollars. Her horrified reaction nearly cost him the game. It was all he could do to keep his face straight.

"Is th-that what you're asking?" she squeaked.

"And if I were?" he countered. "Would you remove your clothing for me, Indigo?"

She gulped and hurled a dread-filled glance at the lantern. "The lamp is burning."

"The better to see you by." He rocked farther back in his chair and gave her the most lecherous look he could muster. "The blouse first, I think. Not from across the room, though. Come over and stand beside me. And take it off slowly. Anticipation is half the pleasure."

She looked ready to bolt.

In a voice thick with suppressed laughter, he added, "Come, dutiful wife. I haven't got all night."

Bending her head, she moved toward him. When her hip touched the corner of the table, she stopped and crossed her arms to grasp the bottom of her doeskin blouse. He kept expecting her to give it up, felt absolutely certain she would, right up until the moment she actually drew the blouse off over her head and tossed it to the floor.

Jake felt like someone had just doused him with a five-gallon bucket of ice water. His lungs froze from the shock, his heart felt as if it stopped, and he couldn't have moved if God Himself had commanded it. She stood before him like a sacrificial lamb waiting for the knife, her head hung in shame, her body atremble. The muslin of her chemise, worn nearly transparent by numerous washings, clung softly to her breasts, more a tease than cover.

The front legs of Jake's chair hit the floor with a resounding *whack*, and she jerked. Jake sat there in stunned silence. It hit him suddenly, with blinding clarity, that she hadn't been acting. She sincerely meant to accept any edict he handed down, even if it seemed like the end of the world to her.

A memory flashed from yesterday, of Indigo giving way to her father's wishes and saying she would never defy him. He recalled her pallor during their wedding ceremony and after, then her fear last night. The last thing she had wanted was to marry him, yet she had. And why? Because her father had requested it of her.

What supper he had managed to eat suddenly felt like a pile of rocks in the pit of his stomach. He had been an ass a few times in his life, but this took the prize.

"Indigo . . ." he whispered.

At the sound of his voice, she sucked in a little sob of air and untucked her chemise from the drawstring waist of her pants. Jake grabbed her wrists to stop her. Her head came up. Blue eyes, shimmering with unshed tears and aching with humiliation, clung to his in silent question.

"I didn't mean it. I was joking." The words, raspy with emotion, hit the air and hung there, so discordant and awful that he wanted to call them back. A joke? She was right; he was a selfish, arrogant bastard. And a stupid dolt as well. "I never dreamed you'd actually—I thought that—"

There were no words. Looking up at her, he realized, too late, that it wasn't in her to manipulate anyone, or

to tell a lie. The closest he'd ever heard her come to
speaking a falsehood was when she denied being afraid,
and that stemmed from stubborn pride rather than an
intent to deceive. Jesus, why hadn't he read that in her
eyes? They were as clear as tinted glass and revealed her
every thought and feeling.

Is that your wish? Must I? Is that your final word? He
recalled the distressed look on her face this morning
when he had asked her to be careful feeding the animals. *I really don't approve of your feeding that cougar.* He
hadn't forbidden her to do it. That hadn't been necessary. His disapproval had been enough. Denver Tompkins's voice came back to haunt him. *A squaw will do
whatever her man tells her.*

Jake felt as if he might be sick. She had laid herself
out like a rug to be walked on, and he had ground her
pride into the dirt with the heel of his boot. He released
her wrists and sank back in his chair.

"I'm sorry, Indigo. You can put the shirt back on."

She angled one slender arm across her breasts and
bent to retrieve the blouse with a palsied hand. Jake's
gaze snagged on the knife wound that slashed her right
forearm. She was nothing like Mary Beth; he'd been a
fool to make a comparison.

She clutched the leather to her chest. "If you're finished, may I go to the bedroom?"

If he was finished? Jake cringed. He felt pretty sure he
had done all the damage he could possibly do. He was
finished, all right.

14

The moment Jake gave Indigo permission, she turned and fled the kitchen. When she gained the dark bedroom, her feet dragged to a stop, and she whirled to stare at the shadowy walls, feeling like a trapped animal. *Joking*? She clamped a hand over her mouth and swallowed down the rising panic. He was toying with her; there was no other explanation. Being married to him was going to be worse than her most horrid imaginings.

On rubbery legs, she made it to the bed. She squeezed her eyes closed and forced her mind to go blank. It was either that or scream, and she wouldn't give him that satisfaction. . . .

After he had called himself every dirty name he could think of, Jake pushed to his feet, picked up the lantern, and walked through the house. He found Indigo stretched across the bed, her face pressed into a pillow. After placing the lantern on the bedside table, he sat next to her and put a hand on her back.

"Indigo, please, don't cry."

She turned up a stricken but tear-free countenance. "I don't cry."

Jake let his gaze wander to the wall. "I owe you an apology. I never meant to ridicule you. I thought—well, I misunderstood, and I'm sorry."

His delivery sounded so damned stiff and formal and so totally unlike how he felt that he wanted to groan. He dragged his gaze back to her. She had her face pressed into the pillow again. Tendrils of tawny hair had escaped her braid and lay like molten threads of copper against her silken nape.

"It's all right," she said in a muffled voice.

It wasn't all right. She was terribly upset, and he had been deliberately goading her to get a reaction, never dreaming that her upbringing forbade her to retaliate. The responsibility that placed upon him was frightening. He had been handed authoritarian rule over her life? Half the time he didn't even understand the girl.

"I acted like an ass, and it isn't all right." He skimmed his fingertips up the leather of her blouse and toyed lightly with the curls that wisped so temptingly at her nape. "You see, I thought—"

He felt her shrink from his touch and realized how she resented it. He sighed and moved his hand. He didn't blame her.

Bracing an arm behind him, he leaned back so he could see the side of her face. "Indigo, would you look at me?"

She turned her head and fastened injured blue eyes on him.

"I don't deserve it, but could you find it in your heart to forgive me? And try to forget I did something so despicable?"

Her expression said more clearly than words that she didn't see one good reason why she should. Jake had to accept that.

"I know it's no excuse, but I have a sister—Mary Beth. You remind me a lot of her—not in looks, but in temperament. And she . . ."

Looking down into those gigantic spheres of shimmering blue, Jake kept talking, scarcely hearing what he said, hoping and praying that he could make her understand if he told her about his sister and their famous battles of will. When he finally fell silent, some of the hurt had been erased from her face.

"She truly broke all the dishes? What did you do?"

Jake smoothed a lock of hair from her cheek. "I hid the Chinese vase and yelled at her to stop. What else could I do?"

"What do you eat on at your house now?"

Jake's stomach clenched. He had momentarily forgotten that he was supposed to be a man of limited means. Thank God she didn't seem to realize how expensive a Chinese vase could be.

"We had to buy more dishes. Anyway, back to my reason for telling you about her. When Mary Beth wants something, she'll do almost anything to make me change my mind, including trickery, if she can pull it off. Sometimes, she won't speak to me for days at a time, and it drives me wild. I thought—when you—"

"You thought I was doing the same thing," she finished.

Jake nodded, still feeling a little sick when he remembered the look on her face in the kitchen. "When I asked you to undress, I never dreamed you'd actually do it. I figured you'd turn tail and run."

"Where would I go?" she asked in a hollow little voice.

The question caught at Jake's heart. She had nowhere to go, he realized. Wolf's Landing was the only world she knew. "I'll never ask something like that of you again," he promised.

"To undress, you mean?"

He hated to dash the flare of hope he saw in her eyes. "I won't ask you to humiliate yourself," he amended. "Do you forgive me?"

Her eyes softened to a cloudy blue. "Yes, I forgive

you for making me take off my blouse."

He heard a conditional note at the tail of that sentence and smiled. "But you don't forgive me for making you stay at home."

She made no reply, which was eloquent in itself. Jake looked away. "I wish I could change my mind, Indigo, but I can't. I'm sorry my decision has made you so unhappy and angry."

"I don't feel angry now." Her eyes closed. "Just empty."

God, he felt like such a bastard. The most awful part of it was, he really hadn't meant to be. He ached to gather her into his arms, to soothe her. But after their set-to in the kitchen, he didn't want to do anything she might misconstrue.

He sat up, scooted backward on the bed, and braced his spine against the headboard. Patting the pillow beside him, he said, "Why don't you come over here and sit beside me. Maybe if we talk, we can come up with some solutions so you'll feel a little less empty, hm?"

She pushed up on her elbows and eyed the spot next to him.

"Come on," he urged gently. "I promise not to bite."

Looking none too enthusiastic, she rose to her knees and came forward. As she settled herself beside him, Jake draped an arm around her shoulders. The moment he touched her, he felt the trembling rigidity of her body, and he realized the very last thing she wanted was to be close to him.

An awful suspicion slipped into his mind. *Is that your wish?* Tucking in his chin, he regarded her bent head. He'd be wise to find out exactly where he stood, he decided, before he dug himself in any deeper.

Lightly touching a wispy curl at her temple, he said, "You know, I love your hair in a braid. But I think I like it best when you wear it down."

She lifted her hands and began plucking hairpins.

With an ache in his throat, Jake watched the tawny rope of braid loosen as she combed her fingers through it. Silken tresses spilled onto his arm, then over onto his lap. He hated himself for what he was about to do. But, dammit, he had to know.

"I didn't mean for you to take it down right now, Indigo."

She dragged her hair back from her eyes to regard him. Never more than in that moment had Jake noticed the blend of both her parents' features, her mother's fragile beauty, her father's proud regality, all molded together to create a face as striking as it was lovely. Indigo, a puzzling combination of pride and humility, strength and vulnerability. He'd never understand her.

Jake's heart caught at the confusion he read in her expression. Then she averted her face and began gathering her hair to rebraid it. She was going to think he had a serious problem making up his mind, but at least he had his answer.

He leaned his head against the wall and stared at the ceiling. "Now that you've taken it down, Indigo, just leave it," he said in a gravelly voice.

From the corner of his eye, he saw her lay the hairpins aside and settle her small hands on her lap. Silence. For the moment, Jake welcomed it. The magnitude of what he had just discovered nearly overwhelmed him. God, no wonder she had rebelled against marriage. Since the first day he had known her, three things about her had stood out, her wild streak, her fierce pride, and her fidelity to her father's beliefs. Now, as she saw it, she had become a white man's chattel.

Jake thought back, trying to recall those times when he had seen Hunter issue an order. The only times Jake had witnessed had occurred last night, the first a subtle lifting of his hand to silence his wife when she protested Indigo's marriage, the second a stern denouncement when Indigo dared to protest the marriage herself. *Do you defy me, Indigo?* Jake closed his eyes as he recalled her quavery response. *No, my father, I will never defy you.*

Now the ultimate power Hunter had wielded over his daughter had been handed to Jake.

Slowly, the reality of it sliced through the fog of revulsion in Jake's mind. Not that he didn't believe the male head of a household should have authority. He did. It just nauseated him to think that his every wish had become Indigo's command. If he continued to ask, how long would she sit quietly beside him, braiding and unbraiding her hair? Jake had the sinking feeling that she'd do it all night. Whether or not it made sense didn't seem to play into it.

He wasn't cut from the right kind of cloth to live up to this. It frightened the hell out of him to think Indigo might take everything he said literally and obediently do it. In a fit of anger, he might tell her to go stick her head in the horse trough or to go drown herself in the creek. Where Jake came from, people said things like that. *He* said things like that. Mary Beth's reaction was to poke out her tongue or thumb her nose. Jake couldn't count the times he had threatened to strangle her. Indigo might take a threat like that seriously.

Jake had the horrible urge to laugh. The entire situation was incongruous when he thought about it. In a white household where authority was often questioned, there was no doubt who the boss was because, in varying degrees, he blustered, threatened, and sometimes resorted to physical force to see his orders carried out. In Hunter's household, where his authority was absolute, no one could tell who ruled who because Hunter seldom felt a need to assert himself.

Jake supposed it was a good way to live. Everyone in Hunter's home seemed happy, more so than most. The only problem was, he wasn't at all certain he could walk in his father-in-law's footsteps. He had never felt a need to weigh his every word before he spoke. No one had ever kowtowed to him, carrying out his smallest wish. Having that kind of power over someone was frightening.

It was also tempting.

For the first time in his life, Jake came face to face with a dark side of his nature. What man hadn't harbored secret yearnings at least once to have a lovely dream creature at his beck and call, part slave, part seductress, who would satisfy his every whim? In most instances, the fantasy was just that and perfectly harmless. Only for Jake it had become a reality.

Within the circle of his arm sat a beautiful, sweet, innocent girl who would do anything he told her. Even now, she sat quietly, waiting for him to speak. Seductive images slipped unbidden into his mind of Indigo kneeling over him, gloriously naked, her hair a coppery curtain around his face as she bent to let him suckle her breasts.

Jake slid his hand from where it rested on her shoulder until he found the silken slope of her neck. Absently rubbing his knuckles along the column of her throat, he envisioned her lying before him, lifting her hips and opening herself so he could taste the honeyed moistness of her. His pulse quickened, and he pressed a fingertip against the underside of her fragile jaw to raise her face to his.

With her dusky lips inches from his own, her breath so warm and sweet, Jake didn't know for a moment if he could resist kissing her. She was his. Not even God would condemn him. He not only didn't have to wait, but he could demand anything he wanted from her.

That was a potent and heady thought. *Is that your wish?* God help him, he wouldn't be human if he weren't tempted. He swallowed and shoved the image away. Maybe to be tempted was human enough, but if he carried through on it, he'd be the world's most heartless bastard.

Her eyes shimmered up at him, their usual milk-glass blue darkened to silver by what he could only guess was fear. All of this might be a revelation to him, he realized, but not to Indigo. She had entered into this marriage knowing she would be thrust into a lifetime of servitude. As early as last night, she probably had considered the possibilities and accepted that her fate was entirely up to him. Was it any wonder she leaped when he got close to her?

Jake felt as if someone was squeezing his throat. "We were going to talk about ways to make you feel a little less empty."

"The feeling will pass," she replied softly. "In time I will grow accustomed to things as they are."

An ache spread through Jake, accompanied by an unprecedented tenderness. He couldn't name the emotion and didn't want to take time right now to analyze it. For the moment, it was enough to deal with the fierce feeling of protectiveness that welled inside him. She was more vulnerable to him than any other person had ever been, completely and irrevocably vulnerable, a precious gift presented to him in marriage by her father. Jake knew Hunter loved her, which meant he had handed her over on an act of faith. If it was the last thing Jake did, he wanted to prove himself worthy of that trust.

"I suppose that in time we'll both grow accustomed to things, Indigo," Jake told her gently, "but there's no point in your being more unhappy than necessary, is there? In the last twenty-four hours, you've had a number of things taken away from you. I'm thinking that maybe we can lessen your feeling of loss by coming up with a few substitutes."

Though he still had his fingertip pressed against the underside of her jaw, she averted her face. Jake curled his fingers loosely around the side of her neck, acutely aware of the pulse point in her throat.

In a taut voice, she whispered, "Some things can't be replaced."

"That's true. I can't bring Lobo back to you."

"No."

"I do think I can do a few other things, though."

She lifted curious eyes to his. "What things?"

Jake smiled. "I know you're really unhappy because you won't be allowed to wander in the woods. I don't suppose it'll be the same if I tag along, but I'm willing to leave the mine early enough every day to take you walking."

"You are?"

"Sure."

She didn't look overjoyed. "That would be nice, Jake. Thank you."

He wasn't going to be discouraged too early in the game. "And until you can go back to the mine, I'll be happy to sit with you along the creek while you pan for gold. Would that help?"

A trace of the silvery darkness faded from her eyes, and she nearly smiled. "Yes, that would help a lot."

Jake paused a moment for effect. "I know you're probably worried about meat for Toothless, too, since I've forbidden you to go into the woods hunting. So until you can resume that activity, I promise to keep the smokehouse supplied with plenty of fresh meat. It'll mean your having to give up your walk one evening a week, but if you get outdoors the other days, maybe that won't bother you too much."

Her head came sharply around, and she fastened startled eyes on his. "Toothless? But you said you didn't—"

Jake slanted a finger across her lips. "I know what I said. The problem was, I didn't say exactly what I meant. I don't really disapprove of your feeding the cougar. It just worries me." He shrugged. "A little worry won't kill me."

"You mean you'll let me feed him?"

"I never meant for you not to, Indigo. It was all a misunderstanding. I'll try really hard from now on not to say things I don't—"

His words were cut short by the impact of her small body against his chest. Jake was taken so off guard that he nearly lost his balance. She wrapped both arms around his neck to give him a strangling hug.

"Oh, Jake! Thank you. I've been so sad all day about Toothless. Thank you!"

For a moment, Jake wasn't sure what to do with his hands because he didn't want to unsettle her. But he had only enough willpower to resist one fantasy a day, and this one tempted him far more than the last. To have Indigo, willing and responsive, in his arms. . . . Pressing his face against her silken hair, Jake let instinct take over and embraced her.

In sharp contrast, instead of making him feel black and ugly, this fantasy was golden. It was also brief. Within a heartbeat, he felt her stiffen, and he loosened his hold so she could pull back a bit. It was all he could do not to chuckle when he saw her face. Her expression told him she wasn't at all certain how she had come to this pass and that she was even less certain how to extricate herself from it.

In keeping with his decision to make their relationship as easy on her as possible, Jake solved her dilemma by drawing away first. One day soon, maybe she would come into his arms and want to stay. Cupping her chin in his hand, he leaned forward to look her in the eye. "Let's clean up the kitchen and go feed that damned cat so he doesn't keep your parents awake all night."

Moisture that looked suspiciously like tears glistened in her eyes. Then her chin dimpled and started to quiver. Jake wondered what he had done, but before he could ask, she whispered, "Topper was right. You didn't say all those things about me to Denver, did you?"

His heart stilled, then raced with dread. "What things?"

The glistening tears pooled behind her lashes and spilled over onto her cheeks.

"Sweetheart, what things?" Jake asked again.

She gave her head a little shake. "It isn't important. It's enough just to know that Topper was right and that you didn't say them. I won't honor lies by repeating them."

Jake knew by her tears that whatever Denver said had hurt her, and badly. "Indigo, Shorty heard every word that passed between me and Denver this morning. If you have a question, all you have to do is ask him. Or me, if you trust my word."

She brushed at the wetness on her cheeks and shook her head. "I have no question. Not now."

Jake couldn't let it drop, not when it brought tears to the eyes of a prideful girl who never cried. "What did he say, Indigo? Would you mind telling me?"

She flashed him a stricken look, and her face flushed scarlet. She curled her hands into tight fists.

Jake sighed. "Honey, if it's that hard to say it, just forget it."

She shook her head. "He said that as soon as you grew bored with me that——" She caught her bottom lip between her teeth and bit down, turning the surrounding flesh white. "He said that I would have to do a lot of——entertaining to earn back the bride price you paid my father and that he would be seeing a lot of me." She sucked in a breath, then exhaled with a little sob.

"Jesus." The word erupted from Jake as though projected up his throat by a blow to his midsection. "Indigo, why didn't you come and tell me?"

Her eyes clung to his. "I, um . . ." She lifted her hands in a wordless gesture.

Jake swallowed around a lump in his throat. "You thought maybe it was true?"

She stared at him a moment, then finally nodded. "Have I made you angry?" she asked in a tremulous voice.

He groaned. "No, Indigo, not at you."

Catching her around the waist, he moved off the bed and stood up, carrying her with him. Holding her tightly against him, he made a fist in her hair and tipped her head back.

In a ragged voice, he whispered, "I'm going to promise you two things. I want you to listen closely and never forget them. All right?"

Eyes wary, she seemed to consider that and finally nodded.

"The first is that I happily agreed to pay a bride price because I wanted to honor your father's customs. I don't give a damn about the money. I didn't think of it as buying you then, I don't now, and I never will. Is that clear?"

"Yes."

"The second thing I promise is that if any other man but me ever so much as touches you, it'll be over my dead body. There isn't enough money in the world to ever tempt me otherwise. I don't want that thought to so much as pass through your mind. I know that kind of thing must happen. Maybe it happens often. But it isn't going to happen to you. Not ever. Understand?"

She gave a tearful nod. Jake pressed her face against his chest and swayed with her for a moment, so angry he was shaking.

"If anyone ever says anything so despicable to you again, I want you to tell me about it right away. Will you do that?"

"Yes," she replied in a muffled voice.

Jake squeezed his eyes closed, thinking of all the hours she had held those ugly suspicions inside her. He had made a vow to Denver Tompkins, and he was a man of his word. He was going to take Indigo's tears out of his hide and then fire him.

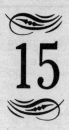

15

True to his promises, Jake tried to make his restrictions on Indigo's activities more bearable. The next day, he went hunting and returned with two deer so she would have meat. In addition to that, though it was nearly dusk and pouring rain, he insisted on taking her for a walk, which he did each evening after, always insisting he wasn't so hungry that he couldn't wait until dark for his supper.

His efforts didn't go unappreciated. Though she still felt uncertain and jumpy while with Jake, Indigo knew he was trying in every way he knew to make her happy. In turn, she made every attempt to hide how truly miserable she was.

Pretension didn't lessen her misery. It took only a couple of hours each morning to clean Aunt Amy's house. She had no need to bake because her mother, accustomed to feeding a family, always made extra and sent it home with her. Consequently, Indigo rose in the morning, walked with Jake to her parents' house to feed the animals, returned home to do her chores, and then spent the remainder of the day listening to the clock tick. The only variation in that schedule occurred when she hauled the tub into the kitchen to bathe, a necessity unless she wished to perform her ablutions at night when Jake was present.

In contrast to the long and boring days, her evenings bolted by like horses racing for the finish line. It seemed to Indigo that Jake no sooner took her for a walk and ate his dinner than she found herself lying beside him in bed, convinced that tonight would be the night he would decide to assert his conjugal rights. When he twitched so much as a muscle, her heart leapt. When he held her close, she lay there, breathless and half sick, waiting for his gentle touch to turn demanding and grasping.

After four nights of such unpleasant expectation, Indigo began to wish he'd just do it and get it over with. Anything would be better than night after night of lying there, knowing he wanted her and wondering, half hysterically, when he planned to take her.

She had prepared herself as best she could. Thus far, he hadn't discovered that she'd put the rock back under the mattress, at his feet this time so he wouldn't notice. Though she had little appetite, she was managing to force down at least one helping of red meat a day. She felt confident that when he made love to her, once would get the job done. After that, she hoped he'd go to the Lucky Nugget for his pleasures, as so many other men obviously did. Not that she wished Franny and May Belle bad.

On the fifth day of her marriage, Father O'Grady made ready to leave, listening to last-minute confessions, one of which was Indigo's, and saying a final Mass. After the service and lunch were concluded, the priest announced that he had several goodbyes to say and left. The moment he was gone, Indigo put water on to heat and began helping her mother to clear the table.

"If you'd like to go, I can get these," Loretta offered.

Indigo shook her head. "I'm happy to have something to do, Ma. The afternoons seem endless just sitting around that house."

Loretta sighed. "The first few months of humdrum

married life are always a trial. I'll never forget how I felt when your father finally got this house built and began leaving every morning for the mine. It seemed like the whole world stopped."

Indigo worked the soap between her palms to create suds in the dishwater. She tried to picture her mother listening to the clock tick. For as long as she could remember, Ma had been a cheerful whirlwind of activity. "I reckon I'll adjust in time."

Loretta sighed. "I reckon. Now that I think back, I had Chase by then, and I was expecting you, so there was plenty to distract me once I got used to having your father gone."

"Like I said, I'll adjust."

Loretta heaved another sigh, and Indigo nearly smiled. When pondering a problem, her ma had a way of sighing that was almost musical, a shrill sound that trailed slowly away into silence. "What you need are some projects, knitting or needlepoint."

Indigo grinned. "I could knit a quiver for my arrows."

Loretta chuckled. "Or a sweater for your husband."

Indigo pictured Jake's broad shoulders. "Ma, I'd be knitting for a year. Besides, you know how bad I am to drop stitches. He'd unravel in the first high wind."

Loretta giggled. "You could make yourself something."

"Lawzy! I'd rather he unraveled than me. I've got enough problems getting my baths out of the way before he gets home."

A blush rode Loretta's cheeks, and she applied herself to drying dishes. Indigo's mouth went dry. There it was again, the unspoken taboo.

"How about sewing?" Loretta asked. "I'd let you borrow my machine. Mr. Hamstead has a lovely selection of fabric."

"What would I sew?"

Loretta considered that for a moment, then visibly brightened. "Dresses! You'll be needing a wardrobe shortly."

Indigo's hands stilled. "For what?"

"Why for your new life, Indigo. You'll be leaving soon." Pain filled Loretta's blue eyes. She gave a shaky smile. "Lands, how all of us ladies in Wolf's Landing are going to envy you. You'll see new places and exciting things. When you come home to visit, we'll hang on your every word."

"You sound anxious to see me go."

Loretta blinked. "Don't be silly. I'm just being realistic and trying to prepare myself. Jake never made a secret of the fact that he was only stopping off here. Before we know it, he'll be gnawing at the bit to move on."

Indigo's legs felt as if they had turned to water.

"Oh, honey," Loretta crooned. "Don't look so stricken. You'll love your new life. Hasn't Jake treated you fine so far?"

"Yes."

"Well, then . . ." Loretta placed a stack of plates on the shelf. "I'm sure he'll always do fine by you."

Indigo couldn't help but wonder why her ma was so unsympathetic to her plight. She wondered if her father had forbidden her to speak against the marriage.

Loretta rubbed industriously with the towel, then held up the saucer she was drying to study her reflection in its shining well. "Jake's a good man—strong and handsome and seems easy to get along with. Many a girl would be thrilled to marry him."

Indigo stared at the sudsy dishwater. With trembling fingers, she grasped a bubble and popped it. "I'm not any girl, and this marriage has ruined my life."

Loretta grabbed up another saucer. "What's done is done, Indigo. Make the best of it. It's time for you to forget your childhood dreams and face life, not as you wish it to be, but as it is. Stop fighting what you can't change. It'll only bring you heartache."

"Do you think this marriage won't bring me heartache? You say not to fight what I can't change, as if

I'm behaving immaturely. Well, let me tell you something, Ma. I faced the things I couldn't change long ago, and I accepted them. Now you're telling me to be something I can't be."

Loretta turned saddened eyes toward her. "You should do your best and start preparing to be a fine wife."

"I can try till the day I die and never be the kind of wife any white man would want." Indigo grabbed her mother's hand. "Look at my skin next to yours."

Loretta curled her fingers around Indigo's. "Your skin is beautiful. If you're concerned because you're darker than most, try rinsing your face and hands with lemon water. I've heard it will bleach the effects of the sun. It might work for you."

Indigo turned back to the dishes. "Sun didn't do it."

"Are you ashamed of that?" Loretta asked.

The question left Indigo feeling as though the wind had been knocked out of her. "I'm proud of what I am, you know that."

"Then act like it," Loretta replied firmly. "Be the beautiful girl you are and stop hiding behind stained buckskins and that awful old hat. Your leather skirts and dresses are fine for Wolf's Landing, but they won't do where the ladies are decked out in flounces and ruffles."

Hiding? Her mother thought she was hiding? Feeling oddly disoriented, Indigo reeled her thoughts back into line and attempted to concentrate on the conversation. Flounces and ruffles? In all her vivid imaginings of the world beyond the mountains, she hadn't considered what sort of clothing she'd be forced to wear.

Somehow, she managed to finish the dishes, listening all the while to her mother prattle about patterns she'd seen in *Harper's Bazaar* and how nicely this or that bolt of fabric would work up. Indigo headed for home with visions of corsets and petticoats and lemons swimming in her head.

Feeling drained, she knelt by the bed to begin the penance Father O'Grady had given her in confession, three rosaries. She felt that was more than fair, and fully intended to say an extra round of Hail Marys for good measure, just in case her mother's God was good at division. Sometimes, Father O'Grady was too lenient. Three rosaries went into seventeen lies five times, with two left over. She wanted to make sure there were no taints left on her soul. Lies were mortal sins, and Father claimed lying to her husband was about the worst kind she could do.

Two hours later, the ache in Indigo's chest was rivaled by a new ache in her knees. Three rosaries required a powerful lot of praying, especially when she kept forgetting where she was and had to start over. *Dresses. Ladies decked out in flounces and ruffles. Lemon water.* Indigo's throat tightened, and tears filled her eyes. She was sorry for lying to Jake, she truly was, and if she didn't do her penance, she was sure as rain going to be eternally damned. But what difference did it make? Going to hell couldn't be worse than the punishment her life had become.

The rosary slipped from her fingers, and she dug her fists into the bedding. The soft chenille made her think of Lobo's fur. She pressed her face against it and wept, tortured by images of a few days past when he had trotted beside her through the woods. She bent her body over the edge of the mattress. She felt as if a hundred little knives were slashing her innards.

A deep yearning filled her, not just for the wolf but for all he had represented. She imagined the shadows of the woods and could almost hear the wind whispering to her. How could she live the rest of her life confined? How would she bear month after month of not hearing her heart's song, of not feeling the breeze against her skin? Why, oh why, had her father done this to her? He of all people understood her affinity with the wild and her aversion to confinement. Why had he made her marry a white man who would never be able to comprehend how she felt?

She pushed to her feet, driven by a primal need. Jake's face was a blurred image. His orders that she stay in the house had become meaningless whispers. All that seemed real was her hunger to be embraced by those things familiar and dear to her.

Just this one last time. . . .

Jake looked up from the sluice to see Father O'Grady. Mud streaked the priest's cassock, and his plump cheeks were red with exertion from the steep climb. Well aware that a man in Father's physical condition wouldn't willingly embark on such a grueling walk, Jake's first thought was that something awful had happened.

"Is Indigo all right?"

Fighting for breath, the priest nodded.

"Has Hunter taken a bad turn?" Jake peeled off his gloves.

"No one's come to harm, Jake me man, but there is a matter of some importance I must discuss wit' ye." With one hand clamped to his chest, the priest huffed for breath. "I'll be leavin' today, ye see, so I'd be appreciative if ye could give me a moment of yer time. In privacy, if ye can arrange it."

Jake gestured at the surrounding woods. "We've got a whole mountain at our disposal."

Still out of breath, the priest nodded. "Just so long as ye lead me downhill, lad, and not up."

Jake led Father to a little clearing where he frequently escaped to eat his lunch. Bearing in mind the priest's penchant for yelling, Jake judged this spot to be far enough away from the mine to afford them some privacy. With a shaky sigh, the priest collapsed onto the fallen log where Jake usually sat. Jake, though concerned about what might be wrong, refrained from pressing for answers until the older man got his breath.

Finally Father spoke. "'Tis not my habit to break a confidence, understand, and I'd never divulge a word said to me by anyone during a confession."

Jake nodded, growing more perplexed by the moment.

The priest threw Jake a distressed glance. "This is a circumstance, however, where I have become privy to information during a conversation, and though 'tis essentially breakin' a trust, I feel I can do naught else. Hunter is bedridden. His son and Swift are gone. There's no one but me to take ye to task."

"To task?"

The priest swelled his chest and fastened fiery blue eyes on Jake's. "I'll admit it's me hope to avoid unpleasantness, lad, but don't let me age and this collar of mine fool ye. In me day, I was a fine boxer. And if ye get me dander up, I can still execute a fancy step or two."

Jake raised an eyebrow. "Father, are you threatening to kick my ass?"

"What's that ye say?"

Jake leaned closer and boomed, "Are you threatening to kick my ass?"

The priest reared back a bit. "Ye won't be intimidatin' me by gettin' in me face. If the only way to settle this is with our fists, then so be it. God will surely be my champion."

Jake couldn't believe his ears. "What have I done?"

O'Grady narrowed an eye. "That's what I'm hopin' to discover. The wee lass came to me in great distress, she did! And I demand ye mend yer ways. 'Tisn't right for a man of yer stature to be harsh with a girl who's so defenseless against ye."

Jake digested that. In a loud voice, he replied, "I can't agree more. Would you care to divulge how I've been harsh?"

The priest jutted his chin. "Bein' the loyal little miss

that she is, she just blushed and wouldna say. But I'm sure ye must know. Ye're the cause of her fall from grace, after all."

Jake focused on the revelation that his wife had fallen from grace. In his estimation, it would be a mighty long tumble. "Did she actually say I had been harsh with her?"

"She didn't have to. I've a nose for trouble after all these years. When a lass who's confessed to lying a half-dozen times in all her life tells me she's lied to her husband seventeen times in five short days, I start askin' questions."

At that, both of Jake's eyebrows shot up. "Seventeen times? She's lied to me seventeen times? That's—"

"Three to four times a day," the priest finished.

Jake eyed the priest with growing alarm. "Has she been sneaking off into the woods while I'm at work? If she has, Father, you'd better tell me. She could get hurt."

An angry flush crept up Father O'Grady's neck. "Do ye truly believe a lass who's lied six times in all her life would disobey ye?" The priest's brogue thickened apace with his building anger. "Ye're a blind, hardhearted man, Jake Rand, if ye don't be knowin' what a good sweet girl she is. Sneakin' off to the woods! Hmph. She'd ne'er do such a thing."

"What has she lied to me about then?"

"That's what alarms me!"

"I can see you're alarmed, Father, and now so am I. Would you mind making your point?"

"I'll be makin' it. Just let me do it in my own way. 'Tis no easy thing, ye understand. After our conversation, the lass made her confesson. I'm a walking a very fine line here. I must weigh every word carefully. Before I proceed, I'll have yer word that ye'll not be punishin' the girl for what she's told me."

Jake slapped his gloves against his jeans. "How in hell can I promise that? It depends on what it is she's done."

"'Tis not what *she's* done that worries me. And ye can

stop with those gloves. Ye look like ye're warming up to go home and be harsh again. If ye do, I'll have yer hide, Jake Rand, God is my witness."

Jake gave an incredulous laugh. "What in God's name has she told you? I've never laid a hand on her!"

"Do I have yer word ye won't punish her?"

Jake raked a hand through his hair. "Only if I have your word she hasn't been up to something where she might get hurt."

"Ye have that."

"Then I won't punish her."

Father straightened his shoulders. "Yes, well . . . now, where was I?"

For the life of him, Jake couldn't recall.

Father held up a hand. "Oh, yes. I was tellin' ye she came to me in tears, saying she'd lied to ye. Seventeen is no small number and was indicative to me of a serious problem, so I felt compelled to ask the nature of the lies. She explained she's told ye seventeen times that she wasn't afraid of ye, when in truth she was." He hardened his jaw. "I want to know what ye've been doin' to terrify the poor wee thing."

For a moment, Jake was so taken aback that he just stood there in stunned amazement. Then he threw back his head and barked with laughter. When his amusement ebbed, he said, "She confessed to that? I can't believe it!"

"We'll be leavin' her confession out of this, thank ye. And I'll remind ye 'tis no laughing matter. Ye've got the lass so intimidated she's even afraid to admit to ye that she's afraid! How can ye find that humorous? Ye've got a black heart, ye have, and I ne'er woulda guessed it. It's a first for me, bein' so far off mark in my assessment of a man's character."

Jake sat on the log. "Father, if you'll just calm down, I think I can explain."

"So begin."

Jake grinned and shook his head. He looked over at the priest. "Given the circumstances and the suddenness of our marriage, I haven't as yet exercised my conjugal rights."

"What's that ye say?"

In a roaring voice, Jake repeated himself. Then he cringed, wondering how far his voice had carried. It was one thing to tell a priest he hadn't yet bedded his wife, but he didn't want the whole damned world to know. In a slightly lower tone, he added, "Indigo doesn't really know me that well, and she's—reluctant. I've been giving her time to relax around me."

Father sniffed. "I can commend ye for that much, at least. I guess there must be some wee bit of good in ye, after all."

Jake braced his arms on his knees and leaned forward slightly. He couldn't help but chuckle again. "Unless I'm very much mistaken, Father, the lies Indigo told must have occurred at those times when she thought we were"—he glanced over—"in near occasion. You get my gist?"

"I'm a priest, not a moron. Go on."

"Well, at those times, when I could see she thought I was going to—well, you know—I could also tell she was uneasy, and I either assured her she didn't need to feel frightened or I asked if she was. In both situations, she was too proud to let me think she was scared and insisted she wasn't."

Father mused on that for a moment. "And that's the truth?"

Jake nodded. "Do I really look like the kind who'd mistreat a woman, Father?"

O'Grady sighed. "No, Jake me man, ye don't. I was sore disappointed in ye. Filled with guilt, I was, to think I'd been so fooled by ye and that I sanctioned the marriage." A twinkle crept into his faded blue eyes. "So that's how all this came about. I've told Hunter a hundred times if I've told him once that pride would be his downfall. He canna understand how being prideful leads to sin. Now we have a fine example of it."

Jake narrowed an eye. "Father, if you think those harmless little fibs Indigo told me are sins, I'm never becoming a Catholic. You'd swallow your teeth during my first confession."

The priest smiled. "Yes, well, it's all a matter of conscience, ye see. A man who has ne'er been taught that murder is wrong could kill and go to heaven. But Indigo, believin' as she does that a wee fib is a black lie, could be eternally damned for the tellin'."

"Do you truly believe that?"

"No, I think God will throw the gates wide when He sees the wee lass comin', but 'tis not what I believe that counts. To her, 'tis serious business." His eyes warmed with affection. "On yer wedding day, she told a lady her ugly dress was pretty. During our conversation she expressed her concern that she may be becoming a compulsive liar." Father narrowed an eye. "I'm tellin' ye this only because I think ye ought to know how deep to heart the lass takes the commandments. There's no such thing to her as a wee white lie, ye understand. Her father has taught her that every word she utters must be the exact truth."

Jake grinned, remembering Elmira's silly resort dress and Indigo's compliments. "She considered *that* a lie?"

O'Grady rolled his eyes. "I must admit that the lass's foul deeds have oft been the source of a smile or two. They're refreshing to an old man who spends half his life hearin' about the truly vile things people have done."

A distant expression crept across O'Grady's face, and he chuckled. "She once rode her Molly mare clear to J'ville and interrupted me mornin' reflections to confess she had eaten her brother's half of a peppermint stick instead of taking it home to him as she was told. Given to her by the man at the general store, 'twas." He shrugged. "She'll forgive me for tellin' that, for she was a wee thing then and the whole family laughs and teases her about it. To this day, she loves her peppermint."

A funny little ache centered in Jake's chest. For an instant, he saw Indigo's clear blue eyes and recalled the times he had felt that he could see to her soul. Was it any wonder? There was no darkness within her to obstruct his view.

"Bless her heart, I can't believe she kept count every time she fibbed to me."

Father's shoulders shook with laughter. "Seventeen times, and once by omission. Ye asked, and she didna answer ye. I let her off on that one." The priest curled his fingers over his knees and took a deep breath. "Well, Jake me man, I guess I owe ye an apology."

"There's no need for that. I can understand what you must have thought. In future, I'll try not to ask her if she's frightened." Jake couldn't help but laugh again, though deep down the priest's revelations made him feel poignantly sad. "Otherwise, I'll be making trips to Jacksonville every time I turn around, to take her to confession."

Father's smile faded, and his wise blue eyes sharpened on Jake's face. "Ye're growin' right fond of her, aren't ye?"

Jake thought about that for a moment. Fond? A few days ago, he would have settled for that word, but now it didn't seem quite enough. "She's a very special person," he replied. "I'm beginning to care a great deal for her."

Father smiled and nodded. After a long moment he said, "Ye know, Jake, I ne'er woulda thought I'd say this, but despite the fact that ye're a Methodist, I think ye're a fine fellow."

Jake stifled an outraged laugh. "I can return the compliment. On occasion, I nearly forget you're a Catholic."

When Jake left the mine that afternoon, he went by the general store to see if Sam Jones had any letters for him. As had been the case every afternoon for nearly a week, there was no news from Jeremy. Impatience built within Jake. If his father was behind the trouble at Hunter's mine, he wanted to know it. The longer a time that passed, the more difficult it would be to tell Indigo the truth. As it was, Jake wasn't sure she'd ever forgive him. With her penchant for stark honesty, how could he hope to make her understand that everything he had led her to believe about him was a lie?

As he started to leave the store, Jake spied a jar of peppermint sticks and charged four to his account. He could almost see Indigo as a child, hiding between the buildings to devour a whole stick, then feeling guilty over what she had done. From now on she could have peppermint until stripes came out her ears. Maybe eating a sweet every afternoon would stimulate her appetite. She was still picking at her food, and he was beginning to worry that she'd never start eating right.

When he arrived home, the house was ominously empty. In the bedroom, he found Indigo's rosary lying on the bed, the spread around it depressed and damp. He envisioned her kneeling there to say her penance. He guessed that the dampness was from tears.

If he hadn't seen the rosary, Jake might have panicked, thinking that someone had forced Indigo to leave the house. But the signs that she'd been crying led him to believe otherwise. It was far more likely that she'd been upset and gone someplace to have a good cry. Remembering her hiding place in Hunter's hayloft, Jake went there and checked. No Indigo. Next, he tapped on the Wolfs' back door. She wasn't there visiting.

Jake stood in the Wolfs' backyard and gazed into the woods. As hard as he found it to believe that she had ignored his orders, Jake couldn't discount the feeling that she had wandered off. If she had, she'd better have a damned good reason.

16

A hunch set Jake on course toward Lobo's grave. When he stepped into the clearing, he saw Indigo sitting by the mound of turned earth, arms looped around her ankles, head pressed to her knees. Even at a distance, Jake could see that she was sobbing.

Though he had forbade her to enter the woods, he couldn't dredge up any anger. He stood near the trees for a moment and studied her. In the last few days, she had dropped an alarming amount of weight. Her buckskins hung on her now. Jake leaned his back against the pine.

Three lies a day for five days? That meant she had been frightened that number of times as well. It wasn't what Jake would call a very good average, and it bothered him to know he was the cause. Fear, warranted or not, was no fun.

Uncertain how to handle this, Jake pushed away from the tree and walked slowly toward her. As he drew near, the sound of her sobs cut clear through him. When he touched her shoulder, she leaped and began wiping her face with her sleeve, trying, he was sure, to hide the fact that she'd been crying. Jake couldn't bring himself to scold her.

Instead, he sat with her by the grave and drew her into his arms. For a moment, she resisted, but then she dissolved into fresh tears and wrapped her arms around his neck. Close to tears himself, Jake returned her hug, then began to rock her.

At last, he said, "Honey, what is it?" He was afraid to ask if she was upset because she had lied to him. Right now, she needed a confidant, and he didn't want her to lose faith in Father O'Grady. "Can you tell me what's wrong?"

She clung more tightly to his neck. "Oh, Jake, it's everything. Lobo is gone, and I'm so lonely. I'm afraid I'll always be lonely. You don't like me working at the mine, and now that you're my husband, you'll have the authority to deny me that. You aren't happy about me feeding Toothless. Nothing's ever going to be the same again."

These were issues they had already discussed, and Jake had done everything he could to reassure her. "Sure it will."

"No."

He rested his cheek against her hair, aching for her. He had a gut feeling there was more to this than she was saying. "What made you start crying? Can you tell me?"

"Ma."

Jake couldn't conceal his surprise. "Your ma?"

"Yes. She wants me to start sewing white women dresses for when I must go away."

Jake ran a hand over her coiled braid. "Honey, that's nothing to cry over. You'll look beautiful in pretty dresses."

Her sobs broke out afresh. "We'll have to go soon. I'll have to leave Wolf's Landing, and nothing will ever be the same again. I'll never see my mountains anymore. I'll never hear my songs in the wind. Even if we come back to visit, it'll never be the same. Never. The animals will forget me, and the magic will be lost."

Jake squeezed his eyes closed. He was the source of

all her pain, yet she clung to him as though they were balanced on the edge of a precipice and he was her only anchor. It occurred to him then that maybe he never should have married her. She might have suffered less by weathering the gossip.

What had he done to her? *Wild things are like that. They do the choosing*. Indigo hadn't been allowed a choice. And now she was trapped. She was right; they would have to leave soon. Even if he brought her back here for visits, nothing would ever be the same. Toothless would probably meet his end in a steel-jawed trap. The deer would stop coming. When she returned here, she would hate him for stealing it all away from her.

Jake's thoughts drifted to Portland. He not only didn't belong here in Wolf's Landing, but he had no way to make a living if he chose to stay. Madness . . . What was he thinking? He couldn't decide to stay here. His livelihood, his family, his home—all that he was lay beyond the mountains. He'd be insane to settle for a life of penury in a three-room house.

Yet how could he expect Indigo to survive in his world? He tried to imagine her surrounded by his sophisticated friends who told polite lies with every other breath, bound to him more by greed than a sense of loyalty. She'd never fit in unless she changed.

Jake envisioned her becoming materialistic and hard, like the other women he knew. She was so infinitely precious as she was, in the way she looked at the world, in the way she lived. If he took her away from here, her rare innocence, which was such an integral part of her, would be destroyed.

He could go to Hunter and discuss the possibility of an annulment. His marriage to Indigo wasn't consummated yet. Jake stroked her back, his body absorbing the shudders that racked hers. Even in tears, she made him feel as if his insides were being warmed by sunshine. If he annulled their marriage, he would never have the right to hold her like this again.

The thought made him go cold. The feel of her face pressed to his neck, of her hugging him, was as close to heaven as he ever hoped to get. Her every sob sliced through him. Like a boulder in the chest, the realization hit him. He was falling wildly, crazily in love with this girl.

Of all the insane, ridiculous— Jake's thoughts shattered, and his feelings took over. God, he needed her. He didn't know what it was he needed. Far more than sex, that was a certainty. Thus far, things weren't looking too promising on that front. No, it was more a need for. . . . For what? Jake couldn't put a name to it. All he knew was that she filled his empty places. Before he left Portland, he had asked himself what the point in everything was. Now he didn't feel that way. Somehow, Indigo gave him a sense of purpose and a feeling of rightness.

He tried to imagine giving her up and couldn't. Once a man had tasted sunshine, how could he settle for grim reality again? A smile touched Jake's mouth. Grim reality. Indigo was the exact opposite of that, a girl who walked on moonbeams and heard music in the wind, a girl who talked with animals and looked into things instead of at them. She was fanciful. Most of the time, he couldn't understand her. Half the time, he thought she was crazy. But, oh, what sweet madness.

He wouldn't give her up. He couldn't. Somehow, he had to make this marriage work. Hunter's voice echoed in his mind. *Choose your way carefully so she can walk beside you. Listen to the song in your heart, yes? It is there that you will find the answers you seek.* Jake wasn't certain if he even had a song inside him, but he knew one thing. Indigo's world was here, and somehow he had to keep it intact for her.

Placing a hand on her braided hair, he listened to the wind and tried to hear her songs there. Though all he could hear was trees rustling, he accepted that Indigo heard something more, a beautiful something that nourished her soul.

Jake bent his head so he could whisper next to her ear. "Would you be happy if I promised never to make you leave here?"

She went still in his arms. "What?" she asked in a muffled voice.

"I won't ever make you leave here," he repeated.

She drew back slightly and turned a wet cheek against his jaw. "You mean you'll stay in Wolf's Landing?"

Jake swallowed, wondering if he was losing his mind to be making such a wild promise. "Sometimes I'll have to be gone."

"And leave me here?"

She sounded so hopeful that his guts twisted. "Yes, here in Wolf's Landing, with your parents. That way you'll never have to leave your mountains, hm?"

She hiccuped. "But we're married."

"Yes, well, lots of married people are separated now and again. I'll try to be gone as little as possible. It might be difficult, but we'll make it work somehow. Your life can continue much as it always has."

She took a ragged breath. "Oh, Jake, my father would be disappointed in me. My place is beside you."

"I'll talk to your father. He'll understand. Besides, this is our marriage, not his. We can do things however suits us."

She lifted her head and twisted to look at him. Tear droplets sparkled on her lashes. Gazing down at her sweet face, Jake felt his heart swell. This was what he had missed in his relationship with Emily, the radical swings from pain to gladness, the feeling that he was either utterly empty or so full he would burst.

"Well, Mrs. Rand? Do we have a deal?"

She looked so incredulous that he smiled.

"Do you mean it? Forever, you'll never make me leave here?"

Jake couldn't resist and bent to kiss her wet cheek, savoring the salty warmth of her tears. "Forever and ever, it's my promise to you. Who knows. Maybe in time, you'll want to take short trips with me, hm? You might enjoy seeing new places if you knew you could come home soon."

She gave a dubious nod. "Maybe."

"Can I see a smile? It doesn't have to rival sunshine. Just a little one will do."

She pressed against him again to hug his neck more tightly. If she smiled, and Jake suspected she did, he was robbed of the pleasure of seeing it.

"Oh, Jake! Wolf's Landing, for always? I—you're the best husband anybody ever had."

For a proclamation like that, Jake was willing to forgo seeing her smile, and gladly. "The best?" He wasn't proud. He'd fish to hear that compliment again.

"Oh, yes, the very best!"

Repositioning his arms around her, Jake settled one hand around her ribs, his splayed thumb touching the soft side of her breast through the leather of her blouse. She didn't stiffen or pull away. He gloried in the realization and intoxicated himself with the scent of her skin.

"You're the best wife anybody ever had, too," he whispered. "You're all my dreams come true, Indigo."

"Not yet. But I will be," she vowed in a fierce little voice. "I'll be the best wife you ever saw. I promise. I'll clean and scrub and bake. I will! When you come home from your trips, you'll be able to use the floors for your shaving mirror."

He chuckled. "That shiny, hm?" In truth, all Jake really wanted was to have her naked in his arms. But that would come in time. "We'll see about that. If you're going to work at the mine, I may have to hire someone to clean."

He felt her grow still. After a moment, she said, "You really do intend to let me go back to work?"

The question made Jake's insides tighten. But for the moment, he had enough to contend with just dealing with her feelings. His own could be addressed later. "I told you I would. Do you want it in writing?"

She shook her head. "You can't afford to hire someone to clean. I can work at the mine and keep the house. You'll see."

Jake felt sure she would try. One day, she would realize he could afford far more than she thought.

In no hurry to let go of her, Jake simply held her for a while. When she finally began to fidget, he grinned and released her, confident that they would share other embraces, far more fruitful if he had his way.

"Are you about ready to go home?" He lifted her off his lap. "I have a little surprise for you when we get there."

She cast an alarmed glance around the clearing, then fastened luminous eyes on his. "A thrashing?"

Jake followed the path of her gaze and remembered she wasn't supposed to be out here. For an instant, he thought she was teasing about the thrashing business, but when he searched her gaze, he saw she wasn't. It bothered him that she thought he might resort to striking her as a form of punishment, but what disturbed him far more was that she seemed to believe he'd lure her home, smiling and promising her a surprise, only to beat her. Did she trust him so little?

The revelation staggered him. The best husband in the whole world, was he?

"Are you angry?"

Jake was the one to break eye contact. He didn't want to frighten her, but on the other hand, he didn't want her thinking she could come into the woods any time she chose. "No matter how angry I might be, I'd never strike you," he said softly. "As for your coming here, did you have a good reason?"

She took a long time to answer. Finally she shook her

head. "No." Her eyes darkened, and she lifted her chin. "I just felt the need to be here, and I came. I suppose you will think I've been a very bad wife."

Jake's throat tightened. Was that truly how she saw it? That she had no right to her own wants and needs. He knew damned well she hadn't come here on a whim. The bedspread at home was damp from her tears. Was that her perception of marriage, that the husband was omnipotent and if his wife disobeyed him, he might resort to striking her? From what Jake had seen of her parents' relationship, he couldn't understand how she had drawn that conclusion.

"What do you think I should do about your disobeying me, Indigo?" he asked her gently.

A muscle at the corner of her mouth twitched. "You could take away my privileges. But you've already done that."

"What would your father do?"

She looked startled by the question. "My father?"

"Yes, your father. Would he give you a thrashing?"

She seemed to ponder that for a moment. "I—I don't know. I never disobeyed him."

Jake watched her expressions closely. "So he never beat you?"

Her blue eyes widened. "My father? No, never."

As far as he knew, Hunter was her only point of reference. If he had never beaten her, why would she immediately assume her husband would try? Jake had a feeling he wouldn't like the answer to that question. Piece by piece, the puzzle of Indigo was beginning to fall into place. He knew he was still a long way from completely understanding her, but day by day, the picture was coming clearer. What he had learned in this last few minutes made him ache for her. And for himself.

"What were you thinking when you decided to come out here?"

"About the wind in the trees and the taste of it here."

Her voice caught. "I was thinking of leaving, and I wanted one last time in my woods."

"So you were feeling sad."

"Yes, very sad."

"And you had a powerful urge to come here alone, just one more time?"

"Yes."

"I can understand that, I think." He paused for effect. "Now that you know you don't have to leave, you won't have to worry about saying goodbye again. Right?"

"I didn't know that when I came here, though."

Jake cupped her chin in his hand and lifted her face. "Do I have your promise you won't come into the woods alone again until I tell you it's all right?"

"Yes."

He searched her gaze. "You could come to serious harm out here, and I don't want anything to happen to you. You understand?"

"Yes."

Jake released her and stood. "Then let's go home so you can have your surprise."

Still looking unsure, she pushed to her feet. "You mean there truly is a surprise? What is it?"

Jake had a hunch Indigo's life might be full of surprises over the next few months. He curled an arm around her shoulders and drew her into a walk. "Something almost as sweet as you are."

Indigo said she couldn't eat the peppermint sticks until she had fixed dinner and said her penance. It had been Jake's hope that the sweets might stimulate her appetite, but she looked so convinced she shouldn't enjoy the treat until later that he didn't insist.

"Is it against your beliefs to have treats before you've said your penance?" he asked.

She turned from the stove to regard him, a thoughtful expression on her face. "No. It just doesn't seem fitting to be glad when I should be filled with sorrow. I still have an entire rosary and a round of Hail Marys that I must finish."

Jake leaned back in his chair, his coffee mug poised halfway to his lips. "How many rosaries did Father tell you to say, for God's sake?"

"Three."

He nearly choked on a sip of coffee. "Three? That seems pretty stiff. You just went to confession five days ago." He was dying to ask her if she'd gotten all that penance for the measly little fibs she had told, but he couldn't. He settled for saying, "You must have done something pretty serious."

Her cheeks flushed a comely pink. "Yes."

Jake watched as she turned the meat and clamped a lid on the skillet. Then curiosity got the better of him. "What on earth did you do? Rob a bank?"

She bit her lip. The flush on her cheeks deepened to a guilty red. "I lied."

"And that was it?"

She looked scandalized. "I told several. More than several, actually. Lots and lots. Lying is a very bad thing."

Jake took another sip of coffee. He knew full well that if he pressed, she'd tell him what the lies had been about and to whom she had told them. He didn't want to put her in a spot like that. "You'd better watch it, so you don't get in the habit."

She returned her attention to the meat she had on the stove. "Yes. I must try very hard not to do it anymore."

A smile touched Jake's mouth. Little did she know that it was going to be a joint effort.

That night when Jake joined Indigo in bed, he sensed that she didn't seem quite as tense. He lay beside her in

the darkness and remembered the promise he had made
to her about never making her leave Wolf's Landing.
God help him, somehow he had to find a way to keep it.

A gust of chill air came through the open window.
Jake rolled onto his side, not at all surprised to find
Indigo awake and gazing out at the moonlit darkness
with a poignant expression on her face. Trading on the
newfound feeling of friendship that was budding
between them, fragile though it was, Jake touched her
cheek and asked, "Can you tell me why you like to leave
the window open every night?"

She drew the covers snugly to her chin, looking
uncomfortable. "I'm afraid to tell you for fear you'll
laugh."

Jake had long since guessed that she left the window
open for Lobo. He considered her troubled profile,
wishing she would trust him enough to tell him that. "I
won't laugh. I promise."

Eyes shimmering like silver in the moonlight, she
turned to regard him. "It's just silliness, but I can't
shake the feeling that Lobo may be out there," she finally admitted in a taut voice. "If he tries to find me, I
don't want him to be locked out and think I've forgotten him already."

The last thing Jake felt like doing was laughing. He
slipped an arm under her and drew her head to his
shoulder. Stroking her hair, he gazed out at the shadows
and listened to the wind. At the Geunther cabin, she
had told him it was her Comanche belief that wolves'
spirits lingered. He wondered why she seemed hesitant
to come right out and admit that now. "I think Lobo
knows how much you loved him," he whispered
hoarsely. "And how much you still love him."

Indigo sensed Jake's empathy in the way he held her
and by the tone in his voice. She knew most white men
would laugh at her. For an instant, she considered
telling him the entire truth—that she believed Lobo was

still alive, not in the flesh, but in spirit. The convictions of a lifetime held her tongue.

Until tonight, every time he had held her this way, she had been uncertain where to put her hands. Now she dared to rest a palm on his chest. Coarse, springy hair tickled her fingertips, and she could feel the steady beat of his heart under her wrist.

Though still afraid he might press her to perform her wifely duties, she closed her eyes and found a measure of comfort in his embrace. His warmth cocooned around her. A smile curved her lips as she drifted into the mists of slumber.

The next morning, Jake was nearly halfway to the mine before he dragged to a stop. He kept remembering how forlorn Indigo had sounded yesterday by Lobo's grave.

A sudden memory hit him, and he closed his eyes. Damn, what a dimwit he was. In all the days since the wolf's death, he had never once thought of Lobo's pups.

Pulse quickening, Jake pivoted and headed back down the mountain. Pray God that Gretel's owner hadn't given the pup that resembled Lobo away yet, or worse , shot him. It was the perfect solution. Jake could have kicked himself for not thinking of it sooner.

When Jake knocked on the Wolfs' door and told Loretta what he planned, she applauded the idea and gave Jake directions to Mr. Morgan's farm. Jake made fast tracks to get there, only to discover that a farmer named Christian had already adopted the pup. Not to be beaten, Jake asked directions to Christian's.

Deke Christian, a tall scarecrow of a man with a silver stubble of beard on his pointed chin, scratched his head and went *tsk-tsk* when Jake explained his problem to him. Pocketing a wad of chew inside his cheek, he said, "I reckon I can see you wantin' the little fella. The thing is, I done give him to my kids three day ago. They've already taken a shine to him. You ever heard seven kids cryin' all at once?"

Jake hated the thought of breaking seven little hearts. "I don't suppose they'd be just as happy with another pup?"

A speculative gleam crept into Christian's gray eyes. "Might could. Children can be fickle. Of course, a wolf cub ain't easy to come by. His pappy was from way up north, you know. Not another one like him for hundreds of miles."

Jake sensed a possible bargain in the air. "The children probably wouldn't care about their pup being one of a kind."

Christian scratched his head again. "Depends, I reckon."

Jake slid his hands into his hip pockets. "I'm willing to make the trade worth your while. You got the wolf pup for free. As compensation, how does fifty dollars strike you?"

Christian didn't look impressed. Jake narrowed an eye. "All right, I'm willing to go as high as a hundred. You could buy each kid a sack of candy to ease the blow, get them another pup, and have a wad of money left to console yourself. You have to admit, it's a mighty fine price for a worthless mongrel."

Deke smiled. "Triple that, and you've got yourself a wolf."

Jake laughed. "That's outrageous. Three hundred dollars?"

"Sounds fair for a one-of-a-kind pup you want mighty bad."

Jake jerked his hands from his pockets. "There isn't a dog on earth worth that kind of money."

"I reckon you could get one like him cheaper if you was to go to the Yukon. Mighty long way, though."

Jake shook his head and struck off down the rutted drive. There was no way in hell he would pay that for a dog. He was about halfway to the farmer's gate when he drew to a stop. He would never miss the three hundred. Was he going to quibble about money when it came to Indigo's happiness? Hell, he might as well spend three hundred as one. Either price was ridiculous. He trudged back up the hill.

"You've got yourself a deal," he told Christian. "I'll pay the three hundred for him." Jake pulled out his money clip, counted off the bills, and handed them to the farmer. "Where is he?"

Christian grinned, revealing a set of snaggleteeth. "I got him in the barn."

The farmer led the way, Jake on his heels. The pup was locked inside a stall. Farther down the center aisle, a thin boy of about ten was sitting on a hay bale, oiling a harness.

"I sold that pup," Christian told him. "This fella here offered such a fine price that I couldn't turn it down."

The youth shrugged. "That pup's so fightin' mean it don't make me no nevermind." He eyed Jake. "You bring a gunnysack?"

That was Jake's first indication of what he was getting into. "No, why?"

"You'll be needin' one to carry him," the boy replied.

Christian smiled and gestured for Jake to open the stall door. "He's yourn, and we wish you happy."

Jake looked over the door. In the dimness, he could see a ball of fluffy silver-and-black fur huddled in one corner of the stall. Jake grinned with excitement and unfastened the latch. "Oh, he's a fine-looking little fellow, isn't he?"

"Yep." Christian smirked. "Wolf to his core, though."

Jake drew the door open and stepped into the stall. He was about to bend over to coax the puppy forward when the fur ball cannoned from the corner, snarling and snapping. Before Jake could dance clear, sharp little teeth snagged hold of his jeans. He stared down, scarcely able to believe his eyes. If not for his high leather boots, he felt sure he'd be sporting fang marks.

"Hey, little guy," he soothed. "Don't be afraid."

The pup braced his feet and leaned back, straining the denim of Jake's pants. Glowing golden eyes sparked in the dimness.

"I knew your papa." As Jake spoke, he slowly inched a hand downward. "I'm a friend."

When Jake's fingers were within jumping distance, the pup abandoned the britches and went for blood.

"Son of a bitch!"

Jake tried to jerk his hand back. The cub locked its jaws. Pain shot from Jake's thumb to his wrist. With his free hand, he grabbed the pup's jaws, dug in with his fingers, and forced his razor-sharp little teeth to give. The instant Jake's thumb was freed, he caught the cub by his ruff and held him at eye level.

"You ornery little bastard."

"That ain't sayin' it by half," Christian said.

Jake knew when he had been had, but he wasn't about to admit it. "Do you have a spare gunnysack?"

Christian rolled his chew. "For two bits, I do."

Jake swore and dug in his change pocket. Christian caught the dollar and pocketed it. "Don't got change."

"Just get me the damned gunnysack," Jake said.

17

An hour later, Jake entered the house, holding the gunnysack at arm's length. He found Indigo lying across the bed, her gaze fixed on the wall. He could scarcely wait to see the expression on her face when she saw what he had brought her.

"Indigo?"

She started and sat up. "Jake? What're you doing home?" Her gaze shifted to the wiggling sack. "What is that?"

"A little something I got for you," he replied. "Move back. Instead of you biting into this surprise, it may bite into you."

She bounded off the bed and watched in bewilderment as Jake upended the sack. The pup rolled out, found his feet, and whirled to snarl at them. It was like looking at a miniature of Lobo. Jake grinned and turned to see the expression on Indigo's face, expecting rapturous pleasure and hoping for a little adoration as well. For him, not the puppy. Instead, she acted as if someone had struck her. After a horribly long moment, tears filled her eyes, and she averted her face.

"Get him away from me!"

Jake stared at her. "What?"

She turned her back to the puppy. "You heard me."

"Indigo." Jake gave a soft laugh. "Honey, you don't mean that. Lobo's puppy? I thought you'd be pleased."

She dragged in a ragged breath. "How could you?" she cried. "How could you bring him here?" She cupped a hand over her eyes. "Do you think I loved Lobo so little that I could let a puppy replace him? Never, not as long as I live."

"Honey, just look at him."

"Please don't ask that." She heaved a ragged sob. "Take him away! Please, Jake? Take him away . . ."

Reclaiming the gunnysack, Jake grabbed the puppy by its ruff. Anger flooded through him as he strode from the bedroom. He came to a stop in the sitting room and stared at the snapping, snarling ball of fur in his hand. Three hundred dollars, and she didn't want it? Well, Jake sure as hell didn't. He had no idea what to do with the nasty little cur. He was tempted to stomp him into a grease puddle and wring Indigo's neck.

Golden eyes agleam with vicious intent, the cub grew tired of flailing and finally hung still in Jake's grasp. Jake sighed and stuffed him in the gunnysack. Maybe Loretta would take him. Jake doubted it, though. Only Indigo would be able to tame a pup like this. No one else in his right mind would even want to try.

The thought made Jake recall his first night in Wolf's Landing and Loretta's concern that no one would adopt a wolf cub. He glanced over his shoulder toward the bedroom, and a grin settled on his mouth. In a voice that he intended to carry, he said, "You poor misbegotten little fellow. I gave it my best try. That's all I can do." Jake cocked an ear. He heard nothing but silence. Indigo was listening, all right. "Maybe if you didn't look so much like your papa, somebody else would take you. As it is, all I've done is prolong the inevitable."

With that, Jake left the house. He strove to keep a suitably grim expression on his face when he spied Indigo peering out at him from behind the bedroom curtain. With what he hoped was a look of steely determination, Jake walked down the street toward the Wolfs'. He was a little surprised when Indigo hadn't caught up with him by the time he reached the porch. Determined to carry this act through to the end, he stomped up the steps.

The weathered planks of the chicken coop felt rough beneath Indigo's palms as she pressed close to the wall and peeked around the corner of the squat building at her parents' back porch. Where was Jake? Had he left by the other door? Oh, God. He meant to shoot that puppy. Scarcely a minute passed that she didn't think of Lobo, and now she would have to look at his son a hundred times a day. In a fit of pique, she kicked at the dirt.

The creak of door hinges sounded from across the yard and brought her head up. She watched as Jake emerged from her parents' house, a rifle in one hand, the gunnysack in the other.

After taking a fortifying breath, Indigo stepped away from the henhouse. "Jake?"

He spun at the sound of her voice and cast around the yard. A slow smile touched his mouth when he finally spotted her, and he relaxed his stance, one hip slung outward, a long denim-clad leg bent at the knee. With the wind whipping his black hair and his dark eyes twinkling, he looked virile and handsome, totally at odds with her image of a heartless puppy killer.

Indigo tried not to look at the wiggling burlap. "What are you going to do?" she asked.

His jaw tensed. "Why don't you go inside and have a nice cup of hot cocoa with your ma?" he suggested in a kindly tone. "I'll be back in a few minutes and walk you home."

Indigo's pulse quickened. An urge came over her to pound his chest with her fists. How could he do this to her? "I can't let you shoot Lobo's baby, Jake," she informed him shakily.

He pursed his lips and slowly exhaled. "Honey, sometimes life is tough. I'm sorry for putting you through this. Lay it off on idiocy. I just didn't think how it would make you feel."

The gunnysack twisted and swayed against his thigh. Indigo's gaze was caught by the movement. "I—I can't let you shoot him. I'll give him a home."

His eyebrows drew together. "I know you mean well, but you wouldn't be doing him any favor. Pups need a lot of love. It wouldn't be right to raise him in an environment where he was always measured against his father and found lacking."

"I'll love him," she insisted in a shrill voice.

Jake heaved a weary sigh. "What you said over at the house, about disloyalty to Lobo. You were right. It'd be fickle of you to get another wolf so soon. I wasn't thinking straight."

"But he's not just any wolf! He's Lobo's son."

"True." He cast a worried glance at the bulging burlap. "That's why I went and got him. He's the image of his papa, and I thought—well, sometimes a replacement can ease a person's grief. But that was before I saw the hurt he brought you."

Indigo shifted her gaze from the gunnysack back to Jake. He seemed bent on carrying through, and the thought made panic well within her. How she felt didn't matter. The puppy's life was at stake. "I'll get over the hurting," she cried. "Please don't shoot him, Jake."

He raised both eyebrows. "Honey, do you think I want to? Give me an alternative and I'll jump at it. Can you think of anyone who might want him?"

Indigo searched her mind. "Chase would take him,

but he's miles away." She licked her lips and lifted her hands. "And, of course, my father, but he's in no condition to care for a puppy. M—Maybe I could just take him temporarily."

Jake shook his head. "He'd bond with you, and it'd break his little heart when you gave him away. No, honey, my way's best, quick and clean. You go on into the house and have that cocoa. I'll be right back."

With that, Jake turned and strode away toward the woods. Indigo stood there watching him, entrapped in a whirlpool of emotion. She didn't even want to look at that puppy.

She broke into a run. "Jake, wait!"

He spun to look at her. Indigo raced to reach him. Not allowing herself to think, she grabbed the gunnysack. He tightened his grip and resisted the tug of her hand.

"Indigo, go in the house like I told you."

She wrenched the sack from his grip and hugged it to her chest, horribly aware of the struggling bundle of furry warmth within the burlap. "I'm going into the house! This is Lobo's baby, Jake! He'd never forgive me."

Looking down at his wife, two thoughts struck Jake simultaneously; he had succeeded in making her want the pup, and for the first time since their marriage, she was defying him. God, but she was beautiful when that fierce Comanche pride snapped her spine taut. She stood with her chin lifted high, her blue eyes blazing with purpose, her narrow shoulders braced.

It hit Jake with the force of a rock between the eyes that *this* was the girl he had believed he was marrying, not the quiet, subservient mouse she had become after making her vows. In a flash of clarity, he saw her sitting beside him on the bed, braiding and unbraiding her hair upon command. Every man's dream come true? Maybe. But it wasn't his. He wanted this Indigo, a girl who was one part angel and one part wild temptress, a curious blend of sweetness and flame. What had begun as an attempt to make her yearn for the puppy took on other proportions. Jake gazed down into her vivid blue eyes and ached a little for both of them, for himself because he felt cheated, for her because her beliefs and her experiences with white men were forcing her into a mold that would slowly suffocate her.

As if it suddenly occurred to her what she had done, she got a stricken expression on her face, and her eyes darkened with confusion. Watching her, Jake held his breath, afraid she might give the puppy back to him. Go ahead and stand up to me just this once, he wanted to say. The world won't end. But he didn't dare rip at the fabric of her upbringing like that. If she was going to find solid footing in their marriage, he couldn't shift the foundation. Eventually, maybe she would find a happy medium in which she could be herself, yet still fulfill what she believed to be her wifely role. That could only come with time.

Jake saw her arms relax around the puppy. Then she bent her head. He knew what she meant to do. Before she could, he said, "If keeping him is that important to you, Indigo, take him home."

She slowly lifted her chin. Tears swam in her eyes. Jake searched for a flicker of the fire he had seen there an instant ago, some trace of the pride that had flamed so brilliantly. But there was no sign of either. Just a hollow nothingness, as if she had tamped down and put a lid on her subversive emotions.

He tried to imagine how it would feel to be enslaved and forced to swallow his pride a hundred times a day. For her, that was what marriage constituted. His wishes came first, always, no matter how strongly she felt about something. For an instant, she had simply reacted and forgotten that. Now, she was reassuming the meek demeanor she believed appropriate.

"Go on. Take him," he repeated.

She hugged the puppy close and retreated a step, looking at him in bewilderment. Jake couldn't help but wonder what she had expected. A thrashing? He tried to reassure her with a smile. Maybe she needed this experience so she could see he wasn't an autocratic monster.

"Are you angry?" she asked softly.

The worried look in her eyes made Jake's smile broaden. "Do I look angry?"

She didn't appear to be reassured by that. "No."

"Then I must not be." He balanced the rifle over his shoulder and glanced at the gunnysack she held so protectively. "Is he old enough to eat meat?"

She gave a hesitant nod.

"Then you'd better check the smokehouse."

She nodded again. Then she turned and fled as if the devil were nipping at her heels. Jake watched her go. When she disappeared from sight, he took a deep breath and exhaled, feeling as if he had just done battle with giants and lost.

Indigo had already started supper when Jake came in that evening. Her stomach knotted when she heard the front door open, and her nerves leaped at his every footfall as he walked across the sitting room to the kitchen doorway. A blur of denim and blue chambray, offset by burnished umber and ebony, he seemed to fill the opening.

She pretended not to see him and continued stirring the stew, putting off the moment when she would have to look into his eyes. Was he angry? That question had plagued her all day, and it was one for which only he could provide an answer. *Do I look angry?* She had learned long ago that white men could hide their darkest emotions and intentions behind a charming smile.

She felt the puppy tug on her moccasin. His playful growls couldn't be ignored. She laid aside the spoon and forced herself to look up. Jake's dark eyes twinkled into hers, and his firm lips slanted into a teasing grin.

"It looks like you've got more trouble than help with a companion like that on your heels," he said lightly.

"He doesn't seem to know when it's time to play."

Jake leaned out to watch the cub's antics. "All the time is playtime, from the way it looks. You've done wonders with him. I can't believe that's the same little fellow who bit me."

Indigo gave her foot a tug, trying to free it. The puppy took that as encouragement and gave her moccasin a shake. "He was afraid this morning. Now that we've had time to become acquainted, he doesn't feel threatened."

Jake arched a dark eyebrow, his expression indulgent. "You two had a long *talk*, I take it?" His gaze searched hers. "I'd like you to teach me how that's done one of these times."

Indigo had suspected he knew about her gift because of the curtained expression in his eyes when she tried to look into him, but she'd hoped she was wrong. Now he had confirmed it. A chill niggled its way up her spine. How did he feel about having a wife who communicated with creatures? And if he had nothing to hide, why did he shut her out? Now she knew he did it deliberately. At times like now, his eyes were warm and communicative. It was only when she attempted to see deeper that the walls went up.

He straightened and stepped into the kitchen. With a glance at the stove, he said, "Is that fresh coffee I smell?"

Dragging the puppy along, Indigo stepped to the dish board and took a mug from the shelf. Jake chuckled as she worked her way back to the coffeepot, one foot ensnared by tugging teeth. He sat on a straight-backed chair and stretched out his long legs, boots crossed at the ankles. She could feel his gaze trailing slowly over her. Her nerves prickled. Did he have a dark side he was afraid she might see? Her hand trembled as she lifted the coffeepot.

"You're wearing a skirt. What's the occasion?"

Indigo turned to give him the filled mug. He leaned forward and crooked his finger through the handle.

"He wet on me," she murmured.

"He what?"

Embarrassed, she repeated herself. Jake grinned and perused the fringed hem of her knee-length skirt with an appreciative gleam in his eyes. "Britches and bloomers both?" At her nod, his grin broadened. "Maybe having him around won't be such a hardship after all. I assumed the only skirt you had was the white doeskin."

Indigo shook her head. "I have several for everyday. I just don't wear them much when I'm working." The puppy jerked harder on her moccasin, and she glanced down. "At least I didn't. Now I have no choice but to wear skirts until I get my pants cleaned and treated. The process takes a spell."

"You've got only one pair?" he asked mildly.

"No, two. But given his bent for springing leaks, I'll save the extra pair for just in case." She glanced up. "You did say I could go back to work as soon as you felt it was safe."

He nodded. "That's what I said."

Indigo relaxed slightly. If he was angry, he was a master at camouflage, and if he had a dark side, he was a consummate actor. The puppy spied a potato peeling she had dropped. Abandoning her moccasin, he scampered across the floor, plumed tail wagging over his back. With a yap and a snarl, he attacked the peel, gave it a shake, and ran with it into the sitting room.

"You ready for your walk?" Jake asked.

She bent over to open the oven and check her biscuits. "I thought I'd skip it for tonight. I'm afraid the pup might wander and not come when I call. By tomorrow, he'll know us better."

The heat seared her eyes. She reared back and averted her face, then closed the oven.

"What're you going to call him?"

Indigo straightened and brushed at a falling strand of hair. "I haven't decided yet. A name is very important. I'd like it to be something significant."

He tucked in his chin and looked thoughtful. "How does Sonny strike you? Temporarily, that is."

"Sonny?" Indigo wrinkled her nose. "It isn't dignified."

Jake shrugged. "But significant. He's Lobo's son. Besides, he's a little tyke yet. By the time he grows up, you'll have thought of a better name."

She rolled the name across her tongue again and managed to smile. "I'm warming to it. All right, Sonny it is."

His dark gaze trailed slowly over her and settled on her legs where her moccasins and skirt didn't meet. His expression sharpened, and he leaned forward. "Honey, are those scratches?"

She bent to look and was surprised to see several red marks on her shins and calves. "He jumps up. Wolves have claws. As cubs, they can be a little treacherous when they play."

"Jesus." He curled a hand behind her knee and drew her toward him. "He's cut you to ribbons." He arched a look at her. "And you're afraid of me? That's amazing."

"I'm not afra—"

Before she could finish, Jake reached up and clamped a hand over her mouth. "Forget I said that."

He started to move his hand, and Indigo said, "But I'm—"

He smothered the words again, his eyes dancing with mischief. "Indigo, just don't say anything. That's an order."

When he removed his hand from her mouth again, she nibbled her lip, gazing down at him in bewilderment. He winked at her, then resumed his examination of her legs.

The feel of his warm fingers made her bare skin tingle.

She tried to pull away, but he held her fast and drew up her skirt with his other hand to assess the damage. No men but her father and brother had ever seen her bare legs, and that had been years ago. Only her mother had seen or touched her since. Indigo's face flamed.

Jake didn't seem aware of the liberty he was taking. She felt his fingertips, feather-light and gentle, seek out each scratch. "Did your Aunt Amy keep any salve here?"

"There's some in the top bureau drawer." All Indigo wanted was to escape his touch and get her skirt back down. "I'll wash them and put salve on after dinner."

"After dinner, hell." He released her and stood up. "Animal scratches are bad to get infected."

He left the kitchen and returned moments later carrying the tin of medication. After motioning her to a chair, he drew a linen towel from the drawer, moistened it with water from the jug, and then knelt before her on one knee. Grasping her right foot, he propped it on his raised thigh and pushed her skirt up.

Indigo's breath caught. She wasn't wearing bloomers. With one of her legs lifted, he could probably see clear to tomorrow. She tried to tuck her skirt. Jake glanced up, and his white teeth flashed in a lazy smile.

"I *am* your husband," he reminded her.

Somehow, Indigo didn't find that very reassuring. "I—I can do it by myself. Really!"

He gave her a look charged with meaning. "I don't mind."

She stared at the back of his bent head. When he ran a hand above her knee, she jerked and clamped her thighs together.

He lifted laughing brown eyes to hers. "Indigo, would you relax? All I'm interested in is the scratches."

She kept her thighs pressed together, but tried to relax otherwise, to no avail. He cast her another questioning glance.

"Don't you trust me?" His voice was deep and rich.

"If I was bent on seeing whatever it is you're working so hard to hide, don't you think I would have had a look before now?"

He had a point. He lowered her right foot, lifted the other, and applied himself to cleaning the remaining scratches. When that was done, he applied salve.

When the last scratch was tended, he replaced the lid on the tin container, set it on the table, and flashed her a slow smile. "Still in one piece?" he asked softly.

Indigo gave a jerky nod, her one thought to get both feet back on the floor. He seemed loath to release his grip on her ankle, however. She had difficulty meeting his gaze.

"You're as pretty a pink as any rose I've ever seen," he informed her huskily. "And you have beautiful legs."

That brought her eyes up. She stared at him, pulse slamming, her hands curled into tight fists over the edge of the chair seat. "Your biscuits are going to burn," she said shakily.

"Now *there's* a tactical maneuver if ever I've heard one," he replied with a chuckle. He lowered her foot to the floor and pushed to his feet.

Sonny reentered the kitchen, still playing with the potato peeling. Jake returned to his chair and took a leisurely sip of coffee while he watched his wife. He couldn't be certain, but he thought some of the shadows had eased from her eyes.

When she joined him at the table for dinner and ate a hearty portion of stew, his spirits soared. It was the first enthusiasm he had seen her show for food since Lobo's death. With every few bites, she picked out a bit of venison and gave it to Sonny. Her feeding the dog at the table didn't meet with Jake's approval, but he said nothing. Hell, as far as he was concerned, she could put a bib on the pup and sit him on a chair. What made her happy made him happy. That was the long and short of it.

He fished a piece of meat from his bowl and leaned

down with it extended on his palm. The wolf cub fastened gleaming golden eyes on the meat and slowly approached to take it. Jake wiped his hand clean on his napkin and met Indigo's shimmering gaze.

"Thank you for bringing him to me," she whispered in a tremulous voice. "He's the nicest gift I've ever received."

Jake straightened his shoulders. For a man who had just thrown away three hundred dollars on a dog he didn't want, he felt absurdly proud of himself.

18

Over the next few days, Jake learned the true meaning of frustration. He wanted Indigo as he never had another woman, so much so that he thought of little else. Living in the same house with her, sleeping in the same bed with her, and knowing she was his made it damned hard to keep himself in line. Only concern for her feelings forestalled him from carrying her to the bedroom and making love to her.

Since their conversation by Lobo's grave, Jake suspected that Indigo harbored more than one misconception about him. If he demanded that she perform her wifely duties, he was afraid he would be living up to some of her worst expectations. She needed time and gentle wooing. He was determined to give her both.

That decision made, Jake had only to convince his body of the wisdom of it. In addition to his long days at the mine and his afternoon walks with Indigo, he felled and chopped eight cords of firewood in the space of four days. When the amount of wood in the Wolfs' backyard began to reach embarrassing proportions, he tackled the dry rot in their front porch, working long after dark by lantern light. At night when he collapsed on the bed, every part of his body screamed with exhaustion.

Every part but one. . . .

On the sixth night, Jake fashioned some crutches for Hunter, then helped the older man to take his first faltering steps after so many weeks of being bedridden. Loretta fixed a lovely dinner to celebrate the joyous occasion. Afterward, Jake walked Indigo home and then took a freezing swim in the creek, which served to numb every part of his exhausted body.

Every part, that is, but one. . . .

By the seventh day, Jake decided new tactics were called for. If he didn't woo his wife into his arms soon, one of three things was bound to happen; he would work himself to death, die of pneumonia, or lose control and forcefully make love to her. Given his age, Jake didn't relish the thought of going to an early grave, and because he loved Indigo, the alternative didn't have much appeal, either. The last thing he wanted was to lose ground with her, which he most certainly would if he resorted to strength of arm.

Since he knew his young wife was as nervous about making love as a long-tailed cat in a roomful of rockers, he decided to use a subtle approach, which would require a smattering of acting ability, a slow, very light hand, and limitless patience. He had high hopes it would work well on Indigo, his aim being to arouse her before she quite realized what he was up to.

Things started off well. During their afternoon walks and long evenings together, he took advantage of every opportunity to touch her, tracing light circles on her neck, feathering his fingertips over her lips, and caressing the center of her palms and the bend of her arms. Jake measured his success by watching her eyes. When she became aroused, they turned a slumberous, stormy gray. Over the course of the third evening, he was happy to note that her eyes were gray more than not.

By the fourth afternoon, he was mentally rubbing his hands together in anticipation. Tonight would be the night. With that goal in mind, he took her for her walk. As had become his habit, he draped an arm over her shoulders. Only this time, instead of curling his fingers around her arm, he let his hand dangle limply over her right breast. Given the nature of walking, especially on uneven ground, it was natural that her body movements should jostle his arm, and since his dangling hand was attached, it also followed that his loosely curled fingers brushed her nipple.

At the first "accidental touch" Indigo started and threw him a suspicious glance, which Jake deflected with a bland expression of no interest. She finally relaxed. He bided his time, then aimed at his target again. It was all he could do not to smile when he felt how hard and erect her aureole had become. On the third pass, her nipple thrust against the soft leather of her blouse, eagerly peaked and straining for attention—attention Jake would be more than happy to provide.

He found a grassy spot beneath an oak. A little thing like damp ground wasn't going to discourage him. He sat with his back against the tree and drew Indigo down beside him. Looping his arm around her, he set his fingertips to work on her collarbone, tracing its shape and talking nonstop about Sonny's antics, pretending to be absorbed with the pup so the touch of his hand would seem innocent. Every once in a while, he let his fingers stray from her collarbone to feather across her upper chest.

A downward glance told Jake that success was nearly within his grasp. Her nipples were as erect as little cadets at muster. He turned toward her and bent to kiss her cheek. Placing a hand on her rib cage, he began a subtle ascent until his fingers curled around her right breast. She gasped and went rigid when he captured the peak of her nipple between thumb and forefinger.

"It's all right," he assured her in a husky whisper. He trailed his lips toward her mouth. "Trust me. Just relax."

Naturally, Jake hoped she would do just that and let him continue. But he didn't expect total limpness. He claimed her lips in a passionate kiss, running his tongue past her parted teeth to taste the sweet moistness. When he did, she went as starchless as drenched silk. For a horrible moment, he thought she had fainted. His hand froze on her breast, and he slowly drew back. Her eyes had a blank, distant look.

"Indigo?"

She blinked and focused, looking slightly irritated. "Yes?"

Jake searched her gaze. Panic, he could deal with. He wouldn't have been surprised by stiffness. Or even a little resistance. She was quick-witted and had to know what was on his mind. But limpness? It was a far cry from quivering surrender, and it left such a nasty taste in his mouth he lost enthusiasm.

"Are you all right?" he asked.

She gave him a dreamy little smile and blinked again, for all the world as if she was drowsy. "I'm fine."

Jake didn't want "fine," he wanted mindless abandon. He drew his arms from around her and settled against the tree, uncertain which stung more, his ego or his aching groin. His lovemaking had elicited a gamut of responses, even a slap or two, but never in his recollection had a female dozed off.

"Are *you* all right?" she countered.

Jake regarded her with dry amusement. "I'm just dandy."

After a lot of forethought, Jake cornered Loretta the next afternoon and asked if she had explained the facts of life to her daughter. Loretta turned crimson and exited the house, saying she had eggs to gather. Jake felt badly about embarrassing her, but his marriage was on the line. He needed answers.

With that goal in mind, he approached Hunter, who was still confined to bed. As before when Jake sought advice from him, Hunter circled the questions and gave Jake vague replies. From their conversation, Jake gleaned that Hunter had no idea what Loretta had told Indigo about sex. That was woman talk and unimportant. In the space of a few minutes, a husband could teach his wife far more with his actions than words could ever impart.

Jake left the Wolf home with the unmistakable impression that Hunter considered Indigo's education to be Jake's problem. To Jake, it had begun to seem an insurmountable one.

While Jake wrestled with his confusion, Indigo dealt with her own. Jake was nothing like she had expected. Though she had seen him display his fair share of male arrogance and knew he was capable of ruling her with an iron fist, he was, for the most part, endlessly patient and solicitous, completely at odds with her expectations of a husband. When he touched her, he was always gentle. He seemed to go out of his way to please her. God help her, she was even starting to like him. Not just a little, but a lot. She tried not to, but she couldn't seem to stop herself. He made her laugh more than anyone she had ever met. And he made her feel—special. Even in his sleep, he held her as if she were made of fragile glass. Sometimes, just recently, she had snuggled against him, feeling more protected than she did threatened by the muscular circle of his arms.

Since the incident under the oak tree, she had even begun to wonder, in weak-minded moments, what making love with Jake would be like. When he touched her, it was like being brushed with gossamer, and he made her feel— Indigo couldn't put a name to it. Frightened, yes, because she knew what he intended to do to her might be very unpleasant. But he made her feel good as well, as if she was butter on a hot biscuit. Her fear was that if she allowed herself to melt, he'd take a hearty bite.

And if he did? How could anyone appear to be so gentle and unfailingly kind if he was planning to do something horrible?

That question led Indigo to face an undeniable fact. Against her better judgment, despite all her past experiences with white men, she was slowly beginning to trust him.

The realization terrified her.

One week after the incident under the oak tree, the long-awaited letter from Jeremy arrived. Rather than risk Indigo's curiosity, Jake took the letter into the woods to read it before he went home. The news wasn't good. After further investigation of Ore-Cal's files, Jeremy felt certain their father was behind the accidents at Wolf's Landing. He told Jake that he planned to visit there soon so he and Jake could do some sleuthing.

With a shoulder braced against a pine, Jake stared at his brother's handwriting for a long while and remembered that distant afternoon when Jeremy had revealed his suspicions. So much had happened since. The breeze picked up and rustled the expensive stationery, which bore the Ore-Cal letterhead. He ran his thumb across the fine grain of the paper. These last three weeks, the world he had left behind in Portland had begun to seem like a distant dream. Now it all came rushing back to him with such clarity he could almost see Jeremy standing before him.

He no longer felt certain where he belonged. He had a wife here. The Lopez house was beginning to feel like home. He had calluses on his palms. Yet how could he turn his back on his employees, his family, and the affluence he had worked so hard to acquire? He cared little for his father, but he loved Jeremy and his sisters. Those ties couldn't be severed easily.

He folded the letter and slipped it into his shirt pocket. This evening when Indigo wasn't watching, he would toss it in the fire. It wouldn't do for her to see the Ore-Cal letterhead and discover the truth about him before he could explain it to her.

Jake sighed. Explain? God, he dreaded that discussion. Indigo wasn't going to be overjoyed to learn she had married the son of the man who had nearly killed her father. Though he had been careful never to lie to her, he had spun a web of half-truths. What would she think when he told her about himself? How would she feel when she learned he had a fiancée? Damn, he hadn't even found a private moment to write Emily yet.

Jake grimaced. A private moment? The truth was, he hadn't found an opportunity to get a letter written behind Indigo's back. That made him feel guilty as hell. Indigo was honest to a fault, even when she feared it might earn her a beating. How could he make her understand his motivations for living a lie?

Jake was no longer certain he even understood his motivations himself. In Portland that long-ago afternoon, coming here incognito had seemed a perfect solution. But that had been before he met the Wolfs, people who told the truth as if every word they uttered was under oath. He had to deal with the possibility that his harmless little deceptions might break Indigo's heart and destroy his still shaky marriage.

Indigo sensed that something was wrong the moment Jake stepped in the house. His dark eyes had a hooded, troubled look, and his burnished features were settled into grim lines. She stepped to the kitchen doorway.

Her first thought was the mine. "Has something happened?"

As if he heard her voice through a fog, he tipped his head and settled unfocused eyes on her. After a moment, he smiled. "Nothing momentous. I just received a letter from my brother."

Indigo didn't think he seemed very happy about that. She recalled the afternoon in the hayloft when he had spoken of his family and the feeling that he was one of six yeast rolls in one muffin tin. "Did he send bad news?"

He brushed his cuff across his forehead. "Not unless you consider company bad news. He's coming to visit."

Indigo felt as if her stomach dropped to the region of her knees. "He's coming here?"

Jake lifted his hands. "I don't know when. Soon, he said." He gave the sitting room a cursory glance. "He can sleep on the settee. His feet'll hang over the end, but that won't kill him."

Indigo tried to martial her thoughts. "He's tall like you?"

"That's where the similarities end, believe me. Jeremy's too handsome for his own good. If he starts sweet-talking you, run the other direction."

The least of her fears was that Jake's brother would try to sweet-talk her. He'd probably take one look at her and ask Jake if he had lost his mind. "Does he know about me?"

Jake walked toward her, shaking his head. "No. I haven't taken time to write."

She had to force her next words. "Will he disapprove?"

Jake's dark eyes met hers, and his face softened with a smile. "I approve. That's all that matters, Indigo."

It wasn't what she needed to hear. Accustomed to Jake's undivided attention, she was alarmed by the distant, preoccupied look in his eyes. Returning to the kitchen, she banked the cooking fire so the bean soup wouldn't scorch while they went for their walk. One thought swam endlessly in her mind. Jeremy didn't know yet that his brother was married to an Indian.

After the dinner dishes were done that night, Indigo asked Jake's permission to go visit her mother. He gave it without hesitation and offered to escort her since it was already dark. Since she didn't really want his company, she explained that she wouldn't be long and left before he could quiz her.

His brother was coming. . . . Indigo hurried along the boardwalk toward her parents' home, remembering her mother's warning. *Your leathers won't do in another town where the ladies are decked out in flounces and ruffles.* Indigo pressed her palms to her cheeks. Why hadn't she listened? If she had started using the lemon water on her face that day, it might already have started to bleach her skin. Now it was too late.

Indigo's feet dragged to a stop. She stood there in the darkness and stared blindly down the street. Learning that Jeremy might visit had forced her to face feelings she had been trying to deny. Somehow, Jake had wormed his way past her defenses. She didn't want to put a name to the ache that was building inside her, not yet. All she knew was that she wanted him to feel proud of her.

What if Jeremy was shocked? What if Jake looked at her through his brother's eyes? He might regret marrying her—if he didn't already. He hadn't looked elated when he told her Jeremy was coming. Why should he? Unless he came from an extraordinary family, his Comanche wife was going to raise eyebrows.

She could lose him. . . . Oh, God, she could lose him. He'd go away to the world beyond the mountains and never come back. She'd never hear him call her name again when he came in the door after work. She'd never again hear his deep voice whispering next to her ear. She'd never again fall asleep at night held close to his heart.

Indigo felt as though something inside her was breaking apart. She dragged in air and hugged her waist. According to white law, until Jake made love to her, he could have their marriage annulled. Was that why he hadn't touched her yet? Maybe he had been planning all along to leave her.

Tears sprang to her eyes. If that was the case, she should be deliriously happy. She hadn't wanted to marry a white man in the first place. So why did the thought of his leaving make her feel like this? The question was unanswerable.

Jake became suspicious when Indigo came home from her parents' house with a bundle in her arms. He became even more suspicious when she headed straight for the bedroom. He stayed at the kitchen table and finished sharpening the kitchen knives, expecting her to emerge and explain. When she didn't, he started to grow concerned. She had been acting strangely all evening.

Pushing to his feet, he moved silently through the house. When he reached the bedroom door, he stood there a moment and listened. He heard movement, so he knew she wasn't in bed. A faint glow of light spilled out from under the door. He frowned and turned the knob.

"Indigo, what are you—"

Jake forgot what he was going to say. His wife stood by the bed, wearing one of her mother's blue gingham dresses. Evidently, she had been jerking garments on and off, for her hair had slipped loose from some of its pins, and her braided coronet hung askew, with long, flyaway tendrils framing her small face. Jake's gaze dropped to the toes of her moccasins, which peeked out from under her skirt.

"Jake," she said weakly.

"What are you doing?" He stepped in and glanced at the pile of dresses on the bed. "Those are your mother's, aren't they?"

Her cheeks flushed to a painful red. "She lent them to me. I was hoping I could wear them until I got some sewing done."

Jake couldn't credit his ears. "I don't know why, but

I had the idea you didn't like white women's clothing."

She averted her face. "I've changed my mind. Not that it does me much good. Ma's dresses don't fit me right."

Jake could see the problem. Her ample breasts were straining the seams of the bodice. "Well, that's no major catastrophe. You can wear leathers for a couple of more weeks while you do some sewing." Personally, Jake was going to miss her fringed skirts. "Blue looks nice on you."

"Thank you." She didn't turn to look at him. "I just wish it fit. I look like a link sausage in it."

Stifling a smile, Jake moved slowly toward her. The tight bodice shoved her creamy breasts high above the neckline. In his opinion, link sausage didn't exactly describe the effect. Not that he intended to argue. As lovely as she was, he wouldn't allow her out of the bedroom with that much bosom showing.

As he drew up beside her, he noticed the stricken expression in her eyes. He stepped closer. "Honey, what's wrong? Just because certain parts of you don't fit in your mother's dresses isn't any reason to be upset."

"Oh, Jake."

He leaned down, trying to see her face. Knowing Indigo as he did, he felt sure there had to be a whole lot more to this than met the eye. "Oh, Jake? That doesn't tell me a lot."

"I can't wear a single one of these."

He concurred wholeheartedly. It was all he could do to keep his hands to himself. "You can make do until—"

"You don't understand! I'll never get any dresses made before Jeremy gets here. Never, not even on Ma's brand-new Wheeler-Wilson!"

"Why would you—" The rest of the question died in Jake's throat. He swallowed and tried again, not at all sure he wanted to hear her answer. "Indigo, why do you have to have dresses made before Jeremy gets here?"

"Because . . ."

The tendons along her throat stood out as she strained to speak. The words never came. Jake drew her hand from her face. The fear and pain he saw in her expression caught at his heart. With a low groan, he drew her into his arms. "Oh, sweetheart . . ."

The moment he held her close, a strange smell wafted to his nostrils. It was so strong that he forgot all else. "What is that odor?"

She stiffened. "What odor?"

He sniffed next to her ear. "It smells like lemon."

"Oh." She pressed her face against his shoulder. "It's lemon water Ma mixed up."

Jake winced. He knew what women used lemon water for; Mary Beth drenched herself with it every summer to lighten her skin. He closed his eyes. Memories washed over him of Indigo sitting under the laurel tree at the Geunther Place. Then he remembered the things he had heard Brandon Marshall say to her. For the first time in her life, Indigo was trying to mask her heritage. And why? Because she wanted him to be proud of her.

As that realization sank home, Jake came as close to getting tears in his eyes as he ever had in his adult life. One of the things he had always admired about Indigo was her fierce Comanche pride. For what seemed an eternity, he had been yearning for some sign from her that she returned his affections. Now that she had given him one, he felt sick. Because of her Indian blood, she didn't feel good enough to be his wife? The exact opposite was true. He was the one who didn't measure up.

Without speaking, he swept her into his arms. With Sonny following in his wake, he carried her to the kitchen, lowered her feet to the floor, and pulled a clean dish towel from the drawer. Stepping to the dish board, he tipped the water jug to moisten it. She reared back when he began to scrub her face.

"What are you"—she sputtered—"doing?"

"Washing off that damned lemon. Look up."

"But I—" She blinked and pursed her lips.

Jake smoothed the cloth across her cheek, then bent to kiss the tip of her nose. "Don't you ever pull something like this again. I love your skin just the way it is."

Her eyes looked like crushed blue velvet. "Y—You do?"

Jake smiled. "I do. Women with milk-white complexions are as common as gnats in a fruit barrel. If that was what I wanted, I would have married one of them." He leaned down and stole a quick kiss.

She didn't look convinced. Jake caught her face between his hands and searched her gaze, his heart breaking a little at the confusion and pain he still saw there. "I love you, Indigo. Just the way you are. I love your hair. I love your skin. I love your leather skirts. I even like your buckskin pants. If I ever smell lemon on you again, I'll wring your little neck. And I want you to take every stitch of those clothes back to your mother. Is that clear?"

"Yes, but Jeremy—"

"To hell with Jeremy. You're married to me."

"But—"

"No buts. Jeremy will love you just as you are. He's going to take one look and think I'm the luckiest man who ever walked."

"But what if—"

He gave her a little shake. "No what ifs. All that matters is what I think, and I think you're perfect."

Jake could see that his words offered her little comfort. He had to accept that. Suddenly, he understood so many things about her that he hadn't before. The question was, did she understand herself?

19

En route to return the dresses to her mother the next morning, Indigo encountered Mr. Christian on the boardwalk. Sporting a new hat and boots, he gave her a courtly little bow and informed her that he had just ordered a breeding bull.

"Oh, how wonderful," Indigo replied. She knew the farmer had been seeing hard times recently. "I'm pleased for you."

He glanced at Sonny, who was busily sniffing grass that tufted up between the boardwalk planks. "I sure appreciated gettin' the money, I'll tell ya, and I'll always be beholden."

Slightly bewildered, Indigo studied his thin face. "Yes, well." She smiled. "Give your wife my best. Good day to you."

As Indigo started to walk away, the farmer called, "How you gettin' along with that ornery cuss?"

For an awful moment, Indigo thought he meant Jake, but when she turned she saw that his gaze was directed at Sonny. "Oh, we're getting along famously."

Mr. Christian tugged on his ear and shook his head.

"Orneriest animal I ever saw. Sure hope your mister don't want to bring him back, 'cause I done spent the three hundred."

With that, Deke Christian walked away. Indigo gazed after him, quite certain she had misunderstood him. A few minutes later, when she reached her parents' house, she was still puzzling over the conversation.

"Ma, has Mr. Christian ever struck you as odd?"

Loretta turned from the oven with a baking sheet of cookies in her mittened hand. "Odd? How so?"

Indigo laid the bundle of dresses on the table. "About a half-bubble off plumb. He just ordered a bull." Indigo frowned. "He said the oddest thing—something about Jake bringing Sonny back and wanting his three hundred dollars."

A startled expression crossed Loretta's face.

"You don't mean—oh, Ma, he didn't!"

Loretta set the baking sheet on the dish board. With a faint smile, she nodded.

"Jake bought Sonny?" Indigo glanced at the puppy in front of the hearth. "For three hundred dollars? Where did he get that much money?"

"It wasn't polite to ask. He knew how much you missed Lobo, and he thought his son might ease your grief. I reckon three hundred dollars didn't seem like much to him if it'd make you happy."

Indigo sank onto a chair. "Then he—why, he never meant to shoot him at all. It was all an act to make me take him."

Loretta chuckled. "You aren't angry with him, are you?"

For just an instant, Indigo did feel angry. Then she looked at Sonny and a fond smile curved her lips. In truth, her days went a lot faster with the puppy as company, and now that she had grown to love him, it seemed right somehow that she should raise Lobo's son. "No, I'm not angry," she said softly.

"I'm glad. Jake's heart was in the right place." Loretta pulled a saucer from the cupboard and filled it with cookies. Coming to the table, she sat it at Indigo's elbow and then took a seat. "A man has to love a woman a lot to spend three hundred dollars on a puppy. Especially one that bit him straight off."

A warm feeling spread through Indigo. "I guess maybe he does love me," she whispered. "A little, anyway."

Loretta helped herself to a cookie. She took a dainty bite, then studied her daughter. "More than a little, I'd say." A question crept into her eyes. "Indigo, I may be treading on forbidden ground, but something Jake said the other day leads me to believe you haven't been honoring your wifely obligations."

Indigo thought of how tidy she'd been keeping the house and the fine dinners she had been fixing every night. "But I—" She broke off. "Oh, you mean *that* wifely obligation."

Loretta's cheeks flushed. "So you admit it?"

Indigo squirmed on her chair. "I haven't refused exactly."

"You've been married awhile. There are things a man expects." She scratched at a fleck of flour on her apron. "I know you married him against your will. It can't be easy." She glanced up. "My fear is that you're going to make matters worse. A neglected man will press the issue. You don't want that."

Indigo didn't. "But Ma—"

"Jake's a good man, and I don't think he's got a mean bone. But there isn't a man alive who can't turn ornery. Understand?"

Indigo understood all right. "Yes, Ma."

Loretta sniffed. "I reckon I sound heartless to you." Her eyes darkened with emotion. "But you're my baby, and I want to save you grief. Don't test your husband's patience."

*   *   *

Indigo returned home worried and upset. Every time she looked at Sonny, she was assailed by guilt. Jake truly did care about her. He had shown it in dozens of ways. So why did she still feel panicky when she thought about the marriage bed?

She went to the bedroom and lay down. She imagined his scent clung to his pillow and closed her eyes. She could almost feel his arm at her waist, his hand splayed over her tummy, the warmth of him at her back.

Pretty soon, he probably would have to leave for a spell. The thought made her feel bereft. She envisioned his dark face with the ebony locks of hair curling loosely across his high forehead. Her stomach fluttered, just as it often did when he looked at her. What if he went away to another town without first making love to her? She imagined him smiling at a beautiful lady and making *her* stomach flutter. What if that lady set her sights on him?

A tight knot of misery settled in Indigo's chest. He had done everything he knew to make her happy. In return, what had she given him? Nothing. Not even her trust. She had to make love with him. He deserved that much at least. If she didn't, he might leave on a trip and never come back to Wolf's Landing. The thought made her want to weep. Somehow, he had become the center of her world. If he never came back, she'd die inside.

Indigo opened her eyes and stared at the ceiling. Confusion tangled her emotions. She didn't want to love him. She didn't. It made her feel horrible inside, and frightened. She slanted an arm across her eyes and sobbed. It wasn't fair that he had made her feel this way. It just wasn't fair.

At noon break, Jake left the mine and headed for home. Since the arrival of Jeremy's letter, he was no longer convinced that Brandon Marshall was behind the incidents at the mine. That being the case, it was also unlikely that the rock slide had been aimed at Indigo. Knowing how much she missed working, Jake had been giving the matter consideration. If the accidents hadn't been intended for her, then why couldn't he take extra precautions to ensure her safety and allow her to come back?

When he reached the house, he found Indigo asleep on the bed. He crept close and touched his fingertip to her silken eyelashes. She blinked and slowly opened her eyes. For a moment, she just stared up at him as if she didn't see him.

"Jake?"

"Who do you think?" he asked with a low chuckle.

She pushed up on an elbow. "What are you doing home?"

"A little bird told me you were being lazy."

"Oh. Is there something I should be doing?"

Jake folded his arms and narrowed an eye at her. "Some partner you are, sleeping the day away. Get up and put your britches on, Mrs. Rand. We've got work to do."

"Where?"

"At the mine."

She bolted to a sitting position. "The mine? But you—what about—do you mean it? You said it wasn't safe."

"I've been thinking it over, and nothing's happened in so long, I'm willing to gamble a little." Jake held up a hand. "With some stipulations. You only work half-days."

She steepled her fingers and looked rapturous. "Oh, yes! Half-days would be wonderful!"

"And you work with me. No wandering off. That's only temporary—just until I'm positive it's safe."

"Oh, yes! Yes!" She nodded emphatically. "I don't

mind that, really I don't, Jake. You'll think I'm your shadow."

"There's more," he warned. "No heavy lifting, and if I see you with a pick or shovel, I'll wrap it around your little neck."

Her face fell. "But what can I do then?"

Jake leaned toward her. "Do you agree to the terms or not?"

Her face brightened. "Just being there will be wonderful."

"Then get dressed."

She leaped to her feet and ran to the bureau. After jerking out a pair of britches, she whirled back around and launched herself at him. Jake unfolded his arms just in time to catch her. She hugged his neck. "Oh, Jake, thank you."

Before he could reply, she wriggled free and started dragging her pants on under her skirt. Jake couldn't help but laugh. He'd never seen such a quick change in all his life.

"Have you had your lunch?" he asked.

"I'm not hungry."

"You have to eat." He swept her skirt from the floor and tossed it on top of the bureau. "No arguments."

Indigo was so thrilled to be back at the mine that she didn't resent the restrictions. Since first meeting Jake, she had sensed that he didn't approve of women working. His allowing her to be there at all was a concession. She wasn't about to complain, and she managed to find plenty to do. Several times during the afternoon, he sought her opinion before making a decision, which made her feel a part of things.

The afternoon flew by, and before Indigo knew it, the men began to leave for home. Jake noted her crestfallen expression and chucked her under the chin.

"Don't look so low in the lip. You can come back tomorrow."

Indigo hugged her waist and took a deep, blissful breath. "Oh, how I love the smell here."

He leaned a shovel against the tunnel entrance, then turned to give her a slow wink. "Me, too. It reminds me of you."

"Me?"

"Yeah. You smell like sunshine and fresh air and pine trees"—he chuckled—"and dirt."

"I don't either smell like dirt." She met his gaze and began to look uncertain. "Do I?"

He threw back his head and laughed. On the way down the mountain, he took her hand. As they walked through the woods, the sun shone in their eyes one moment, then shade fell over them. It was serene, a perfect afternoon kissed with the promise of spring, yet. . . . She felt unsettled and didn't know why.

"How much more sunshine are we likely to get?" he asked.

She frowned. Her feelings felt as stirred up as Ma's flapjack batter. "Not much. When March comes in like this, it usually goes out with a flood."

He smiled over at her. Suddenly the air seemed too thick to breathe.

"Then we ought to enjoy it all we can," he told her in a low, rich voice. "How's about fixing a picnic dinner and eating in the woods this evening?"

Indigo did her best to smile with enthusiasm. She loved the forest. So why did the suggestion make her feel trapped?

Stretched out on his side, his head propped on the heel of his hand, Jake gazed across the meadow. The whisper of pine boughs lulled him. The coolness of the breeze kissed his skin. Though dinner had been simple fare, he felt content, due in part to his surroundings, but mostly because of the woman beside him.

Shifting his gaze, he traced the lines of her profile. He loved the gentle slope of her high forehead. When he looked at her brows, he wanted to run his fingertip along their arches. Her small nose, so like her father's, lent her a regal, wild air, offset by a fragile jaw and sweetly pouted lips. He especially loved her chin, stubbornly squared, but adorable in miniature.

A precious blend of strength and vulnerability. There was something about the way she held herself, head lifted, shoulders straight, that hinted at a spirit no man could ever break. Yet when he touched his loosely folded knuckles to her cheek, the span of his fist stretched the entire length of her jaw.

She turned and caught him smiling. "What?" she asked.

Jake gave her a slumberous look. "I was just thinking."

"About what?"

"About you." Her blue eyes caught the fading sunlight and shimmered down at him, as clear as lightly tinted glass. "You've got such beautiful eyes."

"You couldn't see my eyes."

His grin broadened. "You've got beautiful everything. Especially that dirt on your nose."

She rubbed. "Did I get it?"

"A little to the right."

Bracing herself on one elbow, she leaned down. Jake swiped with his thumb at the nonexistent dirt. "There." He curled his hand around her nape. "Don't go," he whispered. "Stay down here and talk to me."

"About what?"

An ache crept up the back of Jake's throat. He hated to ruin what had thus far been an almost perfect day, but he couldn't handle her with kid gloves forever. They had some serious problems, and now that he sensed their origin, he had to begin dealing with them. Gently, if he could. Facing the truth within one's self could hurt. "You could teach me how to talk to animals. You never know when I'll have to feed Toothless."

Her eyes turned turbulent. "It isn't really talking. Animals just take to me."

"You do it with your eyes. I've seen you with Sonny."

Clearly uneasy, she avoided looking at him and toyed with a tendril of hair. Since finding her in the bedroom last night, frantically donning white women's clothing, Jake wasn't the least bewildered by her denial.

"Indigo, look at me," he whispered.

Her large, apprehensive eyes flicked to his. Jake met her gaze, determined not to shut himself off from her this time. How could he expect complete honesty from her until he was ready to risk it himself? He couldn't continue to cloak all the good in his heart to conceal one miserable secret. There were other things within him that she needed to see—mainly the love and tenderness he felt for her.

He sensed that his repeated reluctance to let her delve too deeply had troubled her. In a way, he understood why. As bewildered and wary as she was, as hard as she tried to camouflage that, her eyes were like windows. Perhaps that was an inherent part of the gift God had given her, and she couldn't help how communicative her eyes were. Regardless, though, she shared all that she was when she looked at you, and it was bound to make her feel leery when another didn't. He had given it a lot of thought and decided he'd rather have her know he had secrets than to think he was hiding something worse.

"It's a special gift, your being able to communicate with creatures. Don't you realize that? Even if I can never learn how, won't you at least try to share it with me?"

Her mouth tightened. "If you're so convinced such a communication exists, let Sonny teach you."

Jake chuckled. "He's too busy chasing bugs. Besides,

I don't want him to teach me." He drew her closer. "Please?"

She nibbled her lip, looking as though she felt cornered. "It's not something you can teach, Jake. It just happens."

"So you do talk to the animals?" He held her gaze, praying she would find the courage to say yes. "That's why Toothless trusts you, isn't it? And why you have no fear of him. You've looked into his heart, haven't you?"

By her expression, Jake knew he had finally hit on the right words. She could deny that she "talked" to the animals. That wasn't really a lie, because it wasn't a verbal communication.

"It's done with feelings, isn't it?" he pressed. "Not something you hear—not messages that can be expressed with language—just a sharing of emotion."

He saw her small hands curl into fists. "Why does it matter to you?"

Jake smiled. Wasn't that the entire problem? She was terrified that it would matter. "It's no crime to be different."

She averted her face and closed her eyes.

"You can't hide what you are," he whispered with gruff tenderness. "Don't you know how precious you are to me? I've known you talked to the wild creatures since the first."

"It's not really talking. It's—" She turned frightened eyes to his. "It's not like that at all."

He ran his fingertips over the delicate vertebrae in her upper spine. "Why are you afraid to tell me about it? I'm not so different from Toothless, am I? If you can trust a cougar, why can't you learn to trust me?"

She pulled away. "I trust you."

His hand still poised in midair, Jake curled his fist around the nothingness and accepted that he had once again failed to reach her. It was ironic that a girl who could so easily delve into the hearts of others couldn't find the truth within her own.

He fixed his gaze on some distant trees. From the corner of his eye, he caught movement, but preoccupied as he was, he didn't pay it any heed. As it drew closer, however, the flash of black and white kicked his sixth sense into gear and a tingle of alarm shot up his spine. He glanced past Indigo and saw— Damn, it was a skunk, and it was marching right up to them as if they'd sent it an invitation to dine.

Jake tensed, then forced himself to relax. A skunk. Of course, a skunk. He had nearly forgotten he was sitting there with Indigo, the champion of creatures, large and small.

"Honey, we've got company. A friend of yours, I hope."

She glanced over her shoulder. "Oh, it's Stinky."

"How apt." Jake sniffed, then wished he hadn't. "He won't spray me, will he?"

"No, of cour—" Before she could finish answering, Sonny leapt out from behind some brush and cannoned toward the skunk, snarling and snapping the air. With a horrified expression on her face, Indigo cried, "Sonny, no!"

Jake immediately guessed how the wind was going to blow. Already tensed to run, he shot to his feet, snagged Indigo's arm, and tore away with her. He heard Sonny yelp. The next instant, he was running blind. His eyes felt on fire. His lungs convulsed on the most awful smell on earth. Then a horrible, gut-wrenching nausea struck him. He heard Indigo gag beside him.

"Shit!"

Jake tripped over a limb and crashed to his knees. The next moment he was vomiting. Between heaves, he kept calling to Indigo, but she didn't answer him. When his sight finally started to clear, he saw that she was lying on her side nearby, looking as green as he felt. Sonny was rolling and scrubbing his nose in the dirt, whimpering pitifully.

"He got us," Indigo said weakly.

For some insane reason, her statement of the obvious struck Jake as hysterically funny and he started to laugh. His arms buckled, and he rolled over onto his back. Slanting an arm across his eyes, he finally managed to say, "I think you're right," between breaths.

"I'm sorry. I should never have made friends with a skunk."

"Better a friend than an enemy." Jake started to laugh again. He clamped a hand over his stomach. "Oh, God, I'm sick."

She slowly sat up. "So will everyone else be who dares to get near us. It doesn't wash off."

Jake sobered. "For how long?"

"Days, sometimes weeks." She plucked at the back of her shirt and gagged. "Oh, Jake, I'm sorry. I think Ma's got some remedy made from tomatoes. Maybe that will work."

He sniffed. "I don't think he got us straight on."

She managed a quavery smile. "You're just getting used to it. In an hour or so, you won't even realize you stink." She worried her bottom lip. "Are you angry?"

Jake chuckled. "Honey, if there was anyone on earth I would choose to be exiled with, it'd be you. I do think we'd better teach Sonny some manners with your friends, however."

She pushed unsteadily to her feet and glanced toward the remains of their meal.

"Just leave it. The basket's ruined anyway."

She nodded. "I know. I was just looking for poor Stinky."

Poor Stinky? Jake started to laugh again.

20

"*Oh, lands! Stay back!*" Loretta pushed the door nearly closed, then peered out at Jake and Indigo through the crack. "Indigo, I swear, when will you ever learn?"

"Stinky wasn't aiming at us, Ma. It was Sonny."

"Aiming or no, he got you good." Loretta waved her hand.

Indigo plucked at her shirt and wrinkled her nose. "Do you have something that might help?"

Loretta sighed. "I've got some tomatoes preserved. But mind, don't get any in your mouth and wash with soap after."

"I thought they proved tomatoes weren't poison," Jake said.

Loretta shot him a challenging look. "Have you seen anybody eat one and live to tell it?"

Jake and Indigo chose bathing spots along the creek some distance from each other. It immediately became apparent to Jake, however, that he couldn't reach the places where he had been sprayed the worst. After donning his soiled pants, he sought out Indigo, whom he found bathing in a bend of the stream, shielded from view by brush and still wearing her chemise. Without a doubt, the girl trusted him with her life.

He smiled and picked his way down the bank toward her, happy for once to live up to her worst expectations. After all, he had tried the other route, proving her wrong about him at every turn.

"I'll scrub your back if you'll scrub mine."

At the sound of his voice, she started and let out a squeak. "Jake! What're you—" She sank in the water and stared at him, looking more adorable than she had a right to with her unbraided hair hanging in wet ropes over her face. "I'm not decent."

He had noticed that, yes. Scratching his ear, Jake eyed her with dry amusement. Sonny scampered by him, stopping every few steps to shake and scrub himself dry on the grass. From the wet condition of his coat, Jake assumed she had already bathed him. "Are we going to let the culprit of all this be the only one to come out smelling like roses? You're wearing your chemise. I can reach under it to wash you. And I'll keep my britches on."

He made it sound safe enough. The trouble was that he didn't look harmless standing there in wet jeans and no shirt. He looked everything but, all bronzed maleness and rippling muscle, his ebony hair tousled and dripping water. She cast a glance at the lapping current. What could happen in the creek?

"All right," she finally agreed.

He came wading toward her, his jar of tomatoes held high in one hand. "I'll go first." He handed her the jar and turned his back to her. "Get the back of my neck and shoulders good. I think that's where I got it the worst."

Indigo was freezing, so she didn't waste time. She

quickly scrubbed him with tomato, then, while he rinsed, grabbed her bar of soap off a nearby rock and lathered her palms. Beneath her massaging fingers, the bunched muscle in his shoulders and back felt as hard as steel, yet silken and warm. She ran her fingertips up the thick column of his neck, marveling at how he was made. Where she had bones poking out, he was padded with strength.

After she finished lathering his hair, he dove under to rinse, then surfaced to shake. A spray of water fanned across her. He grabbed the second jar of tomatoes. "Okay, your turn."

He waded up behind her and groped for the hem of her chemise. When his hand grazed her bare fanny, she leaped.

"What're you doing?"

He chuckled. "I can't see under the water. Sorry."

He didn't sound very sorry. She held her breath as his warm, leathery palm skimmed up her back. He didn't give her time to worry as he smeared on the tomato and began scrubbing.

"I'm afraid your chemise is ruined."

His voice sounded oddly tight and a little hoarse. Indigo decided it was probably from the cold. "I've got others. It's bloomers I'm short on."

She thought she detected a smile in his voice when he said, "What a shame."

There was laughter in his tone, and an unspoken challenge as well. "Ma's got muslin in her yardage barrel. I'll buy some from her and whip up some more bloomers on her Wheeler-Wilson."

"I don't know . . ." He curled warm fingers around her nape. "I can think of better ways to spend my money."

Indigo's pulse quickened. Trying to gauge his mood, she glanced back as he gathered her thick tresses in a fist. His expression was unreadable. When he finished working the remedy through her hair, he told her to hold her breath and dunked her to rinse her off. Then he led her to the shallows.

Indigo plucked at the front of her chemise, feeling self-conscious. The wet muslin was nearly transparent and clung to her skin. It made little sucking sounds when she pulled it away from her breasts, then immediately cleaved to her when she let go. Jake's dark eyes slid slowly over her.

"Honey, relax. I'm not looking."

Indigo had just seen him look. She eyed him suspiciously. There was a mischievous twinkle in his gaze. He seized her wrist and drew her to her knees. His fingers on her scalp felt wonderful. The only other person who had ever washed her hair was Ma, and she had tiny hands. Just one of Jake's covered Indigo's head. His touch was as gentle as her ma's, but firmer, his fingertips moving in circular motions that pulled at the muscles in her neck. Lulled by the sensation, she let the tension flow from her shoulders and surrendered to his strength.

After several latherings and rinsings, he pronounced her hair clean. Wringing it out and drawing it forward over her shoulder, she stood so he could wash her back.

She wasn't prepared for the slick heat of his hands on her bare skin. Her breath caught as his fingers skimmed across her.

"God, you feel like satin," he whispered next to her ear.

Indigo's stomach clenched, and a fiery heat began to build deep within her. She closed her eyes. She felt his hand slide up her side. Had she been sprayed by the skunk there? She supposed the stench was all over her. His hand, slick and hot, glided over her hip to her belly. The heat of his chest and flat stomach pressed against her back. His fingers gently kneaded her abdomen. Then he dove a fingertip into her navel.

Indigo gasped and stiffened. He dropped the soap and slipped his other arm around her. "Just be still," he said hoarsely. "You said you trust me, remember? Just before Stinky came along." The smile still lingered in his voice. "And if you trust me . . ."

He left the sentence unfinished. Even if she had tried to move, she couldn't have. His right arm was like a vise around her. Feeling weak, she leaned her head back. He sank with her into the water to rinse the soap from her skin. The cold curled around her, but his heat held the bite of it at bay. His mouth found hers, his lips wet and cool, yet laced with fire. She moaned when his tongue touched hers. The world went into a spin, the sky, the water, the trees all blurring in a kaleidoscope of color. Then he slid his hand from her belly to her breast.

Hardened against the cold, her nipple was shocked by the warmth of his palm. His fingertips felt like fire when they clasped the rigid peak. She whimpered at the jolt of sensation that zigzagged through her. In the back of her mind, she knew she should at least try to twist away, but she couldn't find the strength of will to make herself do it. He was making her feel so wonderful, weak and trembly, deliciously warm yet shivering.

He lifted his head, momentarily freeing her mouth. On a jagged breath, he whispered, "My God, you're precious."

Entrapped by the tangled sensations erupting inside her, she couldn't find her voice. Jake looked down at the stunned expression on her small face and smiled as another shiver ran over her. With her head tipped back, he could see the wild pulse in her throat. He hated to shatter the mood, but it was too damned cold to make love to her in the creek.

Reluctantly, he moved his hand from her breast and bent to gather her into his arms. Water streamed from their bodies as he carried her from the stream and up the bank. He knew the exact moment when passion lost its hold on her. Her body snapped taut, and she curled an arm around his neck, straining to see.

Jake covered ground fast, his aim to get her into bed as quickly as he could, before she had too much time to think. Despite his haste, she looked wide-eyed and wary when he carried her through the house and into the bedroom. Not that he was surprised. She was innocent, not stupid. When he lowered her feet to the floor beside the bed, she tried to move away.

"Oh, no," he said huskily. "Not this time."

Ignoring the alarm on her face, he grasped her chemise. She foiled his attempt to disrobe her by hugging her breasts.

"Indigo . . ." After her reaction to him in the creek, he knew she was ready; she just didn't understand the signals her body was sending her. "Raise your arms, sweetheart."

She stared up at him. For a moment, he thought she might choose now, of all times, to disobey him. But after a moment, she did as he asked. He jerked the chemise up to her elbows, left it there to entangle her arms, and bent his head to her breasts as he lowered her to the bed. The instant his mouth homed in on its target, she gasped and bucked with her hips, flailing to get her arms free from the wet muslin. Sensing her panic, he drew back.

"Whoa," he soothed. "Just be still." He peeled the dripping muslin off over her hands. "There, you see? There's no need to feel frantic."

Her huge blue eyes sought his through the evening gloom. He could feel her breasts swelling against his chest with every breath, and the longing he felt was so sharp, he shook from it.

"Jake?" she squeaked. She strained to swallow, then licked her lips. "Y—You're getting our bed wet."

Her attempt to distract him was so obvious that he would have chuckled had there been a trace of humor left in him. "I don't give a damn about the bed."

Her eyes grew rounder. "What are you going to do to me?"

Indigo knew, of course. The smoldering heat of his gaze left her in no doubt. Her numb brain registered her nakedness and the warmth of his chest against her breasts. The breadth of his glistening bronze shoulders filled her vision.

"I'm going to make love to you," he whispered silkily. "There's nothing to be afraid of. I promise you that."

And with that pronouncement, he began.

He started off with a kiss that stole her breath. An airless pounding began in her temples, and dread built within her. His heartbeat, quick and hard, thrummed through her. He slid a hand over her hip. She knew by the rigidity in his body and the fast sound of his breathing that he wasn't going to stop.

She wrenched her mouth from his, wanting the kind, gentle Jake she knew, not this hungry, frenzied man who was squashing her into the feather mattress. "A—Are you g—going to hurt me."

"I'll tell you before that happens. Trust me, honey."

Trust him? Indigo strained to keep her mouth away from his.

When he had made several unsuccessful attempts to kiss her, he raised his head. "Indigo, look at me," he whispered.

She forced herself to comply.

"I want you to make this beautiful for you."

Indigo didn't see how pain could be made beautiful.

"Have I ever deliberately hurt you?" he asked.

"No."

"Then trust me now," he urged in a husky voice. "Just lie back and trust me."

Just lie back? Franny had said that. *Just lie back in a field of daisies. It'll be over before you know it.* Indigo closed her eyes. Daisies. A huge field of daisies. A gentle breeze. And warm sunshine on her face. Ah, yes,

daisies. Daisies and birds singing. Daisies and the bab-
bling of a nearby brook. Daisies and Jake's tongue teasing the tip of her nipple.

Her eyes flew open, and she gasped. Making fists in
his hair, she gave him a violent shove. "Don't!" she
cried. "Please, don't, Jake. I—I can't think when you do
that."

"I don't want you to think," he informed her in a
husky voice and lowered his head again.

Before he found his mark, she protected it with a
cupped hand and wailed, "But—Jake, that's—I can't—
how can I think about daisies when you do stuff like
that?"

He pushed up on an arm and gazed into her eyes.
"Daisies?"

Too late, Indigo realized what she had said. Taking a
huge gulp of air, she clamped a hand over her other
breast.

"What daisies?" he demanded.

From the expression on his face, she didn't think he
was going to like her answer.

"Indigo," he persisted. "What daisies?"

"Franny's daisies," she blurted. "It's nothing, really.
Just a way for me to bear up."

She could see that had been the wrong thing to say.
He drew away and arched a black eyebrow. "Bear up?"

Indigo searched frantically for a way to explain.
"While you're—you know—so it won't be so awful."

A curious glint crept into his umber eyes. He studied
her for a moment. "Awful? Indigo, start at the beginning. Who the hell is Franny, and what daisies are you
talking about?"

With more than a little reluctance, Indigo told him
about her fears of making love, her consequent visit
with Franny, and the advice she had been given. Jake
rolled off her and draped a muscular arm over his brow.

"That day under the oak tree—you were thinking

about daisies, then, too. Weren't you?"

Indigo averted her gaze and plucked nervously at the chenille. "No, about Lobo. Franny's daisies didn't work."

"Franny, the little blond?" With a low laugh, he said, "You went to a—" He groaned. "Indigo, why in God's name did you ask Franny, of all people, for advice?"

She jerked the bedspread over herself and put some distance between them. "She's an expert?" she ventured.

"She's that, I guess. Has anyone else given you any advice I should know about?"

Indigo felt pretty certain he was angry with her for discussing something so personal with her friend. "No one else would talk to me," she admitted. "Ma just says never mind."

He lowered his arm a bit to peer out at her with a dangerously narrowed eye. "Did you ever consider coming to me?"

She sputtered at that. "I couldn't talk to *you* about it!"

"Why not? We're talking about it now." He sighed. "Honey, if you're worried about something like that, you should come to me. At least that way I know what your concerns are. How can I deal with something if you hide it from me?"

Indigo didn't want to be dealt with. Especially not by him. She stared at the bulging muscle in his chest, the rippling tracks across his belly, the dark swath of hair that ran in a dark triangle to the waistband of his jeans. Dealt with?

"I—you—it's not something you *talk* about. It's—" She wished with all her heart he would stop looking at her. He made her feel like a bug in a jar. "It's not ladylike."

"You aren't supposed to be a lady with me," he replied gently. "I'm your husband, and there's nothing you should feel uncomfortable telling me. What if something goes wrong inside you and you need to see the doctor? Franny can't take you."

Heat flooded Indigo's face. "I reckon I'd just go."

"And pay for the visit with what?" The slashes at the corners of his mouth deepened. "You're going to have to be open with me. And I think right now is a good time to start."

She thought next week would be better, maybe next month.

He rolled onto his side, and propped his head on the heel of his hand. She jerked when he grasped the bedspread, then felt foolish when all he did was tuck the edges around her.

"I wish you had told me how frightened you were at the first. As it is, you've worried needlessly all this time. I could have told you what to expect and eased your mind."

"I'm not frightened exactly," she inserted in a quavery voice. "It'd be more correct to say I'm unenthusiastic. It's sort of like tapioca—some people are wild about it, and others gag at the thought."

He brushed a knuckle over her chin, his eyes crinkling at the corners with what looked like amusement. "I'm going to tell you what to expect now, okay?"

That was the last thing she wanted. "I already know."

His mouth twitched. "I see. And what font of wisdom do I have to thank for that? Franny again?"

"No, of course not." She stared at a point just below his larynx. "Once I saw two cougars do it."

"Marvelous," he said beneath his breath. "If they go at it like house cats do, no wonder you're trembling. Honey—"

Before he could launch into a description, she inserted, "And Useless! I've seen him with the sows lots of times. And one time my Uncle Swift put his stallion in with Molly. He sent me to the house, but I heard enough to know she didn't like it."

"What if I were to promise you that you will like it?"

She lowered her lashes and tried to think of a delicate way to answer. "I'd think maybe—" She licked her lips. "Not that you'd stretch the truth or anything, but—"

He laughed under his breath. "Indigo, what purpose would it serve if I fibbed? In a few minutes, you'll find out for yourself. Then what?"

"It wouldn't matter then. I'd have already let you."

"Once," he amended. "What about after?"

Indigo sincerely hoped once would do it.

He toyed with her hair, his touch sending shivers down her neck. "I promise you're going to love it. Does that ease your mind any?" He feathered a fingertip across her lips. The ticklish sensation made her want to scratch with her teeth. "The first time, there'll be some discomfort. There's a fragile barrier inside you"—he dipped his fingertip to touch the moist inside of her bottom lip—"that will tear when I enter you. The pain will only last a few seconds, and then you'll feel nothing but pleasure. There'll be a tiny bit of blood—from the torn membrane—so don't be alarmed when you see it."

At the mention of blood, Indigo bolted to a sitting position, clutching frantically at the bedspread. "I don't think—I'm dying for a drink of water suddenly. Aren't you?"

"We just crawled out of a whole creek full of water," he reminded her in a warm voice.

"Nonetheless, I feel parched."

He trailed a fingertip up her bare arm. "As soon as we're finished, I'll bring you a dipper and a whole bucket of water."

She jerked the spread over her shoulder so her arm was covered. When he touched her, her skin prickled everywhere. "There's no need. I'll grab a drink on the way to the privy."

"Why do I have the feeling you'll be hungry next?"

That was a thought. "You know, I—" She broke off

when she saw the knowing twinkle in his eyes. "It's easy for you to laugh," she accused. "It won't be awful for you."

Somehow he had worked a hand under the bed-spread. He ran a fingertip down her calf, then traced her instep. She found it difficult to breathe. She fastened pleading eyes on his.

"It won't be awful for you, either," he whispered. "I promise."

In a low voice, he started describing exactly what he was going to do to her. Indigo wasn't surprised to hear her worst fears confirmed. "Are you absolutely bent on it?" she asked.

His hand slid to the back of her knee, then along her thigh. The heat of his touch made panic well within her. She tried to swallow it down as his fingertips climbed higher.

"Honey, let me start, okay? If we get to a part that's awful, you just tell me, hm?"

His hand came dangerously close to the apex of her thighs. Black memories flashed in her mind—things she tried never to think about—of cruel hands grabbing at her, of digging, brutal fingers. Sweat beaded on her scalp and forehead. Her heart started to slam, and she felt as if she might get sick.

Before she could stop the words, she cried, "It'll be too late then." A sob knifed through her chest, bringing a sharp pain like when she swallowed air. Only it wasn't air; she couldn't breathe. "You won't stop! I know what you'll do."

His hand stilled and curled warmly around her thigh. "What will I do?"

"You'll just keep on. Even when it hurts. You—" She stared down at him. "You won't care how it feels for me. And since you're bigger, I won't be able to make you quit."

A question crept into his eyes. "Indigo, think ratio-nally about this. Think of all the thousands—millions—

of women who make love. A blind person can see how your ma adores your father. Would she love him if he did awful things to her?"

In a high-pitched voice, she cried, "They've only got me and Chase. Maybe they only did it twice."

"That's nonsense," he said firmly.

She shoved at his hand. "You can't compare me to Ma. She isn't a squaw, and she isn't married to a—" She broke off and stared down at him, the words dying in her throat. The unfinished sentence hung between them, stark and resounding.

Jake winced as if she had struck him, and a glitter crept into his eyes. He pulled his arm from under the spread and sat up. "She isn't married to a white man? Is that it?"

The hard, bitter edge to his voice frightened her. She cast a wild glance around the room, not quite sure why she had said such a thing. It was as if a black ugliness had boiled up from a hidden place inside her. She longed to call the words back so she wouldn't see that awful look in his eyes. "I—that's not what I meant."

"Isn't it?" His face drew into harsh, dark lines that made him look like a stranger. "I think it's exactly what you meant." With a curse, he forked a hand through his hair and said, "You know, Indigo, I'm sick to death of being compared to Brandon."

"I—I don't compare you to—"

"Like hell you don't." He pushed off the bed and stood up, turning to glare down at her. "There aren't two people in this marriage, but three. You know what the saddest part is? I don't know if you realize it. You're packing around so much garbage inside your head because of what that bastard did to you that you don't know which way's up."

She reared back, her eyes as large as saucers. Jake realized he was yelling and took a deep breath, trying to cap the unreasoning anger that was trying to erupt from within him. The weeks of frustration had taken a toll. He was overreacting. In the back of his mind, he knew it. But he couldn't seem to stop himself.

He paced across the room, trying to calm down, then turned to fix smoldering dark eyes on hers. "What do you want from me?" he asked softly.

The question hung between them, an unanswerable wedge.

"N—Nothing," she finally managed.

With a low laugh, he said, "Sweetheart, don't tell me nothing." He walked back toward her. "What more can I do to prove myself to you? Name it, and it's yours. Anything."

As he swung his arm to indicate her options were limitless, she flinched away, as if to dodge a blow. For Jake, that was the last draw. "Dammit, Indigo, don't cower from me."

"I—I'm sorry!"

"You're sorry? And you think that fixes it? Do you have any idea how it feels to have you duck like you think I might strike you?"

He felt the anger taking hold of him again. He tried to shake it off. This wasn't the time or place for the words that were roiling within him. But reason eluded him.

She opened her mouth as if to speak, then snapped it closed.

He moved closer, so furious he wanted to shake her. "Do you think I might hit you when I'm angry? Is that it? Another little memento left behind by good old Brandon?" He pressed his face close to hers. "Look at me, dammit. Take a long, hard look! I'm not Brandon Marshall."

Indigo looked into his eyes and saw the pain there. Pain that she had inflicted. Instead of frightening her, his sudden flare of temper was such a startling change from his usual patience and gentleness that she felt a wave of guilt. Was it any wonder he was furious? "Oh, Jake, I—I know you're not."

"Really?" He gave a harsh laugh. "You could fool me. I've bent over backward trying to prove to you that I'm nothing like him." He jerked up the end of the mattress and swept the rock out onto the floor. "Name me another man who sleeps on boulders, goddammit, and I'll put in with you. Have I complained? Even once? Hell, no. And that's just for starters."

Indigo flicked a horrified gaze to the rock teetering on the rug, then looked back at him.

"What do you want from me?" he asked again. "Being good to you hasn't helped." When she said nothing, he snapped his fingers. "Maybe I could marry you and go three weeks without touching you." He moaned and threw up his hands in mock defeat. "But I've already done that, haven't I?"

An electrical silence fell between them. Indigo thought of all the nights when he had held her so tenderly in his arms, and tears filled her eyes. Indeed, what did she want from him? The answer was nothing; he had already given everything any man could possibly give, and then some. She squeezed her eyes closed and tried to breathe around the ache in her chest. The smell of vanilla filled her nostrils.

"Maybe I could stop by the general store every evening and buy you peppermint. Better yet, maybe I could go without my dinner and take you walking every night so you can be in your woods? Now there's an idea. A little hunger after working my ass off all day wouldn't hurt me, not if it'd make you happy. Or maybe I could promise never to make you leave Wolf's Landing." He laughed under his breath. "But I've already done all that."

Seeing her behavior through his eyes made Indigo feel so ashamed she wanted to die. "Oh, Jake, please, that's enough."

"I haven't even started," he came back. He began to pace the room again. In the dimness, she could see that he was shaking. At the bureau, he turned. "You know, I don't blame you. I've committed the unforgivable crime."

When he left that comment hanging, she couldn't resist asking, "Wh—What was that?"

His eyes glittered across the room at her. "I was born white." He lifted his hands and glanced down at himself. "Guilty as charged. I'm a no-good white bastard, always have been, always will be. There's no changing it. And you know what that means. You don't dare trust me. The minute you do, I might turn on you. Just like Brandon did."

Indigo strained to speak, but there were no words. She pressed a hand over her eyes and finally managed, "Oh, Jake, it isn't like that. It isn't like that at all!"

"It's exactly like that. I didn't stand a chance in hell from day one. You never gave me one." His voice throbbed. "Do you know how it felt that day by Lobo's grave when you thought the surprise I had waiting for you here was a beating? Have you any idea how it hurt, knowing you thought I was capable of that? Not because of anything I did, but because I'm white?"

The raw pain in his voice lingered in the air long after he stopped speaking.

"Do you think I can't bleed, Indigo? Well, let me tell you something. It hurts me just as badly as it hurts you to be judged and condemned because of my skin." His voice raked over her. "And while we're on the subject of race, there's another little truth you need to face. You aren't proud of your Indian blood. A near miss, that's what you are, damned near white, but not quite. A squaw who'll never measure up."

The words cut into her like a lash. Even as she shook her head and cried, "No," she recognized the truth in them.

"Take a long hard look inside yourself, sweetheart. A

journey within, isn't that what you called it? You make yours with your eyes closed. Maybe I'm the no-good bastard you think I am, but at least I see my ugly side. You've dressed yours all up with brittle pride, thumbing your nose at the world, pitting yourself against men, hiding behind squaw clothes so you'll never again make the mistake of forgetting what you are. Brandon showed you what could happen if you stepped out of your place."

Indigo clamped her hands over her ears. True or not, she didn't want to hear this, couldn't bear it. "Stop it!"

"No, by God, I won't stop it. If I have to rub your nose in the truth to make this marriage work, I'll do it every damned hour of every day until you open your eyes and face it."

She shook her head.

"You're in a hell of a spot, aren't you? You can't decide who you hate worse, me or yourself."

"No, please, no . . ."

His voice vibrant with disgust, he said, "How can I possibly have any regard for you? *You?* A nothing squaw? You've been walking on thin ice from the second you married me. Correction! Not walking, groveling. So I won't slap you into line. Your mother argues with your father. She may obey him in the end, but she's not afraid to stand up for herself. But do you dare? Hell, no, you're married to a white man."

Indigo clutched at the bedspread and hugged it around herself, feeling as if it was all that held her together. The only sounds that broke the silence were her broken sobs and Jake's uneven breathing. She flinched when he spoke again.

"Where's your knife, Indigo? Since the day you married me, you stopped wearing it. Your parents say you used to practice with it every day."

She sucked in a whine of air. "I—I didn't think you'd like for m—me to."

He gave a shaky laugh. "True enough. Your being that handy with a knife makes you all the more Indian, doesn't it? And talking to animals? What white woman can do that?" He motioned toward the window. "And we can't forget Lobo. The truth is that you leave the window open for him because you believe his spirit is out there, that it'll always be, and you want him to know you haven't closed your heart to him. When I asked, you alluded to that, but you couldn't come right out and say it, could you? It's an Indian belief. It makes you something less. Isn't that right?"

His eyes demanded an answer. When she said nothing, he went on. "You were afraid to be open about any of those things, for fear I'd wake up and see you for what you really are. A squaw. Three-quarters white, but still a nothing."

The accusation stripped her. In her mind's eye, she saw herself more clearly in that moment than she ever had. "I'm *not* a nothing! How dare you say that to me?"

"You aren't all white. In your books, that makes you a nothing."

She stared up at him, unable to accept what he was saying, even though she knew it was partly true. "No! I'm proud to be Comanche."

"Words," he sneered. "They sound good. And you tried to live them. It was your insurance, wasn't it? If you wore those leathers like a flag of glory and that God-awful hat, what white man would look at you, let alone want to marry you? God forbid that should happen. Brandon and his friends showed you how a white man would treat you, didn't they?"

She passed a hand over her eyes.

"Then I came along." He stood with his fists clenched at his sides, the bunched muscle in his arms sharply delineated beneath the bronze overlay of flesh. "And I wanted you, leathers and all. A white man who didn't run the other direction. A white man your father liked, which made me even worse. I spelled trouble from the second you laid eyes on me. No matter how nicely I treated you, you knew I had an ugly side. I had to because I was white."

His gaze routed through the dimness, as dark as obsidian. She moaned and tried to stifle the sound with her palm.

He waved a hand. "And that brings us to now, doesn't it? A squaw about to be used by a white man. Who I am doesn't count. All you can see is what I am." He dragged in a breath. "I'm sorry as hell about that, but this is the skin I was born in."

He walked slowly toward her.

"What am I supposed to do now, Indigo? Do we start with you getting on your knees to me? That's where squaws belong, right? I don't want to disappoint you."

She fastened horrified eyes on him.

"Oh, yes, I heard what he said to you that day, every ugly, sick word. Come on." He snapped his fingers and pointed at the floor. "Right here in front of me. Let's see you crawl. Isn't this what you've been waiting for? For me to see you for what you really are and treat you the way Brandon did?"

"That isn't fair," she whispered tremulously.

"Fair? Have you been fair to me?" he asked in a taut voice.

Indigo stared at him through a blur of tears. She hadn't been fair to him, never once, right from the start. "Oh, Jake, forgive me. Please forgive me. I know I've behaved badly. And I—I'm sorry."

His eyes, dark and shadowed with hurt, searched hers for an endlessly long moment. Then he whispered, "If you're sorry, really sorry, get on your knees and say it. Prove to me and to yourself, right here and now, that you know I'm nothing like Brandon Marshall."

Indigo knotted her hands into fists. "You're nothing like him," she sobbed. "I know you're not."

"Prove it. Face doing the one thing that terrifies you the most and put it behind you," he urged, his voice ragged. "Trust me, and find out once and for all what I think a squaw is good for. I swear on my life you won't regret it."

Memories slid through Indigo's mind, ugly and stark. She saw herself at thirteen, standing in a clearing with five men moving in on her, all determined to make her crawl for them. *Indian slut.* The name echoed inside her head. She looked at the floor where Jake had pointed, and it seemed as if it was a hundred miles away. He was nothing like Brandon Marshall and his friends. She knew that. But God help her, she couldn't get on her knees to him.

Her shoulders jerking with sobs, she cried. "I—I can't."

"Why?"

"I—I'm afraid," she admitted. "I shouldn't be. I know I shouldn't be. But I can't help it. I'm afraid."

His face chiseled with pain, he regarded her for a moment. Then he sighed. "Thank you for that much, at least. The truth, for once. I didn't think I'd ever hear you say it. The two most difficult words in the English language, right? 'I'm afraid.'"

With that, he turned for the door.

She pictured him walking out and never coming back. Her stomach clenched around a ball of pain. "Where are you going?"

He jerked the door back with such force it hit the wall. Pausing on the threshold, he said, "I'm getting the hell out of here before I do something I'll regret."

She tugged frantically on the bedspread, trying to gather the extra folds. "Jake, wait. Please, wait. Let me explain."

"Explain? It's crystal clear to me already." He laughed harshly. "Do you know what the heartbreak is? I could have had you"—he snapped his fingers—"just like that.

If I didn't care about your feelings, I would have—probably a dozen times a day this last three weeks. The fact that I haven't counts for nothing with you."

With that parting shot, he walked out. An instant later, the front door slammed. She bowed her head and swayed from side to side, holding her middle. The pain inside her was almost more than she could bear. He was leaving, and she didn't blame him. He would probably keep going. And why not? She hadn't given him a single reason to want to stay.

The words he had flung at her played back inside her head, over and over, making more and more sense each time she heard them. *A nothing squaw.* Slowly, painfully, she realized what Jake had been trying to make her see, not that he had that lowly opinion of her, but that she did.

Pictures of him flooded her mind. His lazy smile. The way his eyes warmed when he looked at her. He was probably on his way to the creek to get his boots. Then he'd come back to get his things. And then he'd go because she couldn't tell him how desperately she wanted him to stay.

21

The house was dark when Jake returned. After closing the door, he stood until his eyes grew accustomed to the darkness. Moonlight spilled through the window, gilding the furniture with splashes of silver. He listened to the silence, then closed his eyes on a wave of regret. Had he really expected her to be here after all the terrible things he had said to her?

Picking his way through the shadows, Jake groped for the settee and collapsed on it. It was surprising how clear a man's mind could get after sitting outside in the dark for an hour, freezing his ass off. Leaning back his head, he stared at the wash of moonlight on the ceiling. Moonbeams. A girl who walked on moonbeams. Tears filled his eyes. Jesus, what a bastard he was. What right did he have to rip her apart?

Jake propped an elbow on the arm of the settee and covered his eyes with his hand. Every nasty word he had said to her played through his mind. He hadn't left her a shred of dignity or a single delusion. As if she was the only person on earth who hid behind a mask? A fine one he was to throw stones.

Why? Why in God's name had he lost his temper like that? He had made it sound as if three weeks without sex was an eternity, as if she had used him for a doormat the entire time. Poor old Jake. He was one mistreated son of a bitch. He thought she had problems seeing the forest for the trees? Where the hell was his own head buried? Up his ass, he guessed. How else could he expect an inexperienced and frightened girl to roll on her back and spread her legs after knowing him less than a month?

Now what? He supposed he could go to her parents' house and drag her home. After all, he didn't have to worry anymore about what she thought of him. Tonight, he'd sunk as low as he could go. Or he could do the decent thing and set her free. The marriage could still be annulled. He could get out of her life and leave her with what little dignity he hadn't destroyed.

A nothing squaw. Why had he said that to her? Sometimes a person's deepest feelings were too painful to expose to the light of day. But had he hesitated? Hell, no. All he'd been able to think about was the ache in his groin. May Belle had called it like it was; his brains were between his legs. He'd been a prince, Indigo owed him, and he had been bent on getting his reward.

Something cold and wet touched Jake's toe. He started, then leaned over to spy Sonny snuffling around his feet. Indigo wouldn't have left the puppy behind. Afraid to hope, he sat erect and threw a look over his shoulder.

Shivering like a lost child, she stood in the shadows of the hall, a wraith draped in white chenille, her tawny hair ignited by a shaft of moonlight.

"You're still here," he said stupidly.

She glided forward a few steps. "I w—waited so I could see you be—before you left."

Jake's chest tightened. What did he expect? An invitation to stay? He turned back around and draped his arms over his knees, petting Sonny's head with one dangling hand. Tears tickled his cheeks. The last time he had cried was at his mother's grave. That seemed fitting; for the second time in his life, he was losing the most important person in his world. He blinked and prayed that he'd think of something to say that might convince her to give him one more chance. There was no God in heaven. The only word that came to him was her name.

Indigo. A month ago, the word had conjured vague images of blue. Now, he thought of wind songs and daisies, of moonbeams and the howling of wolves, of sweetness and purity. He'd told her to look at the ugliness inside herself. How had he dared?

Intending to beg her forgiveness, Jake said, "Indigo, I—"

She stepped forward. "No, don't! Please, don't say it!"

She twisted her hands in the folds of the bedspread. Shaking so badly he was afraid she might fall, she circled the settee and came to stand in front of him. Before he guessed what she meant to do, she sank to her knees and let the chenille slide down her slender arms.

Nearly strangling on a sob, she cried, "I—I'm saying it on my knees. Will you f—forgive me?"

"Oh, Jesus, don't." Jake grasped her shoulders. The shudders wracking her body vibrated up his arms.

Her small face contorted, and she held her breath for a moment, trying to stifle the convulsive sobs. "I don't think you're like Brandon. I'm sorry for making you th—think that."

"Sweetheart, I didn't mean it. Get up from there. I lost my temper and laced into you when I didn't have—"

She gave her head a wild shake. "No!" she wailed. "What you said. It's true. M—Most of it's true. I d—did feel like I was a n—nothing." She held her breath again, looking up at him with tear-swollen, pleading eyes that shimmered like silver in the moonlight. A sob broke

ree, the air whistling from her lungs in a tearing rush.
And th—then you came. And you started to make me
eel like something." She lifted quivering hands in word-
ess appeal. "P—Please don't go away. If you'll give me
one more chance, I'll ch—change. You'll see. I truly
vill. I won't be afraid anymore. And I won't think about
laisies. And I w—won't lie. And when I think you're
;oing to hit me, I w—won't duck."

A thousand words crowded into Jake's throat, but he
:ouldn't force them out past the lump of shame. Dear
God, what had he done to her? She wouldn't duck. For
;ome reason, her saying that hurt him worse than any-
hing else. She had been afraid, and instead of reassur-
ng her, he had yelled at her.

Since he couldn't talk, he did the only thing he knew
o do and slid off the settee. With trembling arms, he
;athered her close and buried his face in her silken hair.

For several seconds, he struggled to say something,
mything. When he finally managed, all he could get out
vas her name and three words, "I love you." Since grop-
ng for words was typical of him and the three he had
lredged up weren't particularly profound, he didn't
:xpect them to work the kind of magic that they did.
ndigo wrapped her arms around his neck and clung to
iim, whispering, "Oh, Jake . . . I love you, too."

There was no mistaking her fear; he could feel it in
he rigidity of her body and the wild pounding of her
leart. He knew what it had cost her to approach him as
;he had, naked and on her knees. That she had found
he courage to do it made her all the more precious to
iim. It also told him just how much she did love him.
He wished he could find the words to tell her that.

Jake tightened his arms around her, glorying in the
eel of her velvety skin beneath his hands. He traced the
ragile ladder of her ribs and smiled at the way she
eemed to shrink beneath his touch. Courageous as she
vas, she was still a long way from fearless. But wasn't

that what love was all about, taking risks?

She leaned back. Her huge, luminous eyes sought his through the dimness. "Do you forgive me? I'll throw the r—rock away."

Relief made Jake feel almost giddy. With more than a little chagrin, he recalled his behavior and wished he could take it all back. Bless her heart, he'd sleep on a whole bed of rocks if it would make her happy. "I think the question here is whether you can forgive me." The hurt in her expression made him want to kick himself. "It wasn't the rock or the daisies or that you were afraid. What set me off was that you still weren't ready to make love. I can't even dress it up and say it was stung pride talking. The honest-to-God truth is that I've had an ache for you since the moment I set eyes on you, and after three weeks of holding myself in check, knowing you were mine to take—" He broke off and swallowed. "It was pure selfishness. I'm sorry."

"I'm ready now," she proclaimed in a tremulous voice. She gave a vehement nod. "Truly, I am."

Jake laughed under his breath. She wasn't exactly oozing enthusiasm. The tips of her nipples grazed his chest, and he felt the jolt in his groin. With a strained effort, he said, "Do you have any idea how much I love you? And how awful I feel about the things I said to you?"

She gulped air. "It was mostly true. Practically all of it. Except the part about h—hating you. And thinking you're like Brandon. I—I've known better for a long time." Her mouth started to quiver and her chin dimpled. "It's k—kind of like being afraid of something in the dark. You kn-know nothing's really there, but you can't stop feeling scared. I can't think it away."

The ache in Jake's chest intensified.

She took a breath and rushed on. "When my father asked me to marry you, I thought maybe you'd—" She squeezed her eyes closed and made a soft sound in her hroat. "It's not the same for men. When they get married, they're still the boss. But a woman has no control, and whether or not she's happy depends totally upon her husband." She strained to swallow. "Some husbands think of wives as possessions only good for serving their wants, and having babies, and taking care of the house."

Jake knew he had appeared guilty on that count.

"It's a thousand times worse for squaws if they marry men like that. A million times worse, because they're nothing people and no one really cares how they're treated."

Jake tried to speak, but she cut him off.

"It's true! I've s—seen it. White men marry squaws and treat them worse than dogs. And I was afraid." Her voice trailed off. "I didn't know you very well." She licked at her upper lip and sniffed. "I was scared if I made you angry, that you'd be mean. And—" Her gaze chased off from his. "And I was afraid you wouldn't be very nice when you—when you—did private things to me."

Private things? At least it was a step up from awful. Jake leaned over and grabbed the bedspread. Using a corner, he dabbed at her upper lip and her streaming cheeks. He could feel wetness on his chest where her tears had trickled down her breasts.

"The 'yes, my husband' part? That wasn't a lie. It truly is the way of my father's people. A wife is submissive in all things. It sounds awful, but amongst the People, it isn't because a husband honors his wife and looks upon her with great regard. It's only awful when she marries a white man who scorns her." She rubbed the heel of her hand across her eyes. "I had no way of knowing how you'd treat me."

"Oh, sweetheart . . ."

A shiver ran over her. "One time we w—went to a fair in J'ville, and a tr—trapper came with his squaw.

She spilled the plate of food that he bought her. It was just an accident, but he acted as if she'd done it on purpose. He called her vile names and kicked her for wasting his money. Then he told her she could just get on her hands and knees and eat it out of the dirt. The other people standing around laughed because she did it. They laughed." A world of heartbreak was reflected in her shimmering eyes. "The trapper bragged that she would do anything he wanted. A stupid squaw, he called her."

She covered her face with her hands. "I know you're not like that now. But I couldn't help feeling scared. Sometimes my father is too trusting. Because he has only goodness in his own heart, he sees only the good in others. I was afraid he had done that with you. I'm sorry."

He gathered the bedspread around her and drew her back into his arms, shaking as badly as she. He tried to imagine how she saw the world, how she felt, knowing there were men who might mistreat her like that if she gave them an opportunity. He remembered her pallor during their wedding, her tremulous fear after, and he understood her as he never had before. Yet here she was, naked and on her knees, asking him for forgiveness?

"Indigo, I'm the one who's sorry." He smoothed a hand over her hair. "So sorry."

Jake swayed with her. Holding her felt so perfectly right. So incredibly and unbelievably right. He never wanted to let her go. He dried his cheek on her hair. Then he bent his head and nuzzled his way to the sweet curve of her neck. If a trace of skunk was left, he couldn't smell it. "Can we agree to forgive each other?" he asked huskily. "Or should we fight about it?"

She rewarded him with a wet, strangled laugh. He drew her gently to her feet. Not sure if she was shivering from nerves or cold, he tucked the folds of chenille around her. Looking down at her face, which had become so precious to him, Jake thought of the squaw who'd crawled around eating her food from the dirt. He wanted to drive the fear of that happening from Indigo's mind forever. Yet he knew words alone would never be enough.

Running his hands up and down her arms, Jake whispered, "I want you to stand right where you are. Don't move and don't speak. Will you do that?"

Though she looked both puzzled and apprehensive, she nodded. Jake gave her shoulders a reassuring squeeze, then released her. What he was about to do went completely against his nature. Until this instant, in fact, he would have stood his ground and fought to the death before he even considered it. After taking a deep breath, he sank to his knees in front of her.

The first feeling that hit Jake was humiliation, wave after wave of it. Then acute embarrassment. Grand gestures weren't his way; he didn't have the eloquence to carry them off. Now that he was down here, he couldn't think of one damned thing to say. Not a single goddamned thing. She'd think he was crazy.

Which he supposed he was. . . . Crazy in love. He tipped his head back to look up at her. Her eyes filled with tears again, but, obedient as always, she didn't speak. She didn't have to. Jake could see the incredulous expression in her gaze, and that told him all he needed to know. He no longer felt idiotic. Bending low, he curled his hands around her fine-boned ankles and kissed the tops of her small feet.

"Oh, don't . . ." she cried. "Jake, don't . . ."

Releasing her, he slowly straightened. His voice thick with emotion, he said, "That's what this white man thinks his squaw is good for."

She covered her face with her hands and started to weep, the cries coming up from her chest, dry and tearing. Her legs buckled. Jake caught her as she sank to the floor. Holding her cradled in his arms, he rocked her and stroked her hair. As difficult as it was to hear her cry, he knew the tears had been six years in coming, and that she could never completely put Brandon Marshall behind her until she purged herself of the pain.

Between sobs, she began telling him about that day. Jake could almost visualize the clearing in the woods and the five men who had lured her there. Indigo, at thirteen. Moisture burned in Jake's eyes. At nineteen, she was still a child in so many ways, shielded as she had been from the world outside Wolf's Landing. He had never known anyone quite so pure of heart. How innocent and trusting she must have been as a pubescent girl in love for the first time. His heart broke a little for that child and for the woman he now held in his arms. Her only sin had been being born.

What hit Jake the hardest was her sense of betrayal. She had adored Brandon and trusted him. Until he sprang his trap in the clearing, he had treated her like glass and showered her with flowery compliments. Was it any wonder she was terrified to feel that way again about another white man? Suddenly Jake was able to see himself through her eyes and understand the uncertainty that must have plagued her. Was he what he appeared to be, a kind and gentle man who truly cared for her? Or was he a treacherous monster playing a cruel game of cat and mouse?

"Indigo," he whispered. "I want you to listen to me and listen good because I don't ever want you to forget this. You're the most beautiful person I've ever known. The last place you should ever be is on your knees—to me or to anyone else. I lost my temper, and I said things I shouldn't have. Asking you to get on your knees was unforgivable. I want that knife back on your hip as of tomorrow. Understand? And I don't care if you give oratories to the animals in the woods."

A wet laugh caught in her throat. "All right."

"And another thing," he added huskily. "From here

on out, it's my wish, my command, my order"—he smiled and brushed the hair from her lovely eyes—"that you never obey me when my wishes put you in a situation that humiliates you. Never."

She fastened a troubled gaze on his. "But . . . you're my husband. I must obey you, always."

Jake grasped her chin. "Not when it means you have to sacrifice your dignity." He trailed his gaze over her face. "I mean it. I'll carve the command in stone if I have to, because I never want you to forget it. Your pride means far more to me than your unquestioning obedience. If I'm ever so stupid as to ask something debasing of you, I want you to tell me to go straight to hell. Have I made myself clear?"

"Yes," she murmured. "Very clear."

Acutely aware that he was asking her to go against all that she believed and that she probably wouldn't do it if the moment ever came, Jake said, "Swear it."

She looked uncertain. "Jake, I—"

"Swear it," he insisted in a raw voice. "Right now, so it's forever out of the way. I never want you to remember that squaw eating from off the ground and worry that the same thing could happen to you." He grasped her chin again and gave her a little shake. "Swear it."

"I—I swear it," she finally replied. "I don't think it's right, but I swear it."

"It feels right to me, and since I'm the husband in this household, that's the way it's going to be."

Jake lifted her off his lap and pushed to his feet, drawing her up with him. His gaze shifted to her shivering shoulders. "You're going to catch your death," he said huskily. "Without fires going, this house is as cold as a tomb."

She drew back and scrubbed at her face with the heels of her hands. He lifted a corner of the bedspread to dab at her cheeks again. When the last trace of wetness was gone, he bent to kiss her shimmering eyes closed and scooped her into his arms. When he reached the bedroom, he lowered her to sit on the bed and went to the bureau for her flannel gown.

"I won't be needing that," she said in a shaky voice.

Jake turned toward her and froze. She sat in a shaft of moonlight. The bedspread lay in folds around her hips. She looked so beautiful with her hair draped around her like molten silver, her dusky-tipped breasts peeking through the strands at him. His gaze dropped to her slender waist, which flowed gently into well-rounded hips and supple thighs.

"Indigo . . ." He curled his fingers in the flannel. "Honey, we don't have to—"

"I w—want to," she insisted in a thin voice. "Really."

Jake's mouth curved in a smile. He had received more enthusiastic invitations. "I don't think tonight is—"

"Please? I don't want to feel afraid anymore."

The flannel slipped from Jake's numb fingers and fell forgotten to the floor. A saint, he wasn't. "Are you sure?"

She answered with a determined nod. Jake took a step toward her. Damn, how could he resist?

In truth, Indigo wasn't at all sure about anything. She was still just as afraid as she had been two hours ago. But she loved this man, and if she had to lie with him to keep him, she was willing to do it, tonight and every night.

As he moved toward her, the fear moved up into her throat and suffocated her. She wasn't positive what she expected him to do. To immediately start kissing her, she guessed. And to lie with her on the bed and start grabbing her private places. Instead, he hunkered down in front of her. She wanted to cover herself so badly that she had to make fists in the bedspread.

In the moonlight, his dark eyes were shot through with glints of silver. His gaze moved slowly over her. It was the most humiliating few seconds of her life.

"Do you have any idea how lovely you are?" He touched a hand to her cheek, then traced her nose and lips with a gentle fingertip. "Sometimes during the night I wake up and lie here just looking at you while you sleep. I'm afraid to move for fear you'll vanish like a beam of moonlight erased by a shadow."

Indigo tried to speak, but all that came out was a squeak.

He trailed a finger across her collarbone. "Honey, you're shaking like a leaf."

She strained to swallow.

He brushed a callused thumb across her mouth. "You're frightened."

She gave a jerky nod. "A little."

Jake bit back a smile. She looked so young sitting there, her eyes giant spheres of dread, her features taut. Taking her by the shoulders, he gently laid her back and settled himself beside her, his upper body supported on an elbow. Placing a hand on her waist, he bent his head to kiss her eyes closed.

"Tell me about your daisies," he whispered as he trailed his lips to her earlobe. "Are they white, pink, red?"

"White," she gasped as his teeth nipped at the sensitive place below her ear. "Wh—White with yellow centers."

"Where are they? On a hillside?"

Indigo squeezed her eyelids more tightly shut, trying frantically to bring up the images so she wouldn't feel his teeth nibbling along her neck. His breath, whisper-soft, washed over her skin and sent shivers down her spine. "They're in a meadow."

"Mm." He nibbled at her throat. "A big meadow?"

"Yes . . . with a brook running through it." She felt his teeth pinch lightly at the beginning swell of her left breast, and her eyes flew open. When he had described the things he would do to her, he hadn't mentioned biting. Not that it hurt. Yet. She watched in frozen horror as he nibbled his way toward her nipple. "Jake?"

"Hm? Daisies, Indigo. Just close your eyes and think about daisies." With light, teasing little nips, he circled her nipple. "White ones with yellow centers, remember?"

All Indigo could see was her traitorous flesh hardening and thrusting eagerly toward his mouth. Her body didn't seem to realize what was in store for it. With each pass, he circled closer and closer to the dusky crest. Between the little bites, he started tickling her with the end of his tongue. The tip of her breast started to swell, and with every beat of her heart it throbbed, as if all the blood in her body was pulsing into it.

His tongue flicked from her skin onto the sensitive pebbled flesh. The throbbing turned to a sharp ache. She took a ragged breath, then gasped when he finally seized the swollen peak. Expecting pain, she stiffened, then whimpered as a shock of sheer pleasure rocked through her. He rolled her with teasing little bites, then clasped her firmly with his white teeth and dragged his tongue over her. Once, twice. Indigo jerked with each pass. It felt—not exactly nice, but not exactly unpleasant, either. Unsettling, maybe. Jarring was a better word. No. . . . Frustrating, that was how it felt. It made her want. But she wasn't sure what. Sort of like when she got to craving something and ate everything in sight trying to satisfy the need. Only worse . . . much, much worse.

With a low moan, she ran her fingers into his thick hair and arched toward him. She sensed that he knew what he was doing to her, and the frustration grew until she had a good mind to give his hair a yank. She hated to be teased, and this was the worst ever. "Jake?"

In reply, he closed his hot mouth around her and gave a sharp pull that curled her toes. She sobbed and held on to him for dear life. Wave after wave of electrical sensation streamed through her. Her belly knotted and began to spasm. Deep within her, a fiery heat started to build. Hungrily, he switched to the other breast and suckled it. Then he began to tease her again with the light nips of his teeth, until she writhed with yearning for his mouth to close over her again.

When he drew away she felt strangely empty and alone. His eyes sought hers. Then he bent to kiss her forehead. "Do you trust me?" he asked in a throbbing whisper.

"Y—Yes."

He cupped her face between his hands. "Are you frightened?"

"Yes."

Jake's heart caught at the myriad emotions swimming in her eyes. Confusion, apprehension, and yearning. There was also a world of love shining there. Far more than he deserved. "There's no need to be afraid. What I just did, was it nice?"

"Yes, sort of," she admitted. "The first part was— maddening. The last part was nice, though. Very nice."

"The rest will be even better."

"It will?"

"I swear it."

She turned her cheek against his hand. "When will the hurting part come?"

"I'll tell you beforehand, just like I promised." He rubbed his thumb along her jaw. "But I don't want you to worry about it. It'll happen so fast, you'll hardly feel it. It'll hurt a lot less than the cut you gave yourself on your arm."

Her eyes widened on his. "And then never again?"

"Never again."

The tenderness in his eyes soothed Indigo in a way words couldn't. His chest grazed her breasts and sent a tingle through her. She wanted to feel his mouth on her again, but she was embarrassed to ask. With trembling hands, she made fists in his hair and pulled his head close, telling him with her body what she couldn't say with words. He gratified her with a thoroughness that left her head spinning. Then he abandoned her breasts and sought her mouth.

Indigo felt as if she was melting into him. She ran her hands over the bunched muscle in his shoulders and parted her lips to grant his tongue entry. He curled a warm hand around her hip, his fingers kneading, then lightly stroking. Then she felt his callused palm slide to her belly. Very lightly, his fingertips slipped into the curly nest at the apex of her thighs.

"Don't be afraid," he whispered against her lips. He coaxed her legs slightly apart. "There's my girl."

His knowledgeable fingers played lightly over her until the place between her thighs began to ache. Lifting his head to kiss her neck, he whispered, "God, you're so sweet. Just touching you makes me crazy."

Lost in a swirl of sensation, she let her head fall back to accommodate his silken lips. Need filled her, and she clamped her thighs around his hand and lifted her hips, uncertain what it was she wanted.

Jake knew. She dug her nails into his shoulders and bowed her back, her breath coming in short, quick little pants. Jake smiled in the moonlit darkness, wondering what color her daisies were now. He watched her face as he brought her to climax. An expression of sheer bewilderment touched her features, and her lashes lifted. At the first spasm, her eyes filled with fright.

"It's all right, honey," he soothed. "Just let it come."

Another spasm rocked her. Jake's heart caught at the confusion he read in her startled gaze. "Sweetheart, trust me."

Afterward, while she lay there quivering and dazed, Jake jerked off his jeans and moved between her legs. When he grasped her hips, she opened her eyes and gazed up at him from beneath passion-heavy eyelids.

With all his strength of will, Jake held himself in

check. He wanted her. Never had he ached so for a woman. After taking such care to get her past the fear, he hated to jolt her back to awareness. But he had promised to warn her. First, he decided to check out the situation. Maybe, just maybe, a miracle would happen, and he could slip in without causing her pain.

He eased his hips forward and pressed into her. His breathing harsh and ragged, Jake eased in a little more. He hated to hurt her. The God's truth was, he didn't know how bad it would be. He'd made it his habit to avoid bedding virgins, so his experience in this arena was nil. By the way her mouth was drawn, he knew he was already causing her discomfort, and he hadn't even begun yet.

"Indigo," he whispered hoarsely.

She focused large, trusting eyes on him. "Now?" she asked in a faint little voice.

Before she could tense up, which he felt certain would increase her pain, Jake whispered, "Yes, now," and drove his hips forward. Her body went rigid, and she gave a shrill cry. Jake broke out in a cold sweat. After sinking himself into her, he drew her into his arms and went still. She clung to his neck.

"It hurts," she cried.

Jake clenched his teeth, in an agony of regret because he was bringing her pain, and guilt because, even though he knew he was hurting her, he didn't want to stop. Being inside her felt more wonderful than anything he had ever experienced. Her body sheathed him so tightly. That alone could have pushed him over the edge.

"Oh, God, Indigo, I'm sorry."

Unable to hold back, he moved his hips. She gasped and held her breath. Loath to hurt her, Jake forced himself to go still again. While he lay there embracing her, trying to soothe her, the building pressure inside him exploded, and he spent himself like a randy youth with his first woman. He squeezed his eyes closed and quivered, letting it come since he didn't have a hell of a lot to say about it.

Indigo gasped again as his heat flooded through her. With a little sigh, she whispered, "Oh my . . ." He felt the tension drain out of her. Then, like a novice drummer marching to her own beat, completely oblivious to the fact that she was out of step with the rest of the band, she undulated her hips.

Jake didn't know whether to laugh or cry. His body felt like a wet, wrung out rag, and now she was responding? On arms that quivered with weakness, he suspended himself above her, determined to come through for her if it killed him. Which it might, he decided. His heart was slamming like a sledge.

In the moonlight, he could see the silver tracks of her tears on her cheeks. She lifted a luminous gaze to his. An incredulous, glowing little smile touched her lips. She raised her hips in artless, awkward abandon, a little off center, and without the force that he knew would bring her pleasure. But even so, the muscles in her face tightened. With a joyous moan, she retreated, then bumped against him again.

"Oh, Jake," she whispered. "I love you. Oh, yes . . ."

Jake's thoughts were more along the line of "Oh, no . . ." But then every man had at least one miracle coming to him in his lifetime, and while watching his innocent little wife discover the pleasures of lovemaking, Jake finally got his. Unbelievably, incredibly, he felt another flash of fire course through his loins. Still trembling from one release, he felt the pressure of another begin to build. Carefully, he moved forward to meet the clumsy little thrusts of Indigo's slender hips, letting her set the pace, filled with an aching pleasure at the sound of her shaky little moans and shrill cries as she experienced her first jolts of ecstasy.

Then passion pulled him into the vortex with her. He

took over and set a more masterful rhythm, one which he knew would bring her far more pleasure. He nearly grinned when she bent her knees and clasped his hips between her thighs to better absorb the impact. She was so infinitely precious, so completely without guile. He wanted this to be beautiful for her.

Suddenly, she arched and stiffened. Jake's body responded with a primal ferocity. As his second climax in less than four minutes rocked over him, he had two surprisingly rational thoughts. One was that he had to be breaking some kind of world record—not that anyone documented phenomena of this sort. The second was a little more profound.

After a lifetime of not being entirely certain, he was now absolutely positive there was such a place as heaven. It wasn't in California, as he had believed years ago, and contrary to popular opinion, a man didn't have to die to get there. Heaven was right here on earth . . . in Indigo's arms.

22

Dawn streaked the leaden sky with wisps of light, touching the bedroom with a rosy glow. From behind his closed eyelids, Jake saw the pinkness and wondered if he had died and gone to heaven after all. He felt Indigo's bare breasts against his chest and her slender thigh clasped between his. If this wasn't heaven, he didn't know what was.

As lightly as butterfly wings, he felt her fingertips tracing the lines of his face and realized what had woken him. He was being explored. He resisted the temptation to open his eyes. If she realized he was awake, she'd probably turn shy.

She touched his nose, following the ridge with a timid fingertip. Then she explored his mouth, his ear, the texture of his hair. When she drew back and skimmed her palms over his chest, he nearly smiled. The male nipple was obviously a curiosity. Tenderness welled within him when she toyed with it, as he had hers, trying to elicit the same response. She captured the peak and rolled it between her fingers. He lifted his lashes slightly. Her huge eyes were filled with childlike wonder.

Evidently bored by his unresponsive nipple, she checked out his chest hair and then prodded the pads of muscle. Next she walked her fingertips down his rib cage. Jake's breath caught when she followed the line of hair on his belly to its destination. A tiny frown puckered her delicate brows when she curled her hand around his limp manhood. She gave it a tentative little squeeze. Her frown deepened. She traced the crown.

Mistaking the tantalizing touches of female fingertips as a call to muster, his flaccid appendage came to rigid attention. She went still, gazing down at the swollen rod she found herself holding. Her eyes widened, and she jerked her hand back as if it burned her. Her startled gaze flew to his.

The game was up. . . . Jake cracked a smile. "Are you looking for trouble, Mrs. Rand? If so, you just found it."

Crimson flooded her face, and she started to scoot away. He caught her around the waist. "Where are you off to so fast? I was hoping it was my turn next."

Her face flushed a deeper red. "You're awake."

Wide awake, Jake realized, the victim of an unintentional seduction. He drew his other arm from under the pillow and mimicked her, tracing the lines of her face and feigning curious awe. He slowly worked toward her chest and explored her nipple.

"What do we have here?" he asked in a husky voice. "Interesting, very interesting. Do they have a specific use, or are they just for pretty?"

Her eyes darkened and turned turbulent when he captured a hard little peak and lightly pinched it. Jake slid his palm under her breast and lifted it. Bending his head, he tasted with the tip of his tongue.

"It's delicious. Do you mind if I have a nibble or two or three?"

Her lips parted and she expelled a soft little sigh.

Jake lay back and grinned. "Selfish with them, are you?"

A heated languor entered her eyes, and her lashes drooped. She leaned forward to put her breast more fully in his hand. He cupped it with his palm and rubbed his thumb over her aureole.

"Well? Cat got your tongue?"

"Yes," she breathed in belated response.

"Yes, what? You're selfish with them?"

"No. You can nibble all you like."

Tightening his arm at her waist, he lifted her slightly, then drew her toward him. When her breast was within an inch of his mouth, he released her. Gazing up into her passion-dark eyes, he whispered, "Last night, I had to take. Will you make a gift to me now?"

Her gaze dropped to his mouth. She swallowed and pressed closer. When he did nothing, she moaned low in her throat. A shy blush stole over her cheeks again as she touched her nipple to his lips. With an unprecedented tenderness, he drew her into his mouth and watched the expressions that flitted across her face as he suckled her.

She was, without question, the sweetest, most precious gift he had ever received.

It was half past nine, Jake hadn't left for the mine, his wife was still asleep, and he hadn't had breakfast. But did he care? Hell, no. Jake sat on the edge of the bed and braced an arm on the other side of her.

"I have to go, you little hellcat," he whispered. "Since I kept you awake all night, would you like to stay home today?"

"Mm . . ."

"Be waiting for me?"

Her kiss-swollen mouth curved in a dreamy smile. Without opening her eyes, she murmured, "I'll throw away the rock, I promise."

Jake nuzzled her neck. "What is it, anyway? A Comanche charm of some kind?"

She snuggled deeper under the down quilt. "No, a remedy," she replied groggily. "So I'd take."

With his lips hovering below her ear, he grew still. "Take?"

"Mm . . . with a baby." Her smile deepened. "So you wouldn't pester me."

Now that Jake thought about it, he remembered hearing once that a rock placed under a husband's side of the mattress might expedite conception, the idea being that the less a man slept, the more frequently he would make love to his wife. Somehow, he didn't think that result had been Indigo's goal, and he chuckled. "Damn, don't just throw the thing away. Bury it." He nibbled his way to her mouth. "Not that I'm against making babies. We can start work on that tonight."

"Tonight," she agreed drowsily.

"Let's aim to have a dozen," he said with a grin. "A hundred tries each. If I haven't run out of steam by then, you can dig your rock back up."

"Mm . . . a dozen, yes."

Jake kissed her goodbye, then rose to gaze down at her for a moment. God, he loved her. He wondered if she had any idea how much. He gave Sonny a farewell scratch between his ears, then slid his gaze to the window. Last night, for the first time since Lobo's death, Indigo had forgotten to open it.

Later that morning, when Indigo finally came awake, she heated a basin of water so she could wash. After dressing, she collected her ruined chemise and Jake's jeans, then headed for the creek for their other smelly clothing. Minutes later, she had a small bonfire going. As she tossed the garments into the flames, she was swept back in time to a night six years ago when she had burned all her white clothing and vowed to never again acknowledge her white blood. Lying in Jake's arms had erased all that pain from her heart. She felt whole again, and healed.

A smile touched her mouth as she recalled the first time

she had set eyes on Jake. If someone had told her then that less than a month later he would get on his knees to her and kiss her feet, she would have bent double with laughter. Now that it had happened, though, she wasn't laughing. To think that Jake, of all the men she knew, had done that, and for her? It brought tears to her eyes.

She tossed her bloomers on the fire and took a deep breath. It was odd when she thought about it. For so long, she had clung desperately to what little pride Brandon had left her. Then, with only a few words, Jake had stripped her of even that. Yet now she felt glorified. It was as if he had emptied her of the ugliness, then filled her back up with only good things.

Smoke drifted into Indigo's eyes. She squinted and hugged herself, enjoying the heat. Laurel, which was far scarcer than pine and more difficult to cut, was a hard wood that put forth a slow, hot, longlasting fire. Like Jake's love, she thought. His wasn't the kind to burn hot and fast, then fizzle out.

In spite of her discomfort from lovemaking, Indigo attacked the housework with gusto when she went back indoors. Though perhaps only temporary, this little house was Jake's home, and she wanted it to be more than just tidy. When he came in from work in the evenings, he would be able to tell just by looking how much she loved him and how proud she was to be his wife.

After changing the bed linen, Indigo decided today would be a perfect time to do some deep cleaning, symbolic of the fresh start she and Jake had made last night. She hauled all the rugs outside and beat them with the broom. Then, before sweeping, she decided to clean the ashes from the cookstove and fireplace. She finished in the kitchen first, then moved to the sitting room. Kneeling on the hearth, she leaned forward over her knees to scoop the ashes and suet.

At the back of the inner hearth lay the burned remnants of a piece of paper. Indigo would have discarded it if her gaze hadn't caught on the partially charred letterhead. A prickle of uneasiness crawled up the back of her neck. Ore-Cal Enterprises? Her gaze lowered to the unburned portions of the letter, written in a distinct, masculine scrawl.

Dear Jake:

I'm sending bad news, I'm afraid. As I feared, further investigation confirmed my suspicions. We're wading knee-deep in shit. A large portion of the paragraph was scorched and illegible. It ended with— *to get the dirty work done. If we can, we'll lay the proof under Father's nose and call it a job well done so you can get the hell out of there and come home. It's boring as hell around here without you, and Emily never gives me a moment's peace, asking when you'll be back so she can set the date. You do remember Em, your fiancée? She's beginning to wonder, since you haven't written. I took the liberty of telling her the same thing I told Father, that you're on a short, much-needed vacation. Less chance of discovery that way.*

*I'll arrive there as soon as I can. It'd probably be safest to keep your story to Wolf as close to the truth as possible and just say your brother's coming to visit. We never were much good at sticking to the same —*more charred area— *our explanations got too elaborate. Ah, but weren't those the good old days?*

Until th—
Your broth—

Indigo started to shake. She stared down at the letter and willed it to disappear. When that didn't work, she reread it and prayed it wouldn't seem quite so incriminating the second time. Jake was somehow connected to Ore-Cal Enterprises? What dirty work was Jeremy referring to? And who was Em?

Oh, God. . . .

Indigo clamped a hand over her mouth. Lies, all lies. Everything he had ever told her about himself had been a lie. She knew what dirty work Jeremy was referring to, the sabotage of the mine. Of course! What perfect sense that made. If they could put her father into a serious financial bind, he would sell out at a low price to Ore-Cal.

It all fell together for Indigo like the scattered pieces of a puzzle. Jake's arrival on the same day that they had expected the representative from Ore-Cal. The lack of calluses on his palms. Even his reluctance to have her at the mine now took on new significance. He wouldn't want her there any more than he could help for fear she might hinder him in his plans.

The pain she felt was unbearable. She huddled there on the floor and held her middle. How could she have let herself trust another white man? Wasn't once enough to teach her?

She was nothing to him. Just as she had been nothing to Brandon. He was using her. He probably didn't even consider himself married, since she was an Indian. Even if he did, he wouldn't hesitate to get a divorce. But worse than that was what he was doing to her father. Ruining him. Destroying everything he had worked for these last twenty years.

How could he? Oh, God, how could he? *Easily*, a small voice in her mind replied. *Your father's a nothing, just like you are.*

With an enraged sob, Indigo sprang to her feet, envisioning her father, broken and unable to stand. She started across the room. Her gaze froze on the spot where Jake had gone down on his knees to her. She stumbled to a stop as the memories of that washed over her. Confusion swam in her head. She recalled his gentle lovemaking, his husky whispers. Her legs felt as though they might buckle, and she sank onto the settee to stare at the letter. A liar? A consummate actor? How could any man as tall and strong and proud as Jake Rand go to his knees and humiliate himself like that for a woman unless he sincerely cared for her?

* * *

When Jake threw open the door late that afternoon, the last thing he expected was to see Indigo sitting on the settee, her face swollen from crying and streaked with black suet.

"My God, what's happened? Is it your father? Your mother?" He cast a glance around the room. "Where's Sonny?"

Indigo stared up at him. "He's asleep under the bed."

Jake closed the door and leaned against it. His heart began to slam. "Honey, is it Toothless? What made you cry?"

She didn't answer, just kept staring at him. Framed by black suet, her eyes looked so light a blue, they reminded Jake of endlessly deep, clear pools of water. He looked into them and felt as if he was drowning. A loud silence settled around them. Then an eerie sensation slid over him. He felt as if she was looking clear to his soul.

Then it hit him that she might be doing just that. She had gone unnaturally still, and there was a faraway expression on her face, as though she was listening to something he couldn't hear. Jake felt vulnerable in a way he never had, and naked. He wanted to look away. He nearly did. But he sensed that to do so would be an irrevocable mistake.

After a long while, she pushed to her feet and extended a trembling hand toward him. He saw that she held a charred piece of stationery in her slender fingers. His gaze whipped to the fireplace.

"All of it didn't burn," she said simply.

Jake groaned. "Damn it to hell."

"I'm afraid that's not what I want to hear."

Jake held up his hands, then dropped them. "It's not as bad as it—" He gave a bitter laugh. "Actually, it *is* as bad as it looks. That's why I didn't have the guts to tell you."

"Tell me now," she said softly.

Jake swallowed. "I suppose you've already told your father."

Pain flickered in her eyes. "I nearly did." Her mouth trembled slightly. "If things are the way this letter makes them look, I owe you nothing but a knife in your gut. And then, of course, I should spit on your grave."

Jake closed his eyes. "Jesus, Indigo. After all that we shared last night, you can't mean that."

A glitter crept into her eyes. "Did we share something special? Or were you just using a stupid squaw? Who is Emily?"

"She's, um . . ." He threw up his hands again. "She was my fiancée."

Indigo looked him dead in the eye. "Have you broken the engagement? Or do you plan to return to her once you've had your fun with me?"

Jake gave a humorless little laugh. "You can't believe that. I married you, for God's sake. I'd say that effectively ended my engagement to Emily. I just haven't had time—" He broke off, no longer able to color the truth. Since knowing Indigo, he had a whole new definition of honesty. "Actually, I've had plenty of time to write her. I just couldn't find a way to do it behind your back."

"Because I would have found out about her?" She lowered her arm and let the paper flutter to the floor. "So I'm married to a man who's engaged to another woman? To a man who loves another woman?" Her body went rigid. "When I think of the things I allowed you to do last night—I feel so dirty and used. Worse than Brandon made me feel. At least I fought him. He tried to rape me with force, which was at least honest. You rape with lies."

"Indigo, you have to listen to me."

Her narrow shoulders straightened. "Why do you think I'm still here? I felt I owed you that much. Even though it appears that your 'dirty work' nearly killed my father. Even though it looks as if you have made a bigger fool of me than Brandon ever dreamed of."

Her voice shook with the intensity of her feelings. "Even though it seems that everything you led me to believe has been a lie, I couldn't betray you without first hearing what you had to say." She slid her arms around her waist and stared up at him. "If there's anything you can say to make the hurting inside me stop, please do it."

Jake brushed his sleeve across his mouth. He wanted nothing more than to cross the room and take her into his arms. He was afraid to try. She looked as though she might shatter if he touched her. But there was hope. She must still love him, or she wouldn't be here.

"I love you," he said hoarsely. "That isn't a lie, and it never was. And no matter how bad it looks, I came here to help your father, not hurt him." On legs gone quivery with nerves, Jake strode to the settee and sat down. The crushed look on her face was scaring the hell out of him. "It wasn't my dirty work Jeremy was talking about in the letter. It was our father's."

Haltingly and not at all sure he was making any sense, Jake dragged the story up from his guts. She stood listening in a frozen, awful silence.

"I never told you an outright lie." He gestured with his hands. "I know I haven't been honest. I've lied by omission. Believe it or not, where I come from, that's not considered lying. I know that doesn't make a damned bit of sense to you, not the way you see things, but in my world, if your intentions are good, which mine were, and hiding the truth facilitates matters, it's more power to you."

She still said nothing.

"Indigo, when I came here, all of you were faceless. I never intended to hurt anyone with the deception, only to help." He strained to swallow. "I never meant to fall in love with you. By the time I started to realize how much I cared about you, I'd already dug my grave. I wanted to tell you the truth, but I put it off, praying Jeremy would find proof our father wasn't behind it all. Then, at least, the telling wouldn't have been quite so awful."

She still didn't speak.

Jake dropped his head into his hands. "I suppose you're still waiting to hear about Emily."

"How astute of you."

He glanced up. "I never really loved her. We spent a lot of time together. I enjoyed her companionship. She came from an acceptable family. I was nearly thirty. Asking her to marry me seemed like the thing to do. I've regretted it since—long before I met you, I began to regret it. I'm fond of her. I'd never deliberately hurt her. But there was no magic there for me. Not the way there is with you."

"Is she beautiful?" she asked in a hollow little voice.

Jake longed to say Emily had jowls like a hound and constantly drooled. "Yes, she's pretty." He knew those words would cut, but he was finished with lies. "She's a lovely woman and a lovely person. You'd like her, I think." He clenched his teeth, then sighed. "But I don't love her. I love you. I can't even remember exactly what she looks like."

"D—Does she wear flounces and ruffles and lacy petticoats?"

Jake knew he was on dangerous ground. Indigo felt inferior to women like that. "I've never seen her petticoats."

She fastened bruised-looking blue eyes on his. "You say she comes from an acceptable family. You're— You're rich, aren't you? The house you told me about that day in the hayloft, the one that's so big your family can get lost in it, is a very fine house, isn't it? A rich man's house?"

Jake thought of his home and the many elegant rooms. He could lose her over this. And for what? His life in Portland? He couldn't settle for that now. For years, he had thought poverty was what he had experienced as a child. Now he realized the most wealthy of men could be starving. Here in Wolf's Landing he had found things money could never buy—love, loyalty, laughter, intrinsic honesty, purity of heart. The most priceless of all, of course, was the girl standing before him. How in God's name would he live without her now that he had discovered how beautifully sweet life could really be?

"Yes, it's a rich man's house," he admitted hoarsely. "Except for one room—my office." He searched her gaze. "It's probably the only room there that you'd love. It is the only one I love. Everything's handmade and simple." He swallowed. "I'm wealthy. I can buy just about anything I want." With a shrug of one shoulder, he said, "A seven-hundred-dollar wife, a three-hundred-dollar wolf pup. Everything else I ever bought didn't mean squat to me. So I had my office to hide in, and I filled it with pictures of all the things my money couldn't buy. Mountains and trees and clear streams. I grew up in this kind of world, and I missed it. I first began to realize that the day we had the picnic at the Geunther Place."

She rubbed her arms as if she was cold. There was a stricken look in her eyes. "You should be married to a lady, someone you can be proud of when you introduce her to your family. A woman from an acceptable family."

Jake heaved a sigh. Raking a trembling hand through his hair, he said, "Actually, I'm far more worried about being proud when you realize the kind of life I've led. I can take you anywhere and be proud of you, Indigo. But I can't hold my head very high knowing what my father has done. It sullies everything I ever believed myself to be. You're so worried about being good enough for me? Honey, the truth is, I'm the one who doesn't measure up."

"I'm not married to anyone in your family but you," she replied softly. "Another's sins aren't yours."

Jake felt the first stirrings of hope.

She licked her lips. "I think you should go speak to my father. He deserves to know everything you've just told me."

Jake tried to imagine Hunter's reaction. "Before I do

that, I have to know where I stand with you, Indigo. What if he throws me out on my ear?"

With an aching sadness, her gaze clung to his. "I will pray that doesn't happen. But if it does—" She looked at the suet on her hands, then lifted them in supplication. "If you truly love me and want me as I am, then I—"

"Oh, I want you," he assured her in a ragged voice. "I want you, Indigo."

Tears sparkled in her eyes. "Then I'm willing to say you've been a very stupid man and start again with no lies between us."

Jake couldn't quite believe he had convinced her so easily. He? The man whose tongue got tied into knots around one-syllable words? He slowly rose from the settee. "And if your father tells me to get the hell out of his house and the mine?"

Her mouth quivered. "I think you will find my father listens with his heart and that he hears more than words. He will look into you, if you will let him, as I have, and he will see the goodness shining through all the lies you have told."

Jake remembered how she had looked into his eyes when he entered the house, the naked feeling. "What else did you see within me, besides some goodness?" he asked softly.

Her eyes turned cloudy. "I think you know. You looked back this time and opened yourself up so I could see."

Jake's throat felt tight. "You must have seen love then. And fear, because I was scared to death of losing you." He moved slowly toward her. "And sorrow, because I wish I'd been honest from the first. I'll never lie to you again, I swear it."

She gave an almost imperceptible nod.

"And I'll write Emily tonight. You can read the letter and mail it yourself. Will you forgive me?"

Her reply was to walk into his waiting arms.

23

Indigo was in the kitchen trying to wash the suet from her hands and face when she heard the front door open. A deep voice boomed, "Well, I'm here, dammit. So where's my welcome?"

Though she hadn't expected Jake to conclude his talk with her father and come back so quickly, the voice sounded like his, and the tall, dark man she glimpsed through the kitchen doorway looked like him.

"In here," she called back. "I'm covered with soap!"

She leaned over the wash basin and rubbed at her face. "I'm trying to get the black off." She rinsed, then groped for the towel. After dabbing her eyes, she squinted at the blurry, broad-shouldered figure in the doorway. "What did he say?"

"The only he I've talked to said Jake Rand lived here," a rich voice replied. "Have I just done the unforgivable and walked into the wrong house?"

Indigo blinked and tried to focus. The darkly handsome face grinning back at her didn't belong to her husband. She slowly straightened and blinked again. He looked very like Jake, so much so that they might have passed for twins.

"Oh. . . . No, you've got the right house." She felt heat rising up her neck and prayed she had all the suet washed off her face. "You must be Jeremy."

He snapped his fingers, leveled a finger at her, and gave her a wink. "You have me at a distinct disadvantage, and when it comes to a lovely young lady, I can't have that. Who are you?"

In all her worst imaginings, she had never once considered that Jake wouldn't be present to introduce her to Jeremy when he arrived. She didn't have the nerve to mention their marriage and face his brother's disapproval alone. "I'm Indigo."

His dark eyes traveled slowly over her and warmed with appreciation. "Indigo? . . ." He inclined his head, urging her to complete the introduction.

"Wolf is my maiden name," she squeaked. "Indigo Wolf."

"Ah, your father owns the mine where Jake works." He flexed his broad shoulders and straightened. His blue chambray shirt looked off-the-shelf new, unlike the earth-stained blue wool Jake was wearing. "And you're here doing . . ." He glanced around the doorway at the hearth. "Housework?"

That was true enough. "Yes," she replied, relieved that he had come up with the explanation. "Housework, yes."

His twinkling eyes slid back to her. Pointing to his cheek, he said, "You missed a spot."

Indigo rubbed. "I, um, suppose you're looking for Jake." She realized how stupid that sounded and gave a nervous laugh. "But of course you're looking for Jake or you wouldn't be at our house." Her heart did a flip. "His house."

With a slight smile, he studied her for a moment. "Do you know where he is?"

"He went to see my father. He should be right home. I mean back, he should be right back." She wiped her hands on her pants. "Would you, um, like some coffee? I can put some on. And I've got some cake. Do you like chocolate?"

"I love chocolate." He lifted an eyebrow. "You do the cooking here, too?"

Indigo turned toward the stove and realized she'd have to lay a fire. She glanced down at the black smudges on the sleeves of her work shirt. Jake was accustomed to her wearing the stained work leathers when she did grimy chores, but what would Jeremy think? She looked like a pig that had been routing in dirt. This was her worst nightmare. It would have been bad enough to meet Jake's relatives when she was at her best. "I—yes, I do both the cooking and the cleaning."

A growl from Sonny made Jeremy turn. Indigo darted over and reached past his leg to capture the wolf cub by his scruff. "He's not used to strangers." She straightened and hugged the puppy close. "I'll, um—if you'll let me by, I'll go lock him in the bedroom. He bites, I'm afraid."

Jeremy stepped back. Indigo darted past him. Once she gained the bedroom, she took a frantic look in the mirror above the bureau and cringed. Scrubbing at her smudged cheek with one hand, she jerked open a drawer with the other and dragged out a clean leather top. She changed in record time, then smoothed her hair. Not good, but better, she decided.

Jeremy was sitting at the table when she returned to the kitchen. His gaze settled on her clean blouse, and his expression turned quizzical. Indigo winced. She hadn't stopped to think how it would look if she reappeared in a clean garment.

Jeremy's dark eyes lifted to hers. "Are you living here with my brother, Indigo?"

She fixed horrified eyes on him. "Not exactly, no. Sort of, though. Not the way—that is to say, there's nothing improper about it."

"What does your husband say about that?" He watched her carefully. "You did say Wolf is your maiden name, so I assume you're married?"

Indigo gulped and sent up a frantic prayer that Jake would come back. "My husband, he, um, doesn't say anything. He doesn't mind, I mean." Another nervous laugh erupted from her. "He wouldn't have it any other way . . . really."

Jeremy nodded. "I see," he said, his tone implying that he didn't see at all.

Indigo retreated a step. "I think I'm going to just run along." She waggled her fingers at the front door.

A muscle in Jeremy's jaw began to tick. Indigo had seen that same look on Jake's face when he was becoming angry. "It was a pleasure meeting you," he said.

"Yes, a pleasure. Meeting you, I mean, not me." She laughed again. "Jake should be here any second. If you wait right there, you can't miss him."

Turning, Indigo made a beeline for the door, her one thought to get out of there and not come back until Jake got home. Just as she touched the latch, it swung open and Jake walked in. Unaware that they had company, he looped an arm around her waist and lifted her feet off the floor to swing her around.

"Your father's the most understanding man I've ever met," he said warmly. "I feel like a thousand pounds has been lifted off my shoulders." He slid his free hand to her bottom and bent his head to kiss her. "God, honey, you feel so damned good. After what I just went through, I want to hold you and never let go."

"Jake, we have—don't." She arched away, in a panic to keep his hands in polite places. "Stop it. Your—" Her eyes flew wide when she felt his hand slip under the waistband of her britches. "Jake, please, your—stop it!"

"Stop it? That has an echo in it," he said huskily, bending his head to nibble on her neck. "Give me two seconds, and I'll have you begging me not to." A floorboard creaked. He broke off and stiffened. As he looked up, he said, "Jeremy!"

Indigo squeezed her eyes closed. It was the only

option when her new brother-in-law was standing less than ten feet away watching her husband slowly draw his hand out of her pants.

"The feeling's mutual," Jeremy said icily. "Surprise, surprise."

Jake kept his arm clamped around Indigo's waist. "Have you met Indigo?"

Jeremy's eyes sliced toward her. "Yes."

"And she explained."

"I believe I understand the situation, yes," Jeremy replied.

Indigo clutched the front of Jake's shirt and gave a wild shake of her head. "He doesn't."

Jake's mouth twitched as he looked back at his brother. "Do I see a glint in your eye, Jer?"

Jeremy propped a shoulder against the doorframe and flashed Indigo a smile. "We'll discuss it as soon as the lady leaves."

"She isn't leaving," Jake answered with a mischievous grin. "She lives here. Jeremy, I'd like you to meet—"

"I don't believe my own eyes," Jeremy bit out. Glancing apologetically at Indigo, he said, "Excuse me. Could you give me and my brother a private moment?"

Jake tightened his arm around Indigo's waist. "Jeremy, before you say anything more you might later regret, I think you ought to know that Indigo is my wife."

"That's no excuse," Jeremy shot back. "I can't believe that you, of all people—after all the times you've given *me* hell? What is this, Jake? And with a girl her age? With the daughter of the man you supposedly came here to—" He broke off. "What did you just say?"

"Indigo is my wife."

A flush crept up Jeremy's dark neck. He slid a glance at Indigo, then looked back at Jake.

Jake chuckled. "Indigo, this is your new brother-in-law, Jeremy. He sometimes appears to have rocks between his ears, but he's not a bad sort once you get to know him."

In an agony of dread, Indigo watched Jeremy's face for his reaction. After initial surprise, his mouth turned up in a grin. "Are you serious? Your wife? You went and got married?"

Jake nodded.

"That's unforgivable. How could you get married without any of us here?" Jeremy walked slowly toward them, his gaze fixed on Indigo. His eyes lit up with laughter. "Why didn't you just tell me, Indigo? I thought—" He raked a hand through his hair. The habit reminded Indigo of Jake, and some of her nervousness fled. "I thought my brother—well, it's obvious what I thought. I was ready to kill him."

"Or die trying," Jake amended.

Jeremy ignored that and took Indigo by the shoulders to draw her from Jake's side to get a good look at her.

"Well?" Jake asked proudly. "What do you think of her?"

Jeremy's gaze warmed. "My only question is, where did you find her? She doesn't have a sister, does she?"

Jake chuckled. "No such luck."

Jeremy winked at Indigo. "Did he warn you what kind of a family you were marrying into?" He turned a meaningful glance on Jake. "Does she know what scoundrels we are?"

Jake nodded. "She knows everything, Jeremy."

Jeremy bent and kissed Indigo's cheek. "Jake, she's lovely. Leave it to you to find the most beautiful girl in Oregon and marry her before I could even get a shot at her." He straightened and stepped back. "Welcome to our family. Right now it's lacking a bit in respectability. But hopefully, Jake and I are going to rectify that."

Indigo moved toward the kitchen. "I'll get the fire laid and put on coffee and start dinner."

Indigo heard Jake speak softly to Jeremy. A moment later, he came up behind her in the kitchen and grasped her shoulders. "Honey, are you okay?"

"Relieved," she whispered. "I didn't know what to

say when he walked in. Without you for moral support, I was afraid to tell him we were married. And then I—"

"No, I mean okay otherwise." His dark eyes searched hers. "Just now, when you walked in here, it looked like you were a little stiff."

Color flooded her face. "Oh, that. It's nothing."

He tucked in his chin and gave her a mock scowl. "Nothing? Honey, are you sore? From—"

She clamped a hand over his lips and shot a worried glance toward the sitting room. "It's nothing," she whispered. "It'll go away."

He steered her toward the table. "Sit. I'll take care of the coffee and dinner. What you need is a nice long soak in a hot tub." He pressed her down in a chair. "Don't argue."

"Be quiet," she squeaked.

He gave her a quick kiss and turned toward the stove. "Come on in, Jer. It looks like we're cooking tonight. Indigo's feeling a little poorly."

Indigo winced, and her flush deepened. Jake noted the painful red creeping to her hairline and grinned.

Jeremy came into the kitchen. "You're not feeling well?"

Jake laid wood in the stove, struck a lucifer, and lit the fire. "She's just a little sore," he explained, sliding a mischievous glance at his wife. "Yesterday, she engaged in some unaccustomed activity and overdid a bit."

Jeremy slid a curious glance from Jake's twinkling gaze to Indigo's scarlet countenance. He took a chair and smiled. "The best cure for that is more of the same."

Indigo bent her head and scratched at a nonexistent spot on the tablecloth.

"Now there's a thought," Jake said with a chuckle. He turned to the dish board with the coffeepot and pulled out the crock of freshly ground beans. "So, Jer, have there been any new developments since your letter?"

Jeremy glanced toward Indigo. "I can speak freely?"

Jake sat the coffeepot over the heat and gave a relieved sigh. "Yes, thank God. Indigo is aware of everything."

Jeremy settled back in his chair. "Father's behind it. I'm certain of it."

Jake turned from the stove, his expression suddenly grim. "You sound mighty certain."

Jeremy nodded. "Unhappily so. I found record of three bank drafts Father made, all to Hank Sample. In each case, the draw was made about a week before there was trouble here. That's too much to be coincidence. Hank hired someone here to do the dirty work. He used those draws to make the payoffs."

Jake leaned a hip against the dish board and folded his arms. His expression darkened. "I still can't believe it."

"Believe it," Jeremy said softly. He propped a boot on his knee and studied the heel for a long moment. "That's not the worst of it." He lifted a solemn gaze to Jake's. "Another draw was made five days ago."

Jake stiffened. "So you think we should be expecting more trouble?"

"If I'm correct in my suspicions, yes, and I believe I am. If things go according to schedule, we can expect something to happen the day after tomorrow, maybe the next day."

Indigo glanced up at Jake, her eyes filled with alarm. "Another cave-in, do you think?"

"There's no telling." Jake scratched his jaw. "We should start watching the mines tomorrow night then." He shot Jeremy a look. "Each time before, the tunnels were sabotaged the night prior to the accident. It'd be my guess our man will stick to the same methods, since they've worked well. You couldn't find any information that hinted at who their contact here might be?"

Jeremy shook his head. "Father's too smart to leave written evidence of that sort. I'd guess it's all been handled by verbal agreement, payoff in cash so it can never be proved." He turned to regard Indigo. "You can't know how sorry I am—about what happened to your father and everything. What must you think?"

"I think it's very good of you to try to stop it," she said softly. "And I pity your father. He must be an unhappy man."

The coffeepot began to boil. Jake moved it off to the side so it wouldn't spill over. To Jeremy, he said, "Are you up to some midnight vigils? I think we should watch both mines, just in case. If we can catch the bastard messing around at either site, we can get all the proof we need to confront Father."

Jeremy nodded. "And then what, Jake?"

A tight feeling spread through Jake's chest. He had never particularly liked his father, but the blood ties were there, and he couldn't help but care. It hurt to think of bringing about the old man's downfall. Then again, Jake couldn't forget the harm done to Hunter Wolf and his family and countless others.

Not to mention his mother. . . . In a way, maybe it was fitting that her sons should destroy the man who had so callously destroyed her. Jake looked at Indigo. His wife. Now that he had lain with her, he felt a thousand times more protective. Never, he vowed, never in a thousand years, would he repeat his father's mistakes. Nothing would ever be so important to him that he would jeopardize Indigo's well-being.

Dragging his mind back to Jeremy's question, Jake replied, "I don't know, Jeremy. I can't think that far ahead yet. Let's get the evidence, then worry about what to do with it. Retributions must be made, that's a certainty. Beyond that, we'll have to decide."

Jeremy pressed his lips together, his face drawn. "Yeah, I guess you're right." He took a bracing breath. "So what's the plan, you watch one mine and me the other?"

Jake nodded.

Indigo straightened. "I want to go, too. Three pairs of eyes are better than two."

Jake looked over at her. Without any hesitation whatsoever, he said, "Absolutely not."

Indigo stiffened. Jake's stern tone brooked no argument, but this was far too important to let slide. "Jake, my father's whole life is on the line. Everything we've worked years to build. If you're worried about the danger, please don't. It's my risk and my decision."

His jaw tensed. "Correction. It's my decision, and I just made it. You're not going anywhere near there."

"But I—"

He riveted her with his gaze. "Correct me if I'm wrong, but I don't believe I said the matter was open for debate."

"Jake, there's a large area to watch up there," she cried. "We'd have a better chance of catching him if three people were in position. You're being unreasonable."

Looking into Indigo's blue eyes, Jake could see how important it was to her that he allow her to go. Unfortunately, all he could think of was the possible danger. Letting her work was one thing, but he'd be damned if he would deliberately put her into a situation where she might get hurt. Her father's damned mine wasn't that important. Nothing was that important.

"If the need arises, I can take care of myself," she assured him.

"You have a husband to take care of you now."

"Please, Jake, this is important to me." She curled her hands into fists. "Whoever it is, nearly killed my father. I have a right to my little piece of revenge."

Jake's expression remained implacable. "I've made my decision."

"Not a fair one."

"I don't have to be fair. You're my wife, and you'll do as I say, about this and everything else. End of discussion."

Indigo felt as if she'd been slapped. Cheeks stinging, she sat there a moment and stared at the floor, acutely aware of Jeremy sitting across the table from her. A

tense silence fell over the room. She remembered how
solicitous Jake had been about her feelings last night
and couldn't help but feel he'd just done an about-face.
She glanced up to find that Jeremy was smiling, as if he
found the exchange between her and Jake hilariously
funny. She wondered if Jake's change in attitude had
anything to do with his brother's arrival.

"Some things never change," Jeremy said with a
chuckle.

Jake cleared his throat. "I hope you'll excuse us. Like
all newlyweds, we run into the occasional wrinkle that
has to be ironed out."

Indigo didn't particularly appreciate having her feelings about something so important referred to as a wrinkle. She pushed up from her chair and, without looking
up, said, "I believe I'll lie down for a while."

"I'll haul in some water and put it on to heat," Jake
said.

Indigo paused at the door. "I'd really rather not take
a bath this evening." She shot a meaningful glance in
Jeremy's direction. "If I'm not better by morning, I can
take one then."

Jake drew the bucket from under the dish board. "Then
you'd be sore all day tomorrow. I'll holler when I've got the
tub all ready. Jeremy can stay in the sitting room."

Indigo's nape prickled. He expected her to bathe
when his brother was in the house? She stared at him.
"Jake, I really—"

"Just leave it to me," he came back.

For the second time in as many minutes, he was
being arrogantly authoritative. Indigo flashed him a
mutinous glare and left the room.

24

For the next several nights, Jake dropped Indigo off at her parents' house at about midnight so she wouldn't be left alone while he and Jeremy kept vigil over the mines. Contrary to Jeremy's prediction, no trouble occurred, and they saw no one lurking near the tunnels. One night Jeremy thought he spied a shadow moving near the entrance of Number Two, but when he crept close, there was no one there.

Reasoning that any vandalism would probably occur in the dead hours after midnight, the two men left their stands at about three and headed back for Wolf's Landing. Jake wasn't oblivious to the fact that Indigo resented being excluded from his and Jeremy's nightly forays. He knew she would have preferred it if he hadn't gone by her parents' to fetch her each night on his way home. His only comfort came from the knowledge that his decision to keep her safely uninvolved was for her own good. One day, once she got over being angry, he felt sure she'd realize that.

Jeremy's return from *Wahat,* the number two mine, took an hour and a half longer than it took Jake from Number One. That lapse in time gave Jake an opportunity to stay at the Wolfs' to eat the snack Loretta had waiting for him each night and still have the necessary privacy to make love to his wife after he walked her home. He didn't let Indigo's initial reluctance forestall him from doing just that. He had never been one to resist a challenge, especially when the rewards were so incredibly sweet.

Indigo. . . . She was a fever in Jake's blood. Even when she tried to resist, she responded to his touch with a passionate abandon that he had never expected. Jake tried a dozen different times to cajole her out of being angry with him, but, as always, words didn't serve him well. In his urgency to impart his feelings to her, he pressed his attentions on her with more passion and possessiveness than he might have if eloquence had been his.

He wasn't certain how Indigo felt about making love with him when she was feeling resentful toward him. He knew it stung her pride a bit that a brush of his hand could send her senses reeling, but she surrendered so sweetly, Jake couldn't resist. At least when she was in his arms there was no anger between them. Like the explosives she so expertly handled, once he got her fuse lit, she went off like a little bundle of dynamite.

One night during preliminary lovemaking, he looked down into her passion-heavy eyes and couldn't resist easing her. "For a girl who didn't want any part of this, you've sure taken to it."

Breathless and trembling, she strained up on her tiptoes to kiss him. "The same thing happened with asparagus."

Jake chuckled and cupped her fanny in his hands, lifting her against him so her mouth could reach his. "Asparagus?"

"Yes." She nibbled impatiently at his lips. "I took one look and thought I'd hate it." She ran her hands into his hair and drew his head down to accommodate herself. "Ma finally forced me to eat some, and for weeks, I couldn't get enough."

Jake's last thought before he acquiesced and kisse
the little hoyden was that he hoped she didn't lose he
craving for him in a few short weeks. He would need
lifetime of loving her like this to satisfy his own.

As had become her habit, Indigo lay in the circle o
Jake's strong arm after making love that night and won
dered what had come over her. Since their disagree
ment, she had made the unnerving discovery that sh
couldn't resist his touch, not even when she was angr
with him. A strategic brush of his hand could make he
quiver like a plucked bowstring.

The most humiliating part of it was that he knew th
power he had over her. Sometimes, in the throes of pas
sion, Indigo's head would clear and she would look u
into his eyes and see a possessive, satisfied gleam tha
said more clearly than words, "You're mine—complete
and irrevocably mine. Try to fight it if you like. When
touch you, you can't hold onto your anger."

And she knew it was true. The realization frightene
her. Jake tended to be overprotective. If she gave in to
easily over this, he might be just as autocratic abou
other things. It was crucial that she take a stand no
and let him know she couldn't be happy if he coddle
her. If she melted in his arms every time he touche
her, he wasn't going to take her feelings seriously.

But melt, she did.

It was ironic in a way. All her life, she had dreade
being owned by a white man. Now she belonged, bod
and soul, to Jake Rand. He possessed her, not wit
force of arm, but with fragile threads of love and fier
tendrils of passion that curled around her and licked he
into an inferno of need.

On the seventh night, Indigo immediately sense
something was wrong when Jake came by her parents
house to walk her home. He usually began an assault o
her senses the second they stepped off her parents
porch, lightly caressing her cheek, her neck, her shou

der, her arm. By the time they reached the house, she was always tingling with eagerness for his kisses. But tonight, he seemed preoccupied.

"Jake? Has something happened?"

He looked mildly startled. "Happened? No."

"You seem distant."

He chuckled and looped an arm around her. "I'm sorry. I was woolgathering." He traced a circle around her ear. "As soon as I get my thoughts together, I promise to concentrate on you."

Indigo's cheeks burned. "I wasn't hinting for attention."

"What a disappointment. You're a fickle little thing. First you burn out on asparagus and now on me." He bent his head to give her a kiss. "Mm, that doesn't taste like no interest."

Indigo rolled her eyes. "What were you woolgathering about? Is it something to do with the mines?" She leaned forward to look at him. "You can include me in that much."

He sighed. "I'm not trying to exclude you, honey. I'm just not sure what it all means." He shook his head. "Seven nights, and we haven't seen a thing. I'm beginning to wonder if my father realized we were on to him and told Hank Sample to call off the dogs."

Indigo chewed her lip. "If that's so, then we'll very likely never find out who caused the cave-ins. Your father will just move on to another mine, and the contact here who nearly killed my father will never be punished."

"Exactly." Jake sighed. "I've been hoping they'll make a move. But it doesn't look like they're going to."

As they stepped off the boardwalk, he whirled her into his arms and ran a hand under her skirt. The shock of cold air in contrast to his warm hand made Indigo gasp. She tried to resist and hated herself when she felt her pulse quicken.

"I've got to get more bloomers made," she said breathlessly.

"I haven't got a cent to spare for bloomers."

His fingers slid to the cradle of her thighs. Indigo's head fell back. "You're wealthy. You can buy anything you want."

In a ragged voice, he said, "What I want is to feel your bare little bottom."

"Someone's going to see!"

"It's the middle of the night." He tightened his arm around her waist. "You are so sweet, so unbelievably sweet."

Indigo moaned under her breath and arched her back over his arm to stare up at the spinning sky. Tree limbs. A cloud-swept moon. Dim stars. And an upraised arm, holding a club. She focused just as it arced through the air at the back of Jake's bent head. A sickening thud of wood buried itself into flesh and bone. Jake's body buckled.

Before she could register what had happened, Indigo hit the ground on her back. Jake pummeled into her like a two-ton dead weight. She blinked and struggled to draw oxygen into her lungs. She heard Sonny snarling. Then he yelped and went silent.

Dazed, Indigo was slow to grasp reality. Jake, unconscious. The shadows of two men looming as they circled her. The feel of her husband's lifeless hand lying on her leg. Lifeless. . . . A scream welled, but with no breath inside her to give it impetus, all she got out was a squeak. Jake, oh, dear God, Jake. . . .

One of the men knelt near her head. "One more sound, Indigo, and I'll slit the bastard's throat."

Slit—throat—bastard. The words spun eerily inside her head, not making any sense. That voice, she knew that voice. She blinked and tried to see through the fuzziness. Brandon. Oh, dear God, it was Brandon. Movement on her other side snagged her blurry gaze. She dragged in a whine of breath, suddenly terrified. She wrapped her arms around Jake's limp shoulders.

"Wh—What have you done to him? What have you done?"

Brandon leaned closer. She could see him now. Moonlight shimmered on his blond hair and glittered in his blue eyes. "So far, all I did was give him the makings for a giant headache. One false move from you, though, and he's dead. Understand? It's touching, you with your arms around him and all. But forget that and give me your knife. Real slow, Indigo."

She drew one arm from around Jake and groped for her hip. As her fingers curled around the hilt of her knife, she considered her options and realized she had none. Brandon held a blade against Jake's neck. She pulled her weapon from its scabbard and let it fall to the dirt. With a smile, Brandon knocked it away.

"Now I have you the way I want you. Defenseless." He glanced up. "Gag her, Denny."

Denny? A shadow leaned over her. Cruel hands forced her jaws apart. A rag was stuffed between her teeth. Denver Tompkins . . . Denny. She closed her eyes as he knotted a band of cloth over her mouth.

"My cousin, Denver," Brandon said with a chuckle. "You never made a connection, did you, you stupid little bitch. He was my inside source until your husband got rid of him."

Pushing to his feet, Brandon gestured to Denver. "Pull her out from under the asshole so we can tie her up. And watch her. She's quick."

Cruel hands hooked Indigo by the armpits and dragged her from under Jake. Instead of focusing on the pain, she concentrated on Jake's warm, limp hand as it trailed down her thigh and slid off to plop on the dirt. She heard him moan.

Jerked to her feet, Indigo staggered dizzily and threw a frantic glance at the dark buildings along the street. Even if she could have screamed, there was no one to hear her. No one to come. She slid a sick gaze to Sonny and prayed he'd wake up and start barking. She couldn't see a serious wound. Denver wrenched her arms behind her back Rope dug into her wrists.

"There she is, all wrapped up, Bran, and tied with a bow."

"Good work. Now let's get the hell out of here."

Each man gripping her by an elbow, Indigo was half led, half carried between them into the dark woods behind the buildings. She heard the low rush of Shallows Creek. They made a sharp left. Minutes later, the two blonds took her right across her parents' backyard. Indigo yearned to scream. Her father lay just beyond that rear window. Even on crutches as he was, Indigo knew he'd come help her if she could only wake him.

The brief flare of hope died as Brandon and Denver dragged her along between them toward the mountain Indigo's eyes bulged over the gag. Some of the cloth had inched up over her nose, and every breath she drew was an effort. The mine. They were heading toward Number One.

When the way grew steep, Indigo gave up hope of someone helping her. They were quite a ways from town now. No one would be passing this way in the dead of night. Jeremy's route home carried him down the mountain a quarter mile to the east. Oh, God. . . . If Jake regained consciousness, he'd have no idea where she was.

Evidently her two captors shared her feeling that any chance of interference had passed, for they slowed their pace and turned loose of her arms. Indigo's relief at being unhanded was short-lived. Brandon dropped back a few steps and planted the toe of his boot on her bottom. With a shove, he sent her careening. With her arms tied behind her, Indigo couldn't break her fall. She hit on her knees, crashed face first, and slid a few inches down the incline. Only the gag saved her face.

Feigning sympathy, Brandon grasped her shoulder and rolled her over. "I'm sorry. I thought you'd be better at crawling by now." He clamped her chin in a cruel grip. "But I guess nobody's taught you yet. That's okay. I give lessons."

He straightened and motioned her to her feet. Indigo twisted to sit up, then struggled to stand. He stepped close. "You look so surprised. Don't you remember my promise to teach you how to crawl, Indigo? Like squaws are supposed to? Sure you do." His scarred mouth twisted in a horrible smile. "It's time to pay, love." He drew his hair back to reveal his notched ear. "You should never have fought me, you know. It would have been so much easier to just spread your legs. Now I have to teach you how squaws should grovel for it."

Denver laughed. "Tell her. Tell her what we're gonna do."

Fear roiled within Indigo, stark and chilling. Her legs quivered under her, and she feared she might fall. They had planned this. And whatever they had in store for her, it was going to be diabolic.

Brandon leered at her. "It's simple, really. Tonight, you're either going to crawl and beg me to do it to you, or you're going to be buried alive. It's your choice, sweet."

"And me, too," Denver inserted. "I've got mine coming after what Rand did to me."

Even through the haze of fear, Indigo caught that and slid a bewildered glance toward him. Anger burned in Denver's eyes.

"He never told you?" He barked with laughter. "The bastard beat the shit out of me and fired me."

Indigo stared at him. Jake had fired Denver? She thought back to her half-day at the mine and suddenly realized she hadn't seen the blond there that day. It had been a happy miss, so she hadn't thought about it then. Why hadn't Jake said anything?

Denver moved closer. "Do you know why? Because I dared to get out of line with you. Can you believe it? Out of line with an Indian slut? He acted as if I'd insulted the goddam Queen of England or something."

Brandon seized Indigo's arms and jerked her into a

walk. "Your reign was short. Now it's back to reality."
He chuckled. "God, I can't believe the time is finally at
hand. I've waited six years for this, six years." He gave
her a little shake. "Don't think that asshole husband of
yours will come to your rescue. The fact that we have
you shows we outsmarted him."

Denver interrupted with a laugh. "We've been
watching him watch for us for almost a week!"

"What he didn't reckon on was that I wanted at you,
not the goddam mine. When we saw he wasn't going to
let you near there, we took matters into our own hands
and jumped you on the way home. The stupid bastard
walked right into it."

Indigo wheezed for air through the gag, pumping her
legs to keep up. Her mind could focus on only one
thing. The mine. Oh, God, they were taking her to the
mine. *Buried alive.* She knew what they intended to do.
Dear God, she knew.

Brandon glanced over at her and smiled another
twisted smile. "You've got it figured already, don't you?
I reckon it's all the white in you. More brains than most
of your kind. So what do you think, love? Are you
gonna strip down and plead with me and Denny to let
you pleasure us? Or would you rather die inch by inch
hundreds of feet inside the mine?"

Revolted, Indigo tried to jerk her arm free from his
grasp.

He chuckled. "Don't think I won't do it, Indigo. I've
owed you for six years." He gestured at his mouth. "You
ruined my face, you little bitch. Did you really think I'd
just fade from your life and never make you pay?" He
pressed close. "At first, I was just going to kill you. The
first time, I damned near killed your father instead. That
turned out okay. It was nearly as satisfying to watch you
grieve over what had happened to him."

Indigo suddenly felt dizzy. She blinked and stumbled
to catch her balance.

"And then the wolf. God, that was rich. I meant to hit you and got poor old Lobo instead. I sat up there on that hillside and laughed myself sick."

Indigo's toe caught on a rock. Brandon kept her from falling.

"After the rock slide failed, I decided more specific aim was necessary. Denny and I thought of a dozen different plans, but the one thing that stuck in my mind was how much fun it had been to watch you squirm. So we came up with this idea. Squirm or die. If you crawl real pretty for us and tempt us enough with your charms, we'll let you live. Understand?"

Indigo understood, all right.

He gave her another shove, this time not quite hard enough to send her sprawling. "Your grave awaits, ma'am."

As they walked the remainder of the way to the mine, Brandon painted a vivid picture of her fate should she decide not to do some crawling. This time, he had carefully chosen the timbers that he damaged. When the tunnel collapsed, a small section at the end would remain intact. That was where she would draw her last breath, hundreds of feet into the earth, in total darkness, chilled to her bones, the oxygen slowly running out. A large grave, carefully chosen so she would die slowly and in terror.

Indigo almost wished the two men would rape her and get it over with. But she knew sexual gratification wasn't really what Brandon craved. In his twisted mind, she was a piece of dirt to be used, and she had not only dared to deny him, but had left him scarred for life, trying to defend her virtue. As far as he was concerned, a woman like her had one use, and being chaste wasn't one of them. To feel avenged, he had to degrade her. In exchange for her life, he expected to see her crawl and beg him to dishonor her. As far as he could see, that was her only recourse.

What Brandon didn't understand was that without her honor, she truly would be the nothing creature he had always believed.

When they reached the mine, both men lit lanterns, then hauled her deeply into the bowels of the earth. The deathly cold penetrated to Indigo's bones. They turned right into a reconstructed drift. It seemed to her that they walked forever. When they had nearly reached the drift's end, Brandon passed beneath some closely grouped timbers and paused, holding his lantern high to direct Indigo's gaze to them. She could see fresh axe marks in the darkened wood.

"Shored up," he said softly. "A weak spot they walled in with timbers when they got this section dug back out." As he spoke, a clod of dirt dropped from the earthen ceiling. He smiled. "I'll bet your husband sweat blood down here helping them get these up, never knowing he was constructing a trapdoor to his wife's tomb."

He pointed to two ropes that were knotted around as many timbers.

"Weakened like those timbers are, what do you think will happen if Denny and I uncoil the extra lengths of rope and give them a good jerk when we reach the mouth of this drift?" He swung his lantern and made a *sw-shh-sh* sound. "In a blink, it all comes down. The collapse will probably be only a few feet wide, but it's enough to serve our purposes." He flashed her a slow smile. "Because guess what, sweetness? You're going to be on the grave side of the collapse in a little pocket of space, with no air holes. You'll last a few hours, at most." His eyes gleamed into hers. "A few hours that will seem like eternity."

With that he gave her a shove. On legs that felt like appendages of cold rubber, Indigo walked toward the blackness ahead. Her grave. Fear crawled over her.

When they reached the end of the drift, Brandon set his lantern aside and untied her gag. Taking a step back, he ran a glittering gaze over her. "How pretty can you beg, squaw?"

Denny plunked his lantern in the dirt and sidled toward her. "Let's jerk that top up and see the pretties, Bran."

"No," Brandon snarled. His face contorted, then settled into a strained smile. "She has to beg me to look." He moved closer. "Tell me how sweet they are, Indigo. And how they burn for my kisses." His eyes seared hers. "Beg me to pull your shirt up, hm? Beg me to take them? Say it real sweet. Or die."

Indigo worked her mouth and spat in his face. For several seconds, Brandon just stared at her. The shocked surprise in his gaze told Indigo something she had failed to see years ago. Brandon didn't have any inkling of what dignity was because he had none. He had been crawling all his life and didn't know it.

"Go straight to hell, Brandon," she whispered. "I can't stop you from raping me, but I'll never ask slime like you to touch me. Not with my last breath."

He started to shake with rage.

"You gonna take that?" Denver cried. "Slap the shit out of her."

For a moment, Indigo thought Brandon might do just that, but at the last second, he seemed to regain control.

"No. If I start hitting the little bitch, I won't be able to stop. I want her to die clearheaded." Breathing hard, he backed away and leveled a finger at her. "You chose it, you stupid little breed. You just remember that. I wouldn't have you now if you groveled for it."

Denver laughed. "Come on, Bran. We've got plenty of time. I'm all worked up for it."

Brandon shot his cousin a glare. "Go see a whore. You're not messing this up for me just to get a shot off. I've waited too many years. This was the plan all along, she had to beg or die. You knew that when you said you'd help."

Denver held up his hands. "Well, who'd've thought she'd choose dying? Come on, Bran. It isn't ever as good when you gotta pay for it."

"I said no!"

Indigo watched as Brandon collected his lantern. Denver reluctantly followed suit. Brandon pulled another length of rope from his coat. "Hold my lantern, Denny."

Indigo stood motionless while Brandon tied her ankles. When he rose, he flashed her a cold grin. "Just so you can't run to safety. Who knows? Maybe you can roll as far as the timbers and get buried. It'd end quicker that way."

He slowly backed away. "Goodbye, Indigo. Tell the devil hello."

With that, the two men walked away. Indigo waited until their lanterns became tiny bobs of light in the blackness, and then she dropped to her side to do just as Brandon had suggested and roll. Dirt and rock cut into her. She ignored the pain. The timbers. She had to work her way past them. Had to.

Dizziness washed over her. She shoved with her feet and rolled into an earthen wall. The blackness around her had become absolute. Was she even rolling in the right direction? She had lost her sense of place.

"Goodbye, you no-good Indian slut!"

Brandon's voice echoed around her. *Good-bye-bye-bye.* The sounds died out with *slut-slut-slut*. Then a low rumble punctuated the call. The ground beneath Indigo rocked with vibration. Particles of dirt rained on her. Then silence descended, a horrible, black, endless silence. Indigo lay there, frozen with disbelief. It couldn't be. It was too horrible to be real.

She was buried alive.

25

Blackness swirled around Jake. He groaned and tried to swim out of it, beckoned by a distant voice, Jeremy's voice. He tried to pinpoint the direction from which it came and move toward it. Moonlight knifed into his eyes. He reached to touch the explosion of pain at the back of his head.

"Jake, for God's sake, what happened? Where's Indigo?"

Indigo. The panic in his brother's voice brought Jake to painful consciousness with a jolt. "My God, what hit me?"

With a rubbery arm, he pushed to a sitting position and blinked to clear his vision. To the east, he saw ribbons of faint pink streaking the gunmetal black of the sky behind the brooding peaks of the mountains. Dawn? He shook his head. How long had he been—

He looked around and spied Indigo's knife lying in the dirt. Fear shot up his spine. "Indigo? She isn't here?" He focused watery eyes on Jeremy's concerned face. "What in hell happened? We were—" He broke off, trying to remember. All that came clear in his mind was seeing Indigo's sweet face tipped back, her lips parted with breathless pleasure. Then sudden blackness. Jake shoved to his feet. "Sweet Jesus, where is she?"

Jake staggered sideways before he got his balance. A wave of nausea rolled over him. He braced his hands on his knees and took several deep breaths. Meanwhile, Jeremy scanned the dirt.

"Two men on foot," he said gravely. He straightened and gazed toward Shallows Creek. "They took Indigo with them."

Jake squinted against the blinding pain to peer into the blackness of the woods. His heart started to slam. How long had he been lying here? Two hours, maybe three? He had picked Indigo up about three-twenty. It had to be close to six now.

Jeremy turned toward him. "We'll have to wait for daylight. We can't see the end of our nose in the dark like this."

Jake staggered again. "We can try tracking them on horseback with lanterns." He spied a length of wood lying nearby and touched the tender throbbing in the back of his skull. "Son of a bitch. I kept her to hell away from there, trying to protect her, and now something's happened to her anyway."

"We can't track anyone with lanterns, Jake," Jeremy argued. "It'll be daylight in less than an hour. Let's wait until we can see what the hell we're doing."

Jake headed for the barn. "You do what you like. It's my wife out there somewhere."

Once in the barn, Jeremy accepted the situation and helped Jake saddle the horses. Jake had just led Buck outdoors when he heard a sound that sent cold chills up his spine. He froze and cocked his head, listening to the forlorn call of a wolf as it lifted eerily to a sad crescendo in the distant darkness. He couldn't quite believe his ears. Lobo. He had heard the wolf howl only once, but the sound was unmistakable. Not a coyote. Jake had heard plenty of those howling around Wolf's

Landing, and there was a marked difference in the cries.

"Sonny, do you think?" Jeremy asked.

Jake gave himself a hard mental shake. He cast around for the pup, only just now missing him. He had evidently followed Indigo. "Sonny's too young to howl like that," he said hoarsely.

Jake turned back to scan the darkness, trying to place the call. The pain in his head was forgotten now. The howl came again, long and forlorn. Another unearthly chill crept over him. It was Lobo's death howl—exactly like it. The call was engraved in his memory, every note a heartbreak he would never forget. As the cry died away, Jake whispered, "Jeremy, that's Lobo."

"I thought Lobo got shot."

Jake stared at the black silhouette of the mountain and strained to speak. "He was shot. He's—dead."

Jeremy leaned against his horse and peered through the darkness. "That hit on the head rattled you good."

The howl rose again. Jake waved Jeremy to silence and homed in on it. "He's up at the mine," he said shakily. "That's Lobo, Jeremy. I'd know his call anywhere."

"Have you lost your mind?" Jeremy gave a low laugh. "What in hell are you thinking, Jake? And where do you think you're going?"

Jake circled around to Buck's left flank and swung into the saddle. "I'm going up there. What do you think? That's Lobo, I tell you."

Jeremy scrambled to mount his horse. He rode abreast of Jake. "You're crazy. Would you stop and listen to some sense?"

Jake kept riding.

"Your wife's out in the woods somewhere," Jeremy yelled. "And what the hell are you doing? Instead of tracking her, you're chasing after wolf howls? Goddammit, Jake. Pull up. You're not thinking straight. It must be the blow to the head. Listen to me, dammit!"

Jake was listening to another wolf howl rising in the

night. He couldn't explain himself to Jeremy. He couldn't sort his feelings and make sense of them himself. All he knew was that something deep inside him, where reason couldn't reach, told him that wolf cry came from Lobo. He believed that so strongly that he was willing to bet Indigo's life on it.

The icy, damp air had grown thin. Indigo's eyes burned from staring into the blackness. Shuddering, she drew a shallow breath and finished the last refrain of her death song. "*Nei, Indigo, habbe we-ich-ket*, I, Indigo, am seeking death."

Silence. She could hear only the sound of her breathing. Soon, she wouldn't have enough breath to sing her father's songs or say her mother's prayers, and she would die buried in the awful silence. She tried to fight back the panic.

"Ja-aa-ke!" she screamed, giving way to the terror. "Jake!"

His name echoed around her, then died away. She knew he would move heaven and earth to save her. Trust. Complete trust. It had been so long in coming.

Jake. . . . Tears rolled down her cheeks, and she sobbed. Faced with death and blinded by blackness, she could finally see with clarity. The differences in their two worlds weren't so gargantuan. Now, all the things she had feared beckoned to her like the promise of heaven. To go away with Jake to the world beyond the mountains. Oh, yes. . . . If only she could have that chance. With him beside her, what was there to fear?

She pictured him kneeling before her, his hair glinting blue-black in the moonlight as he bent low to kiss her feet. This last week, she had bridled constantly because he had forbidden her to come near the mines. She had feared his arrogant refusal was a prelude of things to come, that he would forbid her to do other equally important things and make her life a misery. She had resented the way his touch could make her burn with longing for him. And why? Because it was symbolic of his control over her. Even surrounded by his love, she had clung to the old fear of becoming a white man's chattel.

Jake's chattel. Here in the blackness, Indigo could take her fear of that out and examine it. Jake's possession, his slave, his squaw? Oh, yes. . . . She'd be those things forever, if only she had the chance.

Was he even alive? She prayed he was, and then she prayed that God would somehow find a way to spare her as well. Just one more chance to set things right between them, that was all she asked. Maybe Jake would keep her confined to home and hearth, mothering his children. But would that be such a horrible fate? He was good and kind and thoughtful in every other way. Even if he took her away from Wolf's Landing to a world where she would be an outcast, at least she'd be with him. He was all she needed in her world, anyway. . . .

It was full daylight by the time Jake drew Buck to a halt near the entrance to the mine. He swung slowly out of the saddle and scanned the surrounding hillsides for a wraith of silver and black. Lobo. His throat tightened as he moved toward the gaping black hole of the tunnel. Jeremy rode up and leaped from his horse.

"Well, we're here, and there's no goddam wolf," he said. "Can we go back down now and follow the tracks?"

"Shut up, Jeremy. Go back if you want, but if you're staying with me, shut the hell up."

Jake bent to grab a lantern. He quickly lit it and held it high, stepping to the yawning black entrance. Fear pounded through his body. He half expected to see Indigo lying dead before him. Instead, he spied gleaming, golden eyes. His pulse quickened. Then a shrill howl echoed out at him.

"Sonny," he said with a tremulous laugh. "Hey, fella."

Clearly spooked, Jeremy laughed, too, the sound shrill and shaky. "Well, that explains our wolf howl. Inside the tunnel like that, the echo made him sound louder than normal."

Jake no longer cared who had done the howling. "Jeremy, if Sonny's here, I know Indigo is."

Without waiting for a response from his brother, Jake held up the lantern and hurried into the mine. A deathly cold closed around him.

Drifting . . . drifting in blackness. Indigo fought against the feeling, but it felt so comforting to succumb to it, to feel apart from her frozen body. Words jumbled in her head. Her mother's prayers, her father's songs. A heavy numbness had crept over her. Her aching lungs drew breath shallowly, the pace fast and frantic.

"Our Father—blessed is the fruit of thy womb—heartily sorry . . ."

The words spilled ceaselessly from her lips, her only comfort, the only weapon she had to fight off the panic. Indigo Rand. Rand, Rand, Rand. She closed her eyes on frightened tears. So afraid. She didn't want to die alone, a speck of nothingness in utter blackness. A speck that was being absorbed and becoming smaller and smaller. A tiny spinning speck. She pictured Jake's face. In her swimming mind, he seemed so real, so close. She imagined his arms closing around her, strong and warm. . . .

And then Lobo. His wet tongue touched her cheek. Ah, yes, Lobo, her good friend. He gave a low, mournful howl that rose around her and cascaded from the ceiling in rippling echoes. Lobo, her loyal wolf. She had remained beside him to sing his death song, and now he had come to sing hers. She wasn't alone after all.

"Lobo," she whispered.

He whined and licked her face again. Then he lay down

beside her. So real, so real. Indigo longed for her arms to be free so she could wrap them around his thickly furred neck, as she had in life. Instead, she settled for pressing her cheek against his fur. His warmth seeped into her and surrounded her. Her tears trickled through his ruff.

Lobo. . . .

"Oh, sweet Jesus, no . . ." Jake stood frozen and stared at the collapsed section of the drift, his heart slamming with a fear so cold it turned his blood to ice. From out of the rubble trailed two ropes. He took one look and knew what had happened. He set down the lantern, panic seizing him. "Jesus, Jeremy, she's in there."

Jeremy came up behind Jake. "You don't know that, Jake. The thing to do here is try to stay calm."

Jeremy no sooner spoke than Sonny bypassed Jake and scratched frenziedly at the wall of dirt. Jake swore and started throwing rock. "Brandon Marshall! Jesus Christ! It was him all along. I should have watched over her every second. The bastard buried her in here!"

Jeremy caught Jake's arm. "We need shovels. Jake, for God's sake, get a hold on yourself. You can't dig her out with your bare hands."

Jake jerked his arm from Jeremy's grasp and proceeded to do just that. He tore at the dirt and rock like a wild man, swearing, praying, sobbing.

"She may be—"

Jake whirled. "Go get me a goddam shovel!"

Jeremy retreated a step, frightened by the crazy look in his brother's eyes.

Four hours later, Jake dug through the last barrier of dirt with bloody hands. The opening he and Jeremy had tunneled was narrow, and too much movement might cause it to collapse. Jake knelt before it and stared through at the pit of blackness beyond, more terrified than he had ever been in his life.

"Indigo?"

Silence bounced back at him. He shot Jeremy a tortured glance. "I'm going in."

Jeremy grasped his shoulder.

Both men knew that Jake could easily be buried alive if the earth shifted. Jeremy would never be able to dig him out in time. Jake met his brother's gaze. For once, words weren't necessary. Some emotions couldn't be expressed, and even Jeremy was reduced to speechlessness for once.

Jake turned back to the opening and carefully started through. At this point, he had become so afraid he could no longer feel. Death held no threat. Living without Indigo was what terrified him.

An awful airlessness hit Jake's face as he gained the other end of the makeshift opening. He fell into bottomless blackness. His lungs immediately convulsed and grabbed frantically for oxygen. He knew then. . . . He knew but he couldn't turn loose of that last bit of hope.

Groping in the blackness, he found her. So small and cold. Air, he had to get her out into the air. He crawled with her toward the shaft of dim light. When he reached it, he called through to Jeremy.

"I've got her, Jer. I've got her. I'm going to hand her through to you. Grab her shoulders and pull her on out."

Carefully, oh so carefully, Jake shoved her toward the light. Jeremy crawled forward to catch her by the shoulders. From there on, Jake could only watch and pray that Jeremy got her through before the earth collapsed. To the light. Surely God would grant him that. If not for Jake, for Indigo, a girl made of moonbeams and wind songs. She didn't belong in blackness.

When Jeremy pulled her through, Jake nearly cried with relief. Safe, she was safe. Struggling to fill his lungs with the air that wafted through the opening, Jake fought off a wave of dizziness brought on by lack of oxygen. Then he started through himself, hand over hand, a foot at a time. Toward the light and Indigo. When he crawled free, he slid down the other side in a shower of collapsing earth. An instant later, the tunnel he and Jeremy had clawed in the earth closed its jaws behind him. It was a miracle they had both gotten out in time. A miracle. God had given him another miracle.

Jake staggered to his feet, filled with leg-trembling joy. He turned and saw Jeremy standing between him and the huddled form of his wife. From the way Jeremy stood, his legs braced wide apart, Jake knew. But his mind couldn't accept.

"Jake." Jeremy's voice shook, and a horrible expression came into his eyes. "Oh, God, Jake, I'm sorry."

A shudder ran through Jake's body. He stood there a moment, staring at his brother's stricken face. Then he moved his gaze to the lifeless body behind him. "No . . ." The word hit the air in tremulous denial. "No . . ."

With battered, shaking hands, he touched her cheek, then her neck, searching the cold, lifeless flesh for any sign of a pulse.

"Jake, she isn't breathing," Jeremy whispered. "I know you see that."

Not breathing. Lying her across his thighs, Jake cupped her face between his bloody hands and touched his lips to hers. He'd make her breathe, goddammit. He sucked in air and forced it from his lungs into her mouth. It stopped at the back of her throat. He tipped her head back and forced her teeth apart.

"Breathe, Indigo. Do you hear me. Breathe, dammit!"

He forced another breath into her body. And another.

"Jake, for God's sake." Jeremy turned away with a broken cry. "Get ahold of yourself. Please."

Jake came up for air and shot his brother a wild-eyed glare. "Pray, goddam you! Don't stand there doing nothing!

Pray!" Turning back to Indigo, he pressed his hands frantically to the sides of her face. "Breathe, Indigo. Do you hear me? Breathe, damn you! You've done every other thing I ever asked of you. I'm telling you to breathe. Do you hear me? I'm your husband, and I'm telling you to breathe."

When she didn't respond, he started to weep. "I love you. You can't die. I didn't give you permission to die, goddammit!"

For several minutes more, Jake shared his breath with her. He knew it wasn't enough. In the back of his mind, he knew it wasn't enough. He wanted to give her his beating heart. He wanted to pour his pulsing blood into her. He wanted to give her his warmth. He would have gladly died in her place and given her his very life. But that wasn't the way of things. And sharing his breath with her simply was not enough.

In the blackness, there was a tiny tunnel of light. Someone spoke to her from there. The voice was rich and warm and wonderful, yet strangely sad. The words drifted to her, scarcely more than whispers at times, then deep and resounding, all repeated in echoes.

I love you, the voice said. The words curled around her, warm and sweet. *I don't think I ever told you how much.* Warm hands moved over her. Strong arms held her close. A ragged sob shuddered through her. She drifted closer to the voice. It spoke to her about moonlight and Lobo, of yellow-and-white daisies, of songs in the wind and wild creatures eating from her hands. It sounded wonderful, like heaven. *I know that's where you are. Off somewhere, floating on moonbeams.*

Indigo frowned and tried to lift her eyelashes. She wasn't in a field of daisies. She felt cold, horribly cold. Jake. . . . She tried to reach for him. He was crying. Not silent tears, but great, wracking sobs that shook his whole body. She had to comfort him. But she couldn't

He nodded, clearly unable to speak. In the moonlight, she saw tears spilling down his cheeks. After a moment, he swallowed and said, "We have a second chance, you and I. I'm going to make the best of it and live every second as if it's our very last."

She wiped the tears from his cheeks, then slid a hand to the back of his head. "Don't cry then. I want our last second to be happy."

With a horrible sob, he joined her on the bed and drew her into his arms. Indigo hugged him close, frightened because she had never seen him like this. His whole body was shaking. He held her so tightly that she had the feeling he was afraid to let go.

After several minutes, he drew a ragged breath and relaxed, drying his cheeks on her hair. "Don't ever leave me. Promise me that."

She closed her eyes and smiled, remembering all the revelations that had come to her in the mine. "I promise, Jake. Where you go, I go. Even if it's to Portland. As long as I'm with you, the thought no longer frightens me."

"To hell with Portland," he replied in a husky voice. "I may have to go up for a few weeks to set Jeremy on track, but after that, Wolf's Landing is my home, and it's where I'm staying."

"When you go, I'll go there with you."

"I know," he said with a smile in his voice.

"You don't even sound surprised."

"I'm not." He pressed a kiss to her temple. "You and I are meant to be together. Whatever problems we run into, we'll get them worked out."

"What about Ore-Cal?"

He laughed softly. "I think it's about time Jeremy takes over. And why not? I've carried the load for years. Now it's his turn. He can handle it. I've earned the right to be my own person and live my own life. I plan to do that here in Wolf's Landing, with my little powder monkey and our twelve children."

Indigo stirred, acutely aware of an unstated message behind those words. "Me? Mrs. Jake Rand, a powder monkey? We'll see what tune you sing when it's time to do some blasting."

He ran a hand up her back, loving her as he had never loved anyone. "I learned an important lesson in the last twenty-four hours. I can't protect you from everything. I was with you last night when Brandon came along, remember?"

"Well, he hit you from behind. You can't blame yourself for that."

He sighed. "No. And I can't go through life blaming myself for every other bad thing that happens either, just because I can't prevent it." In a halting voice, he told her about his mother's death. "Nearly losing you made me stop and realize that it's the quality of life that matters, not how long you live."

He took a deep breath and exhaled on a sigh. "The true tragedy about my mother's life was that she was miserably unhappy during her short stay on earth. I can protect you into old age and make every day of your life miserable, or I can give you the freedom to enjoy every minute." He grew quiet for a moment. "I've been wrong, Indigo, about so many things. Mary Beth, for instance. I can only pray it's not too late for me to change."

"You're going to let her study law?"

"I'm finished with wrapping the women I love in cotton." He took a deep breath and exhaled on a sigh. "Take you, for instance. I want to know I gave you happiness. In the end, when we have to say our final goodbyes, those memories are the only things that comfort us."

He sounded as if he had learned that from personal experience. Indigo pressed her cheek against his chest and listened to the even, sturdy beat of his heart. "You mean it, don't you? You're actually going to let me handle dynamite and set the charges."

He tightened his arms around her. "Honey, I'll always be overprotective. That's part of my makeup, just as a need to be free is part of yours. I can't see myself happily standing aside while you do backbreaking labor. We'll have to reach compromises we can both live with. But the dynamite is different. Unless it blows accidentally, it won't hurt you to handle it."

Indigo's heart welled with happiness. "I'll be careful, truly I will."

He chuckled. "You'd better be. I've already made up my mind I'm going to be right beside you when you handle the damned stuff. If you get blown to kingdom come, I'm going with you."

Except for the wind whipping under the eaves outside the house, a peaceful silence settled around them. Enveloped in happiness, Indigo grew drowsy and drifted between sleep and wakefulness. She blinked awake when Jake gently moved away from her and got out of bed.

Unaware that Indigo was awake, Jake moved to the window. He didn't know why, but the sound of the gusting wind drew him. He pressed close to the glass and stared out into the moonlit darkness at the shifting shadows. When he stared long enough, those shadows seemed to take shape. He knew it was his imagination, but in the distance, he thought he heard the forlorn howl of a wolf on the wind.

With a sheepish smile, he lifted the latch and opened the window wide. Since his marriage to Indigo, he had grown accustomed to sleeping in the cool night air. Besides, what could it hurt to leave the window open?

Just in case. . . .

With tears in her eyes, Indigo watched Jake standing there at the open window, gazing out into the night. She knew what was going through his mind. She turned her head on the pillow and listened to the wind's song, filled with joy because Jake had finally come a step beyond the explainable and could share the beauty of it with her.

He turned toward her, his eyes glistening like silver

in the moonlight. Indigo met his gaze and let all that was within her flow out to him. A slow smile curved his mouth as he moved toward her. She knew he heard the message, even though she hadn't spoken it, just as she heard the one he sent to her.

Whether or not Lobo's spirit truly lingered here in this place was a question that no longer seemed important. The wolf lingered in her heart, and it was enough to know that. What truly counted was that Jake had somehow come to embrace those things about her that she had always been afraid to share. The Indian side of her that set her apart in a hostile world. She lifted her arms to him, content in a way she had never dreamed she could be.

As Jake moved from the window, his body cut through the moonlight and his shadow fell across the bed. For a moment, Indigo was swallowed by blackness. When he took another step, the light fell across her again, and she reappeared.

Indigo . . . a whimsical girl made of moonbeams who heard songs in the wind, a girl not quite part of this world, yet absolutely necessary to make it complete. He joined her on the bed and drew her into his arms, cherishing the moment, thanking her many gods for this second chance. He knew it was crazy, insane, totally irrational, but if he lived to be a thousand, he'd always believe she had been snatched from the clutches of death and brought back to him by a loyal silver-and-black wolf whose howls would drift always in the night wind, an intrinsic part of the mountains and the moonlight.

Indigo. . . . She was indeed a most precious gift.

AVAILABLE NOW

INDIGO BLUE by Catherine Anderson

The long-awaited final installment of the Comanche trilogy. Indigo Blue Wolf, a quarter-breed Comanche, has vowed never to marry and become the property of any white man. When tall, dark, and handsome Jake Rand comes to Wolf's Landing, Indigo senses he will somehow take over her life.

THE LEGACY by Patricia Simpson

A mesmerizing love story in the tradition of the movie *Ghost*. Jessica Ward returns to her childhood home near Seattle to help her ailing father. There, she meets again an old friend, the man she's secretly loved since she was a teenager.

EMERALD QUEEN by Karen Jones Delk

An exciting historical romance that sweeps from the French Quarter of Antebellum New Orleans to the magnificent steamboat *The Emerald Queen*.

THE STARS BURN ON by Denise Robertson

A moving chronicle of the life and loves of eight friends, who come of age in the decadent and turbulent '80s.

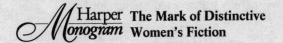

COMING NEXT MONTH

FOR ALL TIME by Parris Afton Bonds

A time-travel romance for today's women. Stacie Branningan, a modern woman, is transported back to Fort Clark, Texas, in the 1870s. There, embodied as her own grandmother, she meets her soulmate, the man she's been yearning for all her life.

WINGS OF THE STORM by Susan Sizemore

When a time-travel experiment goes wrong, Dr. Jane Florian finds herself in the Middle Ages. There, she vows to make the best of things. Unfortunately, she hasn't counted on her attraction to her neighbor—the magnetic Sir Daffyd. An award-winning first novel told with humor and sizzle.

SEASONS OF THE HEART by Marilyn Cunningham

In this bittersweet novel of enduring love, Jessica, an idealistic young woman, falls in love with Mark Hardy, a bright but desperately poor young man. Not realizing Jessica is pregnant, he leaves her to seek his fortune. Years later he returns to find Jessica married to another man.

ALL MY DREAMS by Victoria Chancellor

Set in colonial Virginia in the year before the American Revolution, ALL MY DREAMS is the story of a woman who will stop at nothing to save her plantation—even if it means buying a bondsman to give her an heir. But her plan backfires when the bondsman she purchases is a wrongfully transported English lord.

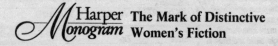 **Harper Monogram** **The Mark of Distinctive Women's Fiction**

If you would like to receive a HarperPaperbacks catalog, fill out the coupon below and send $1.00 postage/handling to:

HarperPaperbacks Catalog Request
10 East 53rd St.
New York, NY 10022

Name _____

Address _____

State _____ Zip _____